RUNEDANCE

by Beth Hudson

Book Two of The Sagathas Bard

This book is dedicated to Eleanor Ray,
Who has been there for me in countless
ways throughout the years

And, as always, to the kids
Dylan, Novembre, David, Gabbie, & Alex

A special Thank You to my generous patrons:

Laura Hudson Kittrell
Bob & Roxanne Quinlan
Eleanor & David Ray

Additional Thanks
To others who have helped me with this book:

David Ray
Amelia Kibbie
Jason Hooton-Tuscher

And to the Monday night group
Including
Bob & Roxanne Quinlan
Bill & Jason Hooton-Tuscher

TABLE OF CONTENTS

Chapter One
Family Friends

A year and a day.

The deadline obscured Traedis' future with a drapery of uncertainty, its folds and seams hiding the dark pattern within. A year and a day from receiving the knife made from the n'korreld thane's breastbone. A year and a day from the thane's pronouncement of doom, which might destroy Traedis' entire country.

A year and a day until she must kill her beloved uncle.

Traedis swung her longsword in an arc, catching her sister's leather practice gear with the tip. Taken off balance, Vandeyr righted herself and lowered her weapon.

"Very good!" Vandeyr said, shaking the tension out of her shoulders. "Either you're getting better or I'm having a terrible day. I'm hoping it's the first." She swept her gaze across the practice field which spanned the rear of the palace, to the high stone wall encompassing the entire palace compound. This month alone had spawned three assassination attempts on Traedis, leaving Vandeyr constantly on alert for danger. Many were unhappy with Traedis' ascension to the throne of Tolin.

Feeling more than a little smug, Traedis rolled her head to relax her muscles, loosing a few copper curls into her eyes. She was still terribly out of practice after her four-year imprisonment, but Vandeyr was working her hard, and her old skills were coming back. Even at her best, she would never have been able to beat Vandeyr, but scoring a touch told her how far she had come.

An impulse seized her, and Traedis swung the sword back up, hoping to take her sister off guard. The bout was not finished until one of them formally conceded.

Without apparent effort, Vandeyr brought her weapon up to block, twisted it, and sent Traedis' sword flying. Traedis shook out her right hand, which smarted fiercely, though not as much as her pride.

Vandeyr rolled her eyes. "You're so predictable, Trae." She shook her head to clear a few errant strands of white-blonde hair from her face.

Traedis bit down on a defensive response. "Perhaps I am," she agreed. "But I still scored a touch."

Vandeyr eyed Traedis with a critical blue gaze. "You did, and I suppose I'm proud of you." She cleared her throat. "I am proud of you. But I could also see what you were thinking. You tensed a dozen muscles before you decided to attack again. That could get you killed in a real fight."

"I've been in real fights—" Traedis began, before she realized that Vandeyr was trying to provoke her. Unable to decide if she were annoyed or amused, she settled on the latter. With a short laugh, she nodded and wiped the sweat from her forehead. "All right. I concede. But I must be getting better—I pricked you."

"You did." Vandeyr stabbed her sword into the dirt of the fenced-in practice field. "Repeat it twenty more times and I'll take you seriously. We're done for now. You're going to be feeling those muscles later. Let's stretch and then get something to drink."

After a quick cool down, they returned their practice swords to the adjacent armory and headed for the side yard which led to the guard's entrance of the palace. A thorny hedgerow twined just inside the wall that surrounded the estate; a screen of trees curtained the palace itself.

The large stone edifice had originally been built as a mansion, then turned to its new purpose after Traedis had become king. The owners had fled her rule; wise, as she would have turned some of them over to the justice of the neighboring kingdoms. Tolin's relations with the rest of the world were historically poor.

That had begun to change, but many from both inside and outside Tolin were unhappy, either with the changes, or a lack of confidence in those changes. Traedis was not a popular ruler. But she possessed the *falmyros*, the godsgiven bond between the king and the land, and could not be easily deposed.

Inside, two guards fell in behind and followed them upstairs toward the family apartments. Vandeyr split off toward the second floor guardpost, leaving Traedis to plod wearily into her sitting room and close the door behind her.

She quickly undid her hair and called for a bath; she would need it before her next engagement. If she could have skipped the obligation, she would have, but it was one commitment she could not shirk.

Dinner with her mother was bound to be difficult.

At least she need not go alone. Her mother had agreed to also invite Traedis' friend Ruth, and Vandeyr was to be a guest rather than a guard. What Mitheira Atenel had planned, Traedis did not know, but it was clear she had some intent if she was willing to have Ruth at the table. She wanted something. And generally, what Mitheira wanted, Traedis did not.

"She just means the best for me," she told herself through gritted teeth. Certainly, her mother believed that. Only, she had not visited Traedis once during the four years Traedis had spent in prison for the crime of desertion. It was hard to understand how Mitheira had meant that for Traedis' good.

Her nerves now frayed to the raw edge, Traedis scooped up her harp case from the floor where Rose Goldsong had waited during arms practice. Usually Traedis carried the harp everywhere, but Vandeyr had put her foot down when she had showed up with a sword in one hand and a harp in the other.

"I don't care if you can't break it!" Vandeyr had told her. "It plays by itself, and I won't have it unnerving everyone on the field while it cheats by singing you some glorious martial music that saps my strength and makes you a paragon with the blade. Leave it back in your apartments!"

"She doesn't—" Traedis had attempted to say, but Vandeyr had cut her off.

"It doesn't matter. You're going to listen to me on the field, even if you ignore me everywhere else."

Now Traedis heard a few airy notes as she opened the case. The harp, an exquisite creation of cherrywood with carven roses that climbed its wooden frame, carried a great treasure: thirty-six gold-coated *sagathas* strings. *Sagathas*, or dragon gold, was one of the most magical substances in the mortal world, and Rose might be worth as much as Traedis' entire city-kingdom. Traedis was aware of the equally precious *sagathas* harp key she wore around her neck, and even more of the single *sagathas* hair at the back of her head that bound herself, the key, and the harp into one inseparable whole.

Sinking onto her settee, she lifted Rose to her lap and leaned her cheek against the soundboard. Her fingers curled over the strings, gently plucking a simple but haunting tune from her childhood. Yes, Rose could play herself, but Traedis preferred the magic her hands and fingers could bring to the music. Besides the *falmyros*, it was the deepest power she possessed: a far greater thing to evoke the heart than to weave the threads of enchantment.

Her mother could wait. For now, Traedis would shore up her spirit with the dance of harpstrings and the sweet murmur of melody.

The Atenel family dining hall was a long but narrow room with age-blackened beams that held up an iron chandelier with two dozen candles. The table was set with porcelain dishes in a blue-and-silver pattern; the cutlery was fine silver. Daylight streamed through the tall eastern windows, so only some of the candles were lit, creating a patchwork of shifting light over the heavy wooden table. Traedis entered, followed by Vandeyr and her brunaidhi friend Ruth whose gray curls bobbed at the level of a human waist.

Then Traedis stopped short. Seated near the head of the table were Kaal Shefferie and his sister Ana.

Vandeyr muttered a curse under her breath.

Mitheira Atenel rose from her seat. As always, Traedis felt disorderly and unkempt in her mother's presence. Her mother was, even in her fifties, one of the great beauties of the City; her hair still shone red gold above a delicate, heart-shaped face and skin as fresh as a much younger woman's. Traedis knew she resembled Mitheira, but did not possess the poise her mother exuded like fine perfume.

That thought faded before the more immediate discomfort of the

Shefferies. Kaal and Ana were from a Council family, and Vandeyr and Ana had once been friends. Still, Vandeyr's loyalty to Traedis was now established.

"Come in and greet our visitors," Mitheira said, her voice hospitable. She introduced Ruth to Ana and Kaal, who responded politely.

"I'm very honored to be invited to your table," Ruth said, no obvious irony in her tone. "And I'm glad to meet you, Lady Ana and Lord Kaal." Traedis could see her friend's lively gaze darting between the two, taking her own measurements.

Kaal stood and seated Traedis between himself and Mitheira. This made it impossible for Traedis to buffer herself with Vandeyr and Ruth on either side of her. Instead, she was forced to smile while his shrewd eyes calculated her response and measured her like a pound of beef bought at market.

Kaal was blond-haired, blue eyed, large-framed, and conspicuously handsome. He was also five years older than she. The last time Traedis had seen him, he had knelt before her throne in open court, presenting her with the unwanted gifts of a valuable necklace and his courtship. He had never taken any notice of her before she had become king, so his intent was obvious. Recently, Traedis had been inundated with suitors who flooded the palace, earnestly and eagerly petitioning for her hand. Most she did not like, and the rest she did not trust. Kaal fit firmly into both the first and the second categories.

"Thank you," she murmured, trying not to clench her teeth.

Mitheira waited until Vandeyr and Ruth were seated before taking her position at the head of the table. She was the perfect hostess; even Ruth's seat was tailored to her tiny frame.

"I'm so glad you've come," Mitheira said, including all five of them by an incline of her head. "Those of us from Council families should not forget each other, though the nature of our roles have changed." It was a subtle needle in Traedis' flesh, but she was used to it by now; her mother would never approve of anything she did.

Servants emerged from the kitchen entrance and brought out the dinner. Chicken with crème sauce and leeks, fresh bread with butter, nut-encrusted trout, candied ginger, and plum tart made an appearance. Despite her earlier nausea, Traedis felt her stomach rumble at the sight. Her mother's table was always impeccable.

Vandeyr unfolded a napkin and placed it on her lap with military precision. "Mother," she said, her voice as even as the cloth, "I think it's admirable of you to keep our friends close after so much strife during our recent transition to having a king." Her smile was perfect, and if she lacked a spark in her eyes, it was barely noticeable. "It's also admirable of you, that since the gods have decreed we have a king, you also welcome *all* her friends to your dinner table."

Traedis knew the signs: Vandeyr was angry. For her to be displeased with Mitheira was unusual, and warmth spread through Traedis' chest.

Kaal gave Ruth a perfunctory glance before turning his attention back to Traedis. "King Traedis," he said, "the dress you are wearing becomes you. If I had known the colors you would choose, I would have brought you gold to match your dress and emeralds to match your eyes. As it is, I have only this small gift, and it does not harmonize as well as I had hoped." He reached into his pocket and brought out a small wooden box, from which he extracted a silver filagree bracelet set with small but deep-hued rubies.

"May I affix it to your wrist?" he asked, his voice too self-satisfied.

"Despite the clash of hues, I think it becomes your natural beauty well."

Traedis swallowed back a very impolitic response. Her mother was watching like a mousing cat, and Traedis could not think of how to refuse him. "Certainly, Lord Kaal," she said, forcing her words out of a reluctant throat. "It is a generous gift." She tried not to cringe as Kaal's fingers swept over her skin.

Ana, another rawboned, handsome blonde, smiled serenely. "Would it not be delightful to be sisters, Vandeyr? I have not seen you so often of late, and it would gladden my heart to share my family with yours." Her gaze was level and calculating; Traedis did not trust her seeming enthusiasm for the match.

Apparently, Vandeyr did not either. She batted her eyelashes at Kaal, then turned her gaze on Ana. With a smile almost identical to the other woman's, she said, "Why Ana, what changed your mind? 'Sister' is not what you called me three weeks ago."

Only the twitch of an eyelid told Traedis that Ana was annoyed. With speech crafted to sound genuine, she said, "I was angry at you. I should apologize, it is true; my temper got the best of me. I should never have let that happen. Of course I understand your desire to support your family in these times of transition. I have never considered you an enemy, Vandeyr. I would be very glad if we became sisters."

"I'm sure you would." Vandeyr speared a piece of plum with her fork and popped it into her mouth. She swallowed, then added, "Since that would mean Kaal would have married Traedis, and the Shefferies had assured themselves of a solid foundation in the royal family."

Ana did not turn a hair, but Kaal reddened slightly. "King Traedis, I hope you don't think my interest in you is merely as a step to the throne…"

Vandeyr gave a snort so quiet that Traedis might not have heard if she had not expected it.

A line briefly appeared in Mitheira's forehead, then cleared. "None of us," she said adamantly, without looking at Vandeyr, "would ever think such a foolish thing. You are a guest at my table, and I would not insult you in such a fashion."

A stir of anger heated Traedis' cheeks, but she could not bring herself to contradict her mother, or to shame her in her own house. Vandeyr's eyes glittered from across the table.

Ruth took a sip of wine. "None of us think that your interest is *merely* as a step to the throne."

The chicken lost its flavor in Traedis' mouth. Kaal might not have leered at her, but Ruth's implication made Traedis feel ill. She could not imagine sharing a bed with Kaal Shefferie, no matter how handsomely he presented himself.

After her experience in prison with a skilled interrogator, Traedis would never let herself be cozened by another man who wanted to suborn her will. She brushed aside the sensation of soft lips on hers and grasped the table's edge with whitened knuckles.

Oblivious or unconcerned with Traedis' discomfort, Ana said, "Traedis, I never got the chance to really know you when you were a child, nor did my brother. I would love to hear about your studies and your time in Kaelennar, as well as why you've made the changes you have in Tolin. Unlike some of my compatriots, I will not simply dismiss your thoughts, nor will Kaal. Please understand that we are at this table out of respect for your rule, not greed or ambition."

Blinking mildly, Ruth asked, "I don't really know much about the

Council families. What did the Shefferies oversee?"

Traedis found herself cutting her trout into increasingly smaller pieces.

Kaal answered, his tone just a bit too condescending, "We supervise the financial aspect of the City, and manage governmental spending. It has always been our pride as well as our duty."

Ruth nodded. "Does that mean you are as solidly behind Traedis' rule as many of the merchants are?"

Kaal drew a breath to speak, but Ana cut in quickly. "Of course we support the gods' mandate. How could we do anything else? If they decree we have a king, we will have a king."

Vandeyr's gaze sparked with malice. "How very prudent." She finished her leeks with neat, even bites, then flashed a bright smile. "It is, perhaps, a politician's answer, but you've always excelled in that area."

Mitheira cleared her throat. "Vandeyr, please be polite while you sit at my table, and do not bring your petty disagreements here."

"Petty?" Vandeyr said, her expression clouding. Traedis gave her a slight shake of the head. Vandeyr contented herself with saying, "I did not mean to insult your hospitality, Mother. Perhaps this is a conversation we should take up another time."

Ana said, "I would be happy to do that, Vandeyr. Believe me, Kaal and I have no ill will toward you or the king."

Yet, Traedis thought, but did not give the word voice.

Ana continued as pleasantly as if she had heard nothing against her. "Traedis, I would like to make up for being relative strangers when we should all have been friends many years ago. Would you come with us on an outing next thirdday? Vandeyr and I can both act as chaperones, and you need not fear that Kaal will be anything but a gentleman."

"I would be most honored if you would accept," Kaal said smoothly.

A vivid memory rushed into Traedis' mind; a red fox with an almost impish expression requesting she come out to play. Elben, the red-bearded Haven knight had also established himself as a suitor. The fact that Traedis and he could both transform into foxes—she into a gray fox, he into a red— was not the smallest lure.

The difference between Elben and Kaal could not have been more evident. Elben had treated Traedis with courtesy and respect, and though he had made his interest clear, he did not press her for an answer. Kaal had embarrassed her in open court, cozied up to her mother, and given Traedis two gifts she could not socially refuse.

If it had not been for the curse laid upon her by a Power of air, Traedis might have accepted Elben's suit. As it was, she had no intention of endangering him. Its ambiguous wording could mean many things, and had already taken most of her freedom.

She could not send Kaal packing the way she wanted. Mitheira had maneuvered her into an impossible position. If Traedis declined, she would offend her mother in her own house.

"I accept your invitation," she told Ana.

Traedis stepped out of the carriage, shaken by her mother's ambush. Perhaps she should have expected something of the sort, but she had not been prepared to deal with the Shefferies.

The carriageway in front of the palace was lined with carefully manicured trees which drooped graceful limbs to the ground as if bowing. They were imports; though they handled winter cold well enough, the ice storms that would sometimes sweep down the mountains could damage their fragile boughs.

Traedis stopped to trail a hand against a long, golden leaf. Someone had loved gardens. She was glad of it, as the trees, shrubs, and flowers were well-grown, and she could simply enjoy them.

Vandeyr's step behind her faltered for a moment. Traedis started to look over her shoulder, when Vandeyr shoved her roughly to the ground, falling on top of her.

"Damn!" came Vandeyr's voice in her ear, venom spilling from it like a viper's fangs. Her weight lifted.

Traedis rolled over to see a terrifying form a few body lengths away: a black wolf, large as a pony and scaled like a lizard. Its hide was the hue of ebony, and the whole of both eyes was a dark, featureless blue. It was a ciriin; Traedis had only seen one before, but they were unmistakable, and beautiful in their own wild fashion.

The creature sat on its haunches, let its tongue loll out, and laughed: not the laughter of a wolf, but a deep, throaty woman's laughter with an edge of mockery.

Vandeyr had recovered her balance, and now held a knife in one hand, a sword in the other. "What do you want here?" she called, her voice ringing against the gray stone of the palace.

Traedis rose to a crouch as the other guards closed around her. Her wrist dagger slipped into her hand, and it took her only a moment more to pull one of the jeweled hairpins from her head and flick off the protective sheath that hid the stiletto inside. She waited, weapons at the ready, wishing she wore trousers rather than skirts. One of the guards shook her head as Traedis moved to exit their protective circle. Frustrated, Traedis could only watch.

The ciriin laughed again, then stood and padded in a long arc around the knot of guards who protected Traedis.

"Stop!" Vandeyr's hand barely twitched, but the knife in her hand changed position. "If you have business with the king, state it. If not, explain yourself!"

"I think not," the creature said.

Before the ciriin had even completed the sentence, Vandeyr's knife flashed in the air. But the ciriin moved fluidly to one side, and the dagger passed by harmlessly. Another dagger followed the first, and again the beast eluded it as deftly as if she had known it was coming.

Of course she had. Ciriin fed on emotions. Traedis opened her mouth to tell her sister, but before she could explain, another knife flew from Vandeyr's fingers, this one hitting its mark. A yelp came from the ciriin, but she continued pacing past the guards. Vandeyr turned with the creature, keeping her back to Traedis.

The ciriin jumped to one side, only to meet two more knives, both of which sank into a soft crease where a line of scales met her shoulder. She grunted in pain, and a satisfied noise escaped Vandeyr's lips.

Then the creature blinked out like a firefly, leaving no trace of herself behind. Vandeyr's daggers dropped to the ground.

The flutter of paper caught Traedis' eye. On the main steps to the palace sat a parchment, its blue wax seal brilliant against the stone. It had not been there moments before.

Vandeyr saw it a moment later, and her expression became grim. Her head turned toward the steps, and she halted momentarily before returning to Traedis' side.

"Atenel blue," she said.

Traedis nodded. "It has to be from Daymet or Uncle Cordelayne."

It was hard to think of either of them without pain. Uncle Cordelayne had acted almost as a father to Traedis: had taught her to play harp. He had also trained Vandeyr in the arts of the assassins. But now that Traedis was king, neither he nor their brother Daymet would accept the ruling of the gods. The two had left Tolin to found a resistance against Traedis, and were now implacable enemies.

"Wait until we get inside," Vandeyr told her, taking a pair of gloves from her pouch. She used them to pick up the paper while she examined the entire entrance. She carefully opened the door herself, passing her hand through the lintel before allowing Traedis to go through.

"Get Master Tagg," Traedis told one of the guards. Tagg was her house mage, and would know if there was magic about—which was likely, considering that someone had put a sealed parchment on the front steps without anyone noticing.

Instead of going to her rooms, Traedis followed her sister toward the staircase to the lower level, where a chamber was prepared to protect at least two dozen people in case of some disaster. It was bound with magic stronger than the spells on the palace as a whole, and reinforced with doubly thick walls. It was comfortable but not lush, furnished with two settees, a table, and several chairs.

Traedis took a seat, her skirts rustling against the cushion. Immediately, Vandeyr took a stance facing her, her expression stormy.

"What happened?" Traedis asked. "I'm surprised you managed to injure the ciriin."

"Is that what she was?" asked Vandeyr. "I thought so. When I realized she could read my movements from my feelings, I tried to feed her confusing emotions. I'd hate to try that for any length of time, though. Right now I've got guards looking for her, but I don't have any real expectations that she stayed around. Still, that piece of paper showed up when she gated out."

Traedis nodded, shaken. Ciriin were strange creatures, a race born of refractions of a true dragon from a crystal-lined cave in the Dragon Mountains. They often had odd powers, and all shared the need to feed off the emotions of others. As a result, many of them fell to evil, their urge to induce the most intense feelings plunging them into cruel and violent actions.

They were not inherently so; Traedis had met one who was not. But the fact that some possessed potent magics made them chancy to deal with. If Uncle Cordelayne had enlisted a ciriin's help, he had brought another level of danger upon her.

A knock at the door proved to be Tagg and one of the mages employed by the Guard. Tagg, a small, rotund man with a round face, lowered his eyebrows in apparent thought. The other, a young man just growing his first mustache, saluted Vandeyr and stood at attention.

"Did you find any traces?" asked Vandeyr.

Tagg tapped his fingers against his thigh. "She obviously gated in magically. The magical signature is strange, though—a little like something that might wash out of the mountains when the river floods."

"She gated into and out of the palace compound," said Traedis wearily. That was bad news, given how strong the magical protections on the palace were. "If all she did was drop a piece of parchment and laugh at us, she's going out of her way to alarm us."

Vandeyr straightened her spine and firmed her lips into a tight line. "It's one of Uncle Cordelayne's favorite tricks. The more unnerved you can make an opponent, the more mistakes they make. He's showing only a fraction of his strength, just enough to let us know he has it, not enough for us to truly gauge how much." She lifted an eyebrow. "Trae, you recognized that creature. I know very little about them. What can a ciriin do?"

Traedis rubbed her arm where she suspected a bruise was forming. "They can often take several shapes, including human. You've certainly heard they feed off emotions—"

"Dream Eaters," said Tagg, nodding.

"I've heard that term." Traedis shivered, though it was not cold. "They're people, though. Intelligent, speaking, reasoning beings, which makes them far more dangerous than simple beasts."

Vandeyr frowned. "And certainly, if this one were able to gate through the palace walls, she could have dropped that letter at night, in stealth. Ambushing us as we got back? That's a Player's trick." She held out the letter. "Master Tagg, my ring says there's no magic about this. Am I right?"

Tagg took a deep breath and his entire frame relaxed. He lifted one hand to hover over the paper, then brushed it lightly. He closed his eyes briefly, then opened them again. "No magic," he confirmed.

Vandeyr jerked her chin up and down, and examined the seal. "Cordelayne's." She broke it without bothering with a knife. Scanning its contents, her scowl deepened. "Curse him, anyway!" She half-threw the paper at Traedis, who caught it neatly before it flapped its way to the ground.

Traedis smoothed out the creases and looked down. In Uncle Cordelayne's neat, elegant handwriting, was a single line: *Your actions will bring about their own consequences.* It was signed, *Lord Cordelayne Atenel.*

"Fearmongering," Vandeyr said. "Showing off. Daring us to come after him." She slipped one of her daggers from its sheath and ran her finger over it. "No useful information, just goading us into making mistakes." She tossed the dagger lightly into her other hand. "I'd say he's gearing up for a move, but it won't be in a direction we expect."

"Of course," Traedis sighed. She rose to her feet. "I don't need to stay here until you've searched every niche in the palace. You've said yourself we won't expect the next move."

"Fine!" said Vandeyr. "It's bad enough playing a three-cornered game of King's Crown with him, but you have to put yourself in danger—"

"I have to rule Tolin." Traedis was still clutching her hairpin. Tethyn wordlessly handed her back the sheath, and Traedis slipped it back inside her braided hair. "I can't huddle inside this room like an oyster in a shell. There is danger in being king, and Uncle Cordelayne isn't the only source."

"I haven't forgotten," Vandeyr said tightly. "Very well. I'll even admit you're right. I just hate this."

Traedis nodded. "So do I." She tallied up her enemies: Uncle

Cordelayne and his followers; the demonic Mother of Curses; many of Tolin's own people. In some ways, it was a miracle that she was still alive.

She met Vandeyr's gaze. "So do I," she said again.

The next day, Traedis sat in her office poring over correspondence and reports. Summer sunshine wafted scintillating particles of dust into the air, making her squint to see the missive she'd just received about Tolin's dwindling moneys. She dropped the packet and leaned back in her chair, debating what to do about the problem in a long-term way.

A sharp rap sounded on the door. "Come in!" Traedis called, guessing it was Vandeyr.

It was. Vandeyr pulled the door open and glided into the office. "We've got an issue, and you need to hear the report I have for you."

Traedis felt a further sinking in the pit of her stomach. "Another problem?"

"Someone is up to a new set of tricks. I'm dubious that it's Uncle Cordelayne, though I can't be sure—it doesn't seem to be his sort of mischief." Vandeyr closed the door, pulled up a chair, and dropped into it, tension in every line of her body.

Traedis leaned heavily on her forearms. "What is it now?"

Vandeyr's mouth twisted unpleasantly. "I've been talking to Captain Dorrell. It seems the City Guard has been dealing with something of an unexpected surge in violence. Assaults against people traveling by themselves or in small groups. It's bad enough just like that, but when you recognize the violence is against the poor and the clergy—your primary supporters—it becomes fairly obvious." She frowned. "A Coran priest was even beaten bloody at the door of his own church. No one saw anything. I just wish Dorrell had brought it to my attention earlier. He seems to think that he should handle everything in the City without consulting the palace about it."

Traedis remained silent as she watched the now-swirling specks of dust drift down the sunbeams onto the desk. Her mind also swirled in futile circles as she tried to decide the best course of action. There were too many troubles and she had neither the experience nor the skill to negotiate them.

Vandeyr waited, obviously annoyed. "You need to do something besides practice to be a dartboard. If you need advice, ask, but don't sit there and gape like a town gate on market day."

Traedis shut her mouth quickly. Then she opened it again to protest, realizing at the last moment that Vandeyr must be worried and strained. Traedis closed her mouth again.

"Or a fish on the riverbank," Vandeyr added acerbically. "It's a good thing you don't do this in court, or half of the City would be convinced that you're a fool."

"Half of the City *is* convinced I'm a fool," said Traedis, finding words at last. "I don't act like this in court because I have to convince them otherwise. I didn't think I had to convince you."

Vandeyr looked down at the toes of her boots. Looking up again, she said, "What are your orders? We need to move quickly, or the City is going to panic, and that will give Uncle Cordelayne the perfect opportunity to edge in. You're in some danger, in case you hadn't realized."

"Enough!" Traedis snapped, stung beyond her tolerance at last. "I understand the situation. I am not stupid. You are simply talking so much that I can't get hold of a thought before you chase it away again."

Vandeyr's surprised gaze rose to Traedis' face. "Very well. Do your thinking," she said more mildly than Traedis would have expected. "Do I need to leave the room?"

"You just need to keep quiet for a short while," Traedis answered curtly, still angered by her sister's taunts. "I need a chance to think."

Vandeyr nodded, her blue eyes still holding a slightly startled look. She folded her arms and leaned back in her chair, gazing out the window.

Traedis sat up straight and closed her eyes to screen out distractions. She needed advice, but there were few she trusted in the City. An image rose to her mind: an elderly but hale woman with a wrinkled face and a sharp, penetrating gaze.

"Slip into your old boots," Traedis said. "We're going to visit the Elder of the Church of Coran."

"The goat woman?" Vandeyr stared. "Why?"

"Because she's not as much of a fool as you think, and because she has very clear sight for—well—goat shit. And we're mired so deep we need to speak to someone with a good nose."

"All right," Vandeyr said, sighing a bit more dramatically than necessary. "We're going to visit the goat woman. I suppose it's more useful than baying at the moon." She made a gesture of futility. "I know you far too well to think that you're going to listen to anyone's reasons but your own."

Then she grinned unexpectedly. "But sometimes your reasons aren't too bad." The corners of her lips turned up. "Just don't tell Mother I said that. She'd disown me."

Traedis was not quite sure whether to smile back.

The goat woman's house sat on one side of a steep pasture. It was a tidy little cottage built of fieldstones and roofed with slate; sadly faded curtains hung in the windows, their patterns remembering the bright colors which had once graced their fabric. Oaken shutters stood open beside the windows and the door was also made of solid oak.

As they neared it, the door opened, and the goat woman came out. "King Traedis!" she said, her mouth splitting into a snaggle-toothed smile. "Come in and have some sausage bread! You look like someone needs to feed you."

Traedis felt a little startled at how tiny the old priest was; the Elder's presence was sufficiently great that memory belied her actual size.

Vandeyr's expression was free of every emotion except polite respect. Traedis knew her sister well enough to realize that this meant she highly disapproved of the goat woman's casual attitude toward the king of Tolin. Taking up a post outside the door, Vandeyr kept one hand on her sword, her spine straight as a lance.

The inside of the cottage was cozy and comfortable, and smelled strongly of the herbs which draped in bunches from the ceiling. A heavy table and chairs dominated the room, and a merry fire burned in the large stone fireplace.

"Sit down," the goat woman said, pulling a chair up to the table for Traedis. "Make yourself at home. What have you come for? Shall I cut you a slice of sausage bread?"

"Thank you and yes," Traedis answered in slight amusement. It felt good to be treated like an ordinary person, much like she might have been treated by her friends in Kaelennar. "As to what I have come for, that will take a little explanation. I would greatly appreciate your counsel in a difficult time."

"You see," the goat woman said, as if continuing a previous conversation. "I thought you were different. No one has asked my counsel in the past twenty...? Yes, twenty or so years. Instead I get a pat on the head and am told, 'Yes, you're venerable and wise, but you're obviously too foolish to be of any assistance to the City.' I would be happy to help you if I can."

Traedis laughed lightly, as some of the tension seemed to ease out of her muscles. "Perhaps you could help me figure out the wisest course of action I may take. People—including priests—are being attacked in the streets, and we're not sure where the danger is coming from. If you have any wisdom, I would be most anxious to know it."

"The goats know, not I." The old priest cut a large chunk of sausage bread, placed it on a plate taken from one of the shelves, and offered it to Traedis. It was still warm and smelled deliciously of savory and sage. "They are sacred, dedicated to the god. I merely read their signs. Do you want some tea with that?" She took a kettle from the hearth and hooked it onto a rod which stretched from one end of the fireplace to the other.

"Yes, please." Traedis took an exploratory bite of the bread; a delicious burst of spice coated her tongue. "If you've learned anything from the goats, I would be grateful to know what they have told you."

"They're trying to cut you off at the knees, aren't they?" The goat woman fetched a mug down from a shelf a little higher than her head and inspected it closely. "I haven't heard anything about these attacks, but I'll be happy to ask the goats and see if they have anything to say." She took a tin and spooned tea into the mug.

"The goats have spoken on other matters," she continued, "and you need to know what they've said. Well, not spoken exactly, but made themselves understood." She took the now-burbling kettle and poured it into the cup. "The goats think that if the people of Tolin reject your governance and their tie with the land, they may get their wish." She frowned. "I don't like the sound of it. They haven't been clearer, though I've tried to get them to elaborate on their prophecy. The god says what he wishes, no more." She plunked the mug down on the table. "Sugar in your tea, dear?"

"Thank you, no." Traedis drew her brows together in consternation. She could make out the goats' foreboding no better than could the goat woman, but she agreed that it sounded sinister. Every citizen of Tolin had a bond with the land and thus to Traedis, whether they realized it or no. It was the way the gods had ordered the world. Short of foreswearing allegiance to Tolin there was no way to break that tie. It would mean a failure on Traedis' part, for regardless of whether she liked her people, she was responsible for them and for their welfare. Cutting them adrift from the land would not prove beneficial: in fact, it sounded threatening. She resolved to do everything in her power to prevent that from happening.

Traedis cupped her hands around the cup's warmth gratefully. The mug looked as solid as the earth, competently but not artistically made, with a glaze of brown and tan. Traedis guessed the goat woman had made it herself.

"Another thing," the old woman said. She pulled a chair out for herself and sat down to face Traedis, her round-cheeked face earnest and compassionate. "I'm afraid it will be a long and hard trial for you, my dear. There is considerable trouble of an unspecified nature in your immediate future. I'm not quite sure exactly what, except the goats say that your sister—the one glowering at my window—well, it's a confusing reading.

The goats say that she is loyal, but they also say you should not trust her. It seems to be a contradiction and I'm having trouble making sense of it. I asked them if she intended betrayal, and they say no. I asked them if she would betray you unintentionally and they say no to that as well. But they keep coming back to the point that you should not trust her."

Traedis shook her head, unsure what to think. After she had finally begun to communicate with Vandeyr she did not think her sister would turn traitor, and the goats seemed to support her in this. But she also did not trust easily, and Vandeyr had never been predictable. A sound of frustration escaped her lips; oracles were notorious for their ability to distress without enlightening.

"I know," the goat woman said, a mischievous smile tugging at the corners of her mouth. "Wouldn't it be nice if the gods simply told us what we wanted to know without making us caper around trying to figure out what they mean? But they don't, so there's no point in getting upset about it. Coran must think this is sufficient warning for whatever you need to know."

Traedis nodded wearily. "I'm sure it will become clear in time. It's just that I'm not sure how to treat Vandeyr, given what you've said."

"I can't tell you that," the goat woman said. "I relay what I am told, though sometimes I can make some sense out of a possible meaning. Not this time, though. Here. Take some of this sausage bread with you. There's far too much of it just for me. Don't they ever feed you at the palace?"

"They keep me hopping so much I never have a chance to eat," Traedis said glumly. "Thank you. I'd like some of it. I'll make sure I eat it, too."

The goat woman pushed back her chair and stood. "Well then, I'll get some ready. Don't get up, dear, I'll manage fine on my own. I'd hate to make the king of Tolin run my errands. I'll just cut off the middle here and wrap it in a towel to keep it fresh. Don't mind me."

Traedis laughed. "I don't mind you. Not in the least."

The following fourthday, Traedis slogged through petitions until open court was finally over. She left the throne room promptly, and headed up the main flight of stairs to her apartments, Vandeyr and Tethyn behind her. Vandeyr's step was so quiet that Traedis looked behind herself twice to make sure her sister was still there.

Tethyn split off at the guardpost, but Vandeyr followed Traedis into her quarters. She took a chair, stretched out her legs, and crossed her booted ankles. Traedis raised a questioning eyebrow; her sister clearly had an agenda.

"What is it?" Traedis asked.

Vandeyr propped an elbow on the arm of the chair and leaned her chin against her hand. "What with lurking ciriin and his own considerable talents, I've been worrying about Uncle Cordelayne getting intelligence on your abilities. What could he learn of your studies if he were trying?"

There lay a terrifying abyss. Suddenly, Traedis felt each brush of her silk dress as if a layer had peeled from her skin; each sound which reached her ears grated like the squeal of boots on a marble floor. Tension gathered in her middle and weighed her down like a belt of stones.

She forced herself to consider the question. Slowly, she said, "It's possible he could find out about spell chording." She picked at the skin around one of her nails. "My bardic master knew the theory I was working with, and could explain it at least as well as I. I've not been able to teach it to anyone but for a single exception—and that was to someone with a greater-than-mortal capacity. I have a facility for improvisation and for modifying a spell in mid-course. I've stretched some of the limits of spell chording since I was in Kaelennar."

Spell chording gave Traedis the ability to bind more than one type of magic into a single song. It was a rare and powerful skill, and one that even experienced bards had difficulty learning.

Vandeyr frowned. "That's bad. Uncle Cordelayne will want to know everything about your bardic gifts, and anything else magical about you that he didn't find out when you were in prison. At least he doesn't know about the *sagathas* modifications to your harp."

Traedis felt immensely weary. "He doesn't know about what my harp can do, or—" She paused, trying to decide whether to tell Vandeyr about her sojourn in the Heart of Winter. Perhaps now was not the time. "Or other things. I didn't tell my closest friends in Kaelennar anything they didn't need to know."

"You'll have to tell me some of those," Vandeyr said dryly, dashing Traedis' hope that her sister had missed the elision. "You're lucky you didn't spill your secrets. There wasn't actually a treason charge against you when the Storm Eagle returned you to the City."

Traedis did not feel lucky, though on the whole she was glad to be alive. The four years she had spent alone in her cell had been nightmarish, harder even than facing the Nightdance or fighting to free the Storm Eagle from the chains forged out of his *falmyros*. The high aelin Cir had, through the land itself, placed thousands of tiny tethers on the Storm Eagle, which had held him inescapably within the borders of Tolin.

Remembering that—and the millennia-long imprisonment of the demon Toledru—she felt petty for bemoaning her own entrapment by Tolin's *falmyros*. Toledru had once been Haven's ruler, and then the City's, after being stripped of the *falmyros* by the gods. His quest for the rule of

Tolin had brought him to make a deadly bargain, and had entrapped him beneath the City in a living tomb. That bargain had also bound the Storm Eagle, and deny it as she might, Traedis was beginning to understand him better than she would have liked.

A knock came: Traedis opened the door to reveal a page, who approached and bowed. "Yes?" Traedis asked, hoping whatever message the young girl brought was nothing she had to address at present.

"Your Majesty, Lady Ana and Lord Kaal Shefferie have sent word that they will meet you at noon in the guardhouse by the west gate."

An exaggerated sense of dread stuck Traedis. She had forgotten all about the planned outing with the Shefferies. She smacked her forehead. "How could that have slipped my mind?"

Vandeyr's expression was as close to sheepish as Traedis had ever seen her. "I forgot as well," she growled. "If both of us had forgotten just a few more hours, we'd only have to make apologies, not excuses."

"I can't do that," Traedis said wearily. "It will cause more problems than it solves."

"I know that!" Vandeyr's voice was a whipcrack. "Leave me my dreams, will you?"

They had planned a leisurely ride through the woods, interrupted by a light meal. Traedis found herself wishing she were back in open court. Many of the disputes might be petty, even heated, but few were malicious. And she was not in the mood for a light outing, much less for dealing with Shefferie deviousness.

"I suppose we have to go." She turned to the page. "Send word that we will meet them, and tell the cooks to cancel my noon meal." She turned to Vandeyr. "We'll have to change. Give me a few minutes and I'll meet you in my sitting room.”

Vandeyr nodded and exited the room, returning a few moments later with Tethyn, at whom she snapped a few instructions. A moment later, Vandeyr disappeared around the corner to her own room, attached to Traedis’ quarters. Traedis stood and ducked into her own bedchamber.

She quickly threw off her court attire, and donned comfortable leathers. Luckily, since they were riding, she did not need to wear jewelry, and either explain to Kaal that his necklace and bracelet were not her favorite gems, or be forced to wear them, burdened with the weight of his expectations. She left her hair braided in its crown, the stiletto hairpins firmly seated.

Traedis, Vandeyr, and their four guards arrived slightly late to find Ana, Kaal, and a manservant waiting astride their horses. Ana’s long fingers tapped her saddle horn; she stopped as they pulled up beside her.

“I am most sorry,” Traedis said, trying her best to look contrite. “I had open court this morning, and it took more time than I’d intended to get ready. Shall we start?”

Kaal smiled, his white teeth flashing. “It is of no great matter. We were perfectly happy to wait, weren’t we, Ana?”

“Perfectly,” said Ana, with just a trace of annoyance in her voice.

The land outside the City was verdant with summer, though autumn gold was beginning to thread through the trees. Surrounding the wide road beyond the city gates were slanting mountain fields, sprouting tall spikes of grain, or holding small herds of cows, sheep, and goats. Pigs foraged in the woods during the warmer months, only gathered into sties during the winter.

Up mountain to the east the land was forested mostly in pine and other hardy trees. The high line of demarcation was where Tolin met the Dragon

Mountains; everything beyond seemed unnaturally clear, as if each scruffy blade of grass, the veining of each leaf, even the hollows of stone had been painted by a master. She could feel the line, too, like an itch against Tolin's skin made of prickling magic more ancient than the mountain roots.

They soon turned off the road towards the lower forest: also mostly pine, but sprinkled with oak, birch, aspen, and other broad-leafed trees. Ana led the way, guiding her dapple-gray gelding with a sure hand onto one of the paths that led into the woods.

Traedis would have been glad to enjoy the ride without speech, but that was not what the Shefferies intended. Kaal pulled his horse alongside hers, causing it to snort and dance sideways. Traedis gentled it, grateful for moments when she could ignore Kaal.

"It is a fine day, is it not?" he asked, as portentously as if he were revealing a long-hoarded secret.

"It is," Traedis agreed, wishing that a deluge would begin so they would be forced to return. "A fine day for an outing."

"We won't have too many days this warm before autumn sets in." Kaal's determination to talk about the weather struck Traedis as being straight out of an etiquette manual.

Deciding that she could play that game as well, she gave him a tight smile. "I expect a few more sunny afternoons, though we're close to the autumn storms. But I enjoy winter as well, despite the hardships it causes. Sitting before the hearth with a mug of tea while the snow falls outside can be a delightful way to pass an afternoon." She made sure to keep her tone light. She would not speak to him of the real reason she loved winter; the deep connection she had with Winter's lord and the land tucked deeply into his heart.

"That sounds lovely," said Kaal. "A good time for visiting and long talks over some mulled wine, perhaps. I would love to sit and look out that window with you."

Traedis sighed internally; she was trying to deflect his advances, not encourage them. "Oh, look, our sisters are getting ahead of us," she said, and urged her horse to go faster. Kaal followed.

The path was steep, and the sun fell in fat, green drops through the overhead canopy. Their horses' hooves crunched through years of fallen leaves. Catching up with Vandeyr and Ana, Traedis stayed just far enough behind not to cause the horses to press too closely. Kaal was next, followed by the servant and Traedis' guard detail.

"...glad that Traedis has chosen to continue the City's training," Ana was saying. "It speaks of her commitment to—" She broke off and looked behind her. "Traedis! We plan to stop in the clearing by the waterfall. I thought it would be a picturesque place for a light meal."

The clearing was not far; Traedis remembered it well. That was where she had released her horse and thrown spare clothes over the cliff when she had fled the City at fourteen. She had hoped at the time that her family would think she was dead. Later she had found they were not fooled in the least, but had chosen not to come after her for reasons she still did not fully understand. She was not sure whether Ana knew this, or whether she had picked the spot entirely by accident. She did not know why Ana would purposely choose to remind her of that piece of her past, unless to put Traedis off-guard. Ana seemed to have inherited a double portion of her generation's brains, and might be laying a more subtle trap than Kaal's courtship.

The site was lovely, but far enough from the gates that it was not a common destination for a casual excursion. The fall cascaded steeply from high on the mountain, dropping in a straight sheet for some distance before meeting a narrow gorge and channeling into a stream. It was fullest in the spring, but even now enough water poured over it to envelop the area in a chorus of water and rock. Near the edge of the gorge, a flat meadow stretched, just large enough for a few horses and a picnic.

As they dismounted and tethered their horses, the servant spread a cloth for them to sit, pulling delicacies from his saddlebags. The rush of water over the narrow but high falls was soothing and pleasant. Ana sat first and Traedis settled next to her; Vandeyr darted in to take the seat on Traedis' other side. Kaal dropped down with the barest hint of a pout on his handsome face.

Traedis breathed a sigh of relief, then decided it was too early to relax. Ana's face showed nothing but concern and pleasant interest, but Traedis did not trust her any more than she would offer her hand to an adder. The manservant laid out their dishes: plates, silverware, and metal cups, along with fruit, cheese, liver pâté, and wine. Ana swatted at a mosquito, then tucked a strand of blonde hair behind her ear.

"Traedis, I've been wanting to discuss how best to support you in your role as king." Ana plucked a blade of grass and twirled it absently in her fingers. "I want you to understand that I don't fault you for the difficult decisions you've made after being given the *falmyros* so precipitously. In fact, I respect you for them, though I don't always agree." She let the blade of grass drop from her fingers and swirl away in the breeze.

"I not only respect you, I admire you," Kaal chimed in, earnest sincerity lacing his words. "You defeated an enemy we did not even know we had, and wiped his taint away from our soil." He reached for an apricot, taking a large bite. Juice dribbled down his chin and he wiped it off with the back of his hand.

Ana patted Traedis gently on the shoulder. Traedis fought the urge to pull back. "My dear," Ana said, "I know that the burden of ruling lies mostly upon the king, but it does not mean that you need shoulder all that burden alone. I commend you in your choice to name your brother viceroy. That is a sage decision, and well-thought-out."

"But?" Vandeyr's voice was a dagger slashing through the thread of Ana's evasion. "You want something."

Ana's lids closed for a brief moment, then opened again. "I have given my life to Tolin, and will always do so." Her words were sharp, but her tone remained cool. "There is no need for divisiveness. We all have Tolin's welfare in mind, it is simply a matter of coming to mutual agreements."

"What agreements?" Traedis believed her. Uncle Cordelayne and Daymet had the welfare of Tolin in mind also, but it did not mean there were agreements to be made.

Ana reached for a cup of wine, moistening her lips. "Whatever changes to Tolin's laws and practices, they must be enacted by the king." A line formed between her brows. "You have all the power in Tolin, Traedis. That does not mean you cannot ask for advice—as you have already done, in fact. I wonder if you could benefit from a small group with specialized knowledge."

"A small group like the Shefferies?" asked Vandeyr, her gaze hardening.

"Vandeyr, please, we've spoken of this." Ana shook her head. "Of course the Shefferies have special knowledge. We have governed the financial quarter of the City for countless generations. I would not offer my opinion on something I knew less well than that stewardship. But I am not proposing I become Traedis' sole counselor." She tapped her fingers against her thigh. "My proposal is quite otherwise." She turned to Traedis. "You are not availing yourself of the knowledge and expertise of millennia. A small group of advisors—"

"Such as a council?" Traedis broke in, finally realizing where Ana was headed. She drew a deep breath to remind herself not to speak hastily.

"You could call it such. I understand why you might have some concern about the old Council. Though individually I respected them greatly, I found them collectively hidebound. And though I think you should not have delivered them to the justice of Telardur, I can understand why you felt you must."

The wine was souring Traedis' stomach, and the afternoon sun was far too warm; sweat gathered under her leathers. "I am not reinstating the Council," she said flatly.

Ana sighed. "That was not my suggestion. My suggestion was to ask for advice from the Council families, since all have studied the governance of the City their entire lives."

"I am not reinstating the Council," said Traedis again.

She cast a sidelong look at Vandeyr, who was unexpectedly straight-faced, a sign that she was suppressing laughter. Traedis shook her head, as much at Vandeyr's inexplicable mood change as at Ana's suggestion.

"Perhaps you simply need—" Kaal began, but Ana interrupted.

"Traedis, I don't want to be your enemy, and I certainly don't mean to make demands. Please, just consider my words." Ana picked up her cup and took a swallow.

Traedis nodded warily. She disliked Ana, but did not want to make an actual enemy out of her—though that might settle the question of Kaal's courtship.

Gazing out over the waterfall, she saw her younger self slip off her horse, take her pack and drop a bundle over the sheer cliff while the spray misted tiny rainbows into the air. She had been so full of anger, fear, and absolute certainty. She would never have guessed where her life would go from there. Six and a half years; it seemed much longer.

She was done here. Traedis put down her cup and turned to the others. "Let's continue."

When Traedis got back to her apartments, a visitor was waiting for her.

A hound occupied her sitting room. He was tall, his back rising higher than Traedis' waist; his soft white hair hung well below his body and feathered his legs. His face was narrow and delicate, his eyes a deep green-blue. He was known as 'the Wise Hound' and he shared his name with Ymre, the fabled land of flowers. It was a place Traedis remembered with deep longing and a sense of peace that she had rarely experienced.

"Lord Ymre," said Traedis, inclining her head with deep respect. He was one of the great Powers of the world, a star who had not shone in the sky since the world's beginning. A smile bloomed on her face. "You are most welcome to my home. How may I help you?" It did not surprise her that none of her posted guards had mentioned him; the palace was guarded against normal magic, but that was like comparing a trickle of water to a flooding river torrent.

Ymre sat and twitched his nose. "King Traedis, pardon my intrusion," he said in a man's deep voice. "When you were last in my land I promised to bring you a runebook. I have kept my word."

There was indeed a book on one of Traedis' incidental tables. She seated herself and looked more closely at the narrow volume. It was bound in green-dyed leather, and bore no stamp on its cover. She carefully flipped it open.

The first page displayed a single bardic rune, precisely inked out on the page. Traedis felt her vision shift; the rune rose off the page and shimmered in the air in front of her.

"It's a rune of light," Ymre told her. "I thought that would be the best choice for your beginning studies. Though I have shown you the first rune—the *quixil*, the irreducible circle of the serpent which bites its own tail—learning this one will give you an advantage as you progress in your study." He whuffed lightly and shook his coat.

Traedis stared at him. She knew Lord Ymre wanted her to learn runecasting for some reason of his own, but he had not explained it to her. The gods did not permit him to divulge everything he saw with his star's vision, but she wished he could speak plainly.

Though runecasting was a fascinating area of bardic magic, Traedis had little time as it was, given her responsibilities. But she was not so foolish as to ignore the Wise Hound's direction.

It had been a long time since she had learned about runes in the bardic college. The general consensus of her teachers had been that they were too dangerous to study. Failure to properly form them could endanger the caster at the very least. Some considered them a cheap route to power, since they were fueled both by a runecaster's ability and the forms of the characters themselves, but took only a fragment of the energy bardic song or dance could consume. Other, darker rumors circulated about possible uses. Best not to set one's pen to an art that could bring about great evil.

But now the author of writing itself was telling her to learn. Despite her reluctance to presume on his goodwill, Traedis raised an eyebrow and said, "Why do you want me to learn this craft? Isn't it dangerous?"

"It is," Ymre said, scratching his ear with a hind leg. "But so is sword work, or riding a horse, or performing any sort of magic at all. If I thought you were likely to misuse runes, I would never have shown you the *quixil*." He thumped his tail on the flags of the floor. "Very few have the mind for runework, but you do. That's only a partial answer, but it is the best one I can give you." He gave her a dog's smile.

"Do you go about giving runebooks to anyone with the talent?" Traedis asked, shooting him a sidelong look. The leather cover was warm under her fingers.

"I said it was a partial answer." Ymre stood and padded over to nose at the table. "Start with the first rune before going on to another. Try to duplicate its shape as precisely as you can. There are many languages and styles of writing that make a rune tight and powerful. But the *quixil* is a piece of every rune, even if you can only glimpse its tail in a curl of the pen stroke or its mouth in the anchor of its meaning. Learn to understand why one shape, and one alone, carries the meaning."

Traedis stared back down at the rune, which shimmered over the page. "Just like that? No instruction, no training? I'm supposed to figure it out?" Her politeness had been wearing thin during her ride with the Shefferies, and was now entirely threadbare.

"I have given you instruction," Ymre said, far more patient than she. "More than many ever get. I've wakened your sight and told you how to study. I am a master of hours, but even I have not so many that I can stay and teach you everything you will need to know." His nails clicked against the floor. "There is value in learning for yourself how the underpinnings of the written character twine and flow into bardic magic. You have the ability. If you will it, you can learn the skill."

"What are the other runes?" she asked, starting to turn the page.

Ymre gently nosed her hand away. "Only once you master the first should you go on to the others. I would advise not trying too many at once; a failed rune can snap back on the caster."

Traedis slowly withdrew her hand. "What are they likely to do?"

"Nothing terrible." Ymre shook himself, sending his ears flapping. "Until you understand how to view a rune without it catching your mind and activating, I will give you no dangerous ones. I would like you to puzzle out for yourself their meanings and their applications. I am not unwilling to answer any questions, but I'd like you to use your own native intelligence first. You will become a far better runecaster if you piece together the magic for yourself."

"I'm not sure I want to become a runecaster," Traedis told him. She was overburdened already with affairs of state, relearning the height of her bardic skill, and training with Vandeyr. Open court and public engagements took far too much of her remaining time.

Ymre sat and turned his long, fine face to hers. "That is your choice. However, it is urgent that you make your own decision on whether to study the discipline or not. I recommend you do, but I do not command you. "

Traedis nodded slowly. "Your judgment is better than mine, and you know things I don't. I'll study the book, since you think it wise." She carefully closed the cover.

Lord Ymre had given her a tremendous amount of help already. She knew this would also work to her benefit, though she could not see as far ahead as the Wise Hound. She ran her thumb down the spine, feeling the lines where the pages were stitched together under the binding. Somehow, she would find the time and strength to study this new discipline.

Rose trilled smugly.

Ymre gave her another smile. "I hoped you would say that."

He rose and turned. Walking toward the wall, his form thinned and dissipated before he reached it.

Traedis set the book down and reached for her harp.

Chapter Four
A Fox in the House

Traedis waited anxiously to be called to the Silk Room, her heart beating like a sparrow caught in a cage. She paced back and forth in her office, while Vandeyr stood by the door watching her.

"You're doing it again," Vandeyr said.

Traedis realized with chagrin that she was pacing out the dimensions of her old cell. Her feet still wandered that pattern when her thoughts were distracted. She stopped and took a seat, touching Rose's frame lightly. Then she folded her hands into her lap.

"That's not much better," said Vandeyr. "Now you look like you're waiting for someone to come for you with a switch."

Traedis blew an exasperated breath into the air. "You're not helping."

"Do you want me to be happy about this?"

'This' referred to a visit from Elben Tallforest, who had requested to come during his week of leave. Traedis had been reluctant, more out of fear for him rather than a lack of interest on her part.

Who will lose their love to the storm? That question echoed through her mind when she allowed her thoughts to drift: darkened her days with foreboding. The words from Wingblade, the deluded champion of self-will, were the terms of her deadly curse. In addition to losing most of her freedom, she must kill her uncle with a blade made from the breastbone of the n'korreld thane.

Eventually, Traedis had decided it was best if she kept her thoughts away from the question of love and firmly in the territory of friendship. She did not intend her curse to affect the Haven knight.

No one could free her now. Traedis had angered the demonic patron of curses, who was unlikely to loose her grip.

A diminutive page girl appeared at the door, and Traedis twitched in her seat. "Yes?" she asked, her voice more controlled than her movements.

"Captain Tallforest has arrived," the page said. "He is waiting for you in the Silk Room."

Traedis' heart gave a small skip. Unsure as to whether it was indigestion or gladness, she rose and went downstairs to join the Haven knight. Late afternoon lit the rare glass windows, making them glitter like gems.

Elben rose as she entered. Traedis had not remembered how tall he was; his lean, rangy form overtopped her slight frame by a head. His shoulder-length hair was gathered at the nape of his neck, and he wore a neatly trimmed red beard. He was not dressed in his Haven greens, but an embroidered linen shirt and breeches.

Traedis gestured at his chair. "Please, sit. You're here as my guest. Have you had refreshments? Are you settled into your room?"

Elben nodded at a partially eaten cake and a cup of fine aelin tisane. "I have and I am. Your hospitality is excellent. Thank you." He waited until she took her own chair before reseating himself.

Vandeyr took a stance against the wall behind Elben. She stood erectly, with a stiffness that belied the usual fluidity of her motion, making it clear to Traedis she was most unhappy.

"I'd like to show you some of Tolin's glories," Traedis told Elben, deliberately brightening her tone. "I've even cleared my schedule for the purpose." She stopped, considering that someone from Telardur and Haven might not think of Tolin as a land of glories. "There are more than you might think."

Following her lead, Elben smiled. "I believe you. Though I have only had a chance to visit the library in my previous visit. Well, that and the plants in the palace gardens."

Traedis' cheeks flamed; they had both been in the form of foxes—a chance that had been responsible for them meeting in the first place—and she could not think as a human in that shape. She had been quite willing to play tag with the mischievous fox who had romped his way into her good graces.

Elben had not been shy about admitting he was courting her. That was no surprise; Kaal was merely the most persistent of her suitors. Men had written to her, sent her gifts, and declared their undying love for a woman they had despised before she had gained the *falmyros*. Anyone who thought they could control her was willing to apply for the title of king's consort. The irony of a Haven knight, once a staunch enemy of the City, courting a Tolin noble did not detract from his appeal. And truly, Elben was the only one she could even imagine marrying.

"Where would you like to go?" she asked. "You've seen the Star Cavern before, but I'm happy to take you there if you want to see it again. The Council Spring is much visited, but there are also fine old churches in the priest's quarter. Of course, the entire city is full of beautiful architecture, much of it from the time of Tolin's birth. There's also the statue of the Storm Eagle—" She stopped and shuddered, remembering the feel of his talons in her flesh as he had returned her to the city she had once fled. She forced the feeling down and continued as lightly as she could. "It's not quite life-sized, but enough to give you an idea of what he was like in the flesh." She poured herself a cup and sipped at it, watching the play of light on the hairs down his long jaw and the fan of smile lines at the corners of his eyes.

"I'd love to go to all of them," he told her, "but I can hardly keep you from your duties for my entire leave. I'd like very much to revisit the Star Cavern first, if you please. And in the time you need to spend ruling, I'd also like to spend some time in the library—if your eldest sister can stomach me leafing through her rare folios."

From the beautifully calligraphed letters Elben had sent Traedis, she had gleaned that illumination was a treasured pastime. She nodded. "Of course. I can understand the draw of the library. I spent many hours there as a child, reading the books I wasn't supposed to while avoiding the ones I was."

Elben drained his teacup. "I'm ready to go any time you are." He chuckled. "Eager, in fact."

His voice was a clear, light baritone with the hint of a burr; it sent a tingle through Traedis' veins. She wondered what his singing range was, and if he could keep a tune.

"Then it's settled," she said. "The Star Cavern and the library it is."

The library—and the Star Cavern below it—were not far from the palace. They walked the distance, conversing while the sun sank into the trees of the Southern Forest on the downslope of the mountain. There were few clouds, and the stars glittered as they appeared just beyond the dome of the sky. Vandeyr followed behind, sinking into the growing shadows.

The library, one of the square-cornered gray buildings that inhabited Tolin like great stone behemoths, had an elegance just beyond its doors that belied its façade. The entry hall arched into the main room, which soared two stories into the air and just managed to contain the wealth of books within. The librarian, her sister Gavaya, moved among the stacks, dusting and checking spines for damage.

The door to the Star Cavern was set into a side wall. Traedis took a lantern off the hook near the door and lit it, then opened the door and headed down the long stone steps to the chamber deep beneath the City. She watched her feet as she descended, trying to stave off the fear of close spaces that had afflicted her since she had been a child. It was a little easier with Elben by her side.

At the bottom, the space opened into an antechamber, once filled with old junk, now clear and ready for visitors. They brushed sides with a n'korreld family of six who were exiting the main cave; one of the children reached only to Traedis' thigh. Traedis smiled as the child raced up the stairs in a scurry of irregular footsteps. Vandeyr took a quick look into the cavern, then stationed herself in the antechamber to grant Traedis and Elben privacy.

Elben breathed deeply as he looked up. The Star Cavern rose high over their heads into a rough dome; the floor was level but not smooth. Several viewing lounges had been set up so that visitors could look at the site's real attraction. Overhead, painted whorls represented stars, each grouped in one of five constellations: the Southern Dragon, the Bowl, the Firebrand, the Twin Lions, and the Great Road. No light was needed; the faint glow of the stars was illumination enough.

Traedis understood; even as many times as she had been there, she could not keep the immediacy and power of these stars in her mind. She sat down on one of the viewing lounges and leaned back, gazing up at the shining stars overhead. Elben followed suit.

"The Southern Dragon seems brighter than the others," he said after a long moment of silence.

Traedis had not previously noticed, but now she looked around at all the constellations, realizing Elben was right. The reason was not hard to guess. "In a sense, they're all awakened," she said quietly, feeling the need to hush; as a sacred place of the n'korreld people, it was very like a church. "But my *falmyros* has touched only the Southern Dragon, and by comparison, the others still slumber."

Elben nodded. "I don't understand exactly how your *falmyros* interacts with this place, but I know it does. It's interesting; I wouldn't have thought n'korreld magic would work well for someone not of their people."

"Perhaps it's because I cared," Traedis suggested. "Their people certainly have few reasons to trust outsiders."

Elben murmured assent and rested his chin on one hand. The two of them spent a little time without speaking, but simply looking at the marvel that had been so long entombed beneath Tolin.

Finally, Elben spoke. "Traedis—Trae—I know you're being attacked by a plague of suitors. If you don't want me to be one of them, tell me. I may not be able to control my feelings, but I control how I express them. I would rather be your friend than drive you away with unwelcome attention. Tell me what you want, and I'll abide by it."

Traedis felt emotions tangle and shiver inside her; she was not sure how to even name them, let alone unsnarl them. All she could comb out of her heart was that she did not want Elben to leave, but was afraid to let him stay.

"I have a curse on me," she told him finally. "It's far too powerful to be removed, and I have offended the Mother of Curses as well. I will lose my love to the storm, whatever that means. I—I don't want that to be you." She closed her eyes as she remembered Wingblade, who had cursed her and her friends. The memory was followed by another: the Mother of Curses, a purple eye gleaming from a cloud of blackness.

Elben expelled a breath of air and nodded. "Thank you for telling me." His lips curved in the smallest of smiles. "I am willing to accept the risk if you are."

"Why?" Traedis asked.

Elben's expression changed to confusion. "Why am I willing to accept the risk?"

"No. Why me?" This was the question Traedis had wanted to ask since he had begun to send her letters. Elben was a handsome man, a Haven knight, and a captain. He would have no shortage of women, nor of men if he favored both.

To her relief, he seemed to take the question seriously, waiting before he answered in a measured tone. "Perhaps it's because the back of your neck looks so scared while you stand there defying kings and demons. Perhaps it's the way you move when you're a fox, as if you were made of liquid *sagathas*. Perhaps it's the sheer glory of your music. And you're absolutely beautiful, though I would love you if you were eighty years old and wrinkled as a crumpled sheet of paper." He chuckled. "I fell in love with you while I chased you around under the furniture in Faldrohaven. Or maybe it was before that, when I first heard you speak. You were willing to challenge Arlen Longspear in the middle of Faldrohaven with the rest of us surrounding you. I love your courage, your principle, and your determination." He cleared his throat. "I'm thirty-four and I've never met another woman I respect and admire as much as you."

Traedis listened with discomfort, but also with a certain gladness; she was unused to hearing herself sincerely praised. And it was sincere, she was sure: Haven knights did not lie. She felt tears gather at the back of her eyes and blinked away moisture. "The curse—"

"Forget the curse," Elben said. "You can't stop living because something *might* happen."

"Better that you know the whole story." It was time to tell Elben as much of the truth as she could. "It's not just the curse. It's—" Raw grief overtook her throat. "I'm not used to having people say good things about me. My family loves me, but they don't have much respect for me." A trace of panic surfaced in her belly. "I suppose some of it is justified. I was unruly as a child, and they only wanted the best for me."

"What did that entail?" Elben asked gently.

"Oh, nothing terrible!" Traedis hastened to say in a sudden urge to explain away any possible misdeed. "They didn't beat me or anything. My tutor occasionally locked me in the closet, but much of the time he only slapped me. Nothing I didn't deserve." She stared at the floor, examining the veining in the rocks and the dirt someone had tracked in.

"Locked you in a closet?" Elben's voice was suddenly discordant. "You don't consider that serious? You think you *deserved* that?"

"Not exactly." She followed a hairline crack with her eyes. "I didn't care for my tutor, and I think he took liberties. Father only meant for him to discipline me, and since I wouldn't learn my lessons, what could he do?"

Elben growled deep in his throat. "Your father knew?"

Traedis drew her brows together. "Of course he did. He knew everything that happened in the City. He was the head of the Intelligence arm; of course he was aware of what his family did."

Slowly, as if he were trying not to frighten a wild animal, Elben leaned forward. Shaking his head, he asked, "How old were you?"

"Six to fourteen, when I ran away." Traedis was beginning to understand that Elben did not consider this normal behavior. "Isn't that what you do in Telardur or Haven?"

"King Emmen—any of us—would imprison someone who behaved like that to a small child." A vein pulsed in Elben's temple, and his wrist twitched. "Six years old and locked in a closet? That would be considered far beyond the pale in Telardur, also." He sucked air in through his teeth. "I'd heard the esch behave that way, but to know you were—" He shook his head. "I'm so sorry that happened to you, Traedis." He squared his shoulders. "What about the rest of your family?"

Traedis flashed a nervous grin. "Merely normal sister and brother things. Daymet catching me in the kitchen and washing my face with the dirty water. Otenemar hanging me out the window." Her grin grew broader. "Though he got quite the scare from that as well; he nearly dropped me. Made me promise that I wouldn't tell Mother or Father. I've never seen him so flustered."

"How old were they?"

Traedis tallied the years in her head. "Otenemar is twelve years older than me and Daymet is fourteen, so if I was eight when Otenemar did that, he would have been twenty. The incident with Daymet was later; he was probably twenty-four or twenty-six."

"Normal." Elben's voice was low.

Traedis felt another jolt of realization that Elben no more thought of this as normal than he did of Master Celdon's actions. "Not normal?"

Elben shook his head again.

"Oh." Despite the Haven knight's clear dismay, it was hard to reconcile Elben's view with everything she had ever been told. Of course she had been difficult; her parents had never needed to be so harsh with her brothers and sisters. She had defied them frequently, and the results had been predictable. She had needed to flee the City, but it had been partly her own fault. Perhaps not all, but partly.

Hadn't it?

She shook her head, feeling as if it were about to fly apart. She was not yet ready to accept Elben's understanding as her own.

"What about the others?" he asked softly. "Your mother? Lord Lang? Your sisters?"

Glad to have a question to answer in order to still her own curiosity, Traedis considered the matter. "Gavaya wasn't bad. She didn't have a great deal to say to me, but she was kind. And she warned me once, or I think she did. Not that I should change, but that I should be wary. She was right." It had been long enough that Traedis did not remember the exact words, but the exchange had been so uncharacteristic of her oldest sister that her memory had caught and kept it hidden, to surface now, when the subject had been raised.

Elben sat quietly, waiting for her to speak. More memories tumbled into Traedis' thoughts. "Lang was impatient with me when I was younger, but after he met Alluve, he changed. He was kinder, less abrupt. Vandeyr…"

What could she say about Vandeyr, who had unpredictably attacked and defended her during her childhood? "She tried. Sometimes I hated her, but I always knew in the recesses of my heart that she loved me. She taught me much no one else was willing to. That was why it was so hard that she didn't visit me in prison." Her sister had been forbidden to visit, though she had tried. Learning that had been a gift.

Elben stroked his beard in apparent thought. "You still haven't mentioned your mother. Did she know any of this? Did she agree to it?"

"She—" Traedis' throat closed, cutting off her words.

"I'm sorry," Elben told her. "You needn't speak of anything to me. I have no right to know. I simply care, and want to understand you, but I don't want to cause you pain."

Traedis forced her words around the constriction. "I want to tell you." She swallowed. "Of course Mother knew. She knew everything that went on in the household. Except maybe some of what Daymet and Otenemar got up to. She would have had words about almost dropping me out a third-story window."

"Third story…" Elben closed his eyes, then opened them again, his jaw set. "Your uncle?"

"He knew. But he tried to make things better." Her throat tightened again. "He taught me to play harp, and defended me against Father when he could."

"I see." Elben's words dropped into the chamber like stones in a still pool. "I think I understand better now." He sat upright slowly. "Traedis, I want to know everything about you, but I *never* want my wishes to hurt you." He scratched his chin. "I'd like to continue this conversation later, but right now you look like a fox ready to go to ground. Perhaps this is a good time for me to go upstairs and look through your books."

Traedis laughed slightly as she assessed herself. He was right; every muscle in her body seemed poised for flight. She nodded. "I have made time tomorrow to show you around Tolin. If you want, we can talk further then." She touched the back of his hand, a feather-light motion which set her nerves quivering. "I wouldn't have answered you if I hadn't meant to. You did nothing wrong."

Elben nodded. "Thank you." He rose and offered a hand to Traedis. "Shall we go upstairs?"

Chapter Five
The Church of River Meda

A light touch on her shoulder brought Traedis to instant wakefulness. She reached for the dagger under her pillow before taking in who had wakened her: Vandeyr.

Vandeyr stood bathed in candlelight, her face ashen even in the dim glow. "Wake up, Trae," she said in a shaking voice which frightened Traedis more than anything her sister could say. Vandeyr was never shaken by anything.

"What is it?" Traedis asked, slipping out of bed, and heading for her wardrobe to dress quickly. "What's the matter?"

Vandeyr took a deep breath, steadying herself, but her voice remained thin and strained. "I know you like him—but Trae, your Haven knight nearly killed Mother." The candle wavered, sending the shadows careening at crazy angles across the room.

Traedis stopped in the middle of the rug, her mind dissecting her sister's words and trying to make sense of them. "Elben?"

"Yes, Elben! Elben Tallforest, Elben the cursed knight!" Vandeyr snapped. "I don't know the details, but Mother is with the healers, and she nearly died. And that man did it!"

Traedis stopped, shocked motionless. Her mother was indomitable, untouchable. How could anything happen to her?

She threw the wardrobe door open, reaching for a sturdy riding dress almost at random. One hand outstretched, she said, "Tell me everything you do know." She braided her hair without even thinking, laced up her dress, then drew on a pair of boots as her sister spoke. Her mind whirled; Vandeyr's words made no sense. She *knew* that Elben would not harm someone without cause. And even if she were to accept the premise that he wished to gain control of the City through her, attacking Mitheira would be a foolish way to do it, and would not win Traedis' favor. In addition, he was a Haven knight, sworn not to harm the innocent with oaths both binding and thoroughgoing.

"I don't know the details," Vandeyr told her, in a more controlled tone. "Only that Mother is with the healers and that she nearly died. And that Elben did it."

It did not make sense. While Mitheira was not entirely without skill, she had never needed to fight for her life. If anything, she would be the sort of person Elben had sworn to defend.

She considered for a moment the possibility that her words had sent Elben into a fit of rage that had turned toward Mitheira. But that made no sense, either. Haven knights did not give in to their baser impulses; they were tested and vetted long before being admitted to the order.

It must be Uncle Cordelayne. Traedis was not sure how deeply enmeshed her mother might be; Mitheira was more than capable of accepting risk for the sake of Tolin. But Traedis did not believe Uncle Cordelayne would endanger Mitheira's safety. Her thoughts whirled with possibilities, always returning to her initial conviction.

"Send for Ruth," she told her sister, wanting someone she knew who could watch her back. Right now, Traedis was not inclined to trust anyone, especially not after the goat woman's cryptic warning about Vandeyr. "How is Mother?" A jolt of fear stabbed through her. "And what happened to Elben?"

Vandeyr strode to the door, all trace of shaking now gone, and spoke briefly with the guards outside the sitting room before returning to Traedis' bedchamber. "I don't know yet. I've sent some people to find out. They'll meet us in the church district. That's where Mother is."

Traedis grabbed her harp case. Armed with a hidden wrist dagger and her ornamental feast dagger, a dainty weapon with a wicked cutting edge, Traedis followed her sister down to the courtyard. If she defended Elben, she herself might need defense. And no matter how efficient Vandeyr was, there was no substitute for caution.

Four guardsmen, two riderless horses, and a pony waited for them. All business now, her nerves apparently under tight control, Vandeyr addressed their escort. "As soon as Mistress Ruth arrives, we need to make haste to the clinic at the church of River Meda. We may run into some trouble on the way, and it's your job to see that no one interferes with the king's business."

As they mounted, Ruth asked no questions, but climbed nimbly up the pony readied for her. Five of Vandeyr's palace guard followed Traedis as she rode down the broad roads of Tolin. Despite the late hour, people milled in the streets like the denizens of an angry beehive. Traedis could feel the restlessness in the *falmyros* as more people woke and gathered to spread rumor and fact indiscriminately.

Tolin had no official clinic as did Kaelennar, but a small group of dedicated healers occupied an extension of the church of River Meda. This quarter of the city was populated by smaller stone houses with peaked roofs to shed snow during the long winters; the church rose tall out of it like a lupine in a field of harebells. Traedis noticed a rapidly growing crowd of people swarming the streets outside; several of the City Guard kept the curious out of the church, but no one seemed to be trying to control the mob. A low murmur of anger swelled from the gathering crowd, a sound both ugly and dangerous. Traedis ignored it; she was far too worried about Mitheira to fear their reaction to her presence.

Vandeyr pulled her horse around toward one of the city guards, exchanging tense words. Finally, she nodded, then returned to Traedis.

"What did you learn?" asked Traedis anxiously.

Vandeyr's expression was rigid. "Mother is inside the church. She's had a terrible experience, but she's alive—the healers got to her soon enough. Elben is at the estate. Apparently, it took some dozen people to restrain him. He's injured, I don't know how badly." *And I don't care,* her voice conveyed.

A part of Traedis melted in relief that the Haven knight was not dead. Another part of her wanted to talk to Elben, to ask him the truth of what he had done. A third part simply wanted to see him. She ferociously stifled the last; she must treat the accusation against Elben with fairness and justice, not sentiment.

"Do you know any more about what happened?" Traedis dismounted, followed quickly by Vandeyr. A few of the City Guard fended off the mob while Traedis and Vandeyr tied their horses' reins to one of the hitching posts outside the church. Traedis started toward the door of the healer's extension, anger pumping through her veins. Ruth hopped down from her saddle and followed.

Vandeyr nodded briskly, but did not speak until they were just outside the door. "He came to visit Mother in the middle of the night. No one knows why, and Mother hasn't said, but they apparently quarreled and Elben— Elben slit Mother's throat. The healers got to her just in time."

Shock shuddered through Traedis' body like a stroke of lightning. She could not reconcile this action with the gentle, good-humored knight she had spoken to only a few hours ago. "Get Elben," Traedis told her, urgency seeping into her voice. "Don't you dare let anyone harm him. I want to find out *exactly* what happened."

Vandeyr gave her a curt nod and selected one of her guard and two of the City's to accompany her. Remounting, they disappeared around the corner of the church. Traedis briskly walked up the steps and entered the healers' house.

"Are you all right?" Ruth asked quietly.

"I don't know." Traedis closed the door behind her. "I suppose I'll find out."

Inside, the air was cool and quiet. Traedis could still hear a few voices outside, but the walls reduced them to an almost inaudible buzz. A young man, wearing a clerical coat with Meda's symbol on it, met Traedis immediately inside the door. He bowed politely. "King Traedis."

"Take me to my mother," Traedis told him tersely.

The priest nodded. "Of course." He led her down a short hallway and led her into a room on the right side of the hall.

Mitheira was covered in blood. Her dress was torn at the throat and the sleeves, but no wound married her throat; the healers had taken care of that when they wielded the magic that had saved her life. She heard Ruth's sudden intake of breath from where the brunaidh stood inside the door.

Traedis barely noticed her surroundings; her attention was focused on her mother. Mitheira sat in a chair next to a pine bed, her back erect, her gaze clear. One of her manservants stood beside her, glowering at everyone indiscriminately.

Traedis' eyes widened as she took in her mother's appearance. There was enough blood on her dress to have been fatal. This was no staged attack, but an all-out attempt to kill, and it brought home the reality of the danger.

Mitheira wore a cloak over her shoulders, though the night was warm. Traedis shivered as well. Thoughts whirled in her head, questions of who was to blame. Haven knights did not attack innocent people, but neither would Uncle Cordelayne have endangered his brother's wife.

"Mother," she said shakily. "How are you?"

Mitheira drew herself up coldly in the chair. "Traedis Liori Eisel Atenel," she said with a blaze of anger which Traedis could almost feel from across the room. "If you don't prosecute that man, I will."

Traedis could not contest her mother's righteous fury; she herself was ready to rage at whomever was responsible. She simply could not believe it was Elben. "What in Kyaan's name happened?"

"I should think it was obvious," Mitheira said. "Your Haven knight tried to kill me. That he did not succeed was largely a matter of good fortune on my part, and the intervention of my servants and neighbors."

"Are you all right now?" Traedis asked more gently. Later she might feel the brunt of the fear that she had almost lost her mother. At the moment she could not afford to think of it.

"As well as I can be," Mitheira said coldly, "for having suffered abuse and attack at the hands of a foreigner, a citizen of the land which has always been our enemy."

It was a less than subtle reminder that Traedis was responsible for Elben's presence. This comforted Traedis rather than upsetting her; if Mitheira were attacking Traedis' actions, she was well enough that Traedis need not fear for her body or mind.

"Then I will leave you with the priests and healers," she told her mother. "I'll be back before too long, and then you may detail exactly what happened." She drew a long breath. "I'm so glad that you're all right."

Mitheira lifted her chin. "Do what you please, as you always do. Go, then."

Traedis gestured the young priest into the hall outside before speaking. "My mother has had a terrible experience, and I am sure she would like to feel like herself as soon as possible. Please arrange for someone to go to her house and fetch clothing for her so that she need not face others in such a state."

The priest shook his head. "King Traedis, Lady Atenel's manservant has already acquired clothing for her. Lady Atenel said she intended to wait to dress until you saw her."

Anger brushed over Traedis, but she pushed it back; there was some logic in her mother's decision. Traedis had needed to see the effects of Elben's actions.

Leaving the church to watch for Vandeyr, she could not still her whirling thoughts. In the back of her mind, a deep fear for Elben crouched, waiting for its chance to rend her nerves, but she did not allow herself to focus on it long enough for it to shiver through her bones and blood. There would be time for that later, and her feelings would not affect the outcome of this disastrous situation.

More guards had assembled outside, trying to calm those in the streets. The hum of the crowd became louder, angrier, as she appeared. Someone shouted, "Really concerned for your mother, aren't you?" followed by yells of agreement from others in the mob. Traedis simply stared at them coldly, unwilling to defend herself or explain to those less interested in truth than in blame. Staying with her mother would make neither of them feel better, and she had a responsibility to find out the details about what had happened, and why. Those of the City and Palace Guard fingered the hilts of their swords and shifted on their feet.

She did not have long to wait. Vandeyr and her guards rode back down the street before Traedis had decided whether to follow her sister or to stand her ground. Across Vandeyr's saddle hung a limp figure. Traedis' heart banged painfully against her chest.

The crowd's focus turned now to the returning Guard. Angry words flew, and there was an aborted surge as if the crowd intended to rush them. Traedis took a deep breath and prepared to rein them in with the power of the *falmyros* if she could find the strength. She hoped she would not have to find out whether it was possible.

Vandeyr's head whipped up; she fixed several apparent leaders with a quelling stare no one seemed able to meet. Her movements were calm and assured, laced with confidence in her status and her authority. It seemed to have its effect on the massed group, for they quieted, except for a few muffled angry voices which sank into the darkness.

"I'm here," said Ruth, her soft voice insinuating itself between Traedis' fears and hopes. Traedis could not manage a smile, but she nodded, grateful for at least one friend at her side.

Vandeyr swung off her horse with a sort of hurried leisure that alarmed Traedis. She pulled Elben's still form off the saddle, swaying a little under his weight. Two of the accompanying guards hurried to take him, hastening him into the church. As she neared Traedis, she muttered through still lips, "He's alive, but we need to get him inside if he's going to stay that way."

Traedis was not entirely sure that her sister wished Elben to live, but she did trust Vandeyr's honor and loyalty. She nodded and led them into the church, leaving all but three of the guard outside. Ruth trotted behind, her hand on her dagger hilt.

As soon as they were out of the crowd's hearing, Vandeyr said, "He's badly hurt. I don't know what you want to do with him, but if you're going to question him, you'd better at least get him bandaged, if not healed."

"We need assistance!" Traedis called, and the young priest popped out of a doorway, his expression concerned and a little fearful. Since he seemed to have either been appointed or have chosen to act as a guide, Traedis told him, "Find the best healer in this house."

The priest stammered a few undecipherable words, then seemed to gather his wits. "There," he told her, and pointed to a small door ahead of them in the corridor. "That's the healer's ward." Traedis jerked her head at Vandeyr and marched to the door, leaving the others trailing behind.

The door led to a medium sized room full of cots, some shelves, a table, and several chairs. A man and a woman, identifiable as healers from the blue silk tabards they wore, talked together in low voices. The man, whose mouth turned down at the corners, looked up sharply as all of them entered, making a sound of disgust.

Vandeyr laid Elben carefully on one of the cots. His chest moved, but shallowly; a rasp rose and fell between each labored breath. Blood caked his face and stained much of his hair and the front of his torn clothing. Several darkening bruises swelled on his face and arms, and he had lost a tooth. Her chest filling with fear, Traedis was not sure if she could bear to lose him.

Ruth immediately took up a stance next to him, her size belying the danger in her movements.

"He's the best healer," their young guide told them diffidently, pointing to the sullen man. Both the man and the woman looked at the floor as if to escape notice.

Traedis said, "Heal him."

The healer scowled. "I need to save my strength for those who *deserve* it. Others may have been injured in the struggle with this would-be murderer."

"Heal him," Traedis said, more softly but with a touch of steel in her tone. This arrogant fellow would obey her or pay with a stint in prison; she was not minded to let Elben die for this man's prejudice. She stared him down, her lips firm with determination, her chin high.

He met her stare for a few long seconds. Then he nodded angrily. "Very well, Your Majesty," he said, politeness barely staining his tone. He approached Elben and knelt by the cot. Putting his hands on the Haven knight's chest as gingerly as if he were touching fresh manure, he closed his eyes to put Elben and himself into the healing trance which would convoke his abilities and allow him to knit flesh and bone back together.

Traedis watched, fascinated, as the bruises on Elben's skin purpled, faded to red and brown, then melted into the flesh beneath. The cuts and scrapes drew together, scabbed over, then turned to thin red lines which whitened against Elben's skin and vanished into nothingness. A new tooth pushed up through his gums, its serrated edge speaking of new growth. Elben's eyelids fluttered, showing a sliver of green before dropping shut again.

The healer opened his eyes and pulled his hands back fastidiously. "He's healed, and will come out of sleep soon. Is there another service I can perform for Your Majesty?" Even though his tone was overtly polite, Traedis could hear the sarcasm.

"Not at the moment," she told him, a touch of the Atenel arrogance coloring her own voice. "But keep yourself available for further service."

"As my king wishes," replied the healer, and stood. He bowed—serviceably—and strode out of the room, letting the door bang loudly behind him. The other healer started.

Traedis turned to face Vandeyr. "Send people to take Elben to one of the small rooms and guard him. I want to find out the truth of this matter. Let me know when he wakes."

Vandeyr nodded briskly and gave a few curt orders to her guards. Two of them moved to flank Elben, bending to rouse him roughly from his stupor.

Elben's eyes opened, blank and confused. He looked around as if were gazing through a heavy mist. "King Traedis? What's happening?"

"At the moment," said Traedis, wanting to reassure him but unwilling to take the time, "you are in the church of Kyaan. Go with these guards, please. I'll talk to you later about what happened."

Elben blinked slowly. Then he looked down at his clothing and his eyes widened. He nodded to Traedis. "Of course, Your Majesty." He levered himself up, keeping his hands in plain sight; he obviously understood that something momentous had happened. Once Elben was on his feet, the guards guided him into the hallway. He went without resistance, no trace of defiance in his stance.

Traedis looked at Vandeyr and Ruth. "What next?" she asked, half to herself.

Vandeyr's face was still and expressionless. She might obey Traedis' instructions, but her lack of response showed just how angry she was.

Ruth stood up, her posture stiff. "I'd recommend that you talk to everyone who had a hand in this disaster. Haven knights don't just attack innocent people for no reason. You need to be able to tell who is lying and who is telling the truth." She frowned. "Can you play a spell of truth, Trae? Of memory? Or does Master Tagg know how to cast a mage's version?"

Traedis could not, and though Master Tagg might, the situation was so delicate that she was afraid that no one would believe the findings of her own mage. "I need to have someone investigate this who Tolin will credit— if Elben was in some way made to attack Mother."

Vandeyr's gaze bored into hers; Traedis could almost feel the heat. "Are you serious?" she asked. "You think *Uncle Cordelayne* did this? You think he would touch a hair on Mother's head?"

It should not have shocked Traedis that Vandeyr had guessed so swiftly what she was thinking. Few could force a Haven knight into any evil action, whether by coercion or magic. But Uncle Cordelayne might have the resources and the knowledge to find some way.

"I don't think," she said slowly, "that he would have put Mother in harm's way unless she agreed to it." Thinking about her mother's haggard expression and pale face, she shook her head. "No. I don't think he would. Only, consider this—you've worked opposite Haven all your life. You don't think one of their knights would hunt down and attack someone in their own home, do you? Vandeyr, you know this doesn't feel right."

Vandeyr's jaw was set, but her eyes flickered at Traedis' words. After a few moments, she said in a grudging tone, "No, it doesn't, but there's no question that he is guilty. Mother and her servants bore the brunt of it, and he was there. Where do we take the investigation from here?"

Ruth tapped her fingers against the sheathed hilt of her dagger. "Perhaps we need to find someone who can both discover the truth and whom everyone will believe. Maybe we need Dame Jae-Jae. Even your worst enemies will listen to her."

Traedis felt her heart give a hopeful *thump*. Dame Jae-Jae had once been a bard in Telardur, but had taken up service with Lord Shorr, the first servant of the gods. As Shorr's herald, she was more than mortal, and spent her life unraveling lies and deceptions. With Rose's help, Traedis might be able to call the bard and ask her to uncover whatever secrets or duplicity were involved in the attack on Mitheira.

"You're right," she said. "I need to call Dame Jae-Jae."

"I need privacy," she told Vandeyr, though that was not strictly true. She simply did not want to demonstrate her abilities before the remaining healer who sat watching them.

Vandeyr faced the healer and gestured toward the door. "Wait outside. Afterward we will want to speak to Lady Atenel."

The healer stood hastily, knocking back her chair with a sort of clumsy eagerness that showed she was not at all happy to be in the middle of this conflict. Traedis listened as the door snicked behind her before taking a seat and unstrapping her harp.

Vandeyr went to the door and laid her ear against it for a moment. "She's going down the hall now. Too far to hear us speak."

Traedis took a seat and picked up Rose, fitting the harp's comforting soundboard against her shoulder. She let her fingers play over the strings for a moment as she gathered her energies for the spellwork she needed to do. A calling spell was simple enough, but it demanded a certain concentration and focus in order to send the spell out like an arrow toward its destination. She envisioned Jae-Jae as she had last seen her: a lithe, dark woman with black hair, green eyes, and an infectious smile.

She began to pluck the melody she needed to carry the spell: a simple, repetitive tune with paired chords that represented both halves of the magic. Slowly, she threaded in a countermelody, a lilting counterpoint that asked the question: *Will you come?* The magic did not compel; it simply asked. Rose's bright sound seemed to spin off into an endless distance as the song sought out Shorr's herald.

Almost immediately, she felt a response. A dancing sequence of notes fell into her ears, the affirmative ringing off her harpstrings. She let out her breath and damped the aftertones. "I got through," she said. "She's coming."

Ruth ran fingers through her short curls. "Good. No one is as talented at getting to the heart of a tangled situation."

Vandeyr scowled. "How long will it take her to get here? The mood of the City is still full of outrage, and it's only going to get worse. Not that things aren't bad enough, what with Elben Tallforest alive and drenched with Mother's blood."

Traedis glared at her sister. "I told you she'll come. I'm not in control of when. I think I conveyed the urgency, but I'm not a god or a dragon that I command her. This whole situation is too suspect for me to assign blame anywhere." She patted Rose's frame. "Including on Uncle Cordelayne. We need to know what happened, because if we get this wrong, it can happen again."

For a moment, Vandeyr reminded Traedis of a fighting cock lifting its spurs. Traedis flinched. Vandeyr stared at her for a moment, then relaxed her muscles. "I admit that you are right, Trae, but I don't like it. Elben tried to murder Mother, and he's going to give a satisfactory accounting, or I'll kill him myself."

Traedis winced at her sister's words, then willed her body to calm. "If I come to believe Elben deliberately and knowingly attacked Mother, I'll be first in line to demand justice."

"All right," Vandeyr said, curtly, but with slightly less anger. "It would be a gods-cursed stupid way for a suitor to behave, nevermind a Haven knight. But what are you suggesting instead? That the witnesses were drunk or half-blind? Baldus the steward saw it, and old Tober, and you know how sharp he is. He was the one who half-brained your light-o-love with a brass vase—which is, by the way, badly dented. How do you reconcile what happened with what you want to have happened?"

"That is," Traedis said firmly, "the reason I have called for Dame Jae-Jae."

Before they could speak further, a light tap sounded at the door. Vandeyr shrugged in apparent annoyance. "What is it?"

The door opened slowly, and a shy-faced girl in acolyte's garments entered, bowing respectfully to Traedis as soon as she entered. "Beg pardon, King Traedis, but you have a visitor. It's..." She looked at her feet. "It's Dame Jae-Jae."

Traedis breathed a sigh of relief. "Send her in immediately."

The girl nodded and exited, closing the door softly behind her. Shortly, Traedis heard the sounds of footsteps and the door opened again.

Jae-Jae stepped into the room and grinned. "Did you call for me?"

Jae-Jae breathed hard, as if she had been running. Her practical leather coat and breeches were damp, as was the lute case she wore over her shoulder. A lick of dark hair hung over one eye; she brushed it aside with a strong, long-fingered hand. Her eyes were full of mischief.

Traedis felt as if her bones would melt with relief. "You're here."

Vandeyr inclined her head respectfully. "Dame Jae-Jae."

Ruth sat up and wiped her eyes with the back of her hands. "Jae-Jae! It's been too long."

Jae-Jae nodded politely to Vandeyr, who had donned a stony mask, grinned at Ruth, then turned to Traedis. "I'm sorry about my wet clothes, but I just gated out of a rain shower. I didn't expect the mob in the street."

She leaned against the door frame and crossed one foot over the other. "What do you need me for?"

Traedis explained in a careful economy of words. "Can you play a spell of truth and memory under which I can question my mother and Elben? You have the power, and no one will contest your right—they've been contesting mine since I received the *falmyros*. Given the mood in the City, I can't afford to misstep."

"Of course," Jae-Jae said briskly. "Even if it weren't my job to sort out truth from lies, even if you weren't my friend, I'd help you. You've changed one of the most dangerous institutions the Interregnum produced, and that's enough for me." Jae-Jae shifted her lute and straightened. "The sooner we get down to business the better."

Vandeyr's expression carried the studious blankness she cultivated when she was uncomfortable. She, after all, was an example of what had made the City so dangerous.

Traedis nodded and rose from her seat. "I'll take you to see my mother so you can hear her account of what happened." She shot a glance at Vandeyr who was still imitating a statue. Hopefully Traedis had not permanently alienated her sister.

In the hallway, the young priest waited respectfully to lead the four of them back to Mitheira's room. Vandeyr gestured for her remaining guard to stand sentry outside the door. This left the four of them with Mitheira and her manservant.

Mitheira had bathed and changed her clothing; she now wore a gown of pale blue silk, an eagle brooch on its high-necked collar; her red-gold hair was bound with a filigreed clip. She sat stiffly, her back as straight as an empress. Upon seeing Jae-Jae, she rose smoothly and inclined her head to her illustrious visitor. "Dame Jae-Jae, we have not met, but I recognize you by reputation. I am not only honored by your presence, I confess myself relieved. Shorr's truth will vindicate me, a wronged woman."

"Of course, Lady Atenel." Jae-Jae unslung her instrument case and opened it, taking out a yew wood lute with a wide neck and an ebony fretboard; the pegs were also of ebony, and the strings gleamed silver. "I'm sure it's hard to speak of it, but please tell me what happened. I know you were attacked, but I need to hear your own words and understanding of what you've been through." She flashed an apologetic smile.

Mitheira nodded and reseated herself. "Very well." She folded her hands in her lap. "If I must speak of it to gain redress, I will."

For a moment, Traedis heard the Mother of Curses' hoarse voice asking her, "Am I to receive no redress?" She shivered before collecting her thoughts with an effort.

"Mother, are Dame Jae-Jae's spells of truth and memory acceptable?" Traedis asked her, keenly aware of her mother's fragile state.

"They are," Mitheira said with dignity. "I have nothing to hide, and I wish you to know *exactly* what your Haven suitor did, Traedis." She turned to Jae-Jae. "Please, good dame, lay your spell."

Jae-Jae unslung her lute in a practiced way and tuned it, which took her almost no time; she barely seemed to listen between the turn of one peg and another. Traedis watched, impressed with her skill. Rose magically never lost her pitch, but Traedis had learned to tune a harp efficiently while studying at Kaelennar's bardic college; the potential for thirty-six strings to go flat was great.

Seating herself on the bed, Traedis let her feet swing just above the floor as Shorr's bard began to play.

Jae-Jae pulled the music from her strings with decisive concentration; the intensity of power was like firm muscles under soft skin. Traedis listened with fascination: the music sounded as if Jae-Jae had extra fingers, or as if the lute possessed more than twelve strings. The magic settled over them like a silken veil, the lightest of feather touches, yet constraining them with threads as strong as steel. The notes, bright as a trickling pool, caused words spoken into it to ring more clearly.

With the spell well established, Traedis gathered her courage. "Mother, please tell us what happened tonight, and don't leave out any details, no matter how unimportant they may seem."

Mitheira's posture straightened even more; she nodded and began to speak without a quaver. "I know how to answer questions under such a spell, Traedis. I did not spend forty years married into the Atenel family without learning that." She set her chin and turned to face Jae-Jae. "I had retired upstairs to my chamber, though I had not yet dressed for bed, when my steward summoned me. This was shortly before midnight. My steward told me that Captain Elben Tallforest waited below and wished to speak with me." She smoothed out her skirt, though no wrinkles marred its clean line.

"I went down to him," she continued in an even tone. "He seemed extremely agitated and restless. He began to speak to me in the most abusive terms."

"What terms?" asked Traedis. Elben's courtesy was exquisite, and she could barely imagine him speaking in such a way.

Mitheira's lips firmed. "They were such things as a lady should not repeat."

Traedis gripped the edge of the bed tightly. Mitheira's composure was impressive, but Traedis could tell it was fraying. "The words may be important, Mother. Please tell me what you *can* repeat."

Mitheira swallowed. "He accused me of all manner of things—most of them connected with you, Traedis. He told me that I had 'cut off your voice' and that I had kept a 'chokehold' on your life." She paused, and a small line etched itself between her eyes. "Had I not known better, I would have said he was drunk, but there was no odor of spirits."

Traedis cringed inwardly. Could her discussion with Elben have been spark for such a fire? It still made no sense. Elben was not only a Haven knight, but Arlen Longspear's second-in-command; in his position, he must maintain complete control of himself.

"After he had made these accusations," Mitheira continued, "he drew a long knife from his sleeve."

Vandeyr made a startled noise. Traedis raised her eyebrows.

"Elben brought it?" Vandeyr cocked her head as if trying to shake the memory down into it. "It wasn't a Haven knife. I thought it was one of ours."

A shock like a close lightning strike went through Traedis' body. "How can you tell?" If the situation had not been so serious, she might have been fascinated. She had thought Tolin's only distinctive knives were the black assassin's daggers. It had never occurred to her that Haven and Tolin might make different sorts of knives.

"The folding of the metal," Vandeyr said absently. "Subtle differences in the length of the hilt. Mostly it's a question of smithery developing differently over time. It's not something most people would notice, not even most assassins. I wouldn't, except Father helped me study for my knife specialization, and we learned about half of the blades in creation."

"Would Lord Atenel know this?" asked Ruth, her brows making a vee over her nose.

"He might. He might not. It's a rather esoteric study." She shook her head impatiently. "There's also nothing to say that someone in Haven didn't imitate our style, or that Elben didn't have some trophy, or even that he purchased it from here. It's just odd."

"It is," Jae-Jae said mildly, "but please let Lady Atenel continue."

"Of course," Vandeyr said, with Traedis echoing the words a beat later.

Mitheira cleared her throat. "As I said, he pulled a knife from his sleeve, and I could not determine how best to force him from my home. I have City training, but I am no match for a Haven knight, and I am not so quick as I once was. He said, 'Learn what it feels like!' and—" Her voice caught for the first time. "He slit my throat. My servants came to my rescue, of course, but that knight fought like a madman. Several were injured."

"Not as badly as you," Vandeyr told her gently. "There were enough to subdue him. Tober had the sense to hit him on the head with that brass vase of yours."

Tension seeped visibly from Mitheira's shoulders. From the shadows beneath her mother's eyes, Traedis could tell she was exhausted. "Thank the Four," Mitheira breathed. Then she stiffened again. "One more thing, Traedis. I do not believe your uncle was involved—he would never jeopardize me in this way. Do not blame him for your Haven knight's actions."

That was as clear as sunlight on water. Traedis nodded and stood, the horsehair crinkling beneath her. She faced Mitheira, her stomach dropping at the thought of what she must do next. "Mother, I must speak with Captain Tallforest now. When I have determined what happened, I will come back and tell you." She softened her voice. "You will have redress, Mother, I promise." She meant it; if there were no extenuating circumstances for Elben's actions, Traedis would account him as guilty.

Mitheira nodded. "Very well, Traedis. I will accept that for now. We shall see what comes of it." She inclined her head. "Thank you, Dame Jae-Jae, for your consideration."

Fearing what she might learn, Traedis went to find Elben.

Elben had been taken to a small chamber filled with spare furniture. His arms were bound, and he sat still and quiet, his only movement a slow, deep breathing. Three of Vandeyr's guard stood watch, leaving only a little space for anyone else to enter.

Traedis took a seat on a slightly wobbly wooden chair that sat against the wall, followed immediately by Vandeyr, who stood where she could easily interpose herself between Traedis and Elben. Ruth did not sit upon entering, but stood watchfully. Jae-Jae trailed them, closing the door behind herself.

Elben inhaled sharply. "Dame Jae-Jae?" he asked, his voice rougher than usual.

Jae-Jae nodded. "Everyone recognizes me these days," she said in a slightly rueful voice.

Looking at Elben, Traedis could see the toll the night's events had taken on him. Though healed, he was still ragged and filthy; caked blood stained his hair and most of his front and sleeves. His clothes were ripped in several places, and his eyes were bloodshot. He was far from the dapper Haven knight Traedis had welcomed the day before.

"I have a number of questions," she told him, schooling her voice to sternness. "I want the answer to them under Dame Jae-Jae's magic of truth and memory. You are facing some serious charges."

"I understand something terrible happened." Elben turned his head; a motion of the nearest guard stopped him, and he froze. "I don't remember much of anything last night, so you will have to tell me what I'm accused of." His voice was tired and heavy.

A spark of hope lit Traedis' heart. If Elben did not remember, it implied someone else might have controlled his actions.

"You are," said Vandeyr curtly, "accused of attacking and gravely wounding Lady Mitheira Atenel. There are witnesses, and there is no doubt it happened. It only remains for you to explain yourself under the power of Dame Jae-Jae's magic. That opportunity is only given you by the king's grace. Be mindful of her mercy and comport yourself appropriately."

Elben's lips tightened. "I understand. Tell me what you want me to do."

Traedis met his eyes with her own, trying not to think of them as she had last night, warm and full of laughter. "Dame Jae-Jae will play a spell of truth and memory. Answer everything as completely as you can, and don't leave anything out."

Elben nodded.

Jae-Jae repositioned her lute and began a lively tune with an open, skipping rhythm that forbade duplicity and elicited memory, constraining all words to truth. As the pattern of its notes filled the room, the spell took hold. Traedis listened carefully, marveling at the other bard's technique.

Traedis straightened her spine. "What do you remember of what transpired tonight?"

Elben's gaze did not falter. He shook his head. "I talked with you in the library. After you left, I went back to the books. That's where my memory fails me."

"Just a moment," said Jae-Jae. Notes waterfalled from her lute, teasing at the back of Traedis' mind, calling forth half-hidden memories of her own.

Elben grunted. His breathing deepened, as if he searched inside himself for answers; he closed his eyes, and his hands opened and closed spasmodically behind him.

At last, as if the words were insupportably heavy, he said, "I felt a terrible rage—and a sense of choking. I had no transition, no moment when fury overtook me. It's more like a fever dream than a memory, all clouded together with blood and darkness.

"I was at your mother's estate, and—a significant amount of time passed? I don't know how much." He swallowed hard, and opened his lids. "I attacked your mother!"

Traedis felt the jolt of his admission. "What happened?"

Elben bowed his head. "I remember so little." The ragged edge of his words was like an open wound. "I didn't kill her, did I? Please tell me I didn't!"

"She's alive," Vandeyr answered tightly. "Go on."

Slowly, he raised his head. "Thank Selyn!" His chin firmed. "I see still pictures, a blood-red haze. A knife I don't recognize—none of mine. Stars, a cold wind, buildings? Stone. There's no order in the memories. Just pieces of darkness shot through with reflecting mirror shards." He shook his head as if that would force recollection back into it. "I fought with several people. All I could think was that I mustn't kill anyone. Then a terrible pain at the back of my skull, and I woke up in the other room on the cot."

Traedis felt her bones melt, leaving her weak with relief. She had known he was not capable of such a deed, but the Haven knight seemed barely to even remember it. Now the priority shifted to finding out how his will had been subverted. Then she must prove to Tolin that he was an innocent man.

"King Traedis?" Elben's voice was uncharacteristically tentative.

"Yes?"

His mouth took on a wry twist. "If I have deliberately assaulted an innocent, the god will have left me, and I will no longer be a knight of Selyn. If I call on Selyn now, and he comes, it will prove that I am still in his favor. Though I have no claim on your forbearance, it's something of which I would like to assure myself. If I may."

Vandeyr's expression soured. "I wouldn't," she said to Traedis. "It's quite a risk."

Ruth raised her brows. "It seems like a fine idea to me."

"Perhaps," Traedis answered them both. "It's my decision, and I am going to allow it."

Vandeyr shrugged. "Go ahead. You'll do what you want anyway."

"Free his hands." There was no point in keeping him bound any longer; Jae-Jae's magic was far more powerful than any mortal knight.

Without comment, Vandeyr cut his hands free, taking little time despite the strong cord. Ruth leaned forward, tapping her fingers to Jae-Jae's music.

Elben stretched out his arms, then massaged his hands, though they must have hurt considerably. Lines of worry and shame were incised on his strong features. The guards tensed, their weapons ready.

Compassion surged up through Traedis like a well filtering through stone. "Elben. Call the god and see if Selyn answers." She gave him a half-smile. "I'll warrant they will."

Elben closed his eyes, and the lines on his face smoothed out. The god of fire washed over the room in a wake of heat, warmth on a cold night. Then Elben cupped his hands, and a small flame woke in them, a flickering candle of red and gold which did not burn the flesh beneath.

Elben opened his eyes and regarded the flame. "So," he said. "Selyn still claims me." He parted his hands slowly and the flame evaporated. Tension ebbed from his shoulders and the knotted muscles in his neck loosened. A corresponding relaxation of Traedis' spine signaled her sympathy.

"Very well," she said. "You didn't intend to attack Mother, yet you did. We need to find out why."

"I can't doubt Dame Jae-Jae's truth," Vandeyr said through gritted teeth, "but you'd better have the best reason since the sacrifice of the air dragons to have slit my mother's throat with a hidden knife—yours or not."

Elben's shoulders jerked. "Dear Selyn," he whispered. "I didn't know." He looked down at his hands and tried to wipe away a patch of dried blood on his palm.

Traedis turned to Jae-Jae, whose fingers still danced in the intricate rhythm of her spellsong. "Would you chord with me? I might be able to find something buried in his memory that would explain how tonight's events came to pass." Though spell chording was unique among mortals, she had successfully taught it to Jae-Jae, who was no longer numbered among them.

Ruth's gray curls bobbed as she looked around the room. "No cot." She sighed. "I'll still offer my scrying ability if it will help. I'll just be well-rested, I suppose. If it's even necessary with your skill, Jae-Jae." She had once been a mage, but now her abilities were deeply buried; her gift of scrying in ice could only be accessed when she slept.

The dark-haired woman nodded. "It's a powerful gift. It will be a welcome addition to the spellweave." She turned to Traedis. "Let me play the chording. That way, the magic will be shared out between the three of us, and it won't throw the largest burden on you."

"Just a moment," Vandeyr said, her voice controlled but tight. "With your permission, King Traedis, I'd like to ask Captain Tallforest a few questions of my own."

It was a good idea; Vandeyr was the only one of them trained in interrogation, and she might be able to focus on something the others had missed. "Answer her questions," Traedis told Elben.

"Of course." Elben rubbed at his wrists. "Please ask."

The face Vandeyr turned toward Elben was cold as chiseled marble. "First, I am going to ask you some obvious questions, never mind the reasons. Are you prepared to answer?"

"I am." Elben started to lift his hand, then dropped it to his lap when Vandeyr shifted her weight. "Your pardon, Captain Atenel," he said. "My scalp itches abominably, but I understand you would prefer me to still keep my hands in sight."

"You understand correctly." Though not much taller than Traedis, Vandeyr seemed to loom over Elben's seated form, slender and deadly as a triple-forged blade. "You are a Haven knight," she said. "Is that correct?"

"It is." Elben sat like a bronze statue, every muscle contained except for those needed to breathe or speak. Though the bruises and swelling were gone from his face, a trace of darkness showed around his eyes. He had lost his hair tie sometime in the night, and strands of red-gold fell around his face a little above shoulder-length. He looked neither like a suitor nor an assassin.

"Very well." Vandeyr's expression would have done justice to a hawk on prey. "Your father is Lord Tallforest, who holds the *falmyros* of a small fief in the Northern Forest of Telardur?"

Traedis raised her brows: that, she had not known.

"He is." Elben sounded unsurprised. Traedis suppressed a surge of hot anger; of course Vandeyr had gained intelligence on Elben the moment she guessed he was courting Traedis. A good captain would learn any potentially dangerous secrets that might affect the king. Traedis decided to have a talk with her sister later about what Vandeyr divulged and what she did not.

Vandeyr gave a short nod. "You are the second-in-command, after Arlen Longspear, of King Kenrydh's Haven guard?"

"I am." Elben's tone did not falter.

The pattern of questions was emerging. By seeing how Elben answered facts that were incontrovertible truth, Vandeyr would be able to gauge the difference in his responses if he attempted to hide anything. Elben had probably studied interrogation techniques, but aside from long ago casual discussions over the dinner table, Traedis had not.

Vandeyr's next question was like an arrow to the target. "Are you courting Traedis?"

"I am," Elben answered. "She has permitted me to do so." His demeanor was no different than it had been during the previous questions.

Traedis' contrary streak urged her to immediately accept his suit for no other reason than to spite her sister. But that was not fair, and neither Elben nor Vandeyr deserved it. She held her tongue and listened instead.

"Are you courting Traedis for yourself, or for Haven? In other words, does Haven have designs on the City?"

An angry retort burned upward through Traedis' throat; again she choked it down with effort. Her anger subsided almost as suddenly as she realized her sister was trying to protect her the best way she knew how. She felt a pang of remorse; Vandeyr had proven herself more than faithful in the months since Traedis had received the *falmyros*.

Elben appeared startled, but answered with no apparent difficulty. "No, of course Haven doesn't have designs on Tolin. I am courting Traedis for herself. I have no other motives."

Vandeyr's shoulders softened. "Then tell me *why* you are courting my sister."

A slight pucker pulled at the skin between Elben's brows. "Because she is brave and honorable and wise. Why else would I court a woman?" The corners of his mouth lifted mischievously. "Well, that and the fact that she is the loveliest fox maiden in this quarter of the world."

Traedis' cheeks warmed; she looked at the floor.

"And Haven is not directing your courtship in any way?" Vandeyr's words were as precise as her knife skills.

"No," Elben said, the smile vanishing. "Haven is not directing my courtship. Indeed, many of them would be shocked that I am courting any woman of Tolin, most especially its king."

"I'm satisfied for now," Vandeyr stated. Thank you, Dame Jae-Jae, for the use of your spell." In moments, she turned from deadly interrogator back to Traedis' temperamental sister. "You three decide on whatever esoteric spellwork you're going to pull together to find out what happened. I'll just stand here and pretend to be useful."

Ruth scuffed her foot along the floor. "Who's going to put me to sleep?"

"I'll do it." Traedis unlatched her harp case and slung Rose over her shoulder. "Jae-Jae? You've got chording, truth, and memory. What else can you add to this stew?"

Jae-Jae brushed back a stray lock. "A spell of heeding atop it which should enable all of us to experience what happened, not to simply have Captain Tallforest recount it."

Traedis nodded. "Transfer the memory spell to me and I can take some of the burden off you. I also have another of my own which I've been working on—it helps to pull different threads of knowledge together and make sense of them. We chord Vandeyr into the whole, and she can see the truth as well. That will tell us what we need to know."

The three guards were either well-trained or had gotten used to powerful magics; they stood as stolid as the flagstones beneath them. Though, if it were Traedis, she would be less concerned about being tangled in a spell than a target of either Vandeyr's daggers or her tongue.

Traedis looked at Jae-Jae. "Are we ready?"

Jae-Jae nodded. "As a saddled horse."

Ruth lay down on the floor, stretching her short form before settling into a curled position with her head pillowed on her arm. She closed her eyes while Traedis played a short sequence of notes that rang, bright and clear, into the air. Ruth's breathing settled, and the lines of her face smoothed. After a few moments, Traedis stilled her strings and nodded at Jae-Jae.

It was strange to hear someone else play her own spell, especially since Traedis had been unsuccessful in teaching its full expression to anyone else. In truth, she had not really *taught* it to Jae-Jae; the bard had learned from listening to her. It sounded different played on Jae-Jae's extraordinary lute and sung in her deeper voice, but it worked. Traedis could feel it take hold, the notes wrapping around them like a cocoon. It teased at Ruth, summoning her scrying ability like the butterfly hidden within the chrysalis.

Jae-Jae nodded at Traedis, who began her own part in the spellweave.

The strings sang under Traedis' fingers; a high, descending charm of memory entwined with Jae-Jae's magic. Rose's notes fell into Jae-Jae's spellwork, the music as well as the magic, the strings waking harmonies in the air as the notes meshed. She added the stringed and vocal harmonies of connection, laying them against the other woman's as if they were the right and left hands of a single bard. The dissonance between the harp and lute sparked ideas; the chords and countermelodies brought their threads together into understanding. Traedis lost herself in the music: this was what she was for, what the gods had made her to be.

Guiding all their thoughts along the memories, Jae-Jae focused on what Elben had felt bodily. If he had been poisoned, his physical self would have known before his mind. Traedis struggled with this aspect of the magic; it was not what a memory spell was intended to recall. Still, the chording drew out the core element of memory, as Ruth's nascent ability sought out what they needed to know.

They dragged the spell along the time when Traedis had left Elben, slowly inching toward his eventual meeting with Mitheira. Somewhere between now and then they would hopefully find what they sought. As Jae-Jae kept the rhythm of the chording steady, Traedis added Rose's *sagathas* power to stretch out the moments Elben had lived through, the magic of correlation examining each like a jeweler assessing a gem.

The physical event emerged clearly. Not long after Traedis left him, Elben's blood had suddenly surged in his veins, bursting small vessels in his brain, and forcing him to his feet.

Traedis stopped and spooled time backward, running more slowly back over the point where Elben's body had suffered the shock. With the probe of her magic, she hovered over the instant to see what had caused him to react so violently.

Intense pressure rushed into her veins, like a bubble of air in heated glass. Her head felt as if it would split apart. Momentarily unable to control her body, she fell forward onto her knees, dropping her harp on the floor. She heard Jae-Jae kill the chording with a single downward stroke of her hand.

A jolt went up Traedis' arms as she hit the floor. Elben surged halfway out of his chair, then stopped. The guards moved toward him, and he sat again, quivering with tension.

With the cessation of magic, the pressure inside Traedis abated, leaving her limp and exhausted. She picked up Rose, thankful the instrument was unbreakable. The wood vibrated under her hand like an anxious dog concerned about its mistress. She lifted the harp to her knees and stroked the frame, as much for her own reassurance as for Rose.

"That," Traedis said, still shaken, "was no poison. That was a spell, and a powerful one, or I wouldn't have suffered the effects as well." She looked at the others in concern. "Is everyone all right?" She looked up to see Vandeyr with a dagger in each hand, her stillness containing suppressed movement. Ruth was somehow still sleeping.

"That was what I experienced," Elben answered, strain visible in his muscles. "It's still hazy, but I'm quite sure I felt—whatever it was. What was it?"

Traedis traced Rose's carven flowers nervously. "I don't know. It hit me as soon as I tried to isolate it."

Jae-Jae plucked a pair of notes; her expression was thoughtful. "I may be able to get you closer to that memory without harm. Let me try it again exactly like we did before, but this time I want to add a more protective element into the chording."

Traedis nodded and rose from the floor, wincing as she felt a sharp pang in her knee. She would have bruises. She shouldered Rose again.

"All right, then." Jae-Jae repositioned her lute. "Trae, are you ready?"

At Traedis' assent, Jae-Jae began to play again, her instrument pouring out notes like a cascade of water, precise and powerful in their combined force. Weaving her rich voice into the spell with unerring accuracy, she shored up the spell with an absolute refusal to allow harm to flow into their joint magics. With her own skill and delicacy, Traedis ran her fingers lightly down the harpstrings, waking a series of ghost notes in the air. She fingered some preliminary chords, concentrating solely on keeping the memory spell tight and focused. As she slipped into the spellweave, she was keenly aware of Vandeyr and Elben as silent presences within the singing whole.

She slid into Elben's knowledge with a quick *arpeggio*, and felt Jae-Jae pick up the threads of magic, binding them together, tying Ruth's scrying gift into the magic so that they could all see through the lens of Elben's experience. Traedis let her own high, clear voice soar in a descant over their joint enchantments, feeling the thrumming in the air as the notes joined and interlocked. There was no time to listen; she must use her own knowledge of the magic and the music to search through last night's events.

This time, Traedis could feel Jae-Jae's powerful protective magic shielding them all from being swallowed in whatever enchantment could rise up from mere recollection into active life. Lingering over the gap in Elben's memory, she evoked the events slowly, sharing each action so they could all understand what was hidden behind the rush of blood and the near-apoplectic fit imposed on the Haven knight.

His mind clouded after this point, but Traedis was ready. She aimed the memory spell like a lockpick to slip open the door, teasing out a weak point where the suffocating cloud was thinner; where a moment's sanity had crystallized in the knight's thoughts.

Easing into that point, she lifted up the fog, careful not to fall too far into the morass of tangled emotions below. It came up cleanly, now that she had hold of it; as long as she kept control it should not endanger any of them with the same symptoms it had induced in Elben. Slowed to such a pace, each moment could be studied.

Elben took books from a shelf, brought them to a table, and began to page through them. He turned his attention to a beautifully illuminated plate, his long ink-stained fingers gentle on the thick leaves. All that broke the silence was the rasp of paper, the rustle of Elben's hands on the covers.

A scrap of parchment fluttered on the table next to him: one which had not been there moments before.

The instant his gaze fell upon the paper, the fit struck.

Everything hazed into a cloud of scarlet rage. Elben's throat tightened to a choking closeness; his vision narrowed. He rose precipitously from the table, Haven-trained senses alert. Someone lurked nearby, someone who meant ill. He listened for the telltale sounds of breathing, the whisper of cloth against cloth, the faint scrape of a boot on stone.

Elben's feet were already turning him toward the back of a sturdy oaken bookcase. As he rounded the corner, he reached out to catch and hold, feeling living flesh beneath his touch. A man pulled a knife, moving like the slow pour of molten metal. Elben had the man by the throat in the space of a thought. His body moved of its own volition to twist the assailant's neck just as the knife cleared its sheath. A dull crunch sounded. The man fell limply to the floor.

The knife, a keen, long-bladed weapon, clattered over the man's thigh onto the flagstones as the corpse's hand slipped to the floor. Elben picked it up and tucked it into his sleeve before starting toward the library door.

A spark of clarity told him that he was dangerous to innocents. He wandered down the cobbled streets, crossing over when he saw anyone so he would not attack them. His temples swelled, killing rage threatening to break loose at any moment. He picked out the quieter streets, the dim thoroughfares which would allow him to escape notice. He could not unchain the fury from its hold on his mind. He must find someone upon whom he could safely vent his anger; someone who deserved his hatred.

Time evaporated as he wandered, subsumed in the red rage which demanded blood and retribution. Air whistled in and out of his throat, still partially closed as if to contain the frenzy. A few short strides from the Atenel estate, Elben looked up, and the thought was reborn, pounding through his blood: Mitheira had hurt Traedis.

He was at her door before he knew it, hammering and demanding to come in.

Elben's face was slick with sweat, his breathing shallow.

"He was compelled," Traedis told Vandeyr without dropping her spellwork. "Either that piece of parchment was a distraction, or it had some powerful magic on it. It's apparent he was fighting the compulsion the whole time."

Vandeyr said very softly, "There was no trace of any altercation in the library. My people looked it over. This entire affair was professional. That says to me they were top-quality assassins."

Roughly, Elben asked, "King Traedis, Dame Jae-Jae, would you allow me to add something to your spell?"

Haven knights had odd, godsgiven powers. Traedis asked, "What do you wish to add? What will it accomplish?"

"There is an enchantment of fire that our order is taught," Elben answered, "to determine the purpose of magic. If I could cast it through your joint spell, we might be able to understand something about *how* I was overmastered. It isn't easy to suborn a Haven knight's will."

"Jae-Jae?" Traedis asked. "Can you handle another spell?" The answer was yes, of course, but she did not intend to skimp on courtesy.

Without pause, Jae-Jae nodded.

Traedis let the fingers of her right hand make their way up and down Rose's strings. "Cast your enchantment into Jae-Jae's spell chording and she'll catch it for you."

Elben nodded. His jaw muscles worked silently for a moment, as if he recited something under his breath. Then he cupped his hands again, bringing forth another small flame. He stared into it intently for an extended moment, then blew it toward Jae-Jae and her lute. Traedis had the odd sensation that the flame was not so much snuffed as sent into some invisible realm. With a delicate patter of grace notes, Jae-Jae caught the spell as it entered the chording.

Traedis had a confused set of impressions: dark lines on parchment; a choking sensation; insane fury which could not be quelled.

Jae-Jae halted the spellchording abruptly in mid-phrase for the second time, the spell curling undone like a broken harpstring. She stilled her lute and frowned. "Another moment of *that* and we'd all have been in trouble."

"What was it?" Traedis asked. She felt exhausted, as if she had played her bones instead of her harp. "What is powerful enough to reach through time and memory and gain a hold on us?"

Jae-Jae smoothed her fingers over her fretboard. "Have you ever heard of bardic runes? I don't mean runes of the ordinary sort, the kind you put on gravestones or signposts. I mean runes that carry bardic power and magic.”

Traedis felt understanding settle over her like morning sun cutting through twilight pre-dawn. Lord Ymre’s words; the rune book he had given her; the understanding of the *quixil*, the first rune; all fit into their perfectly aligned places.

“I have not only heard of them,” she said, “but I have a book of them in my apartments. Given to me by Lord Ymre.”

“Was it, now?” Jae-Jae stroked her chin. “I saw more than you seemed to have. That piece of parchment carried two bardic runes: one for rage, and another for choking. The work is clean and tight, well-crafted.”

“I recognize the assassin.” The salt in Vandeyr’s voice could have poisoned whales. “One of Uncle Cordelayne’s people. Trae, I was wrong, and you were right.”

“Uncle Cordelayne couldn’t have meant to hurt Mother—” Traedis began to say.

“Of course he didn’t mean to hurt Mother.” Vandeyr’s voice was implacable. “That’s no excuse. He wasn’t careful. Gavaya was in the library last night.”

The room spun briefly around Traedis; she sucked in her breath and let the dizziness pass. Uncle Cordelayne was playing a game with all of their lives, perfectly certain that he had prepared for all eventualities. Only this time, he had not counted on a Haven knight with iron principles and reflexes like a tiger. “How do you interpret the plan?” she asked her sister.

“I’d say Lothain was there to slip the parchment onto the table, then probably to wait and steer Captain Tallforest carefully toward some poor fellow who’d had too much drink and too little luck. I told some of my people to search the library. As I said, we found nothing. No blood, no dead man, not even a pile of books. Which were shelved where they belonged. Someone else was there as well, someone who decided that Elben's state would care for itself in favor of a thorough clean-up."

"Gods." Traedis ran a hand over her hastily braided hair. "What now?"

"I don't pretend to understand magic. But if you're trying to prove Captain Tallforest's innocence, isn't the best person to assert it Mother herself?"

After a flurry of messages were sent up and down the hall, and after proper security had been arranged, Traedis, Jae-Jae, Ruth, Elben, and a small army of guards escorted them into Mitheira's room in the healer's wing. Elben's hands were bound again, mostly for Mitheira's comfort, and Vandeyr's people fanned out to either side of him, hands on their weapons.

Traedis' mother was pale, but her face was like ice. Traedis had seen warmer expressions in the Heart of Winter.

Jae-Jae strode to her chair and knelt on the floor in front of her. "Lady Atenel, thank you for allowing us to bring this case before you. You are obviously a brave woman, and if I were not sure of myself, I would never bring the man who attacked you into this room. But you deserve to know the truth of what happened this night. Will you accept Shorr's truth, attested to under my magic?"

"Dame Jae-Jae," Mitheira said, "do you promise that all words spoken under your magic are indeed true?"

It was a shocking question and a breach of etiquette, coming from someone who knew the gravity of Jae-Jae's position. But perhaps, thought Traedis, her mother had been through so much this night, that even her perfect courtesy had cracked minutely.

"All the words will be the truth as the speaker knows it," Jae-Jae told her. "I swear it before my master Shorr."

Mitheira bowed her neck.

Jae-Jae's fingers sought her lute strings for the third time that night, plucking music as if the strings were stretched on her heart instead of lacquered wood. Traedis felt the binding magic take hold, though more subdued.

It was Vandeyr who told Mitheira the truth about what had caused Elben's rage; Traedis was afraid to risk her mother's disbelief if the words were hers. Vandeyr laid out the succession of events; her own observations about the knife; Elben's long ramble through the streets, fighting the killing wrath that swept through him.

Mitheira narrowed her eyes at first, but showed every sign of listening keenly. When Vandeyr told her what was on the parchment, her lips tightened, and her neck straightened. Finally, Vandeyr stopped, and Mitheira sat in utter stillness before drawing a breath to speak.

"Well, Traedis," she said in a voice carefully free of timbre. "This will be your uncle's work. He put Gavaya and myself into reckless danger, and unleashed a weapon of your Haven knight upon the streets. In this matter, I cannot defend him." She turned to Jae-Jae again. "Dame Jae-Jae, please continue your spell while I ask Captain Tallforest a question."

Elben closed his eyes briefly, then opened them again. He gave a half-bow. "I am ready to answer, Lady Atenel."

For the first time since they had returned to the room, Mitheira acknowledged Elben. "Captain Tallforest, did you intend me harm when you sought me out this night?"

The Haven knight answered slowly, as if collecting his thoughts, but no hesitancy stained his words. "I have never intended you harm, Lady Atenel. I find you a charming woman, and respect your place and position. If I have a dispute with any of your family, it is with your brother-in-law, Cordelayne. And possibly your son Daymet, if he had anything to do with what happened tonight." His arm muscles tensed. "Had I been in my right mind, I would never have attacked you. I am grievously sorry that I caused you such pain and fear."

Mitheira steadily held his gaze. "I no longer hold you responsible for your attack. In fact, I will make it known to the City that you are not guilty. They will heed my words. Never let it be said that I accused an innocent man of any crime." Her voice sharpened. "May I leave, Traedis? Or do you have further need of me?"

"Of course you may go," Traedis told her uncomfortably. "Thank you for your patience, Mother."

Mitheira stood gracefully, and exited from the room in such a grand fashion that she left an almost visible wake of silk and perfume. Her manservant followed, his own dignity obvious in measured, unhurried steps.

Traedis sighed: her mother had accepted the truth. Still, Mitheira's goodwill would only go so far where Elben was concerned. She would clear Elben's name in the City, but she would not forgive him for courting Traedis.

She was also unlikely to hold it against Uncle Cordelayne. She might be angry that he had not taken better care with his actions, but she would find excuses for him and for Daymet, just as she always did.

Jae-Jae stopped playing and turned toward Traedis.

Ruth shrugged. "Settled, then?"

Traedis nodded. Waves of tension rolled off her shoulders; she suddenly realized how tired she was. A yawn overtook her, and she longed for the soft comfort of her bed.

There would be more to do tomorrow. Traedis must find out more about runes and the runecaster who had penned such deadly strokes of ink. If Uncle Cordelayne had access to a skilled runecaster, he had a greater weapon than she had realized. But her head was beginning to fog, and her lack of sleep was rushing to meet the morning.

"It's settled. For now."

Chapter Nine
A Visit to Faldrohaven

Music threaded Traedis' sleep, notes splashing into her dreams like fountain spray. When she finally woke at mid-morning, Ruth perched by her bedside with a tray of bread and cheese. Jae-Jae and Vandeyr were gone.

"Breakfast?" asked Ruth. "It's good, especially the rind."

Traedis sat up, swung her legs over the edge of the bed, and brushed at her skirt, hoping the wrinkles would come out. She vaguely remembered reaching her room; apparently, she had not changed before going to bed. Intensive use of magic sapped the strength, and Traedis had not had a full night of sleep. She must look like an urchin in a hastily-stolen garment.

"Just a moment." She unbraided her hair so that she could finger-comb it before re-braiding it. Patting down the last flyaway hairs, she said, "How is Mother? How is the City? Has Mother calmed them?"

"She has." Ruth popped a piece of bread in her mouth and offered another slice to Traedis. "Your mother talked to a number of powerful people and told them that Elben was innocent and wrongly accused. Her servants are backing her up and spreading the word around town. The mob is out of the streets, so your sister let you sleep."

"Thank Kyaan," said Traedis. "Mother may despise Haven knights, but she's fair, and won't compromise her honor to incite the City against Elben."

"I know." Ruth offered her a heel of bread slathered with honey. "After last night I have more respect for her. She listened, admitted she was wrong, and immediately did her best to clear Elben's name, all right after she nearly died. She's got a lot of courage."

"She does," Traedis agreed, warmth creeping into her chest. "She certainly does." She took the bread and nibbled on it hungrily. "Where are

Vandeyr and Jae-Jae?"

"Vandeyr went to send Elben back to Faldrohaven." Ruth licked a drop of honey from her finger. "Jae-Jae had to leave. She sends you her regrets, but says she has a full schedule this year."

"If she hadn't come..." Traedis wiped her hands and face with her napkin instead of finishing her thought. She knew what would have happened if Jae-Jae had not come. She regretted not seeing Elben off. She regretted even more that he could not stay. But that would only have enraged the people of Tolin and inflamed already existing tensions.

As soon as Traedis finished her breakfast, she rose and dressed, then headed toward her sitting room. She did not get all the way there before Vandeyr walked through the door, her uniform as neat and well-creased as it had been the night before.

"Sit down," said Vandeyr. "I have news for you." She snapped a few words to someone in the hall, then pulled the door closed and rested one hand on a scrolled chair back, looking down with a haughtiness taller than her height. Traedis sat facing her.

"Mother says she might know the runecaster." Vandeyr tapped one finger on the chair's carved design. "She gave me a description. It might be enough for you to work with."

"Who is it?" asked Ruth, interest lacing her voice.

Vandeyr flared her nostrils. "No one to whom she has loyalty or obligation." She moved to the front of the chair and folded herself into it. "Several years ago, a karreld came to the City wanting to be admitted." She turned her attention to Traedis. "We get that sort of thing—got that sort of thing—quite a lot. Someone wants City's reputation, and they petition for admission. Since the City only takes—took—people with significant skills, we used to get all manner of petitions involving strange magics, would-be assassins, and people who thought their own reputation was great enough for us to grant them anything.

"Anyway," she continued, "Mother says this particular karreld brought with him a grimoire of bardic runes. Uncle Cordelayne was interested enough to speak for this fellow, who I gather was a very sniveling sort, not the kind the City wants at all. Eventually they sent him and his runebook packing. Mother thinks Uncle Cordelayne may have looked him up when he needed resources."

"Describe him, please," Traedis told her.

Vandeyr drew her brows together in thought. "Middle-aged, limestone skin, receding hairline, mouse-brown hair touched with grey. Smallish blue-green eyes, a tic in the left one. Average height for a karreld, which is mid-waist on me. Ink-stained fingers when Mother met him, but who knows whether that's still true? A tendency to overdress. Apparently, he was quite a pompous fellow. Mother despised him."

"A good mind, though, if he can cast runes," added Ruth. "Trae, do you need me to go back to sleep?"

A moment's thought was enough for Traedis. "No, though I thank you for offering. I need Tagg. Vandeyr, can you send a page—"

"Already did." There was a hint of smugness about Vandeyr's lips.

"Of course you did." Ruth rolled her eyes.

"He should be—" Vandeyr was interrupted by a knock on the door.

"Come in!" Traedis called.

The door opened, and Tagg entered, a pleasant expression on his face despite the faint wrinkle in his forehead. He was dressed simply but neatly in a linen shirt and trousers. "I understand you asked for me, Your

Majesty?"

Traedis nodded. "I have need of your talents."

Tagg blinked owlishly. "Tell me what you want me to do, Your Majesty."

"Of course. I expect by now you've heard all about last night."

"I would have to live in a drainpipe to miss the gossip," Tagg said dryly. He smoothed a crease on one sleeve, but his gaze was interested and direct. "You were wise to have involved your mother in clearing Captain Tallforest's name. However, there's only half a story. Who managed to compel a Haven knight to attack your mother? Or perhaps I should say how did that someone manage to compel a Haven knight?"

Tagg's ordinary looks belied his brilliance, and Traedis sometimes forgot how keen his mind was. He had managed to pull the threads together and woven an elegant and largely correct explanation out of rumor and suppositions.

"We're dealing with a bardic runecaster." Traedis gathered her skirts with a nervous hand, playing with the silken folds. "Mother has given us a description of the man she thinks is responsible. I need you to find him."

"Tell me." Tagg's eyes narrowed. "It wasn't a karreld, was it?"

Vandeyr snorted. "I see you've met him."

"I think so." Tagg leaned his chin onto his fist. "I was a journeyman, and it was a long time ago, but the Council wanted to consult my master. I didn't even understand why they were considering admitting the fellow—he couldn't look anyone straight in the face, and he was so mealy-mouthed I almost expected him to spit wheat. That was when my master explained to me about bardic runes and why the fellow had gotten to the Council rather than being sent packing at the gates. He was memorable." He gave a short, barking laugh. "Ultimately, I understand, he was deemed untrustworthy and sent back to his home in Telardur."

"They didn't take his runebook?" asked Ruth.

Tagg squinted against a sudden ray of light that had shifted to pierce the windowpanes. "Of course not. The Council weren't thieves."

"Just murderers," Ruth muttered, barely loud enough to be heard.

Such a stroke of fortune was not what Traedis had expected when she had called for her mage; it was far easier to find someone if given a good description, and an even better chance if they were known to the seeker. With Vandeyr's description to bolster Tagg's memory, their odds had risen considerably.

"No point in waiting," she said to Tagg. "I'd like you to *blork* to Faldrohaven if we find this karreld in Telardur. If he is, King Kenrydh needs to know."

Vandeyr's expression grew frosty. "*Blork?* Awful Telardurian slang," she said, directing her comment into the air.

Traedis ignored the comment; she knew when Vandeyr was trying to bait her.

"Of course, Your Majesty. If you please, give me a moment for my spellwork."

Traedis nodded and fell silent. Tagg focused into the distance, as if he were staring at something very far away. Though some mages chose to use words and gestures to direct their power, they were not necessary; the magic came from the strength of their birthfire and the discipline of their minds. It was sometimes uninteresting to watch a skilled mage when they were performing invisible enchantments.

Without warning, Tagg's breathing quickened, and sweat broke out on his forehead and hands. "He's noticed me. He's trying to put some sort of runic hook into my spell. I don't think he can get past my protection, but I have to get a lock on him quickly—this is harder than I'd have guessed." He drew a great gasp before his breathing subsided into panting, then to even, deep breaths. "That's it—he's at an inn in the southern town of Castron. I can open a gate and still keep up the location spell, but it might help if one of you came with me to explain so I don't have to split as much of my attention."

"I'll go," said Ruth.

The two of them winked out abruptly, leaving Traedis with their afterimage in her vision. She blinked several times to clear it, then gripped the arms of her chair tightly. She wanted to follow the two of them to Kaelennar and head the hunt herself, but those days were long past; she could not simply indulge herself by jumping headfirst into danger. She must put Tolin first. The sound of wings blew past her ears; her curse weighed heavily on her chest.

Rose chimed in her case, a soft reminder that Traedis was not alone. Perhaps she could not act directly, but she had power, both magical and temporal. The leash of her curse did not forbid all of her actions.

At least not yet.

It was several hours before Ruth and Tagg reappeared; hours which Traedis spent alone in her office, reading some of the older histories of Tolin. She hoped to learn something that could give her an advantage in turning aside the tremendous weight of tradition that shaped the City's beliefs. Even more, she hoped she could find something that could help her find her uncle before the year was up. Time was rushing past her in a flood wave, and she must not lose her footing.

Feet scuffed outside the door: Tagg's heavy step; Ruth's whisper-quiet feet; Vandeyr's military precision which could change to softer than the flight of an owl if she chose. A knock came at the door.

"Come in!" Traedis called.

Ruth bounced in cheerfully, Tagg close behind, swaying on his feet. Vandeyr slid in and closed the door.

Before Traedis could ask, Ruth met Traedis' gaze. "They got him."

Tension slid from Traedis like an unfastened cloak. She had not realized how clenched her fingers were, or how tightly her jaw had locked. "Thank Kyaan." She inserted a slip of parchment to mark her book's progress and laid it down on her desk. "Tell me. And Tagg, sit before you wind up splattering my floor with pieces of mage." Tagg gratefully grabbed the other chair and planted himself heavily on the seat.

"He was quite skilled," Tagg told her. "That rune he tried to insert into my spell; most mages wouldn't notice my presence. I wouldn't have expected a bard to. He'd set runes to tell him if anyone were trying to find him, and they're powerful."

"Prince Flamechild went after him," Ruth said. "He may be strong, but he was no match for her."

Traedis raised her eyebrows; Prince Feledh Flamechild was the king of Telardur's aunt and a powerful mage. Both she and King Kenrydh were lesser dragons; paragons of their people who, though nowhere as great as true dragons, possessed tremendous powers. It would take more than a bard to defeat her. She was also one of the people Traedis respected most in all Telardur.

"King Kenrydh requests your presence in Faldrohaven, where our karreld friend is being held." Tagg yawned, hastily covering it with a pudgy hand. "Excuse me, Your Majesty, I have been working hard, though I still have some energy for spellwork at your disposal. The king wants your perspective, considering that the prisoner is a bard—your area of expertise—and that the matter is important to Tolin's security."

Vandeyr was halfway out the door and calling for her second-in-command before Traedis could nod. Instead, she tried to keep laughter from her voice. "Yes, Vandeyr, I am going." She assessed her clothing: silken dress the color of the sky, an amber brooch shaped like a fox at her throat, drops of amber in her ears. It was formal enough that she did not need to change. "Tagg, as soon as Captain Atenel collects up a sufficient guard, can you *blork* us to Faldrohaven?"

"I can and will, Your Majesty."

"Good. Because I don't want to waste any time."

The palace in Faldrohaven was a marvel. The entire city was carved into the top half of Mount Gimreis, an undertaking that had spanned centuries. The palace was the capstone and the glory of the faldren people. A colossal deposit of rose quartz roofed one section of the mountain, and it was under this wonder the palace had been set, a jewel beneath a jewel. During the day, the sun filtered through the rock, though dimly, imbuing the rooms with a soft pink light like the glow of dusk or dawn. Even with torches and lanterns providing most of the illumination, it seeped into the corners so that no place was too shadowed to lift the heart.

Despite its beauty, Traedis had not enjoyed her previous stay. That had been before she had become king, and Tolin had agreed to hire her out to her friends: when she had learned the City's deeply buried secrets.

It had also been where she had met Elben, though she had scarcely noticed him until he had changed into a red fox and followed her under furniture as her own fox form strove to find someplace she could consider safe. After that, she had only cared that he not come too close to her.

This time, Traedis was ushered into a small reception room in order for King Kenrydh to properly greet her. Vandeyr and three guards took positions around her, spines straight, eyes taking in all activity around the room. Traedis took one of two offered chairs and sat gracefully, setting Rose's case on the floor; Tagg took the other chair. Servants offered them a small feast of black bread, finger-sized tarts, lemon ice, meat hand pies, sugared nuts, and so many cheeses and fruits that Traedis was not sure she could identify them all, together with wine and cider and mead. She picked up a pear, biting through the skin into flesh as sweet as the first kiss of spring. She had only taken two more bites before Kenrydh entered with his Haven Guard, including Elben.

Kenrydh was a high faldro, and broad through the chest and shoulder; he was tall for his people, nearly reaching her own meager height. In his early prime, with dark golden hair and beard, his brown eyes missed little. He gave a gracious bow—respect, rather than reverence—as she and Tagg rose to greet him. Tagg bowed deeply.

"Welcome to my halls, King Traedis." Kenrydh's forehead was developing worry lines already, though he was still considered young among his people. "I know you do not have much time to spare, but Duinedh and I must arrange for you to visit sometime when matters are more auspicious."

"Thank you for your welcome," Traedis responded, returning his gesture. She did not even glance at Elben, but could feel his presence like sparks dancing against her skin. "I am most glad that you're willing to work with me in this matter." It was certainly beneficial to him as well, that powerful runecasters and potential murderers not walk free in his lands. Traedis' experience of her own people told her that something might be beneficial and still not be considered urgent by those who had every reason to think so.

"Feledh is still here—I asked her to stay, since she was responsible for catching the man you sought, and may have some knowledge that is useful to you. My people have set the fellow up in an interrogation room. I'll arrange for you and Captain Atenel to join them."

That was unexpected, but a pleasant surprise; Traedis had not seen Prince Flamechild in some time. In addition, the presence of the prince would likely deter any canny tricks the runecaster still had that he was waiting to unleash.

"Thank you," she said. "I am anxious to find out what role the runecaster may have played in—" She stopped for a moment, realizing all the Haven guard probably knew exactly what had happened to Elben during his stay in Tolin. She forced the heat from her cheeks with an effort of will.

"Of course," Kenrydh replied, smoothing over her discomfort.

To Traedis' relief, Elben was not one of the guardsmen the king sent down with her to the prisons. She was not sure she wanted to talk to him just then. Besides, she would need all the concentration and alertness she could muster to confront the runecaster.

The way to the prisons was down a long, spiraling staircase carved into the granite, hugging the wall on one side, sweeping away into darkness on the other. Though the steps were broad, made to accommodate sturdy faldrim, they were also shallow, and felt uncertain to human feet. Traedis did not fear heights, but she did not want to fall half the elevation of Mount Gimreis, and kept close to the wall side of the staircase.

They did not descend all the way to the bottom, but instead stopped on a wide landing opening to a corridor on the opposite side. A guardpost was located on this floor, and a small contingent of palace guards ushered Traedis, Vandeyr, and the rest of her people into the hallway and past a number of barred rooms that might or might not have been cells.

Their destination was a large room near the end of the corridor which contained several guards. Traedis stepped inside, and immediately felt her heart knock against her ribs with brutal force.

She paced her old cell, trying to imagine how to fill all the days and nights of her life and make them bearable. The space was too tight, the ceiling too low. Little light shone through the grate in her cell door. The air was heavy, laden with mold.

Before Traedis could dissolve into panic, she spied Prince Flamechild. The knot in her stomach relaxed; the present returned to her. Feledh would protect her.

Chapter Ten
The Runecaster

Prince Feledh Flamechild was a faldren woman of early middle age; gray threaded her gold hair, which she currently wore up and woven into a circlet. Strong featured, her face was lined with furrows of care, but smile lines bracketed her mouth. She was dressed in practical clothing of linen and leather, and wore a short sword in a sheath at her belt. Upon seeing Traedis, her face broke into a broad grin.

"Traedis! Though circumstances could be better, it is always good to see you. How do you fare?"

"Well enough." Traedis moved forward to embrace the older woman. "And you?"

Feledh gave her a wry glance. "I'm less than pleased about having to spend my time on this miserable karreld, but otherwise I'm well. Shall we get on with it?"

At a motion from the prince, a guard—a lieutenant, from the insignia he wore—unbarred the opposite door. He and three others marched in ahead of Traedis and Feledh. They were soon joined by a woman in the uniform of the palace guard whose sharp glance seemed to take in everything around her at once.

The interrogation room was set up with a table and three chairs. On the near side, the two chairs were sized for Traedis and Feledh. On the far side was the runecaster's seat, a piece of heavy stone furniture to which his hands and feet were chained. He wore a set of silvery manacles that Traedis guessed to be enchanted.

He was even less impressive than Vandeyr's descriptions. He was scrawny, and his hair grew in dandelion tufts around balding spots. The chalkiness of his skin gave its gray limestone texture a mottled look as if he had been severely deprived of air. His eyes, a watery blue-green, were shrewd, but the left one twitched at random, which set Traedis' teeth on edge. He stared at them, outrage plain in his expression.

"Qella," said Feledh to the palace guardswoman. "Set truth upon this room, please."

The woman nodded and her gaze unfocused, as if she were deep in thought.

She must be a mage. The spell of truth was not significantly different than when cast by a bard, but instead of singing, a mage must concentrate on the magic. Though it would not force anyone to speak honestly, it would prevent them from lying, keeping falsehoods contained in the speaker's throat. It applied to all within its range; Traedis would no more be able to lie than would the prisoner. It did not constrain the speaker to simplicity or clarity, and would only confirm what the speaker truly believed.

The prince sat, and Traedis took her own chair. She was not sure what to expect, as she had not witnessed many interrogations, but Feledh was more than experienced enough for the two of them.

"This is King Traedis of Tolin," Feledh said, nodding in Traedis' direction. "You know who I am. Start with your name. Then I want to know about your dealings with Cordelayne Atenel and what work you have done for him, especially as of late—since Tolin gained a king."

"My name is Master Gonaa. I already told you that." A whine in the man's voice made Traedis want to slap him. "I'm no rebel from Tolin. Why do you think I've done anything for them?"

Traedis said, "Because you recognize the name Cordelayne Atenel." She wanted to roll her eyes, but that would look less than kingly, and she was not inclined to give him any indication of annoyance. "And you know he's one of the rebels. Now, answer Prince Flamechild's question." To her own ears, her voice sounded strange, her mother's cadences falling into the room's silence like an echo.

"No one cares whether I did anything or not." The karreld seemed to puff himself up like a bantam. "Why does it matter that I'm a runecaster? You drag me into prison, chain me up, won't even feed me a proper meal of mushrooms-and-grubs, then expect me to explain what you should be able to figure out for yourselves. Is it my fault I studied runes? I didn't invent them, but you seem to want to blame me because I've used a magic that's there to use, and not forbidden."

"I begin to see," said Traedis irritably, "why they turned you away from Tolin."

Gonaa glared at her, grinding his teeth. "Because your stinking city didn't want to accept a karreld. So high and mighty, those great lords. Only a pair of them saw what I offered. And even they didn't make the others change their minds—"

"Enough!" said the lieutenant who had ushered them into the room. He slapped his hand on the table.

"My question remains," Feledh said again without raising her voice. "Tell me about your dealings with Cordelayne Atenel."

The runecaster shook his head. "I—" He stopped and swallowed. Traedis could almost see him thinking of how to weasel his way out of the question. "I never went back to Tolin. If they couldn't see my worth—"

Traedis folded her hands in front of her. "I know you never went back to Tolin. Did you contact Cordelayne Atenel, or did he contact you?"

The karreld shook his head. "Why would I—"

"It's a yes or no question," Traedis said harshly. "You already know the answer. We want to know it too. Tell us." This time she imitated her father at his coldest. She could see Vandeyr twitch at the edge of her vision.

Gonaa's face set into a stony indifference. "If I'm not going to get any mushrooms-and-grubs, I don't see why—"

"You've had mushrooms," Prince Flamechild said quietly. "You've also had grubs. No one will make you a fine karreldish dish simply because you complain about being a prisoner in the king's city. Now: answer our questions before I become angry." The last words she dropped into the silence barely above a murmur.

Gonaa hunched in his seat, his eyes widening. "I—Your Highness, I didn't mean—" He swallowed again. "Lord Atenel doesn't value me in the least. He only cared about the book. And having me teach an ungrateful..." He trailed off and began to cough.

Something bright flashed across his forehead. Traedis leaned forward and stared at him. He dropped his gaze, but she was not interested in his eyes; instead, she tried to see if the tail of a *quixil* lay on his brow.

And there it was: a rune as complex as any she had seen, visible through the sight Lord Ymre had given her. She was not sure of its meaning, but she guessed its purpose.

The mage said dispassionately, "Your Highness, Your Majesty, his inability to speak is not part of the truth spell."

"He has a rune on him," Traedis said.

Rose sang a few notes from her case. They did not sound favorable.

"You taught someone." Prince Flamechild leaned thoughtfully into her hand. "And that person is preventing you from telling us anything about him? If that's not the case, tell me. If it is, silence will be the correct answer."

The karreld remained silent.

"I see." Traedis did. Gonaa was so patently untrustworthy that her uncle must have decided to make his own runecaster instead of using the one he had. "What *can* you tell us?"

Looking as if he would be sick, Gonaa said, "Not everyone can become a runecaster. It's a rare skill. I learned from the runebook, though I must say I am—" His gaze darted back and forth. "It is difficult learning. Any successor would be selected by the Atenel, of course, and—gifted. With the benefit of my training…" He coughed again, this time harder.

Prince Flamechild slowly straightened. "He can't speak of the one he taught." She drummed her fingers on the table. "Did you write a rage rune and a choking rune for Cordelayne Atenel?"

The runecaster fell into a spasm of coughing. One of the guards brought him a cup of water, which he choked down before the coughing stopped. "I can't tell you that." By now, he was shaking as if palsied.

Traedis swore a set of blistering oaths in the esch language, which was well-suited to profanity. "That means you didn't." She caught the hint of a smile from Feledh, but it vanished as the older woman turned her attention back to the runecaster. Narrowing her focus to the rune, Traedis tried to make sense of its branching complexities. "I'd bet diamonds this rune keeps him from speaking about multiple things."

"I want to know everything about your interactions with Cordelayne Atenel." Feledh's voice was a whip crack. "I want to know everything from when you first met him to when he decided that you should teach a more promising student. If your throat will let you, you will tell me about every conversation, every interaction, even if you merely discussed what to eat for dinner. Right now, you are facing probable execution. I will discuss the possibility of leniency with the king if, and only if, you do exactly as I tell you."

By now, Gonaa had begun to snivel. "Your Highness, please! He'll kill me, or—someone—will!" He snuffled, wiping his nose on the back of his sleeve. Tears leaked from his eyes.

"At the moment," the prince told him, "you are more in danger from me than from either of them. You are in the heart of Faldrohaven, and you sit in my presence. Now, one last time. *Tell me what I ask of you.*"

Traedis could hear the command in her voice like the pressure of a slap, though it was not directed at her. She was glad that she was on this side of the table.

Gonaa broke down completely, and began to sob.

Prince Flamechild waited until there was a lull in his weeping. "Now is the time to speak." She seemed to pull her royalty over herself like a mantle. "*Now.*"

The runecaster began to speak.

Gonaa had only been able to hint at the existence of whomever he had taught, but he said enough to confirm that it was Uncle Cordelayne who had employed him. Unfortunately, that proved to be the total of his ability to divulge secrets. Afterwards, Traedis returned to Tolin, more frustrated than she had left.

Now the sky outside the window of Traedis' office massed with clouds, possibly readying for a summer thunderstorm. Traedis lit a candle as the day darkened. Leaning back in her chair, she watched Vandeyr stomp around the room as if she were trying to intimidate an entire troop of runecasters. "Uncle Cordelayne has hundreds of bards to choose from, anyone who would throw in their lot with his. He wouldn't pick someone we knew. He's too wily for that."

"Maybe." Traedis frowned. "But runecasting is such a rare ability that he might have to. I don't know enough to guess that, and we have nothing to go on until this runecaster strikes again. The gods only know when and where that will be."

"Wherever it will do the most damage," Vandeyr said. "Uncle Cordelayne doesn't use half measures. If he's out to destroy your rule, he'll aim for your most vulnerable spots. He most certainly knows what those are."

"Yes." Traedis looked at her feet, wishing yet again that somehow it were possible to abdicate and let the land choose a new lord for itself. But she had defied the Mother of Curses to keep her *falmyros*; fear of Uncle Cordelayne would not deter her.

She sighed, then lifted her chin. "I suppose we're going to have to leave the matter of the runecaster for now. At the moment, I need to repair the damage that Uncle Cordelayne did last night."

"Hopefully, Mother's pacified those who count so that they won't be inciting a riot." Vandeyr folded her arms. "She will. She'd better. I'd like to get some people out in the streets before sunset so we can head off any unrest."

Traedis nodded. "Talk to Captain Dorrell and get him involved. The two of you are going to have to work together on this."

Vandeyr shrugged. "If he listens to me, I'll work with him. If not, I'll do what I must and let him do whatever he supposes is useful."

Traedis shook her head. Captain Dorrell headed the City Guard, and was far from incompetent, despite what Vandeyr believed. Traedis might have to tell her sister to take a less aggressive approach with him, but she preferred not to do that; Vandeyr had to manage her own association with the man.

"All right." She sat up straight and smoothed down her skirt. "Keep me apprised of what Mother is doing, and let me know if you can get any intelligence on who Uncle Cordelayne might have found for Master Gonaa to teach. I'll work on that as well. Send me a runner as you go out, please."

Vandeyr nodded and left the room. A moment later a young woman popped into the room, her hair bobbing just above the tops of her ears. She bowed and waited for Traedis to speak.

"Send word to Lord Lang that he needs to take over government functions for me today." Traedis scribbled a hasty note asking about any bards who might be with the rebels. Folding it, she sealed it with a drop of wax from her candle. "Then take this to Lady Gavaya at the City Library. I'd like you or whoever takes it to get a written response back." It was not unusual for Gavaya to have that information; the City Library had once been the hub of spywork for the entire city of Tolin.

The day broke into storm while Traedis opened the runebook Lord Ymre had given her. Such weather was not so unusual in the mountains, but torrents of rain swept against the window like the river in flood, and spears of lightning split the sky into fragments of cloud and blinding illumination. She could feel it quiver through the *falmyros* like energy in her own veins. The entire palace shuddered under the assault of the thunder.

It was hard for Traedis to keep her attention on the runes before her, despite her interest in the subject. She persevered, determined to understand this new weapon that her uncle had brought to bear, despite the prickles in her skin whenever lightning lanced off a high tree or peak.

The first rune in the book was 'light.' It seemed relatively simple compared to other glyphs pages ahead. Traedis looked at it carefully, trying to see where the *quixil* was hidden, and to memorize the precise shape that she would need to imitate.

Taking a piece of paper, she dipped a quill in her inkwell, then began to sketch the symbol as accurately as possible. She felt an unfamiliar tension in her hand, a resistance to the curves and angles that seemed more tangible than simple inexperience would account for. For a long moment, her second curve stretched and pulled at her pen, and power like the lightning outside sparked her fingers.

The ink splatted. The shape on the page rose into the air, shredding and dissipating as she watched. The paper before her was blank.

A sharp rap sounded at the door, followed immediately by the door opening to admit Vandeyr. She dripped with water; her uniform and her hair were sodden. Rain trickled from her sleeves and the hem of her shirt onto the floor, where it pooled into soft, irregular shapes.

"Mother sent criers inviting every citizen to a public meeting near the Council Spring," she said without preface. "For tonight, assuming the storm clears. Tomorrow night, otherwise."

Traedis felt the uncomfortably familiar hollow in her stomach. "That can't possibly be good." She looked out the window, where the rain sheeted down the slopes. "She's already cleared Elben of misconduct. What more can she want?"

Vandeyr's expression was lemon sour. "I'm going," she said as if she suspected her sister would try to stop her. "I want to know what Mother has up her elegantly appointed sleeve."

The tacit admission that Mitheira had less than helpful intentions toward Traedis was still new enough to surprise her. Traedis raised her eyebrow, then nodded. "Of course you're going. And I'm going with you." She drew a breath and waited for the inevitable protest.

Vandeyr rolled her eyes. "You think it's *safe* for you to wander the streets while the City is in this mood? I'm skilled, but I can't work miracles. If someone wants to assassinate you, under cover of the crowd and night would be the best time. Or haven't you thought of that?"

"I've thought of that," Traedis answered patiently. "I can dress as an ordinary citizen. As long as I keep my hair hidden and my face shadowed, it shouldn't be difficult."

Vandeyr started to speak, then caught herself, a thoughtful expression on her face. "That might work—though I don't like it." A line appeared between her brows. "The more I think of it, the less I'm fond of the idea. You might accidentally become a fox, which would give us away faster than shouting your name in the streets." Vandeyr's mouth twisted. "And if you bring your harp, it will be impossible to miss, even under a cloak."

Traedis laughed. "Don't worry—I intend to listen, not play the March of the Haven Knights. Believe it or not, I'm not trying to provoke every citizen of Tolin." She considered whether disguise was sufficient; she liked her other idea less, but it had merit. "Or I can become a wren and sit in your breast pocket." She shivered at the idea of being contained in a mostly dark interior, but it was important to see for herself what her mother intended.

"No—" Vandeyr stopped where she stood, then looked at Traedis thoughtfully. "Actually, that's not a bad idea. No one would see you at all."

"Then it's settled." Traedis squashed the fear that even the idea inspired in her. "When do you want to go?"

"A little early," Vandeyr said, letting out a theatrical sigh. "I want a good place to observe without being spotted. Especially if you're with me. An hour or so before dusk, so be ready."

"I will," said Traedis.

A blast of intense light illuminated the clouds; thunder crashed through the palace, resounding throughout the stone. Traedis blinked at a scintilla of tiny sparks that swarmed briefly through her vision. She screwed her eyes shut, then opened them again, a weak green afterimage quickly fading.

Light, she thought. *I wonder if I could find a quixil in the lightning?*

But that was a question for later. Right now, she needed to prepare for the evening's excursion.

Whatever her mother intended, it was not likely to bode well for Traedis.

A second storm had blown in an hour ago, but it had lifted, leaving the air damp and chill. The expectant crowd stood in the street before the Council Spring; Mitheira would not invite the entire town onto her carefully tended estate. A dais rose beside the water, atop which public speakers would be silhouetted against the setting sun. As more people gathered, torches lit the growing darkness with oily smoke and a sullen red, like a reflection of sunset.

Traedis heard people assembling—a scuff of feet, the rustle of cloth, low and tense voices—though few of those people crossed her vision from her position in Vandeyr's breast pocket.

She seldom employed her wren form, which gave her sense and speech, unlike her fox's wild instincts. Her brief possession by the air god Kyaan years ago had engendered both forms: two sides of the same face. This shape would conceal her better than any dress or cloak. Her only fear was that riding in Vandeyr's breast pocket would resemble too closely the dark closet her tutor had locked her in, or Toledru's suffocating prison in Tolin's stone roots.

She peered out of a buttonhole. The air was close, but Traedis made herself endure the stifling cloth which clutched her like a burial shroud. It helped that she could feel the rise and fall of her sister's chest and hear the faint and hollow sound of Vandeyr's heart. The hardest part of her position was seeing through one eye only; the opening was not large. Traedis tried to ignore her blind side and did her best to take in what she could from the narrow vantage of the button slit.

Vandeyr wore civilian clothing and a cloak as well as a head scarf to hide her Atenel white-blonde hair. Traedis caught the flash of a youth from one of the Council families, possibly a Sedorin, but the lad did not give a second glance at Vandeyr. Her simple disguise allowed her to position herself close to the dais without being recognized. So far, no one had hailed her.

"There's dear brother Otenemar," she murmured. "He's got broadsheets to put out in the morning, and I'm quite sure they'll praise Mother to the heavens."

Traedis tried to catch a look, but she was unable to see far enough to glimpse him. It was probably just as well; he had refused to see or speak with Traedis since she had left prison.

The crowd noise grew from murmurs to cacophony before trailing into a waiting silence. Traedis pressed closer to the buttonhole, wishing for a wider field of vision. If she positioned herself just right, she could see the center of the dais, but it was hard to glimpse anything not directly in front of her.

A man moved into view on Vandeyr's left, blocking Traedis' line of sight. She wriggled, trying unsuccessfully to see past him. Vandeyr moved sharply to the right, freeing up Traedis' view. When the way was clear again, Mitheira had already mounted the dais, perfectly framed by the last rays of the sun. She wore a powder-blue satin gown with a high collar and simple design, and her hair was carefully coifed. Silver dangled from her earlobes and glinted from a brooch shaped like a wyvern: the Atenel crest.

Another man climbed onto the dais, hard to see as the mountains greedily swallowed the day. Traedis could feel the rumble of a growl deep in Vandeyr's chest. A few moments later, Traedis heard the *whoosh* of igniting torches, and the dais was suddenly illuminated.

Now Traedis recognized him. It was Kaal Shefferie. She would have growled herself, if she had dared. He flashed an ingratiating smile to the crowd, and was rewarded by the hushing of voices.

"Good people of Tolin," Kaal said in the smug voice she despised, but several times louder than natural. Someone had likely put magic on him so that he could be heard easily. "I am Lord Kaal Shefferie, son of Lord Berloth Shefferie. You all know me and my family; we have managed the finances of Tolin for generations. I thank you for attending this meeting. I cannot stress how important it is for the future of the City that you are here."

Vandeyr gave a half-snort, not loud enough for anyone else to hear.

Traedis was more alarmed. The Shefferies were making several moves on a game board with a configuration she had never seen. She did not know Berloth well—he was of an age with her father—but Linden Atenel had spoken well of his intelligence on more than one occasion. Ana had certainly inherited the intelligence, and Kaal, though not as clever, was less of a fool than Traedis wished. She had encountered no other Shefferies recently, and was beginning to think that she should have make a point of seeking them out.

Kaal continued, his voice still unnaturally loud. "I am here, not on my own behalf, but to introduce Lady Mitheira Atenel. The entire City knows her grace and beauty. Her wisdom is no less, and she wishes to share her thoughts with you, loyal citizens of Tolin."

Vandeyr took an exasperated breath which swept Traedis forward and back. Traedis squeaked, and her sister rapidly stilled. The crowd quieted as well, waiting for whatever the king's mother might have to tell them.

Kaal took two steps back and Mitheira stepped forward.

"People of the City," Mitheira began, her voice also magnified. "Good people of Tolin, I welcome you to this meeting, and thank you all for coming." Mitheira's tone was cool and clear. "It is my intention to lay out facts tonight which must inform your choices thereafter. We are suffering a continuing crisis, and I believe I have a balm for our ailment." She stood proud, her head erect; her forehead wrinkled with what Traedis knew was carefully cultivated concern. Mitheira could have taught bards about performance, and Traedis had watched her mother on many nights welcoming friends and strangers into her home and at her table with a deftness that bordered on brilliance.

"You have heard that I was attacked by a Haven knight," Mitheira continued. The crowd burst into eddies of speech that grew louder as the circled. Mitheira raised a hand and the people hushed. "That claim is false; the attack was the work of another. Though I have no love for Haven, its knights have always been honorable enemies, and this has not changed."

A murmur of surprise rippled through the crowd: the admission seemed unexpected. Comments drifted from the crowd to Traedis' perch behind her sister's buttonhole. "How?..." "Didn't attack her?" "But the servants saw it!" One drunken-sounding voice, closer than Traedis found comfortable, muttered, "Damned Greens. Doesn't matter if he did it or not. He shouldn't have been here."

"The knight has been exonerated by no less than Dame Jasper Jacorvic, herald of Lord Shoriantemeth." Mitheira seemed a figure of fire, her hair red in the torchlight, her gown a blue flame. "The good dame's word cannot be doubted. Yet, though this knight did not perpetrate the violence on me, it is because he was here in the bounds of Tolin that such violence was done."

Only a trace of daylight remained, dying behind the mountain peak and spilling stars across the night. Traedis could not see widely enough to glimpse constellations, but she knew them by heart; some of them shone in the Star Cavern. She shivered, though Vandeyr's pocket was warm.

"There is a wider cause for the unrest we have felt in the last few months. Our way of life has been cracked open. It should be the part of the new king—since the gods have willed we must have a king—to repair it. Though I regret to speak ill of my own daughter, it was irresponsibility on her part to permit a Haven knight to set foot on the soil of our great city."

Vandeyr shifted her stance; Traedis slipped sideways and ruffled her feathers.

The crowd was quiet now; speaking against authority had always been dangerous, and whatever the citizens would have liked, Traedis was authority. Her mother was apparently counting on them to acknowledge herself as, at the least, a lesser authority. Perhaps even the mouthpiece for old Tolin.

Mitheira continued, "Let it never be said that I do not love Traedis. As my own daughter, of a necessity, I love her. But she leads Tolin down a dangerous path, and I cannot remain silent. I must speak out against the policy which invites enemies to our table, while she remains blind to the peril they pose to Tolin."

A yell of agreement, quickly hushed, sounded to the back and right of Vandeyr's position.

For a moment, Traedis felt again like a young girl who sat in front of her mother, practicing her stitches while Mitheira oversaw her work. *"Your seams are crooked!" her mother said, a frown pulling down the corners of her mouth. "Can I not trust you to do anything right?"*

She blinked several times through a liquid haze, glad that her wren form seemed to inhibit the urge to weep. She was vulnerable enough as she was.

"Traedis has always been a troubled girl." Mitheira's overtones of sorrow rang out through the crowd. With her bardic training, Traedis could pick out the emotions carefully laid out with a hesitation; a catch in the voice; a roughness underlying Mitheira's smooth clarity. It was masterfully done. "Though my late husband and I tried to help and to teach her, she was rebellious and contrary. As most of you know, she deserted her own city at the age of fourteen. When she was returned to the City, the Council judged it best—for her own good—to confine her to prison. I reluctantly assented to this measure, for though it was drastic, Traedis' judgment was so weak that she was a danger to herself and to others."

Vandeyr hissed like an angry cat, but said nothing. Traedis felt her grief sharpen, unsure as to whether her mother believed her own words. It was like dozens of small pinprick jabs to hear them spoken to half the population of Tolin.

Mitheira lifted her chin proudly. "And yet, the gods must have a plan for my youngest daughter, as they gave her the *falmyros* of this City. I do not understand why, but it is not for mortals to question the gods. Instead, we must do our best to interpret their will.

"Traedis' judgment is still weak, or she would not have allowed foreigners such freedom in our beloved Tolin. The gods must expect the City to aid Traedis in her rule: to guide her, to show her the paths she must follow. Such must be the task of all loyal citizens."

The pinpricks of grief lengthened into knives; Traedis could feel each word as if it stabbed into her own flesh. She swallowed hard.

"I have thought long and hard about this," said Mitheira. "I propose we re-establish the Council, not as a ruling body, but to advise my daughter when her judgment betrays her. With such a Council, our city can recover from the devastation it has endured, and can make wise decisions for our future."

The roar of approval which greeted this proposition stunned Traedis. She knew she was not well-loved, but she had allowed herself to hope the people of Tolin were at least growing used to her. Instead, it seemed that Elben's attack on Mitheira had left no question as to what the people truly thought.

Were it her own choice, Traedis would already have abdicated in favor of Gavaya or Lang, or ceded power to a Council of her own choosing. But she had been appointed by the gods, and neither they nor the Storm Eagle had told her she should blunt her power.

"And now," continued Mitheira in her clear, precise way, "I will accept questions or comments from those who wish to speak. I value all of your words, and I do not wish you to embrace mine without due consideration."

Vandeyr grumbled, very softly, "No, of course not."

"If it takes all night with each citizen speaking, I will listen. Who will be the first?"

A solid fellow standing near the front bellowed, "It is a fine idea, and one long overdue. Lady Atenel, I recommend that you serve on this new Council!"

Mitheira's expression remained merely concerned. "Goodman, I will always serve the City, but it is perhaps too much to ask of a girl to listen to the wisdom and experience of her mother. Forming the Council is the important task, far more than any role I am given."

Vandeyr gave a short but silent grunt of laughter which Traedis could feel through cloth and feathers. If Mitheira were not elected to such a Council, she would undoubtedly control at least two of its members. Kaal Shefferie was a likely choice for Mitheira's favored candidate; if she could have him on the Council and in her daughter's bed, so much the better.

A woman's dubious voice asked, "Is this right? We don't want to subvert the will of the gods. They granted the *falmyros* to your daughter, not the Council."

Mitheira looked high over the crowd. "It is a worthy question, my good woman. I have thought long and hard about the Council families' roles, and I have prayed about the question as well. I have come to remember that every lord has his counselors, and the will of the people must be represented. To allow unchecked power is to invite disaster."

It was not entirely an unfair assessment; Traedis' own experiences had shown her how dangerous power could be when there were no restrictions on its use. What her mother did not understand was that Traedis' power was checked by the *falmyros* and by the gods themselves. Toledru had lost the rule of Haven because he had taken his kingship as license to enact only his own desires. If he had not, he would not have come to Tolin, and Haven would be an entirely different place.

She shivered, suddenly cold despite the layers of warmth against her skin. The memory of Toledru's tortured spirit roused within her, speaking in double voices of anger and pain. She poked her beak out of the buttonhole so that she could breathe the chill air more easily.

"Who will you appoint?" called out a man with a deep voice that rasped like a file against steel.

As if she had expected this question, Mitheira gave a small nod. "I propose we call those whose experience and perspicacity are great. Not all need be from Council families, though it would be wise to select some from the high nobles for their greater experience and knowledge. I believe the City should be represented in all its facets."

Traedis listened with growing alarm as the crowd grew more enthusiastic over Mitheira's proposal. How would she be able to deny its passage without alienating half of Tolin? She wished now that she had more political experience. Why *had* the gods given Tolin to her?

The rest of the evening was spent in the midst of the boiling crowd, its eagerness almost intolerable. Though she had faced mobs and a hostile court, Traedis had not really understood how many of her own citizens hated her and the changes she had made. She quivered next to Vandeyr's heart, trying to take comfort in the fact that not everyone had deserted her. Voices began to argue the merits of a council while Mitheira received questions and returned answers that were well thought-out and clearly practiced. Kaal stayed to the back of the dais, his handsome features self-satisfied as he nodded at each word from Mitheira.

Eventually, Mitheira made a small final speech and took her leave. The crowd dispersed into small clumps, still abuzz with eager conversation. Traedis estimated it was near midnight.

"I'm getting you back to the palace," Vandeyr breathed quietly. "I don't think there's much more to be learned here."

Traedis' vision shifted quickly to a jumble of images, mostly people, which kaleidoscoped through light and faded color, leaving only confused impressions. Her heart beat faster now that she had nothing solid on which to focus. The space inside Vandeyr's breast pocket seemed to shrink.

At the point when the closeness stretched her nerves into frenzy, Vandeyr reached a finger into her pocket and let Traedis cling to it with her tiny claws. "I didn't think you could do it. You can come out now."

Released from her prison, Traedis leapt into the air and changed forms so fast it was disorienting. Her body felt leaden, and her hearing muffled. As her feet came down on the floor, it took her a moment to recognize that they stood in the entrance hall of the palace, torches lighting the space on either side. The cave of Vandeyr's pocket had called forth all her fears of being trapped.

Now she knew she was safe, Traedis began to pant, finding it difficult to catch her breath. Breathing hard, she leaned against the wall, then slid down its length to the floor, leaning over to give her diaphragm less resistance to drawing air. Black specks swirled in her vision.

Vandeyr immediately dropped to the floor beside her. "Traedis? Are you all right?"

Traedis had no breath to spare for an answer. She shrugged slightly, not knowing how to respond. She would be fine, but she did not feel well at that moment.

"Slow breaths," said Vandeyr. She took Traedis' shoulders gently. "Deep, slow breaths. You need to get some air into you, not expend it on panicking."

Traedis forced herself to ration her breaths, just as she had learned in the bardic college. The familiar exercise was what she needed to regain her control; air began to fill her lungs and she sighed, expelling the internal pressure. Her eyesight brightened.

With returning thought, she made an effort to push her fears back into the corner where she kept them, out of the way of rational decision. She would deal with them later.

"I'm all right," she managed, smiling wanly at Vandeyr. "We need to discuss the meeting."

"Let's get you up to your apartment first." Vandeyr stood in an easy motion and offered Traedis a hand.

Chapter Twelve
Disturbance in the Streets

As soon as they were in Traedis' sitting room, Vandeyr cocked her head thoughtfully. "You need rest. Mother isn't planning to pull down the palace and burn you alive, so you're safe enough for now. Elben is gone, so the City can't turn its anger toward him. We ought to get at least a few quiet hours. I'll send spies to listen to the opinions of the people about that little performance Mother staged." She hesitated. "It's an attack, but no immediate danger, in my judgment. You rest. I'll talk to you later."

With Vandeyr gone, Traedis retreated to her bedchamber. She quickly changed into her nightdress, then brushed her hair until it shone. There was comfort in the small, simple acts that Traedis clung to like the spar of a broken ship.

She felt exhausted, as if she had spent the day in swordplay rather than spellwork. Though perhaps it was not surprising; she had also not completed last night's sleep, and the nap she had taken was not enough to stave off fatigue. Even so, she did not want to sleep just yet. This new betrayal by her mother cut to the bone.

Taking Rose from her case, Traedis hoisted the harp to her shoulder. At first, she simply ran her fingers over the strings, delighting in the *sagathas* aftertones which susurrated behind the pluck of each string. Harmonics clung to the notes, each a word of comfort.

Gradually, she began some of the harp exercises she needed to keep her fingers nimble. Though she could play the harp by thought, she preferred to practice with her hands. The need to physically play, to earth herself in the act of making music with her body and not merely her heart, was a discipline she craved.

Drifting from exercises, she migrated to spellsongs. She could almost hear her bardic master gently explaining how the strings of her instrument could find and release the magic of melody and countermelody. In her inner vision he nodded quietly as she played her lessons, then showed her how to play them better.

Finally, Traedis relaxed into the simple melodies she played for the sheer delight, and the joy she could pour from the chalice of the harp into the listening air. Only when she wove herself so deeply into her music could she ever forget her responsibilities and her curse. She let herself fall further into song.

So absorbed that she knew herself only as a conduit for her music, she fell asleep in the chair, clutching Rose Goldsong to her like a beloved child.

Traedis opened her eyes; someone was knocking on the door. Looking up, she tried to reframe the world around her, so the interruption made sense. Light streamed through the windows, drenching Rose's gold-coated harpstrings with the fire of dawn. Traedis' fingers still clutched the harp frame.

"Come in," she said after a moment.

Vandeyr strode in. "Gods, Trae, did you sleep in that chair? You've got a rose-and-thorn pattern impressed on your cheek. Can't I trust you to even sleep right without me?"

"I didn't mean to," Traedis said defensively. "It just happened."

"If you insist on playing instead of taking to your bed, you can hardly expect to get proper rest." Vandeyr was in a foul mood, though her uniform was fresh, and her hair pulled back as severely as ever. She scowled. "I might as well just start into what I'm going to say. Breakfast isn't going to make it sweeter. I don't like the way Mother spoke last night. I don't care one way or the other about her Council, but it might be a way to mediate between you and Uncle Cordelayne. No, do *not* say a word. Don't naysay it without considering it seriously.”

A chill rose through Traedis’ body. She could not help remembering what the goat woman had told her. “I thought you were angry at Mother.”

Vandeyr shrugged and dropped into a chair, crossing her legs at the ankle. “I am. But she's no fool. A lot of people showed up last night. Today they’re restless and angry, and I’m afraid of rioting. If she gave them the word, they would.”

“They didn’t the night before,” Traedis observed. “And Mother did do her best to quell any animosity against Elben.”

Vandeyr waved her hand as if brushing away objections. “It was the first weapon in her arsenal. What do you think Kaal was doing there? Fawning over Mother, hoping for some crumbs of advantage to fall his way. Showing everyone who Mother favors for your hand. He’s not smart enough or shrewd enough to maneuver the crowds himself, but Mother is, and Ana is, and they’re setting him up as a figurehead ruler.” There was an acidity to Vandeyr's tone beyond her sister's normal irony.

“I know what he’s doing,” Traedis said. “Mother’s reasoning is less obvious.”

“He’s easy to control. She's obviously the one who came up with this idea, even if he thinks he’s a major player. She can’t put herself at the head of a Council without seeming as if she’s attempting a coup. The priests wouldn’t go along with that, so she’s trying to take power in less obvious ways.”

“You don’t sound as if you agree with her.” Traedis brushed a strand of sleep-knotted hair from her eyes. "Why are you insisting I listen?"

Vandeyr blew air out of puffed cheeks in a frustrated sigh and clasped her hands behind her head. "She has a point. If you assented to a City-appointed Council you'd get less resistance from the nobles, and it's a compromise Uncle Cordelayne might even accept."

Traedis felt a prickle of anger in her chest. "How can you say that? The only thing that will mollify Uncle Cordelayne would be for me to capitulate entirely and let him make the decisions."

Vandeyr slapped her thigh hard enough to make Traedis jump. "Are you *trying* to attract trouble? Of course Mother wants to hamstring you. That doesn't mean it has to happen that way. You've got a connection to the land she can't gainsay, and the favor of the gods. Her intent to create a new Council isn't as important as keeping the nobles and Uncle Cordelayne from your throat."

"It is important," Traedis said quietly. "It makes all the difference in the world."

Vandeyr uncrossed her ankles. "Look. The Council means less to me than the nether end of an esch. But it's the only way I can see for both you and Uncle Cordelayne to come out of this struggle unscathed. Mother sees that, too. Whatever you think of her, she does love you."

"I know," Traedis answered, Mitheira's words echoing in her heart like a thrown dagger. *"As my own daughter, of a necessity, I love her."* She swallowed over a bitter taste in her throat.

"Then why don't you listen to reason?" Vandeyr scowled ferociously. "Sometimes I think Mother is right. You always have to do the most contrary thing you can think of, don't you?"

"I do not!" Traedis fought to control her voice, which had begun to shake with renewed anger. "Listen to me, Vandeyr. I can't possibly agree to such a provision. There are dozens of reasons, but let's start with the fact that the gods gave *me* the rule of Tolin, not a Council. I'd rather muck out sewers in Eschnar, but they want me where I am. That means I have to follow their will, which means my conscience, since they haven't given me clearer instructions. I can't retreat to a Council under Uncle Cordelayne's control."

She twisted her fingers angrily into the sleeve of her gown. "Secondly, can you imagine King Kenrydh accepting such a proposal? He's not likely to take to the idea that all the changes I've made would likely be overturned within a month. And don't think they wouldn't—Uncle Cordelayne will only accept Mother's solution if it gains him control of the City. That what he wants, whether you admit it or not."

Instead of responding with anger, a thoughtful expression spread over Vandeyr's face. "What do you expect me to think? I'm caught in the middle among you, Mother, Uncle Cordelayne, even Daymet. I want to find some solution all of you will accept. Don't tell me nothing can be done."

"It can't!" Traedis snagged a thread with her fingernail and looked down at her sleeve, a little surprised at her own vehemence. "Vandeyr, I love Uncle Cordelayne. I love Mother. I love Daymet. But I won't allow them to keep my conscience. What they want is not something I can give them."

"Stubborn as the hind end of an ass, you and Uncle Cordelayne both." Vandeyr's tone was low and sullen. "I'll follow you. I've made my choice, and I'm sticking with it. But cursed if I'll toady to you and pretend I agree with you when I think you're being a fool."

"I don't expect that." Traedis sighed. "I'm sorry, Vandeyr. I can't agree to Mother's proposal. I have to do what I think is right."

"You'll stubborn yourself right back into a prison cell," Vandeyr said bitterly, and rose to her feet. "Very well, have it your own way. You've never listened to anyone else: why start now?" She stalked out of the room, slamming the door behind her.

Traedis waited until the echoes of her sister's footsteps receded down the hall. She knew Vandeyr was right about being caught in the middle, but she also knew that Uncle Cordelayne would accept nothing less than complete surrender. What his conscience demanded was completely opposed to hers.

Rose began a high keening, a sound born of wind and sorrow rather than a human voice. Traedis let her harp speak for her. She was never able to speak for herself.

A short while later, though still early, Traedis was leafing through a volume of tax laws when the *falmyros* shattered into her consciousness like an earthquake. Voices spilled into her ear, so many that she could make out no individual conversations. She could see shapes at the edge of her mind: doors slamming before wrenching open; people running. A hundred footsteps pressed against her skin. The smell and taste of oily smoke made her gag. Tolin had erupted into violence.

Lieutenant Tethyn burst into the room moments later, followed by Ruth. The smaller woman had unsheathed her white-bladed dagger. Tethyn moved to the window and looked out.

"I know," Traedis said before either spoke. "Someone sparked the tinder that's been building since the other night. Report."

"There are riots in the streets," Tethyn said, lines furrowing her forehead. "Captain Dorrell was attempting to quiet the unrest, but as far as he or Captain Atenel are concerned, it was inevitable. No one seems to know the source, though—it was as if everyone started talking about the same set of 'injustices' at once. It doesn't seem to have happened by itself, but we can't find an instigator. I'm here to keep you safe."

"Magic," Ruth said. "I'd bet on it. Someone has found a way to inflame all those tensions."

Traedis nodded, though her head was so full of the *falmyros* it felt hard to move. She shuddered. "I need to see."

"It's too dangerous, Your Majesty." Tethyn squared her shoulders. "I'd like to take you down to the safe room if you please."

"Not that kind of seeing." Traedis lifted a palm to Tethyn. "I need to know what the *falmyros* sees."

Ruth came around the desk and gave Traedis a concerned look. "Is there time to move downstairs?"

Traedis shook her head.

"Go ahead and look—we'll protect your body," said Tethyn.

Traedis leaned back and closed her eyes, trying not to listen to the rustle and breath of Tethyn and Ruth. She fell into the land, letting it guide her to the points of most danger. Her consciousness arrowed past the swiftness of the river, the sweep of wind, the staunch pines, swirling back to the City itself. Anger seemed to run through the streets, a current of hot emotion that boiled through minds and hearts and left them with no other thoughts.

Where? she asked the *falmyros*.

The anger eddied through the center of town, easing only at the Council Spring. Then it circled, flowed into the merchant's sector, slid past the priest's quarter, and poured into the more cramped communal buildings that housed the poorest of Tolin's citizens.

The City Guard was streaming into the affected areas, but it was having trouble gaining control. Traedis saw distorted faces scream in anger, her vision pulled from one to another like slices of a hideous kaleidoscope. The anger was a wasp's nest, spewing the fury of stingers and poison. Some rioters kicked in precious glass panes, others lit tinder and tossed it into the thankfully rare thatching of a few roofs.

The fires must be dealt with. Traedis dived into the land, the water, the very air that breathed down from the Dragon Mountains. From far away, she heard her body gasp, but she ignored it in her need to wield the *falmyros*. Wind would only push the fires into a conflagration. Instead, she felt her way into the stone of the houses, the slate that roofed most of the storefronts. *You may not burn*, she told the wood. *You cannot burn. You must hold fast against the consuming flames.*

To the wind, she said, *Quiet yourself. Leave the sparks and the embers where they lie. You are the air, not the fire.*

That had a somewhat smaller effect, but better than nothing. Her attempts to address the fire itself proved less successful; fire, it seemed, was not a biddable element, and sought to increase itself by consuming everything around it. But the other measures Traedis was urging the *falmyros* to accept were starting to have an effect, and citizens armed with buckets were now emptying into the streets.

A niggling observation teased at Traedis. Something about the pattern of the rioting was odd, different from the anger that had driven the mob after the attack on her mother. Continuing to feed her will into Tolin's stone and air, she let herself fall into the ebb and flow of those in the streets.

Now that she was looking, she could see it, though what 'it' was, Traedis could not tell for sure. Rootless anger surged from three separate place in the City; the rioters all came from one of these locations. There was something cyclical about the process, like a repeating loop of fury that reinforced itself each time it crossed some invisible source of renewal.

Anger grew to rage. People began with petty vandalism, which intensified to more serious damage. They built more fires. Fistfights broke out in each of the places; weapons were drawn.

Some of the furious crowd moved out into other portions of the city, where, contrary to what Traedis might have guessed, they began to slowly slough off the effects rather than repeating the loop of anger. Eventually, they returned to normal. Only if they went back to one of the three original locations did their violence escalate.

"Horses," she said, pulling herself out of the *falmyros* trance. "I need to get to three places. Get Tagg, and let Captain Atenel know I'm going to the west side market, the communal homes, and the green."

Tethyn frowned. "I'm not sure Captain Atenel would want you to go. It's dangerous."

Traedis raised an eyebrow at her. "Nonetheless, I am going. The question is whether you and Captain Atenel are going with me."

Tethyn huffed a sigh, but nodded.

Ruth said, "I won't take long." She disappeared out the door while Tethyn beckoned in two guards who she quickly briefed and sent on their way.

It took a little longer for Ruth to return, followed by Tagg, whose hair was uncharacteristically windswept, and whose fingers were covered with soil. Vandeyr arrived a moment later with six guards. It took slightly longer for the horses to be readied; Traedis took the time to change into a shirt and breeches, put on a cloak and pulled up the hood, and retrieved Rose. They headed downstairs and out the door in less than a quarter of an hour. Traedis mounted, then pulled her cloak tighter; it would be harder to spot her on horseback than in a crowd and on foot.

Traedis gave their small group the directions. They skirted areas where the disturbances overflowed, but it was not possible to miss them altogether, especially since Traedis and her small party were headed into an area where many rioters were leaving. But no one accosted them as they galloped by, largely because of their speed and the fact that almost all the rioters were on foot.

Halfway to their first destination, another contingent of mounted guards added to their number, making all of them less vulnerable. As they neared the western market, Traedis studied those who came in and out of the area to see where the rioters were originating from.

It was not obvious at first. The western market was an open square of stalls which sold wares ranging from meat pastries to silk scarves to finely crafted knives. Usually it was a bustling area where cityfolk went to find bargains, whether they sought expensive goods or cheap produce. On a normal day, the scents of spices and cooking meat wafted through the air, and the hum of a hundred conversations sounded like an ocean tide.

Now, stalls were overturned, spices spilled over the cobbles, and carts tilted on broken wheels and axles. A small fight was quickly becoming a brawl, and some of the merchants were wielding weapons against the wrathful crowd. Apples rolled underfoot, and a small cook fire had set a man's robe ablaze. Traedis forced the flames out with the power of her *falmyros*, trying to ignore the rest of the chaos while she dealt with the immediate crisis.

"That's odd!" called Ruth above the din. "None of the rioters look right."

Traedis stared in the same direction, realizing Ruth was correct. There were men and women in everything from silks to homespun wool. A few children were among the mob, as were those who should have been too old or too tired to join in the madness.

Madness indeed. Traedis had seen something very like this very recently, when Elben had attacked her mother.

She swept her gaze across the market square, searching for the source. It was hard to make sense out of the chaotic scene. It had been so much neater in the *falmyros*, where the disordered pattern was easy to discern.

Vandeyr pulled her horse up next to Traedis, her mount stamping and squealing. "I see where," she said into Traedis' ear. "Look at the south corner of that barn near the road."

That was it. The road was a major path to the market, and numerous people were passing it on their way in. These now walked near, slowed, then turned their heads toward the center of the corner wall. Almost immediately, they began to shout, run, or exhibit other aggressive behaviors that seemed to escalate as they moved away.

"Ten silver eagles says there's a rune on that wall. Maybe more than one." Vandeyr touched her horse's neck and lifted the reins.

"Betting against you would empty my purse," said Traedis. "I'm sure you're right. But don't get too close to it. As I'm looking at it, I'd say the range is about a bodylength."

"More," said Vandeyr, "though not much more. Keep some extra for safety. It seems to be able to compel anyone who merely glances that way to stop and look."

Traedis nodded. "I didn't have time to tell you, but there are two more of these somewhere else in the City."

Vandeyr cursed and urged her horse forward through the crowd. Traedis followed close behind, with the other guards spreading outward to encircle them. The City Guard should have been there as well, but now that Traedis was paying attention, she saw some of their uniforms among the rioters.

As she neared the barn, Traedis thought she saw something shimmer in the air. She blinked and tried to remember Lord Ymre's teaching. The translucence of a *quixil's* tail rewarded her.

Traedis immediately pulled her horse to a halt. "I see it," she told Vandeyr. "Or at least, a piece of it. Not sure what to do about it, though."

"That's the problem, isn't it?" Vandeyr responded in a frustrated voice. "In order to destroy it, we have to get close enough for it to affect us." She rubbed her horse's ears and was rewarded by a nicker. "On the other hand, we can block off the road, which will give us time to regroup." Her forehead wrinkled. "Do you have any useful magic you can pull out of your pocket like some sort of *dragonsilver* handkerchief? Or will it take a mage to dismantle it?"

"I'm not sure." Traedis shaded her eyes and peered at the barn. "But get the road closed off now."

Vandeyr gave some terse instructions to Tethyn, who chose four guards and rode toward the road. Traedis was glad to see they were heading for the far side; it would be complex to herd away those who had been affected.

The rioters paid little attention to Traedis' companions on horseback, but seemed intent on causing havoc and destruction on the businesses in the market.

A few moments later, a number of the City Guard rode in, making their way over to Traedis. "Reinforcements, Your Majesty," said a young man with the insignia of a lieutenant. "The magic has hold of some of our people. Don't get close to the barn."

"We know." Vandeyr's mouth firmed into a line. "It's got a bardic rune—or runes—on it."

"Hush." Traedis held up a hand. "I need to ask the *falmyros* about this."

Vandeyr and the lieutenant both shut their mouths with a snap.

Traedis reached out to the land, slipping into it easily; it had become second nature ever since the two-day trance she had spent caught in her *falmyros* after breaking the curse a Telardurian lord had cast on Tolin. The land felt like an arm or a hand, or perhaps an extension of her senses; she could affect what happened in it, but not nearly as well as she could experience what the land was telling her. It was seductive, wanting, as far as something so boundless could want, to pull her into its heart and enfold her in the headiness of its power. Traedis did not know how Kenrydh could rule over a country as vast as Telardur when Tolin's small size was almost more than she could handle.

Just now, she needed to be wary, since she was uncertain whether runes could affect her through her *falmyros*. She doubted it, but she was no expert, and it seemed sensible to exercise additional care.

As she extended her land's senses, she felt a vortex which seemed to suck in intelligent minds and warp their emotional state as they passed. This was a surprise; Traedis had not realized that runes could affect someone who was not looking at them. She had assumed that because the runes on Elben had been dependent on his reading them, these would work the same way.

But of course they need not. They were language, and what they could describe, they could affect. The very first rune in the book Lord Ymre had given her was light, and true light at that. It would illuminate just as brightly whether someone stared at the rune or turned away.

She reached out toward the barn, trying to avoid the whirlpool of magic that emanated from it; queasiness overtook her, as if she were spinning in a circle. *Protect me!* she urged the *falmyros*, trying to make sense of the lines etched on the side of the barn.

The nausea abruptly evaporated. Instead, Traedis was left with an amalgam of sight and the strange perceptions the land gave her. Something was odd about the runes, which were obscured just enough—possibly by the *falmyros*—for her to tentatively examine them.

There was more than one. But more than that, the runes were *flat*: flatter than ironed laundry; flatter than a pressed leaf. Yet they managed to reach out through a medium created of magic, of language and words and symbols pressed together like flowers preserved between the pages of a book.

She had no idea how to destroy them. If no one could get close enough to scrape them off, wash them from the wood, or eradicate them in any other fashion, what could she do? And there were at least two other rune clusters elsewhere in Tolin.

She opened her eyes slowly, withdrawing reluctantly from the arms of the *falmyros*. "I don't know how to get rid of it," she said wearily.

Ruth cocked her head. "If it's possible to protect someone against the effects, we could just go scrape it off. There's got to be some way. This isn't the most powerful enchantment anyone has ever wielded. It's not magicworking, after all."

Traedis shuddered: magicworking was the terrifyingly powerful practice of taking birthfire from living things to fuel almost limitless magic, and was abhorred by the gods. But Ruth was correct. If runes were the pinnacle of magic, they would be a better-known quantity. She let a long, frustrated breath escape.

"I'm willing to try," Ruth added. "I don't think you should do it yourself."

Traedis' heart gave a startled *thump*. "I can't spare you," she said, alarm speeding her pulse.

"Someone has to do it," said Ruth. "And I'm volunteering." She smiled. "I'm sure there's a way."

Vandeyr's face took on a thoughtful expression. "There's something to be said for it," she agreed. "If we can get the area or areas cordoned off, we can ask counsel from a bard who might know something about runes." She shifted in the saddle. "I suppose we can even go back and ask that mangy karreld in Faldrohaven what to do about it. He may not be able to tell us everything we want to know, but he might be able to answer more general questions."

"I wish we'd asked more when we talked to him the first time." Traedis rubbed her forehead in frustration. "I need to find the other two locations so we can get those areas cordoned off, too. Ruth, I may accept your offer, but it's not going to be until I've got a significantly better idea of how dangerous it might be." She turned to Vandeyr. "I'll put Lang in charge of calming the City. He'll do a better job than I would. Kyaan knows he'd make a better king."

"I think," said Vandeyr more quietly than usual, "that if he would, the gods would have appointed him. It's something to mull over when you have leisure."

"When do I ever?" Traedis grumbled, and turned her horse's head to leave. The market was still agitated, though some of the rioters were leaving, and with the advent of another contingent of city guards, the area was beginning to quiet. Traedis hoped that with no new influx of people, the frenzy would become more diffuse, eventually dispersing altogether.

The *falmyros* contradicted her sharply: a warning that she should not count on the unrest in the City to die down so easily. Remembering what it had taken to shake Elben from his bloodthirst, Traedis felt her stomach sink. Elben had required several hours and a blow to the head before coming back to his senses after a single glance at a sheet of paper.

"Let's get moving," Traedis said, nudging her horse into a trot. "I've got another two sets of runes to find."

Traedis found the other two locations more easily, now that she knew what she was looking for. The temple quarter was the best of it; many of the priests had already worked out that something was affecting those who passed the stone wall that skirted the corner of the main Coran temple, and had blocked access from all points. They had managed to restrain several citizens who had been caught in the spell, and were sending out acolytes warning of the danger.

The communal living sector was as bad as Traedis had feared. Too many lived there; she could not simply screen it from passersby as she had hoped. These runes had been affixed to one of the main gate accesses, and as result, there was a small war that spilled from the large community dwellings onto the streets. It was taking many of the City Guard and some extra from the palace to contain it.

By the time Traedis got back to the palace she was already exhausted and shaking with the effort of sinking into the *falmyros* and pulling herself back out again.

King Kenrydh was more than willing to agree to another interview with the karreldish runecaster, and had consented to Traedis using her magic to remove the recalcitrant rune that bound Master Gonaa from speaking of the rebels. Traedis soon arrived in Faldrohaven, the runebook Lord Ymre had given her tucked under her arm and her patience so thin it could have worn through with a single breath. This time, Feledh Flamechild did not accompany them; she had returned to Kaelennar. Instead, a woman with the insignia of a lieutenant in Kenrydh's palace guard led them down the steps and into the interrogation chamber. As before, Vandeyr and the same mage who had accompanied them previously entered with her.

When Master Gonaa saw Traedis enter, his limestone skin blanched. "King Traedis," he said, his eyes darting back and forth as if someone had shaken him. "What do you want of me?"

Traedis put the runebook on the table between them. "I want to know about runes, and I especially want to know who is capable of setting runes in my city that can affect entire crowds. You know who it is—the question is how to loosen your tongue." She overrode his immediate protest with her voice. "I intend to pry that magic off your forehead and ask you some real questions. I am tired of my city being attacked by something about which I know little. You are going to make sure I know more."

"Please, Your Majesty," he whimpered, "don't take off the—" He coughed and fell silent.

"Answer me this, first." Traedis leaned forward. "How do we get attack runes off a location without falling prey to its effects?"

Gonaa thinned his lips and swallowed. "It depends."

"On what?"

"I—" he stopped and cleared his throat. "I can talk about this. If it's physically present, you'd have to remove it physically. How safe it is to get close is reliant on whether there's runework that protects it in some way. Then clean it with sacred oil if it's written. Burn it if it's scratched into wood. Scrape it from stone or break it; a blessed tool is best."

"How do we get close?"

He closed his eyes. "How should I know? I don't know what kind of runework you're speaking of." His eyes grew moist, and he sniffled. "I can't be expected to walk you through every step of something I've never seen!"

Traedis was weary of this man already. "It disorders the thoughts, and compels attention."

"That's hard," he mumbled. "Harder than you think."

"I know exactly how hard it is," Traedis told him, clipping her words short, as her father had always done when he was angry. "We have not come to ask you questions for the sake of your delightful company. We have come because you are the only accessible runecaster we know of. *How do we get close?*"

Gonaa's face crumpled like a decaying monument. "A protective rune should let you do it, unless the words are defended. They're probably not, though, because it takes a lot to put a rune sentence that strong on a place. And why do it if no one can counter what's already there?"

"Could you put a protective rune on someone?"

The lieutenant put up her hand. "King Traedis, he is under considerable magical restraints, and can't do any spellwork. It's been deemed most unsafe to allow him any access to his power."

One of the spells in the runebook was a protection spell; those were some of the earliest learned in any magical discipline, if for no other reason than keeping casters alive while they experimented. Traedis flipped it open to the page and showed the runecaster.

"How can I do it?"

The karreld sniffed. "You have to be able to work with runes—"

"I can," Traedis told him.

He sneered. "You have to be able to see the *quixil* in the—"

"I can do that, too." Traedis folded her arms and waited.

He hunched his shoulders together. "You'd have to write it perfectly, which you can't do unless you understand how to adjust the tension. The key is holding the configuration taut while you shape the rune. If you can't keep it together, it will either fail, or it will snap free, releasing all the magic. Some runes can kill if you lose them."

"Protection?" Traedis asked.

"No." Scowling, the runecaster jerked his head in the direction of the runebook. "This is one that will simply die if you get it wrong. It has to be absolutely flat, or the penstrokes won't hold, so you'll be bending it along a level surface. It's important to keep the final form of the rune in your mind as clearly as possible, while you work from the center outward. That's not the direction to draw every rune, but it's right for a protective rune. You need to keep the quill on the page during the entire process, and don't accidentally blot a line. It's not as fancy as some, so a little variation of line thickness can happen, but not much—do your best to copy it in every particular." He cleared his throat. "You'll feel the tension building, and you'll want to let it snap free, but don't. The rune is complete when it—I supposed you could say it *clicks*, though there's no sound. But it will do it on it's own, and if you've experienced it once, the sensation is unmistakable." He nodded, as if confirming to himself that his instructions were correct.

"Thank you, Master Gonaa," said Traedis, hoping that she could get the protective rune to work. Though, if it did not, she had other magics to try; she simply was unsure of how easy it would be to use those other magics against runework. Sitting back, she looked at him speculatively. "Now, how may the rune on your forehead be removed?"

Gonaa blinked several times, as if the light were too bright. "I… I…" He began to cough again.

"You really can't say." Traedis muttered a curse under her breath.

He looked at her with wide eyes, which were watering again, and said nothing.

Trying to organize her questions, Traedis thought over her brief glimpses of the runes left in Tolin. "Tell me, Master Gonaa, are all runes flat?"

He stared at her. "Of course they are. How else could you get them to work?"

That made no sense. Traedis raised an eyebrow.

Her confusion seemed to encourage Gonaa to slip into a more scholarly tone. "Your Majesty, when words are written, they have no thickness, no depth. The ink on the paper has a small amount of thickness, naturally, but the idea of the written word has only height and length. Bardic runes are that idea of the written word, distilled through every language that has ever been penned. The magic flattens them so that even though the ink stands up on the page, the magic of the runes does not. And if one knows how to draw a rune, one can learn to do so without paper or quill."

A new thought struck Traedis. "What happens to a rune if it's broken and not removed safely?"

The karreld rolled his eyes. "Some will dissipate, but some will snap free of the tension and deal harm to anyone close, just as normal magic will do."

That was not good news. "Would a protection rune also protect against that sort of harm?"

"None that you're likely to master," the runecaster said haughtily.

Traedis leaned over and took Rose from her case, idly stroking the harp's carven roses as she considered how she should go about removing the karreld's rune. Now that she understood a bit more of the technique of runework, she realized that he must be frightened that she would break his rune in the wrong way, potentially killing him.

"Master Gonaa," she said, "I do intend to remove that rune from your forehead, but I have some protective spells of my own, and I think I can do it without harm." She turned to the mage. "Master Qella, I have King Kenrydh's leave to perform magic on him, but I could use some assistance. Would you assent to being a part of my spellwork?"

Master Qella cocked her head in apparent curiosity. "How can I help?"

"I have a bardic spell that will combine magics," Traedis told her. "Cast your spells into the matrix I set, the webwork, and I will direct it."

"What spells?" Master Qella asked.

"Can you do a spell of unbinding?" Traedis did not know mage spells nearly as well as bardic ones. "Of freeing, or loosing? Or even opening. Something like that."

"I can," the mage said.

Rose began to sing before Traedis even touched the strings. After a short time building up the chording, she added in a spell of protection, so that if the rune should break, Gonaa would not suffer the backlash. She nodded to Master Qella, whose spell dropped in like a stone in a still pond. Its ripples spread throughout the spellweave. Threading a melody of hearing and heeding as well as one of protection, Traedis sang to the rune, encouraging it to detach from the karreld's skin, to float away into the air.

It resisted, and Traedis kept herself from magically tugging at it, concerned that it would break where it was. Given its position, that would almost certainly kill the karreldish runecaster.

"Stop!" he squealed. "That isn't the way to remove it!"

"What is?" Traedis asked, her hands still playing the notes of her spell.

"If I could tell you that, it wouldn't be very useful," said the runecaster, and retired into sullen silence.

The problem was the flatness itself; though Gonaa's forehead was not perfectly even, the rune had so little thickness that it clung like skin. If the rune contained some dimension, it would be easier to lift it from the karreld without damaging what was underneath.

Words and music both were part of Traedis' art. Perhaps there was some way of integrating runes with the core of her music.

She let herself fall into the spell, matching her vocal resonance with the harp's bright strings and the faint echo from the chamber's stone walls. Hitting a note which set her teeth buzzing, she stretched it out, fitting it around the shape of the rune. Now, she could almost feel edges, or at least some sort of form in a way that made no sense to her normal perceptions. She tugged again, hoping that this time she had a firmer hold on the rune.

She did.

As soon as one of its impossible edges lifted free, the entire rune wisped away into nothingness, the *quixil's* tail giving one final glimmer before it also evaporated. Traedis closed out the spell, surrendering Master Qella's spell and keeping the magic taut. She looked up at the runecaster.

Master Gonaa looked at her, naked fear on his face.

"Who is my uncle's runecaster?" Traedis asked him, her voice hard.

Gonaa shuddered. "Myssa," he half-whispered. "She's no longer mortal. She made herself into a rune."

Traedis was not sure what he was trying to say. "A rune? What do you mean?"

"She's—"

As he had done the previous several times, Master Gonaa coughed. This time, red emerged, dark as heart's blood. His face and hands turned blue, and his eyes bulged.

Before Traedis could even move, he lurched forward and fell face-first onto the table.

The lieutenant and the mage both jumped forward; the lieutenant checked Gonaa's pulse. "Nothing," she said. "Get a healer, fast!"

Master Qella darted out of the room, reappearing again a few moments later with a harried-looking stork of a man with gangly limbs. The man took one look, brushed the lieutenant's arm off Master Gonaa, and placed his hands on the karreld. His eyes closing, the healer spent several moments without making a sound. Then his lids opened.

"There's nothing I can do. His heart exploded."

The lieutenant looked sick, and Master Qella turned her face away.

"It what?" Traedis asked, shocked.

"His heart exploded. There are traces of magic all over it. I can't tell you what kind, though, or exactly how it happened."

"A second rune." Traedis gathered her thoughts and turned to the lieutenant. "Would you open his shirt for me to expose the area above his heart?"

A cursory look and the fading curve of a *quixil* told Traedis she was right. Guilt suffused her. Master Gonaa had not been a good man, but that was not the death he deserved. And it had been her doing.

She looked up to meet her sister's gaze, which included a tight, concerned vee between Vandeyr's brows. "Are you all right?" Vandeyr asked.

Traedis nodded, while letting the guilt and shame wash through her. "That's a terrible way to die. At least it was quick." She swallowed. "I need to find out what he meant about the other—about Myssa—being a rune."

"Fine," Vandeyr said. "But I don't think you're going to find the answer here.”

“I know,” Traedis said softly. “I’ve done enough damage. Let’s go.”

Needing information now, as well as instruction, Traedis found a Tolin bard who knew some of both. Master Andov was an aelin, his brown face smooth and unlined, his black hair pooling to his knees. Traedis had come to see him, not as a king, but as a bard. They sat in his parlor on velvet chairs, sipping the finest tisane Traedis had ever tasted: honeysuckle and a hint of apple blossom.

“Rune bodies are something I’ve only heard of. They’re called ‘*rûntazents*’ in the old tongue,” said Master Andov.

Traedis set her cup down. “Do you know how they’re made?”

“Not specifically. We don’t teach runes to beginners, because they’re easy to misuse. I have no talent for them. A few of us do use them. Runes aren’t evil, but they can be easily turned to evil purposes, and the making of a *rûntazent* is one of the fouler uses.” He licked his lips and took another sip. “A runecaster can choose to create a physical body from their knowledge of runes and rune sentences, and if they describe that body precisely, it can build a real, tangible form. But it has no life until the runecaster puts life into it.” He shook his head. “It’s one of the most foolish things a runecaster can do, but it can give them physical strength and endurance as well as practical immortality, and it can enable the flow of far more power than mortal bodies can endure.”

“Why is it foolish?” Traedis looked down at the leaves swirling in the bottom of her cup.

“Oh, didn’t I say? In order to inhabit a *rûntazent*, the physical body needs to die.” His face smoothed into an expressionless mask. “The runecaster of whom you speak is a walking dead woman, animated only by what she poured into her rune. And if she missed something—wisdom, fingernails, memories, or any other piece of herself—she will never get that piece back. What she is now is what she will always be."

The hair lifted on the back of Traedis' neck: the entire idea was horrifying. "That makes her simultaneously stronger and weaker."

"Say more brittle, perhaps." Master Andov tucked a lock of hair behind his ear. "Most rune bodies are idealized forms of the runecasters, the concept of their most perfect self. Those of us who are wiser realize it's impossible to describe a whole person, even using runes, and refuse the experience."

"Besides," said Traedis, "it seems to me as if it's spitting in the faces of the gods. As if what we've been given isn't good enough."

Master Andov smiled and shook his head. "I'm not prone to contemplate theology. I just know that it's a terrible thing to do, and a very dangerous one."

The possibilities this brought up were disturbing. If Myssa were not bound by mortal limitations, could she use an endless stream of runes without the physical cost that affected people of flesh? Would she age or die? Could her power grow, or was it circumscribed by the forms and shapes of her body's structure? The implications made Traedis' head spin.

"I know," said Master Andov, sweeping his hair off his thigh. "It's almost beyond imagining. Almost. I have quite a good imagination, and don't like what it's telling me."

"Are runes stronger when they're penned by *rûntazents*?"

"It depends on what they've written into their form." The aelin drank down the dregs of his cup. "Usually, though. It's one of the major reasons to transform.”

Traedis’ mind filled with more questions, but the most pressing came to her lips. “How do I protect against runes cast by a *rûntazent*?” The ideas she had about how to clean the collection of runes from where they had been placed around the City was beginning to look more dangerous. But someone must.

Master Andov shrugged ruefully. “I’m afraid I don’t know. I’ve met few skillful runecasters, and no *rûntazents*—for which I thank the gods.”

Traedis took out the runebook and turned toward the page of the protective rune. This was, after all, part of why she had come. “Can you show me how to make this safely?”

Master Andov raised an eyebrow. “Safely? Runes aren’t safe.” He gazed briefly at the page. “As to whether I can teach you, I need to know first if you have the gift. Since I do not, all I can do is tell you the steps and what you should be feeling. Do you still want to try them?”

“I do,” Traedis said. Despite her lack of experience, if Lord Ymre had told her she could scribe runes, then she could scribe runes. “I can see the hidden ones as well.”

His eyebrows arched. “Do you understand the *quixil*?”

“That every rune contains a piece of it? Yes.”

“That’s good.” Master Andov tapped a forefinger on the page. “Then let us begin.”

The sun had begun westering when Traedis finished with Master Andov. She had learned the basics of the protective rune, but did not know if she could draw it effectively. She carried papers with completed runes on them, but hoped to keep them back unless it was necessary to use them, as she did not know how many tries it would take to disable the magic around the City.

They had little time to address the question of the runes before dark closed over them, which in the mountains was early even in the summer months.

After the City Guard had closed off access to the three sources of the magical unrest, the City had calmed somewhat, though crowds were still buzzing like an angry beehive. It would take very little to incite them again.

Traedis, Vandeyr, and Ruth had argued about who should physically remove the danger. Though Traedis was the only one who could see their phantom forms, it was possible that they were written with ink or chalk, or perhaps scored into wood. Vandeyr's counter-argument was that Traedis was the king, and that was all that mattered.

The prevailing opinion had ended up being Ruth's, who trusted Traedis and who understood magic better than did Vandeyr. Traedis hated allowing Ruth to attempt something so dangerous, but she trusted her friend to use her common sense and not be foolhardy.

Instead of riding, Tagg gated them to the market square while the sun continued its journey down the sky. Vandeyr had brought several guards as well, one of whom was a healer. Clad in simple leathers, Traedis felt almost ready to face whatever the mysterious Myssa had in store for her. She took out the paper and pen she had brought for the purpose, then opened a jar of ink. Tethyn handed her a writing slate to brace her paper, while one of the other guards held the runebook open for Traedis to reference. The rune she had worked on would protect both mind and body, though it might not be the most potent possible choice, and could be overcome by more powerful magics. Still, it was by far the safest for Traedis, as a beginner, to attempt.

From the words of Masters Gonaa and Andov, Traedis knew how to begin. She studied the open book, then paged backward in her memory to the image of the *quixil* hanging over the marble column in the land of Ymre. She inked her quill, blotted it on the edge of the paper, and began to draw a smooth curve, ending in the *quixil's* tail. The newly familiar feeling of *stretch* began to take hold, the sensation of pulling a line taut as her pen continued to follow the pattern.

Then it snapped. Traedis let it go in a squiggle of ink; Master Andov had taught her how to minimize danger from a fractured rune. If this took too long, she would be forced to use her spare glyphs. She dipped more ink onto the quill and began again.

It took her six tries to get it right. She knew she had it when the tension stopped its outward pull and began to draw inward, nearly sending the curl of her pen into a wild slide. Recovering, Traedis felt the click when the tensions balanced, and the rune transformed into a single glyph. It was, indeed, gloriously flat; as flat as the idea that stuck it to the page. Traedis hoped that she would be able to learn how to sketch runes in the air, as Master Andov had told her advanced runecasters could do.

Transferring the rune to Ruth meant affixing the paper to her friend's forehead with the rune facing outward toward whatever harm might threaten. It was not a perfect solution, but Traedis had managed to make the rune effective, which meant it was flatter than the page on which it was written. This would have to do; she was hardly ready to start writing runes directly on anyone's forehead.

Ruth waited until Traedis stepped back. "Am I ready?" she asked. Traedis nodded while one of the guards handed over a chisel, hammer, cloth, and oil. Ruth tucked them under her arm.

"You're ready," Traedis told her. "Try not to look at the runes too directly—I'm not sure exactly what they'll do, and the protection on you isn't tested."

"I won't." Ruth shifted the items she carried, and cast a look at Vandeyr. "Tie me up or something if I don't seem to be myself."

"I intend to," said Vandeyr tightly.

Heading through the area cordoned off by the City Guard, Ruth made her way towards the barn where the runes had been laid. As she reached what they believed to be the outer perimeter of influence, she stopped, jerking her head to one side. She backed up several steps and looked at the ground; she appeared, from a distance, to be panting.

Traedis started to step toward her, but Vandeyr laid a hand on her arm. "She's all right," Vandeyr murmured. "Watch what she's doing."

Ruth began to pace a half-circle just into the safe area, letting her feet carry her to the far side of the barn. Turning, she edged a footstep closer to the barn. She stopped and clenched her unoccupied fist, then turned and headed back to the point she had left, but that one step closer. Then she wedged her feet a little closer and stopped before continuing on to describe the arc to the far side.

She was letting the effect take her a little at a time, Traedis realized. It was obvious that Ruth felt the runes, but perhaps the protection on her was giving her just enough resistance to the effect that she could acclimatize herself little by little.

It took far longer than Traedis felt comfortable with, but eventually Ruth reached the side of the barn. Here, she turned her head quickly toward the glyphs and back, presumably just enough to see if she could locate the area she needed to clean. Traedis tensed while Ruth took the chisel and, still looking away, jammed it into the wood over her head.

A soundless blast exploded from the wall sending wood flying and knocking Ruth to the ground. Traedis saw a handful of tiny *quixil* curves flicker into nothingness. Ignoring Vandeyr, Traedis ran forward to where the brunaidhi woman lay.

Several of the guards reached Ruth sooner. By the time Traedis had crossed the space, Ruth was sitting up, little the worse for wear except for a few cuts on her exposed skin where flinders of wood had hit her. She rubbed the back of her head.

As soon as she got to Ruth, Traedis dropped to her knees. "Are you all right?"

Ruth gave her a slightly crooked grin. "Mostly. Though I may not have thought that through as well as I should have. Next time I'll have to remember to duck."

The paper was still stuck to Ruth's head, but it was now blank and in tatters. Traedis reached forward and unstuck it from her friend's brow.

One of the guards also knelt. "I'm a healer. Let me see if you have any injuries we can't see." At Ruth's nod she touched the back of the brunaidh's head with two fingers, then traced along her hairline, sloped down over Ruth's brow, and slid down her arm.

"You're not seriously injured," she said.

"I know." Ruth stood up a little unsteadily. "I just scared myself out of my next three night's sleep." She stretched, then looked around at the ground, picking up the hammer from below where she had fallen. "I'm sorry. I hope that chisel wasn't a good one. I think it got caught by the rune's breaking." She moved a board where it had split and flown free, taking the oil and cloth from beneath it. The flask that contained the oil was dented, but unperforated.

"I'm not sure you should do the other two areas." Traedis stood, brushing dirt from the knees of her trousers, glad she had possessed the foresight to dress simply. Racing through pieces of barn while wearing a dress would have been hazardous.

Behind her, wood groaned. Traedis swiveled and stared at the gaping hole in the side of the barn. Pieces had broken jaggedly, but the entire hole was roughly circular, presumably because of the magical blast. When enchanted items were destroyed, the result tended to be violent.

"I think I *should* remove the other runes." Ruth slapped dirty hands on the sides of her own trousers and looked ruefully at a tear in her shirt. "I've managed it once, so you know I can. That experience of getting close to the runes was something I can repeat."

Traedis fought the urge to order her friend back to the palace. Though Ruth was not replaceable, her friend had the right to decide what dangers she was willing to confront. The two of them had faced worse during their brief time together in Kaelennar.

The moon shone above barren trees which reflected silver in its light. Soft, unmarked snow shone so brightly as to dazzle. Traedis and her friends shivered as the cold began to sink past their skin and deep into their bones where it nestled into the very marrow. Ruth paused to examine an icicle, then crowed in delight. "I can see images in it!" she marveled.

That had been before Ruth's magic had been buried by the assassins of Old Tolin. Which was another experience she had survived and lived to make her captors regret.

"All right," Traedis said. "But be careful."

The nearest street of the temple quarter was mostly empty, since the priests had helped to steer everyone away from the focal spot on the wall beside Coran's church. Traedis stood for several moments trying to determine the exact location where Myssa had laid her runes. There: she had it. It lay just above Ruth's head height and seemed almost to shine against the rough stone.

The shimmer on these runes looked slightly different from the barn glyphs, though Traedis could not tell whether it was her vision, the curve of the *quixils*, or the texture of the stone that seemed so distinct. Perhaps it was her imagination. It was not as if she had spent much time trying to understand runes. If there were more than one sort, she would find out as she studied.

Lord Ymre had told her she should. Traedis had been remiss by taking what the Wise Hound had said lightly. Now she was being forced to learn from necessity what she had not learned from opportunity.

At the moment, however, her past failure mattered less than her present success. And that meant giving Ruth the best chance at removing the runes.

She again focused on writing the protection rune, though it took her one more try than the last. Traedis was beginning to shake with the effort by the time she managed to complete the strokes she needed. She put the finished rune on Ruth's forehead and stepped back to let her friend work.

By the time Ruth circled her way to the wall, she already had the cloth out and was spilling oil over it. Without looking, she reached up toward the stone which contained the runes and carefully swiped her cloth over the entire area, sweeping the glyphs away in a circular motion.

This time there was no explosion of power. The runes simply sank into the stone and vanished. Ruth waited a moment, then took a quick glance at the wall before sighing and stoppering the flask of oil. She returned to Traedis a moment later, her step light.

"Well, that's done," she said brightly. "Let's get the last one while we have time."

Traedis looked at the sky: she had been focusing so much on Ruth's efforts that she had barely noticed the transition of the sun. Now it was weeping the first red drops of sunset. She nodded, and they headed toward the communal housing sector.

She had been prepared for this to be the worst, given how much chaos had been pouring through the streets earlier. In fact, it was better than the market square, now that guards were keeping people away and residents seemed to have figured out this was one source of the disturbances in town. A pair of men opened a distant window and shouted, but Traedis could not understand their words; she shrugged and took the writing implements out.

This time her hands were simply shaking too hard to let her work. She took out one of the prepared runes and armored Ruth with it, her breath ragged.

Ruth began her slow circuit, edging along the perimeter as she pushed herself to reach the gate. Traedis watched while a steady pulse beat in her throat, making her feel half-strangled. A few plum-colored clouds drifted across the sky.

Part way to the gate, Ruth stopped as if unwilling, turning to look at it directly. Her fists clenched, and she let out an angry shout. Half-turning, she seemed to quiver with rage or suppressed action.

Without thinking, Traedis gathered the *falmyros* near Ruth, cocooning her friend in the protective power of the land. A light mist sprang up between Ruth and the gate, obscuring the runes. The sun slipped nearer the mountain peak, and a deeper red stained the horizon.

Ruth stood rigid for a long moment, before letting the air from her lungs out in a *whoosh* audible from where Traedis stood. "No," she said in a clear, carrying voice. "That's not going to stop me."

Traedis felt her pulse beat in time with her friend's footsteps, though she admired Ruth's determination. She would not have blamed her friend if she had retreated, but it was obvious Ruth had no intention of giving up. Instead, the tiny woman resumed her slow progress toward the runes, moving into the mist with assurance. This time she did not cast a glance toward the magic, but took out the hammer, holding it in both hands.

As she reached the gate, she swung the hammer up in a long arc and brought it down on something Traedis could not see.

The entire gate exploded outward into the road; Ruth flew backward before hitting the ground with a *crunch*. Traedis and Vandeyr both darted forward, Traedis almost catching up to her sister as they ran. Dropping on her knees before Ruth, Traedis felt for a pulse.

It was there, weak, but steady. Ruth, however, was injured, and showed no sign of waking. A small amount of blood seeped from several tiny scalp wounds, but her arm lay beneath her at an unnatural angle.

The image rose to her mind of Atchûk, the brave karreldish prince who had rapidly become her friend, and died at the hand of her uncle. Traedis' breath grew short; she could not bear it if Ruth also died for her sake. It should have been Traedis who had braved the danger of the runes, armed with magic she could use and the power of the *falmyros*. Traedis was not sure if her friend had cracked her skull, hurt her spine, or had even worse damage on the inside than showed on the exterior.

"Healer, we need you!" snapped Vandeyr at the guards.

The healer dismounted and raced toward Ruth, where she knelt beside Traedis. The healer rested her fingers lightly on Ruth's neck, then closed her eyes.

"She's mortally injured, but I think I can save her," said the woman, her attention on Ruth. "She's got a skull fracture and a broken arm. Move away, please, so I can do my job without distraction."

Traedis felt herself relax—though only a little—at the confidence in the healer's voice. She rose and backed up several paces, but did not retreat all the way, watching the healer as the woman's breathing grew deeper and more even. It was almost possible to feel the power at the very edge of her *falmyros*.

From the corner of her eyes, she noticed Vandeyr going to speak to members of her own and the City Guard. They began a joint effort to clear debris away from the destroyed gate, teaming up to pull long beams of wood out of the road.

Footsteps began a quick patter, and a sudden babble of voices strengthened as people made their way into the area. Traedis could not pick out individual conversations, but the alarmed chatter grew as more townsfolk surged in. The light level was dropping quickly as the mountains' shadows spread down the slopes and into the recesses of the City's streets. She turned to watch, unwilling to be caught unprepared for danger.

Vandeyr turned to the crowd. "You're safe! Go home!" she bellowed, the timbre of her voice cutting through the other noise. City guardsmen deployed to both sides of the street and began turning people away.

Even with the runes removed, Traedis was not sure how the

townspeople would behave. Her suspicion was that the magic had influenced the disorder, but not caused it; there had been such incidents ever since she had become king, and her mother's attack had certainly incited rioting.

But perhaps everyone was weary of the unrest; the hum of voices lessened, and the crowd began to disperse. Traedis looked back to the healer. The woman's eyes opened slowly, and her hands dropped to her sides.

Traedis rejoined her a moment later, just as Ruth blinked and rolled her head from side to side.

"I seem to be alive," Ruth said with a glint of humor. "I wasn't quite sure for a moment."

Traedis arched her brow at the healer, though the woman would not be able to see it in the growing darkness. "Is she all right?"

"She is," said the healer, dropping back on her heels. "I'm glad you had me ride along. The swelling in her brain alone might have tipped her over the edge."

"I feel like I should have a headache." Ruth sat up and felt the back of her head. "Thank you, Mistress Healer. If what I heard when I hit was an indication, my skull broke open like a clay bowl. I'd like never to hear that sound again, may it please the Four."

"It did," said the healer somberly. "And it does please the Four. You would not be alive otherwise."

Late that night, Traedis sat in her workroom on the top floor, the runebook opened on the table before her. This story was mostly occupied with servants' quarters and dormitories for the pages, but a few shielded rooms had made this one a good choice if she did not want to disturb everyone around her with music.

The workroom was large, and the vaulted ceiling with its centuries-old oaken beams damped the worst echoes, while still allowing sound to reverberate from the mortared stone. Filtered moonlight dripped through the skylights and crawled through the heavy glass windows. Traedis kept her instruments on the shelves that had once held the herbs and poultices of a stillroom.

At this late hour, she was trying to reliably draw the few runes in Ymre's spellbook, a lamp burning at her side. She had gotten as far as replicating the light rune twice, though the second time she had only just managed to hold the tension, and the rune gave little illumination in consequence. After that, she had no success at all.

She considered going back to Master Andov, but what she really wanted was a runecaster whom she could trust to show her the steps by example, rather than tell her what she should feel. She had not as yet learned how to counter runes herself, and she could hardly summon Lord Ymre every time she learned a new one. Ruth's direct approach was demonstrably unsafe, but there were no better ways Traedis could fathom to destroy them.

Obviously, some had a method of removal: the oil had worked on the one written on the church wall. That oil could not have been used on the barn, however, since the glyphs had been etched in. Ruth's success with the stone wall had been at least as much luck as planning. Uncle Cordelayne's runecaster—Myssa—had probably given each of her creations some form of removal, and like any clever assassin, had made sure each was different.

She looked down at the scrap of paper with the better functioning light rune. It had not varied far from the *quixil*, consisting of three-quarters of a circle and three loops of varying size and placements. Traedis glared at it, frustrated by her inability to challenge a runecaster who was herself a rune.

Her fingers cramped around the quill. She blotted it and laid it on the worktable. Taking Rose up in both arms, she relaxed against the soundboard and called a few finger exercises from the strings, comforted by old disciplines. She plucked a pattern up and down a minor scale, then switched to an aelin mode, only possible due to Rose's double row of strings. Drawing together chords, she began to layer and overlap them in a complex rhythm. She followed this with a dancing melody that threaded in and out of harmony like a singing wind.

A sense of calm suffused her. Weaving in her voice, she sang pure tones that called the ghosts of harmonies into the music. It was very different from the taut, inked lines which she had to form perfectly, not only in her hand, but in her mind. Harp and song could flow more freely.

Her mind flashed back to learning the scales, the interactions of the harmonies and the resonances, how to keep her fingers on the taut strings while she repeated each step over and over until she knew them both in her mind and in her fingers.

The taut strings.

Traedis damped Rose's overtones with her palms. Something niggled at the back of her mind; a thought that might join the ideas of bardic runes and song. The idea would not quite come free as she reached for it, sliding away from her consciousness every time she came too near.

Perhaps logic would pull it closer. Bardic magic was the magic of civilization, Selyn's fire expressed through art. Traedis had learned of bardic dance, bardic drawing and painting, and of course, bardic runes, during her time in Kaelennar's college. Theoretically, one could use any art to express magic.

She thought about Elben's letters with their graceful calligraphy, each letter perfectly formed and shaded. Then she considered her own study of runes, and how both she and Elben needed to maintain control of their respective forms to distill the art from the shape. Why was she a natural runecaster and not he? Both must keep their arts held in perfect tension within the mind.

Runes required a different sort of tension, but the idea was the same. What Traedis had done in prison had been to hold the memory of music so tightly that she could alter it and practice within her mind, even without any instrument to enhance that understanding. It was not simply the impeccable formation of the rune that created its power, it was the comprehension of what the rune *meant*, why it was shaped the way it was, and how it distilled the meaning of a word and a concept down to a form that could be inked on a page.

The very flatness of the word was part of that distillation, a compression of meaning. A plan began to grow in the recesses of Traedis' mind, not yet fully blooming, but budding into consciousness.

Rose quietly thrummed a low, carrying note which vibrated off the rafters, despite their thickness. Traedis raised her brows, then settled her harp back against her collarbone, reaching for the light rune with her free arm. She turned it endways, eyeing the line that presented, seeing the rune only as a smudge of dark slightly raised over the page. But that was simply the ink: the rune itself had no height.

That might be something Traedis could exploit. She had been taught to keep the notes of the music tight, but let it dance with the spirit of her song. Music was inherently anything but flat; it was meant to take on dimension, volume, fullness. Rather than compressing many languages and glyphs into one rune, it took single notes and layered them to make a complex structure. The antithesis of flatness was fullness and movement, and Traedis had trained for two years with one of the best bards in the world to learn that.

Rûntazents were another matter, of course, one that Traedis could not yet begin to fathom, much less to unravel. She could still barely write a simple rune. She would not be able to do that had not it been for Lord Ymre's revelation of the *quixil*.

She had been lazy. She needed to make up for lost time.

Setting the light rune back down, she launched herself into a lively but simple melody, a children's dance that she had learned when young. She did not sing the words, though they ran through her head: *Dance and sing! Dance and sing! Gather all into a ring!* It was the lilting tune that was important. She began to weave it into a chording, letting its rhythm guide her instincts as she crafted the spell.

She laughed, the hand of the boy on her right and the girl on her left squeezing her own, her hair whipping behind her as they all circled and spun. She loved Midsummer. It was a joyous time, when she could eat sweetmeats and stay up until the last trails of the sun streaked behind the mountains. But the best part was the dancing.

Almost without thinking, Traedis called the rune into the chording. The room lit as if she had caught the full moon in a crystal bowl.

Elated at her success, she tried to twine the rune into her spell, to move it to the tempo of her song. Instead, the light died as suddenly as it had kindled. She let the magic go, and leaned her face against her hand in thought.

Chording runes would be useful if she could learn to do them faster than a candle burned to a stub. It was good that the spellweave could contain them, as she had designed it to carry magical elements which might have unfamiliar aspects. But she had not mastered runes yet, and lighting the room was not her objective.

She teased at the rune with a tendril of dancing music, trying to pry at its edges and peel it from its flat meaning into something more malleable. It was like trying to pick up light itself: the pressed words had no edge. Nothing that Traedis could do to it seemed to affect that quality.

She tried to nudge the ink, but that was also fruitless. Once it had dried on the page, the ink seemed to have little connection to what was written in it, at least as far as Traedis could tell. She was not sure if someone more experienced would learn something from the written medium, but at present, she could not glean anything useful from its physical qualities.

Frustrated, she stopped playing and set Rose on the floor with a woody *clunk*. The room seemed darker than it had before, with her lamp the only source of illumination.

She stretched and rose, walking to the windows that overlooked the palace gate. From the third floor she could see the street, quiet here, since only those with palace business were likely to approach at night. The windows were made of exceptionally clear glass divided into eight panes per frame; she leaned her forehead against one, savoring the coolness the night air had imparted.

When she had been imprisoned, she had spent so many hours going over the tiniest details of musical form, the most minute magical elements, that she had been able to listen to them in her head and string them together into advanced spellwork. She had gotten out of the habit in the few months since she had become king; perhaps, though she begrudged any time taken from her physical playing, she should make time to continue working through theory as well as practice.

She must find an answer. The hourglass had been turned, and time was pouring through its narrow channel.

Traedis opened the safe she kept in her office and took out a heavy, rough-cut ruby the size of a walnut. Its coarse texture rasped against her skin as she placed it on her palm and looked into it. This stone was one of three that enabled speech at a far distance with the one who held either Telardur's oak and ruby crown, or the other two matching gems. Given the current situation in Tolin, Traedis checked at prearranged intervals for news of Uncle Cordelayne, as well as to keep current with her allies.

The ruby warmed under her scrutiny, and Traedis focused her attention on its deep opacity, its irregular planes and angles. A crimson mist gathered in her vision, and the face of King Emmen of Haven appeared in the ruddy haze.

Emmen was a tall, strongly-built woman with close-cropped brown hair and an elegantly featured face. "Traedis, what is it?" she asked. She smoothed back a lock, and the lines around her eyes crinkled. "You look like you had a bad day, and it's only just morning."

Traedis gave a short bark of laughter. "Yesterday was the bad day, though it could have been worse." She gave Emmen a brief summary of the karreldish runecaster's information, his death, and Ruth's narrow escape.

Emmen remained silent for a few moments, frowning. "That sounds like a concern for all of us. You're the one in immediate peril, but your uncle will use that woman as a weapon. I'd never heard of bardic runes before the attack on Captain Tallforest, but I'm glad you're learning something, even if it's only enough for us to understand the danger."

Traedis gave a deep sigh. "I would have wished that I had never heard of them, but Lord Ymre wants me to study them for some reason. And when the Wise Hound says something would be wise, it's the height of folly to ignore him."

"As to Lord Ymre," Emmen said, "I have a tale to tell you. I had a rather odd dream last night, and it bore some odd fruit. I don't normally dream true, but I can tell when something is sent, which is why I went over to the palace library and rummaged around before dawn."

Traedis raised an eyebrow. "That must have been some dream."

Nodding, Emmen said, "It was. I dreamed I woke after moonset with a light shining in my window. When I looked out, it was a star so bright I was almost blinded. I got up and left the room, only to see the light pass over a series of windows in the hall. Following those led to a sealed chamber. It's a real room, and not actually sealed, but it was in my dream. It's the palace library, which in the waking world is also stocked with rare volumes, since the judges used it extensively before I received Haven's *falmyros*. In my dream, there was an extra window, a high, round one, and the light shone only through that window onto a low shelf with a few gleaming books that seemed a lot more interesting in my dream than they were when I went to look at them." She gave a wry grin. "They're actually dusty tax records from sometime last century, and I really should clean the place out and send them to the archives, but other things have taken priority."

Traedis nodded; she well understood being too busy to do most of the small things that needed doing. She and Emmen had both been kings less than a year, and old records were not a first concern. "Go on."

"That's when I awoke." Emmen smoothed back her hair. "The light was just coming in, so I went to take a look at that shelf. And there, tucked away in one of the books, were three white hairs of differing lengths."

Traedis suspected she knew what sort of hairs Emmen meant, but she made an interrogative noise anyway.

"Dog hairs," Emmen confirmed. "I'm giving one to you, and one to Kenrydh, though the gods only know what you'll do with them. I have to think about what I ought to do with mine. I don't know why Lord Ymre's hairs were inside a book that hasn't been opened this century, but he certainly meant me to find them."

"Thank you!" Traedis said, startled at both the find and the fact that Emmen was sending her something so valuable. She did not know what use Ymre's hairs might be, but he was a star, and made of greater-than-mortal substance. "I am in your debt."

"I also have a favor to ask," Emmen continued. "Though perhaps I shouldn't, given what happened with Captain Tallforest. But I'm in need of a little peace, and I want to get away from Haven for a day or so. I'd love to visit the Star Cavern—I haven't seen it since the Quo'at repainted it— and I'd like to avoid two persistent suitors. I can bring the hair with me, if it's acceptable to visit right now."

Traedis tried for a laugh, but it came out sounding more than a little sardonic. "I understand how you feel. I could wish that half of Tolin's men would stop trying to find a way to get me safely married and take over the burden of rule from me."

"Ah, *that* I can see." Emmen sighed. "No one is trying to take my kingship, but I have bards composing songs about me, and nobles from other countries falling about themselves to become my great and lasting love." She swallowed, and Traedis saw the brief sheen of tears in her eyes.

"If Tiriel had lived…" Emmen's voice wavered. Swallowing again, she firmed her chin and met Traedis' gaze. "If my Lady Tiriel had lived, I'd be her liegewoman, not king of Haven. The love I bore for her didn't need return, and I wouldn't have begrudged her any love of her own. But it's not that I'm averse to finding someone new; it's that two women can't bear children, and Haven needs my line in order to keep it from falling back into the hands of those who corrupted the judges."

Warmth spread upward from Traedis' chest; she sympathized more than a little, though she herself was not quite in the same position. "That's hard if you want to love the person you marry."

"I could be fond of him," Emmen said sadly. "I could even love him as a friend. That's still not what I want in a marriage."

"No." Traedis shook her head, letting it settle into her mind that Emmen's difficulties with courtship were at least as hard as her own. She had less to complain about.

She pursed her lips. "I'm happy if you come, but you might want to leave your greens at home. We've had so much upheaval here the last few days that I don't want to disrupt anything, and I certainly don't want you to be hurt because Tolin has been stirred up like a nest of stinging ants."

"No," Emmen said. "I'll prepare to leave later today. I don't want to give you any more trouble. You've had enough."

"More than enough," Traedis responded. "I'll make arrangements for your visit."

A few hours later, Traedis made her way down to the practice field to meet with Vandeyr. Clouds were gathering overhead, though Traedis could not tell if they would rain out in the higher elevations, or whether they would sweep down from the mountains in a torrent of late summer thunderstorms. The air prickled with energy; that probably meant the latter.

She arrived before Vandeyr, which was unusual. Heading into the armory, she took her practice sword off the rack against the wall and studied the blade, making sure it had been properly oiled and cleaned by the armorers. Stepping back outside, she looked at the sky again, becoming surer as she did that a large storm was massing.

When Traedis looked back, Vandeyr was striding toward her more quickly than usual. Traedis went to meet her. Something about Vandeyr's stance suggested that she was upset.

As soon as her sister had caught up, Traedis headed into the armory, Vandeyr on her heels.

Vandeyr looked around, then shut the door. Without preliminary, she said, "It's your fault, too, but I'm a blithering idiot, because it's my gods-cursed *job*, no less. And don't think of taking all the blame just because you like to martyr yourself."

Traedis tilted her head, trying to understand her sister's words. "What are you talking about?"

Vandeyr began to sort through the practice swords, more as if she wanted to find something to distract herself than looking for a particular weapon.

"You told me not to fix it," she said. "That part of the blame I'll cede you. But it was my own fault I didn't check back to make sure nothing got past the City's magical defenses, because that was the reason we didn't fix the thrice-cursed crystals to begin with. If I'd had the brains of a toad and half the perception of a mole, I'd have had someone monitoring it. But no. Instead, I let assassins into the Library to drop those runes on your Haven knight."

Traedis' stomach gave a sudden lurch. Like her sister, Traedis had also almost forgotten the cracked crystals in the City walls which had been damaged a few months earlier by Uncle Cordelayne's people. She had left the defenses alone in order to entice the rebels into using them and falling into a trap of her making. Her cheeks flamed as she realized how stupid she had been, forgetting such a weakness.

"Not your fault at all." She would not let Vandeyr blame herself. "It's ultimately my responsibility."

"Kyaan's farting fanny, it's your responsibility." Vandeyr's brows drew down in a formidable scowl. "You may have been the one who told me to leave it, but I'm the one who should have had a mage on it day and night."

"Enough!" Traedis said. Her words were underscored by a peal of thunder. "We can argue about whose fault it was all day, but right now, let's just determine how to fix it, shall we?"

Vandeyr growled something indistinguishable, then opened the armory door in time to let in a storm-scented gust of wind. Before she could close it, the patter of rain began, scattered droplets increasing to a veritable orchestra. Another thunderclap echoed over the rocky peaks, and lightning stabbed a jagged blade across the sky.

"So much for practice," she said.

Traedis shivered with the energy in the air that excited the hairs on her arms, as well as her *falmyros*. She almost felt as if she could reach out with her land-sense and take hold of the lightning, send it singing along her nerves and across Tolin's fields and forests.

Perhaps she could. Her *falmyros* was unusually comprehensive; the Storm Eagle had led her through every piece of Tolin that Toledru had clung to with his false bond. She could see birds hatching in tiny nests, or the sound of ant footsteps. But the *falmyros* went two ways, and the king could compel the land to respond.

She should not call on the power of lightning easily or without great care. That would be folly; the old tales were full of the fates of those who tried to wield too much power. No, better she stick to relocating rats and making sure the roots of trees got their share of riverwater, rather than pull Kyaan's fire from the heavens.

A sharp slap on her face brought Traedis back to herself. She looked up to see Vandeyr draw her hand back. "Why," she asked crossly, "did you just slap me?"

"You stopped responding." Vandeyr's teeth were clenched. "I asked you at least three questions, and you simply stared at the door like you were mazed. I wasn't sure if someone had put a spell on you."

The door of the armory was closed again, but Traedis could hear the storm's fury outside; it had struck in full force and was now pelting the building with what sounded like hail. Each stroke of lightning lit the little space where door met sill, and small puffs of wind blew in through tiny chinks, whistling eerily. "I got caught up in my *falmyros*," Traedis said, and looked down at her booted toes.

A pair of faint worry lines grooved Vandeyr's forehead. "I hate that," she said. "I always think you won't come back out of it."

"I've never heard of that happening," Traedis responded. "My bond may be strong, but I wouldn't have the *falmyros* if I weren't capable of holding it. Whether I like the idea or not."

Vandeyr's expression smoothed back out. "You'd better put away the sword. We're not going to get any training done in this weather. It might be useful to spar in the rain, but I don't trust the lightning."

It was a clear change of subject, but one Traedis was willing to let rest. She replaced the practice sword on the rack, while thunder and wind played Tolin's drumbeats in the storm, punctuated by the staccato bursts of lightning.

"We'd better get those crystals fixed," she said. She turned her head so Vandeyr would not see a half-smile emerge. "Care to make a dash for it?"

"It might be possible to trace whoever tampered with the crystals," Tagg said. The rainstorm had swept down the mountain with great speed, leaving Tolin washed clean by its elemental force.

Traedis sucked in a breath; her ears buzzed. It had not occurred to her that they might be able to track the rebels by the same means used to infiltrate Tolin. She was not sure she was ready to find her uncle just yet, but she must; she had only so much time before Thane Bi'ia's blood curse fell on Tolin.

Traedis, Vandeyr, Ruth, and Tagg sat in the palace library, a high room amply stocked with books, chairs, and a few tables. Windows looked out on the palace gardens; clematis vines framed the windows, staining the emerging sunlight a pale purple. The smell of leather and glue and old paper hung in the air like a timeworn memory. Though it was not her childhood home, Traedis could imagine the ghost of her former self haunting the shelves in search of a vivid history or a heroic tale.

Ruth lounged like a cat in an overstuffed chair; Vandeyr sat more sedately at a table, leafing through the pages of a dog-eared book. Tagg stood by the window, his round face half-shadowed by a nearby bookcase.

The four of them had gathered to discuss what else Uncle Cordelayne might have slipped into Tolin while the magical defenses were weakened.

A knock came at the door, and Traedis jumped. "Come in!" she called.

A page entered, his hair tied in a tail at the nape of his neck. "Your Majesty, King Emmen has arrived."

Traedis nodded. "Send her here."

"Yes, Your Majesty." The page left the room.

Emmen was not long in joining them. She wore an embroidered linen shirt and linen pants, and on her feet were a pair of old, scuffed boots. A battered leather pouch was affixed to her belt.

Upon the Haven king's entrance, Vandeyr's spine seemed to inch itself into such a straight position that it looked like it would crack. Ruth waved, but otherwise did not move. Tagg bowed.

"It's good to see you, Emmen." Traedis indicated the nearby chairs. "Sit wherever you want. We're in something of a war council, but nothing formal."

Emmen chose a seat near Traedis and sat erect, her hands on her knees. "Do you want Ymre's hair first, or should I wait?"

"The hair first, please." Traedis leaned forward, feeling like a child at Midwinter.

Emmen reached into her pouch and fished out a long, white strand of what looked like thread. In the dimness of the room, it glowed with a steady, pale light.

Ruth sat up and stared.

The hair was long, well over the length of Traedis' arm. It must have been one of the strands that hung down Lord Ymre's haunches. Traedis took it reverently, coiling it around her fingers.

It felt more like hair than it looked. "What should I use it for?"

"I have no idea," said Emmen. "Would it make a good harp string?"

Traedis suspended the hair between two fingers and plucked it, exploring the sound it might create. Unfortunately, it made no more noise than if it had come from an ordinary hound. "Well, that's not going to work."

Rose sang a deep melody ending with her lowest note, which vibrated through the room far longer than it should. Startled, Traedis looked at her harp, wondering what Rose was trying to tell her.

With a sound almost like a sigh, the harp played the same melody and the same low note.

"I don't know what you're saying." Frustrated, Traedis curled the hair once more around her finger.

This time Rose played only the low note; everything in the library that could move began to thrum along with the sound.

"Is it—" Ruth leaned over and looked at the harp. "Is it telling you to wrap the hair *around* your harpstring?"

Rose began singing a happy set of notes up and down the scale. Traedis chuckled. "It seems you're right. Very well, Rose. Just a moment."

Rose's strings were unbreakable and never lost their tuning, so Traedis had rare occasion to use the *sagathas* key that held the instrument's spirit. Now she slid the Y-shaped harp key she always wore over her neck, set the correct arm over the peg, and released the low string. Pinching string and hair together, she fitted it back into place, then twisted the hair tautly around the string. Replacing the other end, she tightened the peg and looked at her handiwork.

The hair seemed to cling to the metal wire; Traedis could not get a thumbnail between the two. She plucked the low string, hoping the sound was not compromised.

It was not; in fact, it seemed to carry a richer tone, a deeper sonorousness that reminded Traedis of walking the misty purple path to the land of Ymre. She breathed in, for a moment letting the overtones carry her back to the land of timelessness and flowers.

"Very good," said Emmen as soon as the melodic whisper had died down. "That problem just solved itself. Now, what is this about a war council?"

Chapter Seventeen
Snowflakes

Traedis stood, harp in hand, on the top of the City wall, next to one of the cracked crystals. Vandeyr took a defensive stance behind her. Ruth gazed out at the Dragon Mountains, which were currently enveloped in a pink haze. Occasionally they cleared enough to display their peaks before being swallowed again by clouds.

Emmen and Tagg were busy examining the crystal, though neither touched it; none of them were sure how the defenses would behave under the circumstances. It might be especially dangerous to Emmen, as the king of a once-hostile nation.

The crystal was clear quartz the size of a large man's fist; it was set in an iron base that fit into one of the wall crenels. This near, Traedis could feel the discontinuity like a cracked tooth. Her shoulders were uncomfortably tight, and every time Emmen leaned too close, Traedis' muscles stiffened.

"I see it," said Emmen. "It's where the shadow of the merlon meets the stone. That line becomes almost invisible. And since the shadow will always stay in more or less the same place, the crack stays invisible, too."

"Clever." Tagg squatted and looked at it intensely for several long moments. "Yes. This was done remotely, and with incredible skill. I'd guess whoever did it actually worked on them, so that narrows down who we're looking for."

"Who?" asked Traedis, steadying herself against a gust of wind that whipped her hair around her face.

Tagg stood. "The wall spells were first set in place about five hundred years ago, take a decade or two. They've been reinforced since, and hand-picked teams of mages renewed the spells and added refinements as necessary every half year. I was an alternate at one time, though I never actually got to work on them. I do know most of those who did. The two I'm certain were with your uncle are a married pair—man and woman— who taught the rest of us."

Traedis raised an eyebrow, but let Tagg continue.

"They could have done this," he told her. "The problem is that I don't see any way to use the crystals to find them. There's not a whiff of individual magic on it like I was hoping. It's been layered too many times over too many years. However, I can get hold of alternates like myself who should be able to mend the breaks in the defenses.

"Thank you, Tagg." Traedis felt tension slough from her shoulders.

"At a certain point," Emmen said, "good old-fashioned trackers might serve you better." She turned away from the wind. "If you can find me some of their possessions, something we can get a scent or magical trace from, I might be able to find them. If they're with your uncle, I might be able to find him, too."

"I've been looking," Traedis said, lowering her head and staring at her feet. Failure weighed on her, heavy and unforgiving. "Truly looking. I have not been able to find a trace of him since Prince Atchûk was killed. The entire City depends on me, and I can't find him." The last word caught in her throat, and she coughed.

Emmen's compassionate gaze caught Traedis' eyes as she raised her head. "I know you have. He's expecting that. It's not that he's ignored me or Kenrydh, but he knows less of our capabilities, and frankly, Haven hasn't tried to find him as hard as you have. Let me put some people on it. If we find any of them, we'll let you know right away, and you can decide what you want to do then."

"It's not your responsibility," Traedis replied. No: she was the one who had let her love of Uncle Cordelayne blind her to her duty.

Emmen smiled. "Haven and Tolin are sister cities, Trae. What hurts one hurts the other. If your uncle has his way, Haven will be forced to become very involved in the wrong sort of way. Please let me help you with this."

That was true. Traedis glanced at Ruth, and found her friend looking back at her.

"You can't do everything yourself, Trae," the brunaidi woman said. "And you don't need to."

Traedis stroked Rose's frame. Even seven years after she had fled the City, she still had problems trusting. But if the two years in Kaelennar had taught her anything, it was that there were people she *could* trust. The years of her imprisonment could not override that lesson. Even when it was difficult to feel.

She nodded. "Thank you, Emmen. We'll find something for your people to track from."

In the next few days, Traedis flung herself into her role as king. She sat in open court, met with educators and poets and priests, trying to forget that her uncle's runecaster could strike at any moment. She attended sessions with her brother Lang, trying to hash out how to make changes to certain laws without completely alienating the whole of Tolin.

She also practiced her spellwork and tried to draw several of the runes in Lord Ymre's runebook. Unfortunately, she could not reliably draw a single rune with any speed, nor any with surety. They remained a lesson she could not completely absorb, and she could not spend all of her time on their intricacies.

Late summer was giving over to autumn, and frost touched her windowpanes at night. The gardeners were beginning the fall bedding for the roses, and some of the less hardy flowers turned brown. Traedis felt as if her rule were shriveling with the life in the soil, inevitably bringing her closer to the time when Tolin would truly rebel—or when Bi'ia's blood curse would fall in the early spring.

The aspens were just beginning to turn gold when Traedis received a message from Emmen by way of a special courier. It was morning, and Traedis was in her office looking at petitions for court when it arrived. Vandeyr snatched the missive from the courier's hand and tapped it against her ring before handing it to Traedis.

It read simply, *We may have found the rebels. Contact me. Emmen.*

Traedis retrieved the ruby from the safe and brought it into the light where its irregular facets glinted in the sun. Turning her attention to its heart, she called for Emmen with the inner voice that would waken the magic.

As the ruddy haze gathered around her, there was a momentary sense of dislocation. Shortly thereafter, Emmen's face appeared, her hair windblown and her cheeks bright with apparent cold.

"Traedis." Emmen said. "I'm sorry I didn't answer you directly—I was dealing with a minor emergency, and I wasn't sure how long it would take you to contact me."

Traedis shook her head. "I presume you had other things to do, and I could have been busy as well. As it turns out, I have a meeting with the Ladies' Poetry Guild, and you've given me the perfect excuse to avoid it.

What did you find out?"

"There is an old n'korreld site," said Emmen. "I don't know if someone in Tolin was studying ancient karreldish bolt holes or whether it's a true coincidence, but it's been long abandoned. We're not exactly sure where it is, though. We had to divine this much in a roundabout way. Your people know how to hide their traces." She quickly gave Traedis the most precise directions she could: an area in the Kurtish Mountains to the north.

Traedis looked away from the ruby briefly and flicked her gaze over Vandeyr. "An ancient n'korreld site?" she asked.

Vandeyr's brows shot up. "You want to know where Tolin has sanctuaries? We checked them a few months ago—and they were empty— but that doesn't mean the badger hasn't gone to ground since. Get me a map."

"Just a moment," Traedis told Emmen. "Don't leave. Vandeyr's got something to say about it."

Traedis kept atlases, charts, and scrolled maps in her office, detailing everything from Tolin's city quarters to the entire known world. Rummaging through the larger ones on her bookshelf, she pulled off one that covered the area between esch lands and the Northern Sea. Spreading it on her desk and summarizing Emmen's directions, she bent over it while her sister joined her across the wooden surface.

Vandeyr pulled out a chair and dropped into it. Looking at the map, she put her finger firmly on a spot in the Kurtish Mountains. "This is what Emmen described. It's a large cave area, capable of housing dozens of people. It's also isolated and hard to reach."

"Where else might the rebels go?" Traedis asked quietly. "They may not be occupying other locations now, but I need to know where to look in the future.”

Vandeyr pointed out three other places on the map. At the last, on the edge of the Aelin Plains, she shook her head. “No, probably not this. Too exposed. Hard to fortify. This is a base of operations more than it is a safe house. I’m not sure it’s big enough for all of Uncle Cordelayne’s people, either. No, I’d say Emmen’s information is correct.”

Rose’s strings jangled eagerly.

Vandeyr’s gaze rose to the ceiling. “Give me a good dagger and a straightforward target any day. I’m getting plenty sick of the amount of magic you’re swamped in. Kyaan’s breath, Trae, do you ever do anything the normal way?”

“Not much,” Traedis answered with a suppressed smile.

Vandeyr leaned back in her chair. “How many mages should I dig up for you to chord with this time? Or should I just request Lord Shorr’s presence for your convenience?”

“A moment,” Traedis said. “I’d like Emmen to know about these sites.” She quickly relayed Vandeyr’s words to her fellow king.

Emmen nodded thoughtfully. “Since the cave is in the Kurtis Mountains, you should ask Thane Darg if your people can come.”

“I’m not sure he’ll let me,” Traedis said. “He has every reason to hate me.” She was at least partially responsible for the deaths of his brother and father, and n’korreld were not known for their forgiveness.

“Ask him,” Emmen said. “Darg isn’t his father, and you might be surprised. He’s also not going to want your uncle anywhere in his lands, which is another appeal to both his common sense and his need for revenge. I don’t think it’s you he hates.”

Traedis swallowed hard and fought against the memory of the late thane calling the blood spirit in the form of his dead son to kill Uncle Cordelayne and all of his kin. A thrill of horror went through her, and an old, rotten smell came to her nose.

Rose plinked a tune that sounded like splashing water, and the memory subsided, though it would never be far from Traedis' mind. She tapped the harp's frame and was rewarded by what almost sounded like a giggle: if strings could giggle.

"I'd go myself," said Emmen, "but I'd have half the city sitting on me to make sure I don't endanger myself for Tolin. I'd do it if I needed, but this isn't a situation that requires it."

"Very well," Traedis said. "Thank you for all your assistance."

"All right," said Emmen. "Is there anything else you need?"

"Not at present." Quickly scouting the area was something Traedis' people could do. "I'll let you know what happens."

"Thank you," said Emmen. "And Traedis?"

"Yes?"

"Guard your back." The red mist swirled, and Emmen was gone.

Traedis landed in ankle-deep snow which crunched under her boots, Rose's case banging against her shoulder. Around her, six Tolin guards, Ruth, Vandeyr, and Tagg caught their balance amid the fractured whiteness. Traedis hoped fervently that they had gated far enough away from the rebels' cavern so that no scouts would hear their clumsy attempt at secrecy.

They stood in a copse of wind-twisted pines on a rocky incline in the Kurtish Mountains. Heavy forest spread across the lower slopes, but here the pine woods thinned, and the chill in the air was deeper than in Tolin.

A gust of wind blasted down from the heights, cut only marginally by the pines; Traedis pulled her dark gray cloak close around herself and braced against the wind's force. Kyaan was with them; the wind would likely cover the worst of their noise. The guards were similarly clad in faded colors that would blend in with the stone around them.

"If we take one or two of us," Vandeyr said, her quiet words almost inaudible in the blustery air, "we might be able to get a vantage on whoever is inside. We still don't know if Uncle Cordelayne is there…" Her voice faltered momentarily, then resumed without excessive emotion. "Or whether it's Lords Sedorin and Faylias. Or Daymet. Or that filthy runecaster, Myssa, though I'm not sure how we'd recognize her. I wish we could have gotten something more from that miserable karreld."

Traedis let her gaze pass over their party, one aelin, eight humans, and a brunaidh: five men, four women, and one who was neither. All were competent, with bodies well-used to hard terrain. If anyone could creep into view of the rebels it would be those selected for the task by Vandeyr.

She looked around. They were still below the tree line, but barely; the copse was the only sizeable growth for some distance. Yes, experienced people accompanied her, but she stalked some of the most gifted assassins and those who had once planned strategy for the entire city of Tolin.

"I'm not sure how this will work," she said, frustrated by the lack of cover below them. "I don't care how well hidden we are, someone's going to see us moving in the snow if there aren't any trees, and our footprints will stand out. I pictured this differently in my head. We moved too soon."

"We'll make it work." Vandeyr turned so that she could face out over the downslopes. "We can't afford to waste time. If the rebels have a hint that we know where they are, they'll be gone between one breath and the next. I'm not even sure why they picked a place some of us would know."

"Maybe because you already swept the area," Traedis said. She leaned her back against a tree.

This was so different from the Heart of Winter, the timeless night where Lord Harfast dwelled. Here, she stood on stone and pine needles as well as snow. There, the snow was depthless: possibly with no earth beneath it.

Snow crystals, held together by the meltwater and more cold, reflected sun in tiny pinpoints of light that almost prickled in her vision. She blinked, the sparkles illuminating an idea. She had placed trust in Ruth's winter gift over the past few months, but she had a winter gift as well.

Not as useful as scrying in ice, no; the usefulness of singing to snow was limited. In Harfast's land, the snow was ancient, and knew much. In the world of mortals, snow was ephemeral, and often silly.

But high up and in shadow, she stood atop snow that did not melt with the seasons. Perhaps she could learn something useful from it.

"I'm going to do something odd," she told Vandeyr.

Vandeyr rolled her eyes. "Might as well say that the moon will roll along its path." She sighed. "Go ahead. Do something stupid, please."

Traedis gave her an absent grin and took Rose from her case.

She could not simply speak to the snow. The winter gifts had not been selected for mortal utility. Instead, they had arisen from the junction of winter's nature and their own; crystallized into being because of something called out of them by Harfast's heart. Her own core was music.

She raised her harp and plucked a few strings. As the notes sounded, she heard the tiny, crystal voices of snowflakes. Here, in the heights of the Kurtish Mountains, the snowflakes called out to her as eagerly as abandoned children. They chorused and wove a counterpoint to her spellwork as concise and clear as glacial ice. "Who? Who? Who?" was the gist of their song.

It took only a few moments to fold the winter gift together with a flurry of high, precise scales. "I am a friend of Winter's lord," she sang, her words as clear and carrying to the latticework of the snow colony as they were in her chambers at home. "Will you aid me?"

Snow crystals, no matter how long their lifespan, thought and spoke in concert. The tinkle of harmonies sent a quiver of sound through Traedis' mind. "Friend of Winter's lord? We will help you, help you! We will help you! How can we help? Can we help? What help does Winter's friend desire?"

Traedis' fingers played a few swift chords while she considered what to ask. "Do people dwell near you? Warm bodies, with clear minds, not animals? Can you tell?"

"Cave knows, knows, cave knows, cave knows," came the lilting answer.

"Cave?" Traedis played a puzzled trill. "How can the cave know?"

"Cave is ice, ice, ice!" More snow joined in, as if waking from a deep sleep. "Meda sings in her, n'korreld honor her! We sing to ice, ice sings back. Meda sings. Cave knows n'korreld, Cave knows warmth. Cave knows Meda. Cave knows, Cave knows!"

Traedis caught her breath. "Can you sing to the ice now? Ask it if there are living bodies in it? Whether or not it can count them?"

The snow's words focused into a wordless hum full of intense harmonies so high and pure Traedis felt as if they would drill through her eardrums. She grimaced and settled into a recurrent pattern to keep her music sounding while waiting for an answer.

It was not long in coming. The hum split into multiple voices, each one blending into the whole that carried its consciousness.

"Cave says! Cave says! This is what Cave says!"

Traedis immediately snapped to attention, pulling a downward *glissando* into an active awareness of the snowflakes. "What?" she asked, her heart syncopating against her voice. "Are there people?"

"Many, many, many!" The voices sounded somehow smug. "Cave says many! None are n'korreld. Cave is angry. Meda is angry. Fire has been lit in Cave. Cave is angry, angry!"

Traedis let herself sink deep into the spell-mesh until her surroundings faded into gray, and she could feel winter's incipient chill. "Can the cave describe them? Are they human? How many are there?" Her chest tightened. She wondered if Uncle Cordelayne's people had angered the n'korreld people sufficiently to evoke another blood curse. She could kill Uncle Cordelayne but once.

The snow's voice split into several countermelodies, twining together before they reunified. "Numbers? Cave says two and twenty. Cave knows people, can count. Cave sees human, animal. One bear who is sometimes a man, one wolf, one faldro. Eighteen humans. One person Cave cannot see, only knows from footfall. One human gives orders, allows fire. Cave is angry, angry! Fire must not touch Cave. Cave sings to Meda, only to Meda."

Traedis sank even deeper into the snow's awareness. "Can the cave describe the leader? Is it a man or a woman? What can it tell me of the invisible person?" If Meda were angry, this would be far worse than n'korreld wrath. How could Uncle Cordelayne allow it? How could he not know he trespassed on sacred n'korreld ground? It was his business to know such things.

This time the voices split into incoherent babble, merging back to clarity in considerably less time than the first. "The leader is human, not young, not old, has no hair. No hair. Large-large-large for a human. Cave says leader is male. Cave says the invisible one it cannot see, cannot see, not real. Cave says invisible one is not warm, but leaves a print of two feet. All others are warm, some ill, one may die."

"Please ask the cave," Traedis sang, her voice constricting, "if there is a small male human with pale hair, not young or old, who commands others. Can the cave see him? And a younger man, also small, with golden hair?"

"No, no, no, no, no!" the snowflakes chorused back, almost immediately. "No such humans." The precise, eerie voices climbed to a pitch Traedis could only hear through the bones of her head and the strength of her winter gift.

Her voice slid into a musical sigh. She could think of no more questions the snow or the cave might be able to answer. "I must go," she sang. "I will do what I may to help the cave. Thank it for me."

"Come back! Come back! We welcome-welcome-welcome you!" The snow seemed to ring with pleasure. "You are Winter's friend! We will thank Cave!"

Traedis pulled back into ordinary consciousness, 'thank' resounding in her mind. Slowly she concluded the harp notes, ending the song so that no magical traces would linger.

Traedis set Rose beside her in the snow and looked at Vandeyr. "We may have a problem," she said.

"When don't we have a problem?" Vandeyr asked, folding her arms. "It's Uncle Cordelayne's job to give us problems, at least the way he sees things. What is it this time?"

"I changed the plan." Traedis shouldered her harp and looked anxiously out at the gleam of sun on snow. "I got more recent information from—well, from the snow. We should get out of here before discussing it. Someone might hear or see us, and they'll be tipped off." She shifted her weight uneasily.

She could almost see the thoughts gallop through her sister's head like a herd of unicorns while Vandeyr made the connection. "Your relationship to winter," Vandeyr said.

Traedis nodded. "Yes. Let's leave and talk about this elsewhere."

It did not take them long to get back to the palace. Half an hour later, Traedis called for Ruth and Lang to meet them in a private room downstairs. Traedis and Vandeyr got there just before Ruth.

Lang came in last, shaking snow off his cloak as he entered. He was slight, as were most of the Atenels, with reddish-brown hair and eyes as blue as a summer sky. He might not be as handsome as Daymet, or as brilliant as Gavaya, but he understood people, and would not compromise his principles.

He swept Traedis a half-bow, nodded politely to Ruth, and grinned at Vandeyr, who stared mulishly back.

"We've done a little reconnaissance," Traedis began without preamble.

"Tell us what you learned." Lang sat forward, hands on his knees.

Traedis marshaled her thoughts into an organized queue. "I don't think

Uncle Cordelayne or Daymet are there. And not nearly enough people are hiding in that ice cave. There are only twenty-two, assuming the invisible person is an actual person."

"You're not making sense." Vandeyr shook her head in impatience. "Maybe you should have told me what you and your tiny friends were singing about. What invisible person? There are twenty-two of 'them'? Of the rebels, or something else? Start at the beginning, not the middle. You're a bard, you should be able to do that."

Traedis did not mind her sister's ire; Vandeyr was also under a strain. "Very well," she answered mildly. Turning to Lang, she said, "I can sing to the snow; it will understand me and sing back. Mostly I don't bother, because snow doesn't have much mind or intelligence."

One of Lang's eyebrows shot up, but he only nodded and waited for her to proceed.

"This snow, though—it was high enough that it doesn't melt, and it understands more than a snow that only lives for a season."

"What did it tell you?" Vandeyr asked.

"To start with," said Traedis, "the cave is an n'korreld holy place, sacred to Meda. Only twenty-two of the rebels occupy it, and those have desecrated the cave by bringing fire into it. Those that the snow could make sense of include a bear who is sometimes a man; a wolf; and a faldro. They're led by a large, middle-aged man, a balding human. A twenty-third is described as an 'invisible person' who leaves the imprint of two feet."

"If they're desecrating a holy place they need to be stopped," said Ruth, a hard edge to her voice.

"But—" Vandeyr shook her head again. "The cave doesn't have eyes, does it? How can someone be invisible to the cave?"

Traedis leaned back and patted Rose's frame. "I don't know how the cave sees. Let's figure out the others first."

"I can guess at the wolf and the bear," Vandeyr said. "The faldro could be one of a number of people—there weren't a lot of faldrim who went with Uncle Cordelayne, but there were at least a dozen who fled the City after you took the rule."

Lang cleared his throat. "Their leader, I'll venture a guess at. Lord Sedorin was one of the two Council members who left with Uncle Cordelayne. Lord Faylias was the other, but he's smaller and has hair."

Vandeyr grinned. "Politics and principles! Uncle Cordelayne never could stand Lord Sedorin. I wonder what he's doing there?"

Traedis remembered Lord Demmrel Sedorin; he had come to dinner a few times when she was a child. As the man in charge of the City's military, which required close ties with Tolin's information network, there was a certain rivalry between the two families. She mostly remembered his overly hearty voice and his mottled complexion, but he had spoken patronizingly to Mitheira and Gavaya. Traedis' father had tolerated his company well enough, but Uncle Cordelayne had usually been absent during those visits.

"Does Uncle Cordelayne know the cave is sacred to Meda?" Traedis asked after a long silence. "That's asking for trouble."

"Maybe he wanted to get rid of Lord Sedorin," Vandeyr answered promptly. "Anyone would. If the n'korreld know the rebels have desecrated one of their sacred places, they won't settle for anything but killing them all."

Traedis sat back in shock. It had not occurred to her that Uncle Cordelayne's ruthlessness might extend to his own followers. Unease crept into her veins, tightened her throat. "He wouldn't truly do that, would he?"

Lang's mouth tightened. "As much as I'd love to reassure you, I'd have to lie. He would do whatever he needed to achieve his designs, and that is ultimately reclaiming Tolin. He might spare family, but the only family he has with him is Daymet."

Ruth took a pear and bit into it. A moment later, she said, "I'm sorry, Trae, but you give some of your family members too much credit. Your uncle isn't suddenly going to become the person you want him to be. You've already found that out. You need to face that fact, and face it now, so you can wield that bone knife when you have to."

Nausea roiled in Traedis' stomach. Ruth was right. Terrible as the prospect of killing Uncle Cordelayne was, the prospect of n'korreld blood vengeance on all of Tolin was far worse. She could not give him any more chances.

But right now, there was another issue to deal with. Traedis frowned. "What about the invisible person?"

Vandeyr's forehead wrinkled. "Could this person be *magically* invisible instead of bodily invisible?"

Traedis' chin came up sharply as her gaze and Vandeyr's met in sudden comprehension. "The *rûntazent*!"

"Gods." Vandeyr gripped the chair's arms as if she would strangle them. "She's not a living woman. Is her body even warm? Maybe the snow can only sense real things, not—living runes." She cocked her head. "The bear is a fellow named Pergeff, very much in the Sedorin camp. The wolf is Braaval, and he's a real wolf with a man's intelligence; he's worked as an assassin, but he's got some history with the Atenels. If this group were killed while separated from the others, that would both make Uncle Cordelayne's life easier, and absolve him of responsibility for their deaths."

She scowled. "Or perhaps they're just decoys. I wouldn't put it past him. At this point, I'm not sure I'd put anything past him."

"Convenient for him," said Ruth, laying what was left of the pear on her plate. "If he set the runecaster up as his liaison, she oversees everything, and pushes them in the direction she wants them to go while keeping him informed of their activities."

Bitterness spilled into Traedis' throat; she coughed and took a swallow of tea. "What now?"

Lang shook his head. "It's a neat piece of strategy if it's true. We can't afford to wager on that truth, however. Traedis, after what happened to the defensive crystals, we need to completely reexamine Tolin's protections and be ready to change any that fall short."

"That too," said Vandeyr. "But we've got an opportunity here with this party of rebels, and if we don't take it soon enough, we're going to miss it. I'd say he's hoping something catastrophic happens to them, and is letting his runecaster chivvy them into trouble. But how do we get them to understand it?"

"Perhaps," Traedis said with a spreading smile, "we should tell them."

Vandeyr sat motionless for a moment, then burst out laughing. "I think there may be a little Atenel in you after all!"

Traedis sat at the writing desk in her sitting room; it was less crowded than her office. Vandeyr refused to sit still, prowling around the room like a hunting tava. A frown creased Lang's brow. Ruth sat cross legged on a chair far too large for her, twisting a gray ringlet around her finger. Their combined breaths sounded heavy in the silence.

A fire was set in the hearth; it crackled as Traedis dipped her pen into the inkwell, blotting the tip. "'Councilman Sedorin: you have been betrayed.' How does that sound?" She was not entirely happy with it, but letter writing was a more recently acquired skill.

"I like it." Vandeyr joined Traedis at the desk and looked at the empty page. "Short and to the point. But I'm not the bard. You tell me if it's good enough."

Her mind racing to find the best words, Traedis trailed the quill over her lips and tapped a finger on the paper. "Maybe this. 'To Councilman Sedorin and his people, you have been betrayed. Lord Atenel is your enemy.'"

"Not bad," said Lang. "But we'll need to draw him in. He'll be suspicious of anyone we send, and though he might heed the idea that Cordelayne is his enemy, he'll dismiss that idea if it's presented too baldly. He's not a fool, he's just not as clever as our uncle. Oh, and use Cordelayne's first name, because that will make Lord Sedorin think less respectfully of him."

Traedis nodded and bent to her task, glad that Lang had stepped in. Her brother knew the Council members better than any of them. *To Councilman Sedorin and his people: you have been betrayed. The real reason you are here is to rid Cordelayne of unwanted dissenters. The ice cave is a n'korreld holy place, and sacred to Meda. When the n'korreld find you here, they will surely kill you. Cordelayne knew this when he sent you.* Traedis lifted her pen and glared at the words in front of her in dissatisfaction.

"What else?" she asked. "Did I get the tone right?"

Vandeyr turned and walked to the fireplace, taking up the poker and turning over the log with a crash. Sparks flew upward into the chimney. "I'd say it's acceptable. Lang, will it suffice?"

"Mention Myssa?" Ruth offered. "You should try to make them suspicious of her as well, since she's with them."

Traedis nodded and wrote a few more lines. *Consider who accompanies you, and you will see the truth of these words. Cordelayne wants no one with him who is not of his mind. Use caution: Myssa also knows this.*

Traedis read the new lines aloud. "It's not high art, but will it work?"

Lang steepled his fingers. "I don't think we want to polish it too much. We're trying to give out the idea that someone is looking out for Lord Sedorin's people. If it sounds like it's written by a bard, they'll think of you and dismiss it."

"My thoughts were similar." Traedis laid the pen on the blotter. "Ruth, would you come and copy this for me? I don't think they'd recognize my hand, but they might."

Lang nodded. "Best to be overcautious rather than careless. It's well thought of."

Nodding, Ruth hopped down from the chair and waited for Traedis to give up her seat at the desk before copying the letter in a neat, small hand.

"Now to deliver it," said Vandeyr. "I have someone in mind who I think would be the perfect messenger. Trae, are you willing to have him meet you here? I'd like to keep his presence as secret as possible."

Traedis took Ruth's empty seat and settled herself against the cushion. "Please do. If we can sow that seed of dissent, we'll at least be moving toward disbanding the rebels, even if it doesn't net us Uncle Cordelayne." Acid burned in her stomach, but she ignored it as best she could.

"Very good," Vandeyr said. "I'll be back within the hour."

Traedis, Lang, and Ruth passed the time with the sort of conversation that Traedis seldom had time for in her everyday rush of schedules and court appearances and study. She had never known Lang well, and though he was now her viceroy, she still did not know what books he loved; how he had met Alluve; how he felt about being a father. Ruth made the conversation easier, her comfortable frankness and easy speech facilitating a conversation that might otherwise have been awkward.

As promised, Vandeyr returned in less than an hour, accompanied by a thin form in a concealing cloak. The wearer pulled back the hood to reveal himself as a thin, dark man, whose perfunctory smile seemed to belong on another face. He did not bow, but stood straight and proud in front of Traedis as he would have before the Council.

"This is Master Riast," Vandeyr said immediately after closing the door. "Though he's better known as Rook."

Lang's gaze grew intent. "I've heard of you, Master Rook."

"Not too much, I hope," the man said wryly.

"I've heard you're a shapeshifter." Lang leaned forward. "Am I right?"

In an instant, Rook's form melted and shrank, becoming a sleek black bird with a heavy beak. He launched into the air, his form elongating back into a man's shape.

"Useful!" Ruth commented.

"I've explained the bones of the task." Vandeyr went to the desk, picked up Ruth's copy of the letter, and folded it. "I've given him the location and I'll arrange for a gate to get him there." She turned back to Rook. "Be sure," she told him, "that you don't actually enter the cave. It's holy to the n'korreld and consecrated to Meda. We want this left somewhere they will be certain to find it, but we don't want to lose you, either."

"Should I wait until it's picked up?"

"If it's safe," Vandeyr said. "There may be powerful magic guarding the place. You know your business—assess the situation, figure out the best place to plant it, then wait until they read it before returning. I also want everything you can tell me about each of the rebels. If you know them by name, good, but I want a detailed description. I particularly want Lord Sedorin's presence verified. And let us know if Lord Faylias is with them."

Rook nodded. "I can do that," he said in a calm voice. "Do you have a time limit for this mission?"

"As soon as possible," said Vandeyr. "There's no official time limit, unless the group of them leaves the cave before you get the letter placed. In that case, report back immediately."

"Understood, Captain Atenel." He inclined his head to the others in the room "Your Majesty, Lord Lang, Mistress Ruth." He left the room as quickly as if he had taken wing.

"Let's hope this works," Traedis said. "But we still need to find Uncle Cordelayne." The bone knife came briefly to her mind; she shuddered.

"We will." Vandeyr's voice was implacable. "We have to."

Traedis stood on a raised platform next to the Council spring watching a sea of faces. It was hard to ignore the knot forming in her stomach. As a trained bard, she was not frightened of public speaking; what unnerved her was trying to explain herself to a largely hostile audience. But given the recent tensions in Tolin, it was her responsibility to try.

She cleared her throat surreptitiously, trying to keep it from carrying through the amplification spell. "Good people of Tolin, greetings!" Her voice betrayed none of her anxiety, at least. Hopefully, her words would be equally strong.

Traedis had decided to schedule her speech for noon; the glow of morning would still be present, and the dark hours were half a day removed from anything that might anger her listening citizens. Also, the nights were rapidly growing colder, and when the sun was high she could be assured of a greater attendance.

Sunlight glanced off a high window, briefly dazzling her, and she wondered if her timing were not quite as clever as she had thought. Squinting against the glare, she continued.

"Enemies have attacked our ancient city," she said. "Not with force of arms, but with stealthier weapons: not swords, but words; not killing poison, but the poison of magic that twists the will. These weapons have done their damage in the last few weeks, and will continue to do so if we are not vigilant."

Now she had their attention. She looked at the crowd, tallying their individual reactions. Many seemed to be poorer folk, from the garments they wore, but there were a number of Council houses and lesser nobles represented. A well-dressed n'korreld merchant with pink feldspar skin looked at her with an expressionless face. A pair of ragged young men held hands and nodded. She saw no sign of Otenemar.

Very well. Now she had to hold them.

She could almost feel Vandeyr at her back, her quite visible presence both daring anyone to face her down and signaling that not all the Atenels stood with Mitheira. Other guards were posted around the area, some in uniform, others with a quieter, nondescript presence. Vandeyr was not leaving Traedis open to any dangers she could avoid. Lang stood, quiet and watchful, to one side of the crowd.

"The magic these enemies wield is both rare and subtle," she continued. "What reasonable person would question anger that wells up inside? Anger that stirs up deep-held beliefs: enflames them into an inferno. If the anger is your own, the thoughts that run behind it in your own voice, how then could it be imposed on you from outside? But that is the very danger of such magic."

A murmur went through the crowd, punctuated by the cheerful beat of water that rose from the former Council building and splashed its way downhill to join the river. Traedis could not tell whether or not she truly had their ears now, but she thought she could detect the cadence of surprise in some of their inflections. She hoped that was the case, though she could not count on it.

Swallowing against growing nausea, she gave a quick assessment of her diction before continuing. "I hold your minds and your opinions sacred, even when they do not flow with my own." She dropped her register to an ominous undertone, glad of the magic that meant she did not need to speak as loudly as she could. "Our enemies do not show such restraint. They will use anything, from guile to the frank overrunning of your will to accomplish their intentions. They do not care for your desires. They will use you as the high esch use the esch people: as a weapon; as a shield; as an army."

That seemed to startle many in the crowd. A jumble of voices started up. Traedis could hear what sounded like arguments as well as intense, muted discussion. She gave them a moment to react before she went on.

Sweat was collecting on her forehead, despite the chill in the air. A woman with charcoal-colored skin and deep brown eyes stared, unwinking, at her; Traedis could not gauge the woman's mood. A pale youth in expensive silks glared; she thought he might be a scion of the Quill family.

All Traedis could really do was to introduce doubt into their minds. If they were implacably opposed to her, she would not sway them. She would not beg them for support; her words must carry her very real conviction.

She could hear Vandeyr's feet shuffle behind her, but did not look back. If someone had crept onto the platform, her sister was more than capable of dealing with the matter. She could not betray nervousness now.

"The magic set upon the City was built with bardic runes." That would be, at the very least, a surprise to some. "They were used to attack my city, my rule, and even my family." Let them think on that and draw their own conclusions. "The priests were violated in their own churches, while merchants and commoners were also made targets in a bid to overturn my rule. The love you all bear Tolin was the means chosen to assault it. You have been treated like infantrymen in a game of King's Crown."

And now for the turn, the point where she needed to garner their assent and assistance. "Whatever your opinion of me and my kingship, I have been given the *falmyros* of Tolin in trust from the gods. We cannot step backward into yesterday. If you wish changes, I urge you to petition for them fairly and honestly. Bring them to open court, write letters of change. I will consider them. The rioting and unrest that have beset Tolin harms us all. Your voices will be heard, and they will be heeded.

"Just as importantly, be watchful for signs that enemies are attempting to impose their will upon the people of the City. If the madness of destruction descends on a neighbor, keep them from doing harm and make sure they are safe while you see if their will has been hagridden by the magic of another." This part was tricky; she did not want to turn the people against each other, but she did need eyes where even the *falmyros* did not always turn. "Tell someone: a priest, a healer, a guardsman. This is not a betrayal; I will not judge harshly those who have been coerced by magic.

"This is a time when our city will be tested. We are all of Tolin, and must work together for the common good. We are the Eagle, and must help Tolin to soar into the clarity of the upper air. Our greatest weakness now is in division."

She let out a long, controlled breath, and stepped back a pace. There was scattered applause: not as much as she would have liked. Voices broke out in the crowd, though not particularly loud or hostile.

It was possible that those who had attended simply did not know what to make of her short speech. Her people were quite stubborn about making up their own minds, at least when tradition and law did not dictate how they should think. Traedis had learned much about the City's people since taking the throne. She was not as different from them as she had once thought.

"We should get you back to the palace now," said Vandeyr's voice in her ear. Traedis jerked and instinctively reached for her dagger, but her sister's iron grip caught her wrist. "Don't ruin what you've just done!" said Vandeyr. "Let them think about it first."

Traedis nodded, still feeling a little sick even though the speech was over. She headed into a waiting group of her own guards and moved toward her carriage.

In the midst of dealing with this set of challenges, something tantalizingly familiar and yet strange tugged at Traedis' attention. She stopped and tried to isolate the new sensation, but Vandeyr nudged her forward.

As soon as they were in the carriage, Vandeyr said, "You're distracted. What's wrong?"

Traedis raised a quelling hand to her. "I'm not sure. Give me a moment to track it."

"Anything military?"

Traedis shook her head, then closed her eyes and delved into the *falmyros*.

Finding anything proved irritatingly difficult. It reminded Traedis of the unpleasant sensation of hostile runework, but she was not sensing runes; she knew what those were like by now. Perhaps it was the hostility, but even that did not seem quite right. She spat out a pair of curses and redoubled her efforts to identify what might well be a threat.

Sinking deep into the land's bones, she tried to feel pressure above her, the rumors of feet that disturbed earthworms in their tunnels and ants in their delicately engineered nests. If something was agitating the land's face, she should be able to tell. But there were so many feet, and so much pressure that she could not find the steps she sought.

Tolin's earth rumbled deep below; it was not entirely stable. Traedis had known that her whole life; occasionally a minor quake rattled dishes or dislodged a crock from the shelves. Now she saw a crack in the stone which might upend the foundations of Tolin if it slipped.

Alarmed, she shifted her focus and traced the crack from one end of the mountain to the other, careful not to disturb it or give it a reason to move. A few moments, or the land's eternity later, she decided it was safe enough. Minor motion was always possible, but it seemed relatively secure. She abandoned those efforts and went back to searching for what had initially caught her attention.

And there it was again: a presence, she thought. There was a sort of passion about it that gave away its otherwise quiet touch in the *falmyros*. That was what had alerted her. It seemed to both belong and to have an utterly foreign quality to it. Even so, the recognition teased at her.

When had she felt it before? She asked the land, not sure whether it was capable of answering.

It did not, precisely. Instead, her mind jumped back a few weeks in time to the moment she had descended from her carriage only to be struck by Vandeyr and knocked to the ground.

Her eyes snapped open. "A ciriin!" Now she remembered. She had not analyzed what the ciriin felt like in her *falmyros* because she had been too busy preparing to fight. That would explain why its touch on the land was so slight. They were intensely magical. Part dragon, they were known to have strange abilities.

Now that she knew what she was looking for, she again immersed herself in the *falmyros*, following the tiny wake of dragon magic that did not waft from the mountains. There. It snaked past the communal living quarter, padded around the priest's alley, and made its way to the market square. Finally, it came to a halt at the Council spring.

Traedis was not foolish enough to think this was a coincidence. She would not have been an Atenel if she had not learned that good intelligence was the most important part of an attack. Such intelligence had been discussed at the family dinner table, as casually dropped into conversation as the state of the weather or the marriage prospects of a colleague's child.

Then the trace slithered out of her grasp. Traedis started, feeling as if her harp had been wrenched from her grip. Rose gave an answering snatch of song to reassure her. But it was not Traedis' *falmyros* that had failed her. She could no longer feel any remnant of a ciriin in her land.

"I need to know more about them," she muttered, frustration rising like a tide. "They seem to be able to blink in and out of Tolin without anyone noticing, at least as long as the crystals are still cracked." That was the last thing she needed.

Vandeyr leaned forward. "What?"

"How soon are the crystals going to be fixed?"

Vandeyr snorted. "You can tell better than I, can't you? You're the one who gave the order, you're the one who's got the *falmyros*. I'm just the one who sticks swords into people."

"We had a ciriin in town." Traedis frowned. "In the market square, the communal living quarter, the priest's quarter, and just now, the Council Spring."

"Oh." Vandeyr's looked out the window, then back. "Not exactly subtle, is it?"

"It was. Very subtle." Traedis did not know how to explain what she had sensed, but she understood what it meant. "So subtle that I could hardly find a trace when I was looking for it. So subtle that the land had a hard time distinguishing it from something that belonged."

Vandeyr sat in silence for a very long moment while the carriage jounced over a deep rut in the road. Finally, she said, "That's subtle indeed. Tell me again what you know about ciriin. They haven't been much of a study here."

"They're a sort of children of the dragon Kisrien. The black dragon. She didn't give birth to them, though. I understand they are like echoes of her that rebounded from somewhere in the Dragon Mountains. They feed on emotion, and some may become bonded to non-ciriin if the ciriin in question becomes attached to another person's emotions. Then everything they do is for the sake of pleasing that person." She tried to remember what else she had been told. "They're not inherently evil, but they're terribly dangerous. They tend toward odd magical talents, and some of them like inducing strong emotions—such as terror—to feed from."

Scowling, Vandeyr sat back in her seat, her spine setting like steel. "I know they're very new to the world. But we've never had any in Tolin, and had no dealings with them outside, so I didn't hear much but rumor and speculation. Do you want me to go back and check out those locations after we get home?"

"Yes." Traedis looked out the window, her eyes catching the flame of dying leaves. "Please do. We need to know more about this ciriin that Uncle Cordelayne has acquired."

"All right," said Vandeyr. "And if I meet any, I'll be glad to give them some strong emotions to choke themselves on."

The day was waning, and Vandeyr had not returned. When Traedis went to look out her office window, she could see red seeping into the front garden where a few frost-touched blooms clung to their stems. Lighting a taper sent tiny sparks winking upward as they went out. The candle's pool of light was not large, but she was in the mood for darkness.

Her thoughts were certainly dark. How could she possibly protect Tolin if she could not even find an enemy when she knew one prowled in her land?

She was just turning to the light supper which sat on her desk next to seemingly endless petitions, proposed amendments to laws, and requests for funds, when she was interrupted by Vandeyr's sharp step outside the door. Immediately afterward came the expected rap.

"Come in!" Traedis called.

As Vandeyr entered, Traedis pushed a small flat loaf of seasoned bread toward her sister.

Vandeyr shook her head. "Not hungry. I've got some word on the crystals, but I ran into something else as well. You need to know about it as soon as possible."

She seemed preoccupied. She had not yet divested herself of her cloak, but the hood was pushed back, showing her neat coil of hair. She clutched a pouch in one hand.

"Let me show you," Vandeyr said, a little more tersely than usual. "I've got information about Uncle Cordelayne, and it's vital that you see it right away."

Traedis was a little disconcerted by her sister's urgency, but trusted her to know their family business. "Not good news?"

Vandeyr snorted slightly. "Not in the least. Let me show you what I've got here." She waited for Traedis to move behind her desk. "I've told the guards not to disturb us." She went to the windows and drew the curtains, damping the light enough for privacy but not enough to impair sight. Finally, from her pouch, she pulled out two folded pieces of parchment and a pair of quill pens, which she laid on the desktop.

"I was called in to review two witnesses to the attack on Mother," she said, still in the same terse voice. "I got new stories from them; at least two people knew more than they were telling. I have their confessions here. Uncle Cordelayne *was* involved. I'm sorry." She handed the parchments to Traedis.

Traedis patted Rose's case and bent to examine the papers. Focusing her eyes, she scanned the surfaces of both.

I, Garin Beirlieson, she read, before movement caught the corner of her vision. Traedis whipped her head up to see Vandeyr sweep the quill pens off the table and throw them: one at Traedis' chest, and one at the harpcase on the floor. Frantically, Traedis tried to grab the dart heading toward her, but stopped cold, her body frozen as the quill scratched a rune on the silk above her breastbone.

Beside Traedis, the harp case shuddered itself into dust as the quill penned a second rune. The rune itself, still visible in the space above the harp, settled over Rose's cherrywood frame. The wood creaked and groaned for a moment, but nothing else happened.

Vandeyr relaxed her shoulders and shrugged herself into an entirely different posture. It was not until then that Traedis realized this was not her sister at all.

It was Uncle Cordelayne.

He had used no magic to disguise himself, merely skill, makeup, acting ability, a similarity of feature, and long familiarity with Vandeyr's every movement and voice tone. He looked at Rose, and in an astonished tone, asked, "Where *did* you get that harp?"

Traedis' pulse beat rapidly in her throat and her vision grew clear and small, as if she watched the room from the end of a long tunnel. Her temples felt as if they would burst. Uncle Cordelayne had been willing to imprison her; she did not know what else he might do.

She cleared her throat and realized that she could still speak, though her limbs and head would not move. Even so, her thoughts remained empty of words to use in her defense. Only the terror stayed, beating through her body in rhythm with her pulse. It was an effort to breathe.

"At first," Uncle Cordelayne continued in a casual voice, "I just wanted your spell chording. But now I guess I must take it all."

Alarm stabbed through Traedis as every fiber began to throb: her hand, her pulse, her chest, and her thoughts. Panic seized her; her uncle's words were ominous. Her vision flickered with dark flashes that threatened to overwhelm consciousness.

"Vandeyr's safe," Uncle Cordelayne continued in the oddly conversational tone that rang a false note in Traedis' mind. "She'll wake up before her air runs out. She's family, after all." He began to pace back and forth like a restless tava, still speaking.

She knew it was not like him to chatter, and his behavior was odd. It was as if he was waiting for something.

As soon as the thought struck, she knew she was right. Perhaps the rune on her chest was intended for more than immobilization. *At first I just wanted your spell chording. But now I guess I must take it all.* All of her magic?

The throbbing in her body and mind gathered into a heaviness and an exhaustion that sapped her will and her intelligence. The rune sat on her chest like a weight.

There was one thing she could do. Turning her attention to Rose, she reached for the connection that ran between them, forged together in otherworldly fire with the strength of *sagathas. Keep my magic within me,* she implored the harp. *Never let anyone take it.*

A suction began in her head that ran counter to the feeling of the rune. In a rush, energy and creative fire returned to her with a shock like the snap of a bowstring. Though she still could not move, Traedis felt suddenly lighter.

Uncle Cordelayne stopped in mid-sentence and stared at her, casting a sharp glance at something below her level of vision. He frowned. Approaching Traedis, he gave her a hard, stinging blow to the face, which rocked her head to one side. Tears sprang to her eyes.

If she had been using a spell, the blow would have destroyed her concentration. But since it was Rose who had restored her power, it did him no good. Traedis could feel her magic running through her veins like the lifeblood of her soul.

Her uncle frowned again. He grabbed her chin and forced her to look at him. With all his native intensity, he said, "Let it go, Traedis. You know you can't win against me. We can do this the easy way—and believe me, this is the easy way—or we can do it the hard way." Traedis could almost feel his glare against her own frightened gaze.

With all the defiance she could muster, she said, "When have I ever done things the easy way?" She would *not* lose this battle.

Uncle Cordelayne paused, then nodded. He reached down to grasp something which he brought into her view; a narrow carpet needle coated with green. In a movement swifter than Traedis could follow, he jabbed the end into her sinus just below the eye.

She felt a searing pain in her face before the world went dark.

Harp music flooded Traedis' dreams below her awareness. Ballads and dances wove themselves into aural tapestries adorned with lullabies, anthems, and serenades, all emanating from a single instrument. Music Traedis had known all her life intertwined with melodies she had never heard but instinctively recognized. It was as if she floated on a lake of sound, the music cradling her gently. She could feel the buzz of Lord Ymre's hair against the low string.

Gradually, consciousness seeped back. The thought soaked slowly into her mind: Rose was playing, and Traedis' fingers were not on the strings. The back of her neck hurt.

Moments of awareness grew in longer stretches, conscious thought threading them together like a torn seam. Something was very wrong.

Her eyes fluttered open, closed, opened again. Cracks of light seared her vision, and only blurs met her confused gaze. *I must be asleep,* she thought, and bent her drowsy efforts toward wakening. Her body was slow to respond, but her mind roused more quickly. Smears of color resolved into incomprehensible patterns of black and brown bulges which Traedis thought should mean something. But the patterns made no more sense than did the music, which still continued, insistently, in her head.

Several urgent chords shocked her fully awake. In an instant, Traedis could tell that she lay on her back, and the black and brown bulges were part of an irregular, high rock ceiling. Every muscle in her body ached, and the back of her neck stung with white heat.

Memory swept over her with pressing importance, forced back into her consciousness where it had lain asleep. Uncle Cordelayne had trapped her with the quill-pen rune. That frightening realization goaded her into a struggle to move. Her body responded only sluggishly, one command behind her thoughts.

It was then Traedis realized that though Rose still sounded an imperative in her mind, she could not hear the harp with her ears. Not yet ready to make sense of that, she wiggled her fingers to see if the immobility of the rune still lay over her, or whether she had normal function. Her fingers moved, though with difficulty, so she turned her head.

It was a long journey between the impulse and the action, but Traedis finally managed to look to one side, though her head lolled. She felt terribly weak. The surface under her was rock-hard.

She lay in a large cavern lit by torches. The naked figure of a woman, her back turned, bent over a table where Rose sat beside an open book.

As her thoughts gained clarity, Traedis realized that what she felt was an alarm from her harp; the instrument was besieged by some potent force. The white-hot patch on her neck was where Traedis' *sagathas* hair completed the trinity of herself, the harp, and the key. Traedis could feel the connection between them more solidly than she ever had, as if Rose were an arm or a leg.

Not knowing what to do, she tried to feed the instrument her own strength, hoping that would be enough. Whatever power was strong enough to menace the harp's *sagathas* strings and key had trapped and beset the instrument fiercely. Rose Goldsong needed help.

The woman at the table turned sharply as Traedis played her strength along the connection between herself and the harp. "Stop that!" the woman said, her voice like splinters of glass.

Traedis stared at her, still unable to muster the strength to move more than her head. The woman was dark-haired and very lovely, but something about her repelled Traedis. Perhaps it was the scowl which disfigured the woman's face, but Traedis thought there was something more subtle, something which made the hairs on her arms and neck rise in instinctive revulsion.

Ignoring the woman's words, Traedis continued to pour every scrap of energy she could muster into her harp. The woman's scowl deepened; she clenched her fists as if preparing for a fight. "If you don't stop that, then Cordelayne or no, I'll slap a death rune on you so fast—" She paused for a moment, then shook her head. "Oh, why wait?"

Traedis' heart began to knock against her chest. This must be Myssa, the runecaster who had caused Elben to lose his reason and attack her mother. Traedis tried to gather energy to rise, but she was far too weak and could only manage to flop like a fish, while the runecaster snatched the book from her worktable and leafed through it.

Putting down the book, the woman picked up an inkpot and brush and approached Traedis. Her eyes were the color of a sunless well, no distinction between iris and pupil apparent. In an icy voice, she said, "This isn't a death rune. It's a pain rune." She dipped her brush into the ink and painted on Traedis' forehead as if her captive were nothing more than blank parchment.

Traedis tried shaking her head to dislodge the ink, but she had no more strength; she could not even straighten her neck. Instead, she lay powerless as the woman worked.

As soon as the brush left her forehead, Traedis felt the magic take hold. Some force squeezed her head so hard she felt it would burst. Agony flooded her.

The pain damped to pinpricks across her body, intensifying swiftly in places, then dying back to mere discomfort. Traedis gritted her teeth as the pain increased again like a series of impacts or a fall down a flight of stairs.

As soon as this thought crossed her mind Traedis understood the purpose of the rune. She had fallen downstairs at the age of two. Would this magic force her to re-experience all her body had ever endured, one injury after another?

She was able to identify individual blows: her brother Otenemar giving her a clandestine beating, the slap from her father which had made her eye swell shut, the hair which Vandeyr had pulled when particularly irritated. Twice Traedis felt the snap of broken bones. Her tutor, striking her with a book. Sessions in the practice yard; bruises and falls; minor cuts and scrapes which were negligible at the time; all escalated to a pain so exquisite she could only endure.

As her childhood years cycled into her adulthood, more pain comprised the litany of years. A fall from a horse; broken blisters from constant harp practice; the memory of a debilitating flux; all swept through so swiftly it left Traedis panting. She would not let the runecaster know how successful her rune had been. The agonizing cold of the winterlands chilled her flesh; simple aches compounded and built into crippling distress.

In a great wave of monumental anguish, all those hurts were dwarfed by a single sensation which Traedis had tried to forget. It came on suddenly:

acid in her veins which burned hotter than forge fire. Traedis could only lie helpless as she re-experienced the excruciating sensation triggered when magic had cleared her body of latent poison. The City had not let her fly free when it had hired her out. It had kept the jesses on her.

Though most of the suffering tore through blazingly fast, this pain seemed to go on endlessly, perhaps longer than originally. Traedis could not even cry out.

Then it washed away in pulsating waves, replaced by many small hurts from the last few months of Traedis' kingship.

It was not until she again felt the squeezing in her head that Traedis realized the pain rune would cycle back through everything she had just experienced. A single sob escaped her throat. She fought a second cry; she would *not* let the runecaster derive her pleasure from Traedis' pain.

She must still remember to strengthen Rose, for if the harp had not needed her, Traedis would not have woken. But under the excruciating sensations, it was too difficult to concentrate. Traedis had to settle for feeding her harp strength in the brief lulls between the greater pains. Tears leaked from the corners of her eyes; she wanted to dash them away, but was too weak to raise a hand.

Questions rattled through her head. Would the runecaster be able to touch Rose's magic? What would happen if Uncle Cordelayne and Myssa successfully ousted her from the *falmyros*? Was Vandeyr truly safe?

Biting back another cry, she swore instead, searing oaths that she had learned from her armsmaster and taught to some of Kaelennar's bardic students. Her voice crescendoed and ebbed with pain. She could barely salvage her innate pride; every spare dram of strength went to Rose, a steady presence in her mind and heart. The burn at the nape of her neck continued.

She did not know how long the pains lasted, so focused was she on her twin goals of holding back cries and aiding her harp. A nightmare of repeated tortures, each sensation, small and large, drove her to the brink of terror. Bitter words fell uncontrolled from her mouth as she began to anticipate each repeated pain. Now would be the crack of a broken arm; now the anguish of a sword slash in practice; now the peak agony of Arlen's cleansing spell.

A voice penetrated her consciousness: Uncle Cordelayne's. Traedis almost lost her fragile control as she listened to him speak several sharp words. The runecaster answered back angrily, and a tense exchange ensued. Traedis could make few of the words out—only some references to hair and strings—but their tones were furious.

The slap of bare footsteps sounded, and the runecaster's face appeared in Traedis' vision. She held a bowl and cloth, and with careful motions, she wiped the rune from Traedis' forehead with an oily liquid. Traedis sagged with immediate relief. She would have cried out at the respite from pain, but she had no more strength.

The runecaster turned abruptly and walked away. A moment later, Uncle Cordelayne's face appeared over her, his expression unreadable. He looked down at Traedis for several moments as if contemplating a difficult problem.

Traedis felt mingled fear and love as she gazed at him; in her deepest heart she wanted nothing more than to concede him the victory and allow him to mend the rift. But the time for that was years past. There was no returning to the trust of her childhood.

"I am sorry about Myssa," he said in a strangely compassionate tone. "I gave her no orders to torture you. She acted on her own."

Traedis looked at him, noting the changes a few months had made. His pale hair was streaked with silver, and deep shadows underlay his eyes. Lines etched his forehead, though his voice and movement still seemed youthful. She felt a pang in her chest, quickly replaced by the chill of gooseflesh. When they had met after she had been hired out, he had not been kind.

"Tolin does not need a king," he continued softly. "We have never invested our power in a single person." He sounded almost as if he were hoping she would agree. "Other places may need rulers and kings, but not Tolin. It weakens us; no one person should be that important."

Traedis simply stared at him, barely able to move or to think. There was nothing she could do about the situation; the gods had given her the *falmyros* of Tolin, and she was yoked to the land. A faint sound escaped her throat. Then the room spun, and her thoughts with it.

Uncle Cordelayne immediately straightened her head with gentle hands, brushing a curl back from her forehead. "You'll have some weakness with the poison I gave you. Try not to move too much or too fast."

Traedis gave a slow, careful nod. Her pulse had begun to wake to the same understanding as her mind, though both were still sluggish. Rose's need and her own sharp prickle of fear fought with an exhaustion so deep she could imagine herself sleeping through the song of dragons.

After a moment, Uncle Cordelayne continued in the same patient tone. "Toledru was greedy. He wanted to rule, but it did the City no good. Now see yourself—you've been gone for three weeks, and Tolin doesn't need you." He frowned. "You're a novelty, nothing more. The City has never had a king, and the people think such a turn of fate is exciting. They are beginning to see for themselves how matters truly stand." He tucked the curl behind her ear. "I was going to give them as much time as they needed to learn, but then you set that karreldish boy on me. That annoyed me. Now I intend to make Tolin see that they do not need the chains of your rule."

She had been unconscious for three weeks? It had not seemed long, borne on Rose's music and Uncle Cordelayne's poison. She sucked air into a dry mouth. 'The boy' must be Atchûk. Tears threatened again briefly, then receded into utter weariness. She tasted something strange and acrid at the back of her throat.

Mustering her energy and her courage, she rasped, "That 'karreldish boy' was a prince, and Thane Bi'ia's son." Her throat felt dry and raw. "The thane laid a curse over Tolin because you murdered him."

Uncle Cordelayne's eyes narrowed. "What curse?" he asked in a low voice.

Traedis pulled her scattered thoughts together. "He called the Red Man down on you. He was too mad with grief to care that the Red Man would destroy everyone with a blood connection to you as well. And almost everyone in Tolin shares some measure of common blood." Her heart ached as she remembered Prince Atchûk, once her merry friend, later the embodiment of n'korreld vengeance.

"That's not possible," Cordelayne said flatly. "I'd be dead if he had, and most of Tolin with me."

Traedis coughed weakly. "You would, except I managed to turn aside his wrath for a time. He wanted you dead, and by my hand. He sent a knife made of his breastbone to spill your heart's blood." That knife was never far from her mind's eye; its dull ivory sheen figured into her nightmares.

Taking a sudden breath, Cordelayne became very still. His gaze bored into her "Tell me everything." His face remained expressionless.

"I did," said Traedis. "There's nothing else to tell, except that the thane gave me a year and a day. And that was months ago."

Worry lines grooved Cordelayne's face as he stared at her. "I will have to study the problem. In the meantime, your rule of Tolin is my primary concern."

"Then you had better take it up with the gods, because I have no choice in the matter." Traedis' voice was faint, but clearing. Still, she doubted that she could manage to muster a bardic spell, as weak as she was.

Uncle Cordelayne ignored her words as he might a child's outburst. "You know the principle of the carrot and the stick; I trained you in it myself." Traedis felt a surge of dull anger which subsided almost as soon as it manifested. "But I am not trying to use that now when I tell you this—if you wake again, don't cross Myssa. Sometimes we must do unpleasant things in the line of duty, but she truly enjoys them. She is not someone with whom I would choose to work, given a choice of allies."

"I'm not stupid," she said, her words no louder than her breath. "You may not like her, but if she weren't someone you could control, you wouldn't work with her." Their brief struggle over the pain rune proved this plainly; Uncle Cordelayne held the reins.

He nodded. "True enough in some ways, but the matter is more complex than you know. I don't see you as stupid, Traedis, but you are ignorant. And that ignorance is dragging Tolin down with it."

Traedis had no strength left to reply. She simply stared, helpless as the child he clearly thought she was.

Uncle Cordelayne pulled a small jar out of his pocket, unstoppered it, then drew out a flat metal implement which he used to scrape out a waxy substance from the jar. Lifting Traedis' strengthless arm as tenderly as a mother, he tucked her hand under his arm. He smoothed ointment over her forearm, taking care not to touch it himself, then repeated the action with her other arm.

Almost immediately, Traedis felt intense drowsiness. Her eyelids fluttered, though she fought sleep with everything left in her. Her uncle's face was the last thing she saw as she inexorably slipped back into the darkness.

Rose's voice sang amid the black, calling urgently. Again, Traedis felt the back of her neck flame with pain. She reached out to her harp, instinct still guiding her, though consciousness was fleeting. Something tugged at her bones; she pulled back against the force that would tear apart her tendons. She could not—*would not*—let herself be unstrung. Grasping for anything that would give her purchase, she found something like a rope. She heaved herself along it, hoping it would hold the weight of her spirit.

It felt very much like dog's hair.

Chapter Twenty-One
Balm

Harp music sang again in Traedis' mind. She listened to it without thought, instinct following its lines, the rise and fall of notes and chords. She gave herself wholly to the music, which lay beneath all thought at the core of her soul.

Warmth on her face brought consciousness to the surface. Something rough but gentle dragged against her skin. It was wet. She opened her eyes.

A head appeared in her vision, white and shaggy: an immense hound with eyes of clear, piercing green-blue. He washed her face, and she strove to make sense of what she saw. Shouldn't there be a rock ceiling and Uncle Cordelayne's face?

Clarity crystallized in her mind. She knew this creature. It was Lord Ymre; there was no mistaking those eyes. Still, she could not determine why he would be licking her when her last memory was of Uncle Cordelayne drugging her into sleep.

"Are you all right?" asked Ymre, drawing back and letting his tongue loll. "No more bed sores?"

"Bed sores?" Traedis flexed her muscles and found them cooperative. She raised herself to one elbow, feeling springy moss beneath her. The scent of lilacs saturated the air, almost enough to taste, yet paradoxically, not overpowering.

A movement on her other side startled her. She flinched, then relaxed; nothing would harm her here. Turning her head, she saw Dame Tanjarre, the aelin magic smith who had reforged Rose with *sagathas* and made the harp the supremely magical force she now was.

Tanjarre held Rose Goldsong cradled in one arm. A broad grin spread across her face, framed by hair as fiery as Traedis' own. "Isn't she a good harp?" she crowed, and held out the instrument.

Traedis felt the harp as a balm to her spirit; Rose had become so much a part of her that she would rather lose a limb than her instrument.

Tanjarre held out her hand for Traedis and pulled her into a sitting position. Traedis took the harp, cradling her like an infant, fingers exploring each surface, telling herself that Rose was still her own.

"You'll want this as well," Tanjarre added, and pulled Rose's key from a chain around her neck. Traedis took it gladly, securing it around her throat and tucking the key into her bodice. She touched the nape of her neck to reassure herself that the *sagathas* hair also remained.

The land of Ymre spread around her in eternal bloom, blue and purple flowers raising their petals gladly to the sun amidst goosedown-soft moss and leaves. Ancient oaks stretched skyward, surrounded by graceful lesser trees, and lilac bushes grew in profusion as far as Traedis could see. The light was subtly different from that of the mortal world, somehow fresher and younger. Traedis breathed out a long sigh: half in relief at her rescue, half in realization that she would have to go back and untangle whatever had become of Tolin.

She wore a different dress than she remembered, a shift of undyed wool. "What happened?" she asked in some confusion. She looked closely at Rose's strings, and saw that Ymre's hair, twined around the lowest bass string, was shredded and barely clung where she had put it. She pulled out the harp key to remove the string, took off the hair, and held it out to Ymre. "This is yours," she told him. "Do you want it back?"

"I have others," he said in amusement. His coat, the voluminous mass of a sighthound, rippled in the soft breeze. "You may keep it, though I fear it is no longer of much use. I'm very glad you cleverly put it where I intended." He settled down on the ground, his head resting on his forepaws. "As for what happened..." His eyes half closed, then opened again. "While your uncle held you prisoner, his runecaster tried to destroy your harp. She has considerable power, and managed to keep Rose in a—I'll call it a vise rune—while she worked on it. She was drilling her way into the *sagathas*. When Rose felt herself pressed too hard, she first woke you. She could not wake you a second time, so using my hair as a guide, she wrenched herself free of the vise rune and returned to Tanjarre, the only other person she knew could help you both." His long tongue lapped across his nose. "Rose Goldsong and your own strength were able to transport you to my land."

Traedis shook her head, less in disbelief than in confusion. "I didn't realize Rose could do that."

"She's steeped in *sagathas*," Tanjarre reminded her. "The magic of the heart. Objects made of *sagathas* aren't exactly alive, but they can gain a sort of life and intelligence, and certainly a measure of independence. Life and heart meet in the forging of artifacts when I work in that metal."

"Thank you and the gods for that," Traedis told her, again realizing what an incredible gift she had been given. "I know she speaks her mind, but she's never acted *entirely* on her own before."

Tanjarre cleared her throat. "Rose was a little damaged by the vise rune. I've fixed that, and a few—I would call them magical dents—that she suffered from the runecaster. I've also had a firm talk with her about free will, and not allowing herself to be coerced by inimical forces. Next time she's put to the test, she should stand up better."

"Thank you," Traedis told her gratefully. She was amazed Rose had resisted an all-out assault for three weeks from someone as powerful as

Myssa. Or had it been three weeks? "How long have I been asleep?" she asked Ymre, a little afraid of the answer.

"From the time your uncle abducted you, three sixdays, and this is the third day after that. We only just recovered you. If you would like, I will travel to Tolin to let your people know that you are well and will be back soon."

"I should go back now," Traedis said, reluctant duty pricking her conscience. "If they've been without me for three-and-a-half weeks, they'll need me." She clutched Rose's frame for support, fingers digging into the frame's projections. She could almost feel Rose purr under her hands.

Ymre flashed her a doggy smile. "I think you have forgotten," he told her, "that time in this land passes at my bidding. If you wish to stay for a short while and recover your strength, I will see to it that you get back to Tolin promptly."

Traedis brushed the stickiness of sleep from her eyes, wishing she could as easily wipe out the fogginess of her extended slumber. "I had forgotten." She expelled a long breath of air and relaxed on the mossy mat. "Thank you, Lord Ymre. I will gladly accept your most gracious offer."

She pushed aside confused feelings about Uncle Cordelayne, who had acted almost as if he still cared about his wayward niece. She would leave those feelings muted, hoping they would not hide in ambush as they waited for her to forget them. He had made it even harder for her to hunt him down.

"Please tell Captain Atenel where I am," she said. "And Lord Lang, who should be ruling Tolin in my absence." She traced a finger along a cluster of cilla growing beside her. "Would it be asking too much that you also let King Kenrydh and King Emmen know where I am?"

"I've already thought of that," Ymre assured her. He stood and stretched. "It's done."

Traedis relaxed a little more. "Then I may enjoy the hospitality of Ymre all the more without such concerns. Thank you, Lord Ymre." She closed her eyes and let the breeze play over her face, allowing herself to relax for this small space of time.

The undergrowth of Ymre was fascinating for a fox. Scents were plentiful. The delicious aromas of mice, shrews, and rabbits mingled with the heady odor of flowers on the wind. However, Traedis felt constrained not to hunt the smaller creatures which abounded in Ymre's rich soil; despite their tantalizing squeaks and rustles she felt no hunger, though she enjoyed chasing them through the underbrush.

The late afternoon sun poured rays through the trees. The bushes were safe; she knew nothing would harm her as long as she remained under their wild tangle. She would not expose herself, though neither would she dig into the damp earth, despite the call of her instincts. She flicked out her tongue to taste the wind and turned an ear toward a flutter of birds settling into the undergrowth.

A familiar sound alerted her to the presence of another fox at the same moment her nose caught his scent. She bristled slightly, fearing intrusion. Then her alarm ceased. She knew this fox.

He bounded across a small clearing and dived into the spirea bush where Traedis watched warily. "Traedis? How are you?"

The words meant nothing, but his tone soothed her fears. She padded over to meet him, sniffing at his tail and legs. This was indeed her own fox. She licked him on the snout; he responded by jumping back. Then he moved forward, touching noses until a static shock drove them apart. He laughed a human laugh and licked her face in return.

"I don't know what you've gone through," he said gently and a little breathlessly. "I hope it wasn't terrible. I hope Cordelayne didn't hurt you. I insisted Commander Arlen put me on the detail King Kenrydh sent to help find you. When Lord Ymre came to tell us you were safe, I talked him into bringing me here to see for myself. Trae, I know you can't understand me, but I'm here if you need me, whether you need to talk or to play, or to be silent."

Traedis was not interested in words. She nipped his ear playfully and darted toward the more heavily wooded glade. He laughed again, a half-relieved sound, and followed her.

They played until the sun tipped downward toward the sea and afternoon glowed golden. Traedis suddenly found herself on hands and knees in the dirt beneath a patch of tall purple clover. Her skirt was filthy and her hair full of twigs. Rose was strapped across her back like a weapon.

Elben, still a fox, stopped suddenly. Transforming himself into a man, he offered her a hand up. She took it in bemusement.

"Elben? What are you doing here? I knew it was you, but I didn't expect to see you."

"I did tell you," he said laughing, "but you were your charming, furred self and couldn't understand. I was on the detail King Kenrydh sent to Tolin to search for you. When Lord Ymre came to us with the news, I talked him into letting me return with him in case there was anything I could do for you. Thank the Four you're here, and at least safe in body."

Traedis reached her hand to touch her hair, tangled with debris nearly to her knees. "I didn't expect you."

"You said that." Elben smiled crookedly. "I can't say I've been sorry to taste the hospitality of Ymre, but my main reason for coming was to see you." His smile faded. "How are you? Truly? Don't show me a brave face— I want to know."

Traedis tried to tug leafy twigs from her hair. "I must look frightful."

"You look beautiful." Elben did not sound as if he meant an empty compliment. "A little wild perhaps. More like a fox than you usually do when human." He paused. "You don't have to answer my question."

Traedis looked down at the ground, her eyes searching out the tiny florets imbedded in the spongy blanket of moss. She was not certain how to answer either compliment or question.

"Is it that hard?" Elben asked gently. "I won't pry, then. If you want to tell me what happened, I'll be glad to listen, but I won't ask if you don't want me to." He offered his arm as if they were in court rather than in Ymre's beautiful tangle of wilderness. "Walk with me if you please. If you don't object, I'd love to see more of this land while I have the chance."

Traedis took Elben's arm and noticed he shortened his stride to match hers. She blinked aching eyes and tried to sort out her tangled emotions, grateful for the kindness which put her feelings ahead of his own.

She stopped him with a touch and turned, her mouth tentatively lifting at the corners. His eyes, a paler green than her own, bore the crinkle of smile lines, but there were also lines of pain in his features. She wondered what had put them there, and how they had affected him.

"My harp saved me," she said, her voice unexpectedly even. Then, starting from Cordelayne's impersonation of Vandeyr, she told him what she remembered, doing her best to keep her fear and shame at bay. Elben stood quietly, though his lips pinched together as she spoke.

"What I don't understand," she said finally, "is why Uncle Cordelayne told me what he did. He spoke as if what I thought *mattered*. He rescued me from the runecaster's malice. Yet he had no compunctions against taking me and keeping me asleep for over three weeks. I don't understand his actions."

Elben made a sound of disgust. "I think that's what he wants you to feel—confusion. If he can keep you off balance, he gains the advantage. I doubt the runecaster acted completely against his will."

Frustrated, Traedis shook her head. "You don't understand. He *was* angry at her for placing the rune on me. I know him well enough to be able to tell that. He would never consent to torture a family member. He tried to explain himself to me. I'd know if it were mere manipulation."

Elben shook his head. "If he'd had real concern for you, he would never have left the two of you alone. She may not have harmed you, she may not have—damaged you—but she tortured you without leaving a mark. I have trouble believing he couldn't have foreseen that."

Traedis shook her head again, more forcefully. "He didn't know that Rose could waken me. How could he? *I* didn't even know she could do that."

"Your uncle is no fool." Elben's voice was bitter. "He was one of the City's best assassins for years, then a Council member who controlled every single one of Tolin's spies. Perhaps he didn't know you would wake, but he knew you had some extraordinary abilities. He would have planned for the unexpected. He's known for that."

Traedis tried to think of an argument against Elben's words, but could find nothing to refute them. It did not mean she believed them, however. Though it was true that Uncle Cordelayne was intelligent, subtle, and a practiced manipulator, there was more to him than that. Traedis knew it with a certainty she could not convey to Elben. Perhaps Uncle Cordelayne had calculated the effect of his words with the coldness of a striking snake, but she could not quite believe it of him.

Elben pulled a leafy twig from behind her ear, twirling it in his fingers. "It's quite a fetching fashion," he teased. "I expect all the ladies in Tolin will adopt variations in the next year." It was quite clearly an effort to change the subject.

Traedis decided to let him. Her cheeks warming, she said, "Only if the ladies of Tolin develop a fondness for crawling under bushes. Otherwise I fear it will be a fashion which is over before it's begun."

Elben laughed lightly. He placed the sprig in the top buttonhole of his shirt like a lady's favor, and offered his arm again to Traedis. "Will the king of Tolin deign to honor me with her presence at dinner? I understand it is to be an outdoor feast, attended by all the finest people."

Traedis looked at her grubby arms. "I need a bath." Her skin felt gritty, and she itched. "And a change of clothing."

"If Lord Ymre hasn't thought of that already, I'm sure we can remind him," Elben said, smiling through his beard. "I intend to make your comfort my highest priority." He swept her an elaborate bow, the trace of a grin still on his face. "Though I still think you should keep the greenery."

"I'll consider it," Traedis told him, surprising herself with how lighthearted she had begun to feel in his company. "But only if you attend dinner in similar attire."

Elben picked up one of the twigs which had fallen from Traedis' hair, weaving it into his beard until the leaves peeked out at intervals like strange growths across his chin.

The fear, confusion, and pain of the last few weeks suddenly coalesced into half-hysterical laughter. Great hiccupping whoops emerged, and

Traedis found she could not stop. Instead, she plunked herself down on the grass and gave herself over to mirth.

"You doubt me?" Elben asked in a tone of mock disapproval. "We'll see which one of us dares to dress in this fashion come evening. I will not be cowed by simple propriety. Will you gainsay me, milady?"

Traedis was laughing too hard to answer.

Evening came soon. Ymre's people were happy to provide a hot bath and suitable clothing for Traedis. The simple dress she wore was dirty and torn, and disappeared while she immersed herself in the large tub located decorously amid four dense lilac hedges. After the glorious luxury of hot water and soap, she dragged herself from the tub onto moss softer than any weave the finest faldren carpet-makers could create.

She found a new dress draped over a tall silver mirror; it was a delicate gown of aelin silk the color of the gloaming, which boasted a hint of antique lace, and was surprisingly sturdy, given its appearance. It fit every contour of her body, flattering her slender form, and bringing out the vivid color of her hair and eyes. Traedis looked at her reflection with satisfaction, hoping that Elben would like it.

A brush lay wedged into the elbow of one of the bushes beside the mirror. Traedis took it and began the chore of untangling her unruly hair, still sopping wet and curled in all the wrong directions. She was gratified to see that the water falling on the dress did not stain the material; aelin silk was known for its practicality as well as its cost, and could even be washed.

Her hair dried somewhat as she brushed, and she shook excess water out of the brush's bristles. The air would dry the rest of it in time, hopefully before dinner. Looking to her left, Traedis saw a blue velvet ribbon laced onto a lilac twig next to a pair of dainty silk shoes. She was sure neither had been there a few moments before. Shrugging, she stepped into the shoes, then tied back her hair so that its wet length shed its moisture behind her instead of in front.

As soon as she finished, an aelin girl of thirteen or so stepped out of the bushes to lead her to dinner. Traedis was reasonably sure that the girl had not been there moments before either, but that did not feel strange. The land of Ymre was a magical place, and the commonplace rules of her own world did not apply.

Dinner was held in one of the white marble structures which dotted the landscape like columned growths. Torches lit the area, glinting off the gleaming marble like moonlight. No great feast was prepared, though Lord Ymre himself stretched out on the floor. Beside him, a long table held a number of covered dishes and was bordered by cushioned chairs. Low benches were occupied by mostly aelin diners, some of them disconcertingly less tangible from the corner of the eye than they were at full-on sight.

Elben sat in a chair, his long legs extended and crossed at the ankles. A horrified glee suffused Traedis as she realized that, despite a change of clothing, he still wore leaves woven into his beard as if they had taken root. She approached the diners, hiding the smirk on her face for the sake of courtesy.

He rose from his chair as she stepped onto the marble flooring, then bowed and offered the second seat to Traedis. Traedis gave a respectful bow to Lord Ymre, then turned to Elben, who waited to re-seat himself until she had settled into a comfortable position at the table. He picked up a sprig which sprouted a small fan of leaves and, leaning over, tucked it into the hair behind her ear. "You did say you would wear one if I would," he said, mischief shining in his eyes.

Mitheira would be appalled if she saw her, greenery in her hair, dining with one of the great Powers of the world. The thought pleased Traedis in a defiant sort of way; she sat straighter, determined to wear her leaves with the same flamboyant air as Elben.

Dinner consisted of several simple but delicious dishes. Goblets of plain, flawless crystal held a substance that looked like spring water with a sheen of iridescence. Though Lord Ymre did not eat with them, he kept them company as they dined, conversing with them in the comfortable way of a host pleased with his company. Traedis found herself relaxing further. Elben also seemed to be enjoying himself.

When they finished, aelenin appeared to remove the remains, leaving Traedis and Elben still seated. Traedis turned her chair to face Lord Ymre, and Elben followed suit.

The Hound sat up, regarding them with his fathomless eyes. "It is time to talk," he said.

Traedis sat up straighter, tension immediately settling back into her bones with a leaden thump. "Something needs to be done about my uncle's runecaster," she said.

Ymre nodded his shaggy head. "Something certainly needs to be done. When I created the art of writing, I did not foresee the possibility of runecasting." He yawned so all his teeth showed sharp and white in his large mouth. "I intended writing to augment memories, not to give magical power. Of course, it is the nature of mortal beings to discover new things. That's part of what makes you so delightful."

Elben leaned forward, his eyes sparkling. "*You* didn't foresee it? That if words had power, so could their written forms?"

Ymre nodded. "I am not a god. I do err. I may hope that each error brings me to a better understanding, but I cannot see all outcomes." He shook himself, his hair fanning out around him. "Even the aelenin die, and I did not want their knowledge to die with them, should any forget or not pass their lore to the next generations. Some things are too important to trust to memory's keeping."

Traedis licked her lips, trying to phrase her next question, Master Andov's explanation still in her mind. It had made more sense before she had seen Myssa, as alive and apparently real as any living woman. "How could Myssa make herself into a rune? I understand the principle, but how can words do that? I know what music can do, and how profound it is, but I couldn't magic myself into another woman with flowing blood and beating heart: with knowledge and understanding. How can anyone become—a *rûntazent*? How could she describe herself so fully that she looks and acts real?"

Ymre stretched out still farther, resting his head on his paws. "That's a fine question, but you're assuming much. Did you hear Myssa's heart beat? Did you see her shed blood? Most who succeed in becoming *rûntazents* try to create a form that cannot be hurt. She may look very like a woman, but that does not mean that the artistry of bones and sinew and veins or a living heartbeat are present in her."

Elben swallowed several times. "So she's thrown away the gifts of the gods in favor of recreating herself as a perfect being."

"Hardly perfect," said Ymre. He began to pace in a circle around the marble pavilion. "She never had the mind of a god, so her concept of a perfect creature is limited. In that limitation lies her weaknesses. She is built from glyphs on a page, animated by the woman she once was. Traedis, you must find those weaknesses from what knowledge I've given you of runecasting and the *quixil*. Because you are correct; the safety of your entire nation depends on defeating her. You cannot take your uncle without first dealing with her."

"But..." Elben's brows drew together. "How does Myssa not offend the gods? To turn one's back on their gifts for the sake of an artificial perfection and a lust for power? That seems to fall into the realm, not only of great evil, but of the truly *wrong*. Why do the gods allow it?"

"I do not speak for the gods," Ymre said wryly. "They allow some things to exist which they do not smile upon. Thanatomancy, for instance. It does not mean *rûntazents* have their blessings."

Myssa's very existence horrified Traedis; she shuddered. "She wrote in creativity and intelligence, certainly. Are you saying she left something out?"

"Mortals always will," Ymre said simply.

If it had been merely a matter of facing one magic with another, Traedis thought she might be able to find or chord an antidote to the runes. But Myssa wielded the same magic that Traedis herself employed, that of civilization and of art.

If runes were the distilled essence of written language, Traedis wondered if it would be as easy to dilute the effects of the runes as it was to water wine. That, tangled with the idea of dancing runes, tumbled through Traedis' mind. "Might it be possible to water runes down? Not in literal terms, but at least in metaphorical ones? Perhaps they could be expanded, using their own magic against them. I've already tried one approach which didn't work. I couldn't lever flat runes out of their planes and make them dance."

The Hound cocked his head and looked up at her with one great green-blue eye. "Both are interesting ideas, and neither are impossible. You will have to determine how, though. I have given you what guidance I may, and cannot act for you." He snapped at a passing dragonfly. "You have the makings of a runecaster. If you can defeat Myssa, I'd advise you to continue your studies. For some the power is too heady, but you are not such a one."

"I suppose I must accept your estimation," Traedis said. She scratched at her ear, wishing that Elben had not picked out such a ticklish twig for her to wear, but determined not to back out of the dare. She sighed, thinking of the tasks before her. "The sooner I work on it the better."

"You still forget," said Ymre with a doggy smile, "that Ymre's time bows to my desire. You have time to sleep and learn tomorrow what you need to know without losing time in the mortal world."

"Oh." Traedis felt more foolish than ever for having forgotten that fact yet again. "Yes, perhaps it would be better to begin tomorrow when I am better rested." She stifled a yawn, realizing how exhausted she was. Though Lord Ymre had cured the worst of the effects of three weeks spent asleep, he had not taken common weariness.

"I'm tired, too," Elben said with a smile. "I would be glad to be shown a bed, however uncomfortable. I have spent the last three weeks hunting for King Traedis night and day, and I am more than a little fatigued."

Lord Ymre twitched an ear, and an aelin boy with dark hair and a graceful stride emerged from the bushes just downhill. "King Traedis, Captain Tallforest," said the boy, "if you will follow me, I'll show you to your beds. They're not far."

"And not uncomfortable," added Ymre, a smile in his voice. He thumped one hind leg on the ground. "Sleep well. We will speak again in the morning. Until then, have such peace as the land of Ymre may provide."

The boy led them to separate bowers covered with deep moss and blanketed with sweet-smelling rushes. A nightgown hung from a wisteria vine; after the boy left, Traedis changed gratefully, and laying Rose beside her, curled up against her to fall asleep.

When Traedis opened her eyes, morning slanted through the trees, tracing leaf-patterns on Traedis' bed of moss. She sat up and stretched. For just a moment she wished to savor the feeling of being completely alone without danger or fear. She suspected it would be a long time before she could again feel such safety. She tucked the feeling into her heart, treasuring it, and promising herself to return here in her mind when the burden of kingship became too heavy.

She joined Elben and Lord Ymre for a simple breakfast of lavender biscuits and rose tea, served in earthenware dishes painted with violets. Unwilling to leave, Traedis brushed crumbs off her skirt and rose to face the Wise Hound.

"You have given me hospitality and more, and have been more generous than I deserve." Traedis' voice echoed the reluctance behind her words as she spoke to Lord Ymre under a trio of young willows. "But it's time to return home. Vandeyr is probably putting holes in the mortar with her daggers, and Ruth will worry. And I hate to force Lang to rule the City any longer than I already have." She quirked her mouth into a wry smile. "Though I expect he rules far better than do I."

Elben made a scoffing sound, though gently.

Ymre shot a measured look at Traedis and shook his head. "You undervalue yourself. The gods chose *you* to rule Tolin, and *they* do not err, despite what some of your citizens may believe. Your brother has great skill with people, but you have the courage to make the changes which Tolin must undergo if it is to remain a power in the world."

"Now you sound like Elben." Traedis looked at the knight. "He seems to think I am the best thing that's happened to Tolin in the entirety of its history."

"Perhaps not in all of history," Ymre conceded. "But Elben is a wise man. He does not feel as he does simply because he loves you."

Elben grinned. Traedis breathed out through her nose, trying not to feel too flustered.

She looked up to where the sun arced in the sky. It had not progressed beyond midmorning, but as time in Ymre marched to its lord's will, she was not sure how long the day had already lasted. Even knowing that her hours could be stretched into days, she felt a sense of urgency. "I need to go."

Ymre looked at her, seeming to consider her statement. "I understand. There is only so long you can put aside worry."

"Yes," Traedis agreed. "Too much time here would only make me more afraid to return." She curtseyed to Lord Ymre, though not too low; Ymre was one of the great Powers, but Traedis was a king in her own right, and need not abase herself before anyone.

"I'm ready to send the two of you back," said Ymre. "Now it is time to put your own skill and power to use."

"Please thank Dame Tanjarre for me," Traedis said.

"I will," Ymre promised. He shook himself from nose to tail, flinging off bits of twig and leaf, though nothing flew in Traedis' direction. "The thanks she is most likely to desire is for you to put your harp to work against evil."

"*That* I will continue to do," Traedis said somberly. She slung Rose over her back, thinking ruefully that she must commission a new case when she got back. The sheer enormity of her responsibilities hung over her like a bough which threatened to break. She looked around her, drinking in the land so that she could keep a piece of it in her heart when troubles overburdened her. The sun was bright, the sky clear, and the brilliance of the blossoms ornamented the greenery without overwhelming it. Even their scents, redolent with spring, kissed the air without cloying. A chorus of larks burst out from the trees. It could not have been more different from the Heart of Winter, yet both were ethereally beautiful.

For a moment, Elben melted into his fox form, letting his tongue loll from his mouth, and his brush stream in the breeze. Then he transformed back to his human self, reddish blond hair bound in a tidy tail at the nape of his neck, his Haven greens neat as if Elben had only just stepped into them.

He offered his arm to Traedis, who took it thankfully.

"Go through the trees," Ymre told them, pointing with his nose in the direction of a tall stand of birches which lined a plain footpath. "If you continue walking, you will arrive at the Star Cavern. I've told your sister where you will be; I expect she will be waiting to greet you."

"My thanks, Lord Ymre." Elben bowed politely without dislodging Traedis' arm. "I have been honored greatly to be allowed in your fair land."

"You have aided me in great need," Traedis added. "My own thanks are inadequate to repay the debt which I owe to you."

"You owe me no debt," Lord Ymre told her, wagging his tail happily. "You've taken charge of a problem I've long wished to see corrected. Any small aid that I am allowed to offer you is given willingly." He pointed again at the path. "Farewell, King Traedis."

Elben steered her toward the footpath. The silver birches waved slender branches over their heads as if bidding them farewell with words of light and wind and leaves. Traedis felt her step grow heavier.

Elben slowed his step to match hers. He did not comment, for which Traedis was grateful, but effaced himself as much as possible. Traedis could not help feeling he was giving her the choice of how to treat his presence and his continued interest.

The way darkened, and the trees faded to flickering shadows; she felt the path change from earth to stone as they trudged onward. Then the quivering light steadied and became the clear, cold light of stars. The way widened, and Traedis saw three walls of the Star Cavern. Elben beside her, she stepped into the room and cast a quick glance behind. There was nothing but a rough cavern wall covering the space they had come from. Traedis shivered a little; the walls were too close, and their rough texture reminded her of the rocky chamber where Uncle Cordelayne and Myssa had held her. She wrapped her arms around herself, swallowing against the sense of entrapment.

Vandeyr sat on one of the room's low couches; she jumped up immediately. Traedis blinked a few times to adjust her vision, and recognized Ruth on another seat. Both their forms were tense with apparent strain.

"Thank the gods!" Vandeyr said. You're back!"

"I've been discussing the rune problem with Ymre," Traedis said almost lightheartedly, trying to distract herself from the closeness of the cavern. She fixed her gaze firmly on her sister. "How long has it been?"

"About an hour since Ymre talked to us," Ruth said dryly.

"We've been worried sick," grunted Vandeyr, unable to conceal her obvious relief.

"You're not the only one," Traedis said. "Uncle Cordelayne told me he'd ambushed you, but not much else. Are *you* all right?"

Vandeyr scowled. "Fine, if you call it that to be rescued by my own guard and a smug Haven knight. Damn Uncle Cordelayne's scheming, plotting mind! That's not the way you treat an honorable enemy." She ground one heel hard into the stone of the floor. "He's going to answer for this one way or another."

Traedis' eyes opened wide. She had never heard Vandeyr speak of Uncle Cordelayne in this way. He was a bad enemy to have—but so was Vandeyr.

"It's early morning," Ruth said mildly. She kicked her legs against the edge of the couch. "Lord Ymre came at dawn to let us know you were safe. Before that it's been—"

"Twenty-one days," Traedis finished for her. She turned toward the door. "He told us. In Ymre, it's been about a day since I awoke."

"Let's get you out of here before anything," Ruth said. "You look like you expect the ceiling to collapse at any minute."

"Awoke?" asked Vandeyr, narrowing her eyes.

Traedis did not want to speak of that now. "Thank you, Ruth—you're right. I need out of here." She heard herself speak as if from a distance. "I also want to make sure everyone knows I'm back. Bad enough that I was a fool and let Uncle Cordelayne trick me, but my absence can't have been good for Tolin." Despite her sojourn in Ymre, she felt exhausted. All the cares and concerns of Tolin's rule settled back over her like a wool cloak in the hottest summer. At least, the land sensed her return, embracing and enfolding her with a frisson of joy, if a force without a mind could be said to feel joy.

As they exited the Star Cavern, Traedis could almost feel her sister's anger burning behind her. Traedis had seldom seen her so incensed.

She was just glad that it was not directed at her.

Chapter Twenty-Three
Truths

After Elben returned safely to Faldrohaven and Lang ceded his temporary authority, Traedis retreated to her chambers with a pot of tea, then settled in with Lang, Vandeyr, and Ruth to discuss what had happened on all sides.

She tried to ignore the feeling that she wanted Elben to be here, to watch her back, to cheer her with his effervescent playfulness. They had spent only a day together; how could she possibly miss him? Bad enough that her emotions were so raw, but to show such weakness was to court trouble. Certainly remaining separated was best for them both. Wasn't it?

Setting Rose on the floor, Traedis looked sharply at Vandeyr. "You first," she said. "Uncle Cordelayne told me you were unharmed and that you would wake up before your air ran out. What happened?"

Vandeyr scowled. "I received some information—filtered through my own network, no less—that there might be some mitigating circumstances to Uncle Cordelayne's actions. Specifically, that someone might have set a rune on him. I suppose I wanted to believe it, which is why I was so incautious." She turned her head and set her jaw before looking back at Traedis. "He knows me too cursed well. I went to meet with my source, who insisted on complete privacy." She snorted. "After all this time telling *you* to be careful, what do I do but jump headfirst into a snare a rabbit would laugh at? I feel pretty foolish, that's certain.

"I didn't throw out *all* caution. I arrived quietly and secretly, entered the meeting place, and saw myself across the room. I *almost* managed to dodge before the dart caught me, but Uncle Cordelayne is the best." She chuckled mirthlessly. "After that, all I remember is your pet knight and

Lieutenant Tethyn kneeling beside me and half a mountain of broken brick. It seems that Uncle Cordelayne walled me up in a cellar crawl space."

"I'm glad he didn't harm you." Traedis exhaled slowly, trying to regulate her agitation along with her breath. "When I realized you weren't you, I was terrified."

Vandeyr grunted.

"I'm no longer sure what Uncle Cordelayne will or won't do," Traedis said quietly.

Vandeyr slammed one hand down hard on the arm of her chair. "Kyaan take him, it's not honorable to use his knowledge of me against me like that! That's the way you treat contracts, not family. I think I'd prefer it if he *had* tried to kill me. At least I wouldn't have felt like some errant child being patted on the head, then locked in her room while the adults took care of important business." She breathed out evenly, then said more calmly, "I would never have expected this of him. I thought he had more respect for me than that."

Lang said quietly, "You should know by now that Cordelayne is willing to take liberties even with family, if he believes in his cause."

Vandeyr skewered him with a furious glare; Lang returned an impassive face.

"How did anyone find you?" asked Traedis.

"Tethyn tracked me down, with the help of your Haven fox. I gather he wouldn't take no for an answer." Vandeyr's brows drew together in annoyance. "They dug me out, cleared the poison from my system, and woke me up. Uncle Cordelayne left me a number of loose bricks, damn his conniving, patronizing heart. I could have scratched my way out whenever I'd wakened—which would have been at least another day, according to your dearly devoted Green."

Despite Vandeyr's outrage, it comforted Traedis to know that Uncle Cordelayne had left her sister an escape. She wanted to believe that he was still the honorable, if stern, uncle she loved.

"It was as obvious as a thunderclap what he'd done," Vandeyr added, her nails raking the chair's fabric like a lioness sharpening her claws. "But when we couldn't find you, we were worried. Was it your harp case he demolished? I assume that's what left the sawdust on the floor."

"Yes." Traedis tried to recall what had occurred; she clutched the arms of her own chair nearly as hard as her sister, relaxing consciously only to have her muscles stiffen again as soon as she loosed her concentration. "He was trying to destroy Rose, but she was too strong for them. They've probably learned why by now, because Myssa—" Traedis stopped, panic raking her gut. Fighting the tendency of her voice to wobble, she continued. "His runecaster was studying Rose. They might have determined that she woke me from a drugged sleep."

"What do you mean?" asked Vandeyr sharply. "You woke up while Uncle Cordelayne had you? What did he do?"

Traedis flinched from the memory. "Nothing important," she said quickly. "He put me to sleep again as soon as he found out I was conscious."

"What does 'nothing important' mean?" Vandeyr leaned forward and studied Traedis' expression. "Something happened, because you've got the look on your face that you get when you don't want to talk about something. That means you need to tell me."

Traedis grasped at the part she could tell without reliving the memory of the rune Myssa had placed upon her. "Uncle Cordelayne talked to me, briefly. He said that Tolin should not have a king; that it was the gods testing the City, and that he must resist it—something like that. I don't remember the exact words. I wasn't in any condition to listen carefully.”

“He would think that.” Vandeyr's gaze did not waver from Traedis' face. “What else?”

Temporizing, Traedis asked, “What makes you think there was anything else?”

Vandeyr frowned. “The way you're answering my question. If there weren't anything to tell, you'd say so.”

Vandeyr had been through a terrible ordeal herself; she deserved to know. Traedis tried not to think of her sister bricked into a wall, and what that would feel like.

Turning her thoughts with an effort, she haltingly described what Myssa had done to her. She swallowed, distancing herself from the words as much as possible. She could almost feel the shock of rising pain in her limbs, a phantom reminder of Myssa’s agonizing rune.

Ruth's sharp intake of breath made Traedis start. The brunaidhi woman's features were set and cold. “Your uncle sanctioned that?”

Vandeyr's frown deepened to a truly formidable scowl. “Was Uncle Cordelayne there?” Her tone was harsh with anger.

“Not when she laid the rune on me. He made her remove it when he found out.”

“But he left the two of you alone together.” Vandeyr's lips firmed into an angry line. “Uncle Cordelayne doesn't assume anything. He *must* have known there was a chance you would wake.”

Traedis felt her voice tremble. “I don't see how he could have. He doesn't know what Rose can do. Or at least, he didn't. I'm sure he thought I would sleep until he chose to wake me.”

Lang looked at her gravely. "He's quite capable of that sort of ruthlessness, Traedis. We all love him, but trusting him to that extent is folly."

Traedis' mind scattered into a thousand pieces, each contradicting the others. She could neither accept nor reconcile her uncle's actions, past and present. He was her mentor, jailer, torturer, and tutor. What would he be the next time they met?

"He wouldn't do that," she insisted, knowing full well that he would.

"Maybe." Vandeyr's tone was uncompromising. "But Uncle Cordelayne didn't get to be one of the City's top assassins by taking anything for granted." She snorted. "Listen to me—calling him 'Uncle Cordelayne' like his young, besotted niece. I should be saying 'Cordelayne' instead." She leaned forward, hands on her knees. "Trae, every time I say Uncle Cordelayne's name, you get this look on your face like a bird menaced by a snake." Her voice roughened. "But I plan to be a stormy eagle, and eagles *eat* snakes. He's not going to have everything his own way."

Traedis spent most of the day catching up with her duties and discovering what had happened during her absence. Though strictly speaking things were not in chaos, Lang's lack of the *falmyros* had proved to be a serious disadvantage. The land clamored for Traedis' attention. Minor earth tremors quivered under the surface; a creeping fungus was attacking the roots of trees; a minor rockfall had careened into a small house upslope of the walls.

Coming out of her land several hours after she had dipped into it, Traedis discovered that the last of the sunlight had long since disappeared behind the mountain peaks. She waited for her eyes to adjust to the dim, filtered moonlight, then lit a lamp before sitting down to read.

A knock sounded on the door that adjoined Vandeyr's room. "Trae? Can I come in?" Vandeyr's voice was husky, almost tentative.

"Of course," Traedis responded, her thoughts still filled with the land.

Vandeyr was not dressed in her livery, but uncharacteristically in her sleepwear, which consisted of a set of loose linen trousers, a short, buttoned jacket, and silk slippers on her feet. She walked to the window and looked out at the gardens, where the gibbous moon shone a cold, bleak light on seedheads and still-blooming flowers. Her back to Traedis, Vandeyr began to speak.

"When the *falmyros* fell on you, I didn't want you to be hurt or killed, which is why I stayed instead of going with Uncle Cordelayne like Daymet did. I *wanted* to be with them, and I saw you doing so many things I thought were foolish… but I'd committed myself, and knew I'd never forgive myself if you got killed because I wasn't here.

"I always thought Uncle Cordelayne would understand and respect that." She bit her knuckle, still gazing out the window. "That he would treat me as an honorable enemy, the way I'd treat him. I never thought he'd stoop to using his knowledge of me the way he did." She put both hands on the sill. "I thought you were completely misguided. I was wrong."

"You had every reason for thinking that." Traedis laid her book on the table. "Things were different for you. No one ever questioned your ability to take your place in the City, or expected you to fail before giving you a fair trial."

Vandeyr twisted to look at her. "*I* never expected you to fail. I expected you to succeed, and I was always so frustrated when you floundered in the simplest tasks the way you always did—" She stopped herself, perhaps recognizing the inconsistency in her claim.

Traedis laughed sadly. "You see? You expected me to fail, too. Do you realize that after I went to Kaelennar I didn't have trouble with any of the graces or skills that Mother tried to teach me? They didn't expect anything there, so I had nothing to live up to. Everything made so much more sense."

"If you could do that there," Vandeyr asked, "why couldn't you do it for us? For Mother? I had trouble believing some of the things you couldn't get right. Things as simple as buttering your bread the right way."

"Because everyone was watching me," Traedis replied acerbically. "The more I erred, the more everyone expected me to falter. After a while I couldn't do *anything* right." A memory surfaced: a spreading pool of cocoa on the table; Mitheira's cutting voice telling Traedis that she was clumsy and incompetent, that she could not even pour correctly.

"Was that why you ran away?" asked Vandeyr. "Because you didn't think you could do anything right?"

"I ran away," Traedis answered sharply, "because I wasn't sure I was going to survive to adulthood if I stayed."

Vandeyr whirled and stared at Traedis for a long time. When she finally spoke, her voice was cracking. "We were all worried. Do you remember Mauvri Goodrof?"

Traedis knew of the family—minor nobles—but did not remember the girl. "No."

"She was between us in age. Closer to mine than yours, I think." A thick line formed between Vandeyr's brows, and sweat beaded her forehead, despite the chill of the early autumn night. "She was a nice girl most of the time, sweet, accommodating, cultured, but she had terrible fits of anger. Occasionally in public, where it was quite a trial to her family."

She tucked an invisible strand of hair over her ear. "One day she just wasn't there. I asked Mother where she'd gone, and she told me Mauvri had 'gone to live with relatives in the country.' I didn't understand what she meant then, but I figured it out later."

Traedis felt a jolt in her chest, knowing what her sister was about to say.

"When you left, I wasn't sure what had happened to you, either. Mother told me you'd run away, and I asked if it was like Mauvri. She looked shocked, and told me that of *course* it wasn't." Vandeyr blinked, and Traedis was astonished to see her lips tremble for a moment. "I was frightened for you, Trae. Father was so angry. He wanted to go after you right away and bring you back. I'm still not sure why he changed his mind."

"He was probably angry that his marriage plans for me fell through." Traedis had meant to speak without heat, but an acidic bitterness crept into her tone without conscious intention. She twisted in her chair, suddenly uncomfortable. "After all, he should have gotten *something* out of his next-to-useless daughter."

Vandeyr's eyes widened. "You knew about that?"

"He told me." Traedis remembered vividly the last time she had seen her father; they had fought furiously. She had been planning her escape from Tolin, but it had been her father's words that had truly decided her.

"He said that he had a marriage in mind, someone who would 'overlook my flaws in exchange for an Atenel connection.'" Her speech came out clipped and precise in the same brittle tone her mother used when irate. She had no trouble recalling the words: they were burned into her mind, as were most of those she had exchanged with her father just before she fled the City. "He said if I drowned myself in a lake he wouldn't grieve."

Vandeyr stopped motionless. She spoke slowly, as if her words were thorns that she had to pick her way through. "Trae, I know you and Father never got along, but are you certain you didn't misunderstand him? That you didn't misremember his words?"

Traedis' own voice came out thick, too heavy for what it carried. "Believe me, Vandeyr, I didn't misunderstand or misremember. Those words, more than any others, are etched into my memory. He truly said that."

Vandeyr folded her arms, shaking her head. "I don't understand," she said, her voice trembling. "How could he?" Before Traedis could speak, she added, "No, I don't doubt you. I just don't understand. I know you didn't get along, but that is much more than a simple quarrel."

Traedis understood better than her sister. Vandeyr had been Linden Atenel's darling, his lovely daughter who could do nothing wrong. Traedis had been the one he did not want.

Vandeyr sat abruptly on the windowsill, as if her strength had given out. "Trae, I didn't know." A quiver shook her voice. She blinked a few times, and Traedis saw the faintest glimmer of tears behind crescent lids. "And what he said about your marriage—he said that, too?"

"Yes," Traedis told Vandeyr, her own voice flat. "He said that if he couldn't control me, he would find someone who could."

Vandeyr's face paled. "I thought Father didn't know what he was like. I didn't think he would have chained you to a man like Todroi if he had realized. I never thought he would do it deliberately."

"He knew." Linden intended for his daughter's husband to keep a firm hand on her; his reputation had been at stake. Then Vandeyr's words seeped into her mind. "I didn't know who it was. What was Todroi like?"

Vandeyr's voice had calmed now to a level, if soft, tone. Someone who knew her less well than Traedis might think her sister had thoroughly mastered her emotions. Traedis did not make that mistake.

"He was a beast," Vandeyr said almost as flatly as Traedis. "He was over sixty, and had been married before, had children. He married again a few months after you ran away. After that, his wife was seldom seen without some injury or another: she claimed she had caught her hand in a door, or tripped on the stairs, or bruised her face in a fall from her horse. It was the same with the children." She looked down. "The City demoted him some time later; he caused a terrible injury to one of his children, and no healing would take. Poor Cedar had been a promising assassin candidate before that. Afterwards—well, he learned to walk by himself again. But his face still looks a fright."

Ice enclosed Traedis' heart, colder than Winter. "I wondered if it would be someone like that."

"Mother was against it." Vandeyr shook her head yet again, as if trying to shake history into a pattern which made sense. "She said it would be too hard for you, marrying a man several times your age, and trying to run a household as well."

Traedis held her breath until Vandeyr finished, somehow convinced it would hold the impact of her words at bay. "Mother said that?" She had not thought her mother cared enough to stand up for her. In some ways, that realization hurt more than Mitheira's total indifference; if she could worry about such things, why had she not fought for Traedis when imprisonment threatened to crush her spirit and destroy her will?

"Yes." Vandeyr looked keenly at her sister. "They were both terribly worried about you, Mother and Father both. You weren't the only one who feared you wouldn't live if the Council looked closely into your behavior."

Traedis felt suddenly nauseated. "Mother, perhaps. But not Father. He was worried about how such a scandal would affect the Atenel name." By the time she finished pushing the words out, Traedis found herself nearly spitting in anger. That surprised her; she had not thought she still felt the bitterness so strongly.

Vandeyr shook her head. "You're wrong. Father cared. Don't you remember how he looked when you stepped on the skirt of the Hillfolk ambassador's wife?"

That memory stung as well. In front of the entire Council, Traedis had stumbled and stepped on the aelin silk skirt of an important dignitary. Such accidents had been known to destroy contracts. "Daymet tripped me," she said. "Deliberately. Just to shame me, like he always did."

A strange expression crossed Vandeyr's face. "You're joking," she said incredulously. Then she quickly continued, "No, I know you're not joking. But what would possess Daymet to do such a thing? He could have gotten you killed!"

"I don't think," Traedis said dryly, "that he meant me to trip over the ambassador's wife."

"It doesn't matter." Vandeyr's hands clenched into fists. "There is no excuse for that kind of behavior."

"I certainly don't remember Father's expression," Traedis added still in the dry tone which covered the pain she felt. "You hauled me out of the room by my elbow so fast I barely realized what happened."

Vandeyr's hands unclenched, then tightened again. "I was supposed to be looking after you." She dug her fingers onto the sill beside her. "They always made me look after you. I hated it. You were so much younger than

I—eight whole years—and I wanted to be accepted by the adults." She cleared her throat. "I—I resented you for it too. But I was terrified when that happened." She squeezed her lids together as if to shut out the memory. "Father turned absolutely white and told me to get you out of there. He, and Uncle Cordelayne, and Daymet too—he was just as worried as anyone— spent the rest of the evening trying to calm the ambassador and his wife. When I came back in, Uncle Cordelayne was having drinks with the ambassador, while Daymet poured the charm out like maple sap, flattering the ambassador's wife out of two decades." She slapped the sill beside her. "She was wearing aelin silk. It *washes*!"

The memory took hold of Traedis with breathtaking force. "Father confined me to my room for two entire weeks. He didn't even let me come out to eat."

Vandeyr stared at her. "Are you stupid? He was trying to keep you as far out of sight as he could, so that the Council would forget about what happened."

That had not occurred to Traedis. "He did care? Truly?"

"He cared." Vandeyr sighed. "I overheard him talking to Mother later that day—" She met Traedis' gaze and laughed without humor. "All right, I eavesdropped at the door. Anyway, Father was shouting at Mother about how she couldn't even control her own daughter, and how it was her duty to educate us. And Mother just kept saying, 'I know, Linden. I'm sorry. It will never happen again.' I didn't hear that tone in her voice again until the day you ran away."

"I didn't know." Traedis squeezed the words out of a throat which was suddenly too tight. "I never thought he loved me."

"He loved you." Vandeyr stretched out her arm, then lowered it awkwardly. "But you were always so difficult..." She stopped and took a deep breath. "He *said* you were difficult. I thought you meant to be. It was hard for all of us to live up to Father's expectations, you know. But he challenged us all to be our best. Maybe you didn't understand that."

"No," said Traedis. "It's you who don't understand." Her throat was still tight as she swallowed painfully around the constriction. "He didn't challenge me. He wanted me to fail. He questioned me about my studies until he caught me in an error—"

"He did that to all of us." Vandeyr sighed. "He wanted to find out the boundaries of our knowledge. When he discovered them, he would suggest how to go about filling in the gaps."

"Maybe to you," Traedis said sharply. "He simply punished me when I didn't know something. After a while I just started giving him nothing but wrong answers. We ended up in the same place, and it was a lot less painful not to have to go through the entire process."

Vandeyr made an exasperated noise. "If you started doing that, it's no wonder you made him angry. He really wasn't sure if you were that stupid, or whether you were just trying to be contrary."

"Will you *listen* to me?" Traedis smacked her hand down on the table next to her. Vandeyr straightened, and her eyes narrowed. Then the strain eased out of her back.

Traedis continued, "I am saying that Father did not behave the same way toward you as he did toward me. I'm not imagining being punished for lack of knowledge, nor ignoring some careful attempt on Father's part to teach me. Between Father and Master Celdon, it's surprising that I was able to learn how to write my own name."

"You're obviously not stupid, or you wouldn't have been accepted to

Kaelennar's bardic college." Vandeyr shifted uneasily. "Perhaps Father did treat you differently. I don't know. He seemed to have less patience where you were concerned. But what did Master Celdon have to do with things? I didn't like him either, but he was a good teacher."

"Maybe to you." Traedis thought of a book coming down hard on her wrist; a slap stinging the side of her face; the choking darkness of the hall closet. She closed her eyes and ran through a pair of breathing exercises that were meant to help her singing, but which sometimes aided her with memories as well. The dark closet tangled in her thoughts with the four years she had spent in prison, and especially the terrible incarceration of Toledru under Tolin's bedrock. A black mist passed briefly over her vision, and she found herself shaking.

"Trae?" Vandeyr's voice seemed to come from far away. "Trae!"

Slowly, Traedis re-anchored herself to the present: cool air blew across her face; her hands clutched the chair's bony arms; her heart beat in her chest, hammering with unexpected force. With small details she wove the world back together, reminding herself that she was here, in her room, and nowhere else. The curtains over the window were still pale blue, and Vandeyr sat across from her, an alarmed expression on her face. Traedis smiled weakly, trying to pretend to both of them that she was fine.

Vandeyr's eyes narrowed. "I'm not such a fool as to think you'd react that way if everything had been as I remember it. Maybe you'd better tell me everything."

"There's a lot of it," Traedis said, still feeling a great distance between the words in her mind and the lips and tongue which had to shape them.

"I've got nothing better to do." Vandeyr shrugged. "Go ahead."

"Very well." Traedis reached a hand up to smooth her hair, feeling much like the young hoyden her mother always claimed her to be. "I'll tell you."

Traedis began the tale of her childhood: her father's tyranny; her tutor's abuse; Mitheira's constant belittlement; the daily torments and occasional beatings by Daymet, Otenemar, and Vandeyr herself; Uncle Cordelayne's supreme betrayal. "He promised me he would keep my confidences," Traedis said quietly, her shattered feelings as brittle as they had been when she was a child. "Then he took them to Father. I haven't trusted him since."

Vandeyr listened without comment, though her lips were tight and her muscles tense. When Traedis finally stopped speaking, Vandeyr scuffed one foot against the wall. It was a long time before she answered. "Trae, believe me, I didn't know how things were for you. I knew Daymet and Otenemar teased you—I knew *I* teased you—but I never did anything like dangle you out a window! Is Otenemar's head made entirely of wood? He could have killed you!"

"I think he figured that out," Traedis said, weak laughter rising to her lips. "He was terrified when he slipped, and made me promise not to tell anyone. Seeing him that afraid almost made up for the whole thing."

"I don't know what to say." Vandeyr slid off the sill and paced back and forth, her hands clasped behind her. "I don't understand why Father would behave that way. He said you were stupid, and he worried about what would happen to you if you couldn't do even the most elementary things right." She kicked the floorboards. "He was scared for you, he truly was. Maybe he thought being hard on you was the only way to keep you safe. Maybe he thought that since Uncle Cordelayne was investigated for improper conduct as a youth, it would happen to you as well."

For a moment, the words failed to register among the thicket of memories that tangled Traedis' already full mind. Then the echo rebounded in her consciousness, and she sat up straight. "Uncle Cordelayne was *what*?"

"Investigated." Vandeyr stopped abruptly. "Of course. You didn't know that either."

"I… no." Traedis grasped for meaning among her chaotic thoughts. "Why? How old was he?"

"Twelve, thirteen… something like that." Vandeyr walked to the wall and leaned against it. "I understood Grandfather and Father couldn't control him. I don't know too much about it, except that someone managed to bring him around and turn his skills toward the benefit of the City. But it frightened Father, and he was harsher on all of us because of it."

This made sense, though it excused neither of them in Traedis' mind. It did not make anything easier.

"I have to say this for you." Vandeyr resumed her pacing, her energy like a tiger's and possibly more deadly. "There's no more fear for the children. I never liked that aspect of the City, and I never really saw a good reason for it. Children shouldn't be afraid to ask questions, and they shouldn't have to fear for their lives if they do." She stopped again and turned to face Traedis. "Trae, I know Father was *very* hard on you, but is it possible that he didn't know about what our tutor was doing? Master Celdon never locked *me* in a closet, and he was always strictly fair, even if he tended toward the harsh. But if Father didn't know—"

"*He knew!*" Traedis said, the bitterness rising again. "He mentioned it at least once. He said, 'if you don't learn to behave properly, I'll do more than lock you in a closet…'" She trailed off as her eyes began to sting ferociously.

"That can't be right." Vandeyr's voice softened. "No, I believe you, Trae. After listening to Mother at her speech, how she talked about you, I can't doubt it. I just don't understand why Father would allow anyone to behave like that toward his own daughter. And I'm kicking myself because I didn't notice."

Traedis reached out to touch one of Rose's leaves. "Master Celdon was a brute. But so were Daymet and Otenemar."

"And sometimes me." Vandeyr frowned. "I'm sorry, Trae."

"It was so easy in Kaelennar," Traedis said. "I could earn my place there without expectations. I loved it there, Vandeyr. It was home to me in a way the City has never been. And I had friends, real ones, who stood by me even when they discovered who I was and where I came from."

"And you brought Ruth home with you," said Vandeyr. "I hate to say it, but she's been a better friend to you than I have."

Traedis opened her mouth to protest, but Vandeyr spoke again, quickly. "Don't deny it. I know I've complained about everything you've done. I understand it a little better now." She stopped pacing and stared at Traedis. "This doesn't mean I'm not going to argue with you anymore, though."

"I didn't think it did," Traedis responded, with the beginnings of a smile pulling at the corners of her mouth.

"Good. Because you're still doing everything wrong, and someone needs to tell you." But the mildness of Vandeyr's tone belied her words.

"Of course I am." Traedis felt suddenly light, as if she had been shouldering a load that was now shared by another.

"Goodnight, then." Vandeyr stalked toward the door, her back almost as expressive as her face.

"Goodnight," Traedis returned, and leaned back in the chair, her mind in chaos.

Midmorning of the next day brought the return of Master Rook. Traedis received him in her office, while Vandeyr stood guard and Ruth took her place in the corner.

The shapeshifter looked, if anything, a bit thinner, and one long, parallel scratch ran down his cheek.

At Traedis' glance, he gave her a rueful smile. "I'm embarrassed to say I was caught by a flock of persistent starlings. None of Lord Atenel's people touched me."

"Report," Vandeyr said briskly. "Were you successful? Did you identify anyone you knew? And how did the rebels respond?"

His lips curved. "They took the note without seeing me. I did recognize several people. Lord Sedorin does indeed lead them, and from your description, Myssa is the young woman wandering around in the snow without a stitch of clothing. I saw Braaval, Walggis the swordsmith, and two others I've seen before, though I'm not certain of their names." He paused, his seamed face an odd striping of light and darkness. "The results of the note were rather dramatic. Lord Sedorin immediately ordered the torches to be snuffed, and they packed their gear."

He paused again, looking thoughtful. "During the activity, something odd happened. Myssa was inside, shouting, when the floor of the cave shook, knocking her down and tilting toward the entrance. She started to slide. No one else was affected. She wrote some symbols in the air, and everything subsided."

"That is unusual." Traedis wondered if the cave itself had tried to turn against the rebels. It was not the strangest thing she had ever heard of, but it was strange.

"Did they do anything else?" Vandeyr cocked her head as if trying to listen to the man's thoughts. "You did wait to see if they actually left, didn't you?"

Rook nodded. "Lord Sedorin and Myssa had quite a shouting match—I caught more than a few words. I could have heard them halfway down the mountain. Myssa didn't want them to leave. Lord Sedorin sounded angry and suspicious, both of Myssa and Lord Atenel. Finally Myssa screamed something at them and stalked away from the cave. I didn't follow her since she'd left the main group."

"And?" Vandeyr said, tersely, but not impatiently. Traedis knew her sister was sifting through every grain of information in order to put the picture together.

"They left." Rook scratched the side of his nose. "Lord Sedorin made an offering to Meda—a glass bowl of sugar and some white wine. They put it inside the mouth of the cave before leaving. I followed them just far enough to see they were heading south. That's when I flew back."

"You've done a fine job." Vandeyr gave Rook a long, measuring stare. "Go to Lieutenant Tethyn for a detailed report, and she'll tell you where to pick up your pay."

Master Rook bowed to Traedis. "Your Majesty." He nodded to Vandeyr. "Captain Atenel." Turning, he exited the room, shutting the door behind so quietly Traedis could barely hear it latch. She raised her eyebrows.

"He's good," Vandeyr said. "Tethyn will go over the details with him and if there is anything else significant, she'll note it. If so, I'll let you know immediately."

"Thank you," said Traedis. She shook her head. "I wish I knew what Myssa was planning."

"So do I." Vandeyr's lips tightened. "I'm more worried about her than about Lord Sedorin's entire troop." She shook her head. "We'll find out soon enough, I have no doubt."

Traedis shuddered, remembering Myssa's viciousness and cruelty. "I hope we can stomach the answer."

A short time later, Traedis sat alone in her sitting room, stirring a sludge of steaming coffee. Next to it sat the ruby from Kenrydh's crown, shining in the reflected light like a dull ember. She put down the spoon and watched the coffee grounds settle to the bottom of her cup.

Taking a quick sip to fortify herself, she picked up the gem and cupped it in her hand, concentrating on Kenrydh. Moments later, his red-misted face appeared, a laugh still on his lips. "King Traedis. Can you give me a few moments?"

"Of course," Traedis said, and Kenrydh's image vanished.

She knew that catching him at an opportune time was chancy, and had no worries that she was imposing upon him. Kenrydh was more than capable of managing his own affairs. Instead, Traedis took some more sips of coffee while she waited. Shortly after, Traedis felt the searching mind of Telardur's king. She gazed into the ruby and completed the connection between them.

"King Traedis." Kenrydh smiled. "May I help you with something?"

"Not exactly." Traedis gave a short, nervous laugh. The last time she had neglected to tell him what Uncle Cordelayne's people were doing in Telardur he had been understandably angry. "I have some news about the Tolin rebels which also concerns you."

"Oh?" Kenrydh's eyebrows peaked. "They're in my lands, then?"

"Some of them are headed there." Traedis took a deep, steadying breath, and launched into a comprehensive explanation of where she had found Lord Sedorin's people and what she had done to dislodge them from the sacred ice cave. Kenrydh's expression darkened as she spoke, and only Traedis' bardic training kept the shake from her voice.

"This ice cave, where exactly is it?" A distant and regal attitude settled over Kenrydh like a cloak. "I need to be sure that this does not stir up Thane Darg. His mind is more measured than his father's was, but I want to avoid any extreme actions on the part of the n'korreld."

Traedis nodded. "In the southern reaches of the Kurtish Mountains, just over the border into your lands. It lies against the slope of a high peak, tucked against a permanent snowpack. There, the peak plunges sharply from its apex, falling in an almost vertical line."

Kenrydh stroked his beard. A pucker formed between his brows. "I wonder..." he murmured, as if speaking to himself. Then he met Traedis' gaze, concern in his expression. "I believe I know the region you mentioned. Especially since something strange happened in that area of the Kurtish Mountains earlier today."

"What happened?" A chill slithered over Traedis' spine.

"An anomaly," Kenrydh told her. "Something not part of the normal order." His lips tightened. "Most of Telardur's quakes are heralded by a trembling deep in the ground. Tolin has quakes—you've sensed these, haven't you?"

Traedis nodded.

Kenrydh continued, "I notice these before they happen, which gives me time to mitigate the damage. But this..." He shook his head. "There was a quake in the Kurtish Mountains. Very small in area, but disproportionately strong. I can only describe it as a slope shaking itself like a dog shedding water. I noticed nothing beforehand. I'd already decided to investigate it, but your news makes more sense out of this occurrence."

Traedis pushed hair back from her forehead. "Myssa?"

"I suspect so." Kenrydh gave her a direct look. "We must find that creature. She is dangerous, powerful, and a serious threat to all of us."

Traedis took a deep breath. "I'll continue to ask here. Someone may know something, though they're unlikely to talk to my people. Still, it's worth trying. Someone may have been disenchanted by my uncle's behavior. It doesn't sound as if his own allies are entirely enamored of him."

"Assuming they're alive." Kenrydh shook his head. "Wolves fall out when prey is scarce." It was an old saying, but he said the words with a gravity that made it sound like new wisdom. "I'll set my own people on the question, as well as asking my *falmyros*."

"Thank you." Traedis felt a wash of gratitude that Kenrydh was helping her, rather than simply crushing Tolin with overwhelming military might. He had proven a true friend as well as an ally.

"The good in this world must aid each other. Thank you for what you have done to make Tolin a place of decency."

Before Traedis could respond, Kenrydh's image winked out like a closing eye.

A dispatch from Kenrydh came the next day as Traedis sat in her dressing gown and sipped her morning coffee. He had located the source of the tremor; an entire mountain slope had collapsed a few leagues from the ice cave. The rock had fallen in an unnatural pattern directly on top of Lord Sedorin's small band of rebels, leaving all of them dead.

Kenrydh planned to ship the bodies back to Tolin. Lord Sedorin's family would undoubtedly want a large, public funeral. Traedis felt privately relieved that the former councilman had met his end at another's hands; were he still alive, she would be obligated to turn him over to Kenrydh for judgment, which at this point would be more politically damaging than her initial actions upon receiving the kingship.

As Traedis was getting dressed for court, Vandeyr entered, every line of her body expressing anger and disapproval. She threw an opened letter down on the table Traedis had just vacated. "Take a look at this."

Vandeyr did not usually open Traedis' letters. Lacing up her dress, Traedis went warily over to the table. "Who is it from?" Then she saw the elegant, flowing script, almost as fair a hand as Elben's, and knew who had sent it. "Daymet. Why is he writing to me?" She felt suddenly nauseated.

The note inside was brief. *Traedis, there is something you must know, and without Cordelayne's knowledge. I am sending an emissary to you; you may speak with her and determine, if you will, whether you believe her words. Her name is Aris, and she is my bonded ciriin. Expect her at noon tomorrow. She will come by way of the palace gate. Do not invite any not of Tolin to this meeting, or I will withdraw my offer.*

It was signed simply *D.*

As soon as Traedis laid the letter down, Vandeyr said, "You are not going to meet with this ciriin. Under no circumstances. Not if I have to hogtie you."

Traedis' emotions agreed with her sister, but she could not rule simply by emotion. "I didn't know Daymet had a bonded ciriin." Occasionally, a ciriin would become so attached to another's emotions that they would bond; their loyalty was unquestionable and unbreakable. As nearly as anyone could determine, such a bond lasted for life. "That means she won't betray him or tell us something he doesn't want her to say. I need to know what is so important that Daymet has to go to these lengths to contact me."

Vandeyr sat heavily down in a chair and placed her hands on her thighs. "At least I know how he got the letter to you; he slipped it into a rider's parcel of mail from Telardur." Her eyebrows made an angry vee. "It's a trap, obviously. Do you think he'd really go behind Uncle Cordelayne's back? They want you to think the two of them fallen out. Don't be fooled. There's the stench of treachery in every word." She glared at Traedis.

Traedis thought it likely Vandeyr was right. But what if she were not? Traedis knew she must find out what Daymet's ciriin had to say; it might give them a clue to Daymet's location, or perhaps his future actions. "I think it's worth doing."

Vandeyr straightened her spine. "Daymet's been a schemer from the cradle. I don't want you to accede to this. I also know you better than to think I can actually hogtie you without that cursed harp interfering."

Firming herself for an argument, Traedis said, "I will see her. And I will decide what I think about her message." Vandeyr opened her mouth to speak, but Traedis cut her off. "Vandeyr, I *must* make my own decisions. I know it's not safe. I know it's probably foolhardy. But this is a chance to see into Daymet's mind, and I can't pass it up."

"Not even after what Uncle Cordelayne did to us?" Vandeyr's gaze grew furious.

Traedis pushed back rising feelings of helplessness and shame. "Even so," she said quietly.

"Very well." Vandeyr stood and marched to the door. "I'll do my best to make sure you don't get caught in another of our family's traps. Since you seem determined to jump headfirst into their snares." She flung open the door, stepped through, and slammed it behind her.

Traedis sat down shakily, and poured herself another cup of coffee.

Chapter Twenty-Five
Aris

In preparation for Aris' visit, Vandeyr tightened security within the palace, doubling the guard and insisting that magical defenses be renewed anywhere that had been uninspected for more than six months. She even had masons and carpenters come to inspect the stability of doors, windows, and chimneys. Finally, she went to speak with Captain Dorrell of the City Guard. Traedis felt exhausted from merely hearing reports about her sister's whirlwind activity.

Traedis waited for Aris in an audience chamber which could be secured magically if danger threatened. She would have felt better with Ruth, but Daymet had been clear: no outsiders.

Despite the room's safeguards, it was fully arranged with three elegant chairs upholstered in tasteful plum and lavender. A scrollwork maplewood table held fluted goblets and teacakes. The only drawback in Traedis' mind was the room's lack of windows, a precaution Vandeyr had insisted upon. It made the space feel smaller, tighter. Traedis reached down to tap Rose's frame, her heart racing.

Tagg was overseeing the palace security, so another mage, Master Yann, took over the duty of supplying a truth spell. He was a dark-skinned man with tight, corkscrew hair that he wore in three plaits; a quilted coat; and a warm smile. Traedis might have appointed him to the household if he had not been more dedicated to the cause of making sure the poorer sections of Tolin were served with an ample supply of mage's power. As it stood, she was just glad to have an ally here who would not throw a knife past her head.

Four guards, headed by Lieutenant Tethyn, stood watch inside the room, and two outside; Vandeyr was unwilling to make do with less. Vandeyr herself was absent, intent on monitoring Aris' presence from the instant she set foot in Tolin until the moment she left.

Precisely on the hour, the door opened, and Aris entered, closely followed by Vandeyr. Aris had taken the form of an enormous, scaled wolf. Traedis assessed the creature as she neared the throne. This was not the same ciriin who had accosted them at the palace gates; Aris was much larger. Despite her size, she was whipcord lean and moved with a hunter's grace. Her ebony skin was indeed hairless, but boasted scales from her sharp ears to the tip of her tail. Her large eyes shone the color of deep twilight blue, with no white or pupil to soften their emptiness.

Traedis quivered with an instinctive reaction to the ciriin's stark predatory movements. She had never felt this way around Khardys, the only one of their kind whom she knew well, and whom she counted as a friend. This woman in wolf's form radiated both danger and power.

The wolf dipped a graceful, front-pawed bow, but looked steadily at Traedis' face, her stare unwavering. "Greetings, King Traedis," she said in a husky but tuneful voice. "My name is Aris, and I am your brother Lord Daymet's bonded ciriin." She sat on her haunches across the table from Traedis, apparently determined to ignore Traedis' hospitality.

Gooseflesh rose on Traedis' arms; the air felt full of lightning. Daymet would like possessing a bonded ciriin. He would enjoy controlling something so dangerous and unpredictable.

Aris' intent gaze continued to rest on Traedis' face as she sat, refusing to take woman's shape. Traedis felt the stare like an assault; it intimidated her, though she was determined not to show weakness. Aris smiled, showing a row of very sharp teeth.

Master Yann bowed his head in respect. "Mistress Aris."

Aris nodded and licked her lips.

"Now that we are all here," continued Yann, "I will call truth upon this room, so no falsehoods may be spoken here." He let out a breath, which seemed to linger like a trace of smoke on the wind before dissipating. Magic thundered into the room, a rush of air scented with pine. It settled in her chest and throat, keeping lies unspoken.

"Greetings, Mistress Aris," Traedis said, her voice steadier than she felt. "You have gone to a good deal of trouble to speak with me on my brother's behalf. What does he need to say to me that is worth risking you?"

Aris remained seated. "It is in Lord Daymet's mind to seek a limited alliance with you and with Tolin." Her voice hardened. "Neither of us are happy with the walking rune called Myssa, and we wish to be rid of her." She slowly turned her head around the room, bringing her blank gaze back to Traedis before she spoke again. "Lord Daymet has not sent me here to betray Councilman Atenel. The Councilman's followers are loyal, and we adhere to his cause. Lord Daymet will put it before our lives, if necessary." A small wolf's smile played at her lips. "You are not fit to rule Tolin, after all."

Traedis glanced away uncomfortably; Aris' use of Uncle Cordelayne's governmental title was calculated to make a point. "Very well. You don't intend to betray Cordelayne. I wouldn't expect it of you. But Myssa?" She stared straight back at Aris, remembering that she must not let herself be cowed. "What is your proposal?"

Aris's voice was cold. "Myssa is an abomination. She is no woman at all, but a rune in human form." She inched her head forward. "Should she slip Councilman Atenel's leash, she would be a danger to all of us. We don't want that to happen.”

“I know she’s extremely dangerous,” Traedis replied, trying to sit like her mother, back straight, chin firm. “But do you really think Cordelayne will lose control of her?” Her uncle was used to judging people accurately. Of course, Myssa was not a person; she was a rune. But surely Uncle Cordelayne had taken that into consideration.

“It’s possible,” Aris said, her gaze boring into Traedis’ own. “If it does happen, we are not certain anyone can stop her from doing what she chooses. Myssa is vindictive. She might come after you. She might go after Councilman Atenel.” Her voice carried the hint of a snigger.

Aris seemed to relish playing with them. Even though Traedis had expected as much, it was hard to listen to all the undertones of meaning, meant to slice and carve the listener to the core. It was one of the things she hated most about Tolin, and Aris almost certainly knew it.

Breath caught in her throat, leaving a jagged edge on her words. “I know you cannot speak falsely, but why does my brother think I’ll listen? He has used trickery in his dealings before.” She stared into Aris’ eyes, unnerved by not knowing where the ciriin’s gaze was actually focused.

Aris opened her mouth in a wolf’s smile. “Lord Daymet thought you might ask that question.” She licked her lips with a black tongue, showing her teeth again and gave a quick, harsh laugh. “Let me tell you about you and your brother. When you were eleven, you tore your new dress on the table’s edge at dinner, for which your father punished you. What he did not know was that Lord Daymet had caught your skirt as you stood, and hooked it on the table’s edge so that you would be embarrassed before your father.”

A quick inhalation behind Traedis told her that Vandeyr remembered the incident. For herself, Traedis had tried to forget, despite the acute shame of the memory. Now it rushed back to her. She had loved that dress, amber silk trimmed with creamy lace. She had stood hastily when Father dismissed them from the table, had felt the tug at her skirt the moment before she rounded the table's corner, but she had been moving too quickly to stop. Daymet's amused gaze had watched her as she felt the lace rip from the silk, tearing a gap large enough to put her fist through.

She felt heat rise to her cheeks, not only because of the memory, but also because Aris could likely tell how deeply the recollection hurt.

The rational part of her mind told her that Aris was trying to bait her into carelessness. "That story might cast a poor light on Daymet," Traedis said slowly. "Uncle Cordelayne didn't know what happened any more than Father did."

Aris sighed in an exaggerated fashion that seemed to mock Traedis' concerns. "Do you plan to tell him? I have another memory to offer you. You were twelve. Lord Daymet found you in the scullery when the kitchen staff was gone for the night. You hid behind a shelf of freshly scrubbed pots, and refused to give him an account of why you were skulking where you had no business. To teach you better, he took you by the arm, and scoured your face with the dirty dishwater left by the servants. He told you that your face could not be filthier after he finished than it had been before he began."

Traedis recalled that incident as well. Daymet had been at his nastiest that day, which was why she had hidden in the scullery to begin with. It was very like him to remind her of private shames, rather than less painful remembrances. She lifted her gaze to stare at Aris, challenging the ciriin to ridicule Traedis' experiences.

Aris wisely stayed silent this time.

Traedis schooled her features to immobility. "Enough! Instead of trying to shame me, tell me what you want from me."

Aris's ears flattened, and her eyes narrowed. "We have some information which might aid you against Myssa, if you're willing to work with us. If you say no, we will manage without you. But it would be far easier if you say yes."

Traedis shook her head, still unsure what Aris' true motive was. To cover her confusion, she picked up her goblet and looked at her reflection in the curved crystal. It showed her a skewed Traedis, simultaneously crumpled and stretched.

"It's not information I need," she said, her voice sounding loud in her own ears. "I need Myssa's rune. Is it written down anywhere?"

Aris cocked her head thoughtfully, still scrutinizing Traedis' face. Then she said, "It's not written; Myssa seems to be able to shape runes in the air, without pen and ink. However, I have seen part of her rune, the part that involves emotion. It's strong, powerful, and central to the creature she has become." Her muzzle relaxed into a full-toothed smile. "When inscribed in the dirt, it smooths out in moments. Written on parchment, it browns and shrivels. I think it's the part that fuels her desire for power. If you were able to unmake that piece, it might hamstring her." She edged forward again. "If you agree to a truce, I am prepared to show you that part of her rune."

A weight lay in the pit of Traedis' stomach. Something seemed wrong, reasonable as Aris sounded, though she could not fathom what extra advantage she could gain by trading Myssa's rune. But with Daymet—and she knew Daymet had crafted Aris' words—there were certain to be hidden ramifications.

She could not rule out the possibility that Aris herself was influenced by a rune, either concealed or beyond Traedis' power to perceive. That was one of the limitations to the god's truth; it could not distinguish between absolute fact and moral certainty. In that case, Myssa could be the one puppeting the ciriin, and Uncle Cordelayne in turn held the runecaster's strings. She looked Aris over for a *quixil* tail, but could find none.

Silence stretched as Traedis tried to think of useful questions that might help her discern what Daymet was truly offering. All that came to mind was a picture of Myssa creating the landslide that had killed Lord Sedorin and his people. The image was less than comforting.

The initial shock that had suffused her when Aris had first arrived was fading, leaving a sick weakness in its place. She knew she must give the ciriin some answer, but her thoughts would do nothing but cycle, returning to the first questions like the *quixil's* endless loop.

Only time could help her sort through the tangle. Aris' intense gaze was intimidating her, though the ciriin sat in seeming patience, awaiting her response. Traedis swallowed and decided to play for time. That strategy had worked before.

"I think," she said slowly, "that I need to consider your offer. Can you give me time to deliberate and speak with my counselors?"

Aris bowed again. "I will wait as long as you wish, Lord Traedis. Lord Daymet was most explicit on that point."

"Very well. Captain Atenel, will you please have your guards escort Mistress Aris to a suitable chamber?"

Vandeyr jerked her head and two guards nodded, showing no trace of their earlier uncertainty, but fell in before and behind the unnerving ciriin woman. Realizing that her hospitality was incomplete, as Aris had not been able to eat what was provided, Traedis added, "And call for someone to give Mistress Aris some refreshment." Traedis suddenly realized how little she knew about ciriin. "What would you like, Mistress Aris?"

Aris let her tongue loll while showing her long teeth again. "A sheep would be sufficient, Your Majesty. A live one." She chuckled in a way not designed to make any of them feel at ease.

Traedis simply stared for a moment, trying to parse the words. Then, steeling herself against uncertainty, she said, "Get Mistress Aris a sheep."

Aris chuckled again, letting the pair of guards escort her. Traedis watched as they left the room and moved out of sight. Traedis sent Master Yann out of the room, wanting no one privy to her conversation who did not need to be there. She would call him back when the summoned Aris again.

As soon as the door shut, Vandeyr cleared her throat and turned to face Traedis. "Gods," she said. "Did Daymet really do those things? That selfish, honey-tongued pig!" Traedis could see that Vandeyr was working herself into a temper; she was glad it was aimed at someone else. Still, though Vandeyr's daggers never missed their mark, occasionally her words skewered an unintended target.

She blinked a film of moisture from her eyes. "No one ever believed me about Daymet. Especially not Mother."

Vandeyr made a dismissive motion with one hand. "Well, Mother. What do you expect? Daymet's her precious darling. But when you were eleven, he was—let's see—twenty-five? He had no business acting like a child himself." She grimaced. "I remember how he could be. There was one time when Father complimented my grasp of the northern hill tongue right after I finished writing a treatise for Master Celdon. The treatise disappeared, and Daymet came by my room with the biggest smirk on his face, asking me about it. I knew I wasn't going to convince anyone he'd taken it, and I ended up staying awake all night redoing it. Not nearly as well, either. But we're only six years apart, and he and I got along most of the time."

Sighing, Traedis leaned back and ran a distracted hand through her hair, dislodging a copper hairpin. "Shouldn't I give him a chance? Daymet's not a simple man. You know that. Maybe he really does want an alliance. I can't imagine him being comfortable with Myssa." She smiled tightly. "I can't imagine anyone being comfortable with Myssa."

"You've already given him a chance," Vandeyr said flatly. She folded her arms and glared at Traedis. "He took that chance all the way to Uncle Cordelayne, leaving the country he professes to love. Just because he's our brother doesn't mean he's not a belly slithering, poisonous, deceitful snake."

Traedis raised one eyebrow mildly. "Whatever you wish, Your Majesty."

Vandeyr had the grace to look a little embarrassed. "All right, I know who rules Tolin. But when you're about to do something foolish, how do you expect me to act? Daymet is devious, and there's nothing good about this proposition." She shook her head furiously. "It sounds like a trap to me. Aris isn't being straightforward when she speaks of our brother. She can't lie outright, but there's something not quite honest in her demeanor. I also think she's extremely dangerous."

Traedis considered the words. They made sense, and Traedis knew she would do well to listen. She had no reason to trust Daymet. But family was family, and if there were any chance of winning Daymet back, it was worth the effort. She did not think he would harm her. "Maybe I could meet with him if I'm very careful—"

Vandeyr's hand moved, and a dagger *thunked* into the wood of a supporting beam a few arm's lengths away. "You never listen, do you? And then you expect me to keep you out of danger. Kyaan above, does someone need to lock you in a room until you see sense?"

Traedis inhaled sharply: she breathed out slowly enough to wrestle with an angry response. "It's been tried," she said, very quietly. Vandeyr's thoughtless words brought with them memories of her years in prison that stung as much as anything her sister could have said to hurt her deliberately.

Vandeyr stopped in mid-motion. Two red spots appeared on her cheeks: unusual, given her normally trained control over physical responses. Her voice lowered, and her words slowed. "I didn't mean that." Carefully, as gently as a feather, she touched Traedis' arm. "You just madden me sometimes."

Traedis stared blankly at Vandeyr. "What does Daymet *really* want?"

"You should have asked Aris that," Vandeyr said, resting her forearms on the back of a chair. "You seemed to have missed the entire point. Aris didn't ask for anything. Didn't you notice? If I'd thought so much had escaped you, I would have questioned her myself. Assuming she would have answered."

"Oh!" said Traedis, startled. Vandeyr was right. Aris had offered a bargain, but it was very one sided, and greatly in Traedis' favor. "Why would she do that?"

Vandeyr's expression turned stormy. "She would do that because she's up to something that has nothing to do with this supposed 'bargain.' I've seldom heard a person say so little in so many words." Her eyebrows pinched together, and her fingers twitched. "You're a bard, Trae. Words are your calling. Can't you tell when someone is using them to conceal meaning?"

Traedis looked at Vandeyr sharply. "What do you mean? She wasn't lying. She couldn't."

"She wasn't lying, true." Vandeyr shook her head. "She wasn't telling the truth, either. She wasn't saying much at all. Don't forget that words are integral to Daymet's profession, and he's told her *exactly* what to say. Aris said—" She drummed her fingers. "She said they didn't want Myssa to get out of control. Of course they don't, but she didn't say she feared she would. She simply said it would be terrible if Uncle Cordelayne lost control of Myssa."

The realization struck Traedis with a fist of alarm. She cast her thoughts back over Aris' precise words. "She broke her sentences into pieces that didn't connect, but which sounded as if they did. She said some obvious things as if they were revelations. I do see." Her mouth twisted. "Am I really that much of a fool?"

Vandeyr sighed and relented. "Not a fool, Trae. Daymet's experienced in misdirection, and Aris can read your emotions. Daymet could convince people they should feed fire with water, or climb a tree with their ears. The question is—why did Aris want so much to enter the City?" She crossed her legs and leaned back.

"That does seem to be the point." Traedis knew her sister was right: had been right the entire time. She stood up and went to examine a painting that hung on the wall, smoothing its frame nervously under her fingers. "She wanted to get into the City. And I let her."

"You need to listen to me more." Vandeyr's tone carried an odd mix of resignation and frustration. "I know a few things you don't."

"I *am* a fool." Traedis winced. "This bargain is no bargain, and I'll tell

Aris so.”

“Good.” Vandeyr grimaced. “Curse Daymet’s conniving ways! Aris also didn’t say Uncle Cordelayne didn’t know where she was. I’m trying to think of a single thing she *did* say. I’m not sure I’d trust her if she guaranteed each word with *sagathas*.”

Traedis nodded and stood. “It’s a times like this I’m glad you’re at my back.” She gave Vandeyr a half-embarrassed grin. Vandeyr’s mouth did not move, but her eyes crinkled at their corners.

Traedis quickly summoned Aris back. The guards with her looked distressed, but Traedis did not want to question them in front of the ciriin. Aris bowed, but as she glanced up, every trace of a smile vanished. “Oh,” she said softly. “Not wise of you. Not wise at all.”

Traedis felt a shiver run through her; the gaze of Aris’ blank eyes would have been alarming on her closest friend. The ciriin’s entire demeanor had changed the moment she had seen Traedis, and now Aris’ presence seemed menacing and malevolent.

Traedis forced herself to meet the ciriin’s gaze. “I have deliberated over the question of Lord Daymet’s offer. There are too many questions unanswered for me to feel comfortable accepting it. Tell my brother that I decline an alliance with him at this time.” She considered quickly how to leave open the door for possible future negotiations. “I’m willing to entertain the prospect of further talks, but in this case, I cannot make an agreement.”

Aris slowly moved toward them, her predator’s grace raising the hairs on Traedis’ nape. Vandeyr dropped a hand to her dagger’s hilt. The ciriin took a few steps closer, enough to give Traedis gooseflesh. Still, Traedis refused to lean backward; she would not let Aris daunt her.

Aris spoke with a quiet sibilance. "Then do not expect any help from us, should you need it—*King* Traedis. We know how to tell our honorable enemies from the other sort." She flashed a honeyed smile while showing most of her teeth. This time they carried a trace of red.

She spun and exited the door, all but two of Vandeyr's guard trailing her as if they were the ciriin's retinue. Vandeyr's shoulders tightened.

The next thing Traedis did was to call for a page. A young girl dressed in palace livery appeared; she was shuddering.

"What is it?" Vandeyr asked sharply. "Is something wrong?"

Despite her youth, the page stood erect and met Vandeyr's gaze. "No, Captain Atenel, not wrong exactly, captain." Her voice was soft and breathy. "But there's a mess in the room where the visitor waited, Captain. Where the sheep was killed."

"What kind of mess?" Vandeyr's blue eyes narrowed.

"Blood, Captain Atenel," said the page, louder, but still trembling. "All over the room, and pieces of sheep scattered everywhere."

Chapter Twenty-Six
Sheep Bones

The smell was the first thing Traedis noticed: an overwhelming reek of blood and offal, already putrefying. She gagged. Only then did the scene impress itself on her other senses.

Blood was everywhere. The room was empty of furniture, but there did not seem to be a handspan of wall, floor, or ceiling which did not evince at least a few scattered drops of red. The sheep was torn apart so thoroughly that chunks of flesh, innards, and individual bones strewed the entire floor. Wool, matted with crimson, lay in heaps, like bloody snowdrifts. Traedis swallowed twice before she could convince her stomach to settle.

She was not sure that Aris had eaten any of the meat; most of it was scattered in shreds on the floor. After a brief scrutiny, she averted her eyes, her stomach roiling.

"Kyaan's mercy," Vandeyr muttered. "This is no accident. I'll even bargain it's not the way she usually eats, assuming she ate any. No, it's supposed to send a message." She walked around the room, squatting to examine several of the larger bones. Twice she turned a piece over to look at it more closely. Traedis could not understand how her sister could bear to touch the carnage.

"What good would tearing up a sheep be?" Traedis breathed in and out deeply, trying to calm her body's reaction to such extreme violence. "It doesn't make sense."

"Daymet's playing a deep game." Vandeyr wrinkled her forehead. "I'm even more disenchanted with Aris than I was before, and I already despised her before she even opened her mouth."

"What's the aim, though?" Traedis wanted nothing more than to leave this horrible sight. The odor of blood coated the back of her throat, and her eyes were beginning to water. Her stomach heaved repeatedly, though each time, she forced it back into obedience. "Do you need to see anything else?"

"No." Vandeyr straightened, looking with disgust at her blood-covered hands. "Trae, can you reach inside my belt and grab my handkerchief? I don't think I can get it out without staining my uniform."

Unable to bear the sight anymore, Traedis left the room and waited in the hallway for Vandeyr. Now that she knew it was there, she could still smell the blood, though it was fainter here. She tried to relax the tight muscles in her abdomen.

Why had Aris done this? Was it simply an amusement for the ciriin, or was Daymet trying to frighten her? Nothing added up. She shook her head, hoping for clarity.

Speaking to the guards who had escorted Aris in and out of the room gave more information. They stood more stiffly than usual, their expressions as wooden as their stances. One of them, a short and stocky blond man, looked gratefully at Vandeyr, his face relaxing into lines of relief. "Captain! Will we have to deal with that—thing—again?"

Looking at him sharply, Vandeyr asked, "Why? Did she do anything untoward?"

The blond guard cleared his throat and looked down at his boots. "Not except for the sheep, Captain. Not so's you'd be worried. But none of us wants to deal with her. She kept saying things that get under your skin. Things that made you feel like someone looked through your dirty socks. She's got a knack, seems, for picking apart your peace of mind. She's just about the eeriest thing I've ever seen. What do they call creatures like her?"

"Ciriin," Traedis said flatly. "What did she say?"

Vandeyr's brows lowered, but she waited for the guard's response.

The blond guard answered, "A lot of things that didn't sound all that bad except for the way she said them, and the way they meant something that you wouldn't think they would have—oh, I'm not explaining it very well. Like she said to Orhan, 'Did you sleep well last night?' and gave him this big grin, and he turned kind of brick colored and stammered something about not remembering his dreams, and she licked her lips like she could taste him. He swapped places with Tessedar who was on door duty so fast you could almost feel the flagstones smoldering. Like that."

Vandeyr's response was to tighten her lips and walk back into the room. She returned a moment later. "I'm having the guard clean things up—it's better than asking the servants to do it. We can talk elsewhere."

Before she had an opportunity to leave, Traedis was accosted by another page, his face tight and drawn. He bowed and waited for Traedis' acknowledgement.

"Go ahead," Traedis said, wondering what else she would have to deal with today. "What is it?"

The page licked his lips. "Your Majesty, there is a delegation from the Sedorin family, headed by Lord Tarn Sedorin. The family wishes to know when the body of Lord Demmrel Sedorin will be returned to Tolin so that they may hold a proper funeral. They insist on speaking with you personally."

Traedis bit back the curse that rose to her lips. The Sedorins were near the top of her list of people she did not want to see right now. She lifted her chin defiantly. Though it was necessary, it was one unpleasant distraction too many.

She nodded, less resigned than frustrated. "Tell Lord Tarn that I will join his family shortly." At least this audience would be marginally more pleasant than facing Daymet.

The page nodded, bowed again, and headed back the way he had come.

Traedis watched him go, wishing again that the City's future were not her responsibility. But the gods had spoken, and Traedis was Tolin's king; she could not argue with their dictates. They were wiser than she.

Traedis did not have another opportunity to speak with Vandeyr until several hours later. The Sedorins had been insistent, and though Tarn Sedorin had been polite, it was clear he held Traedis responsible for the old lord's death. The irony nearly choked her.

Traedis and Vandeyr met at the palace library. Traedis took a deep breath scented with paper and leather, and tried not to look at whatever was reflecting sunlight into the window from the garden outside. Vandeyr slammed the door behind her, causing a crystal sculpture on a nearby table to ring in sympathetic vibration.

"Why did I ever get along with Daymet, that vulture?" She clasped her hands behind her back and began to pace in fast, furious steps. "What is he thinking, to let that creature anywhere near his family? Has he lost all sense of decency?"

"I still want to know what the entire charade with Aris was about." Traedis moved over to the window and looked out. The garden was thoroughly brown; seed heads hung heavy on the flower stems. "Was it all theater? All of it about making us unsure and afraid? Aris might consider a career as a Player, if so."

"She's a cheat. She knows what you feel." Vandeyr's expression grew stormy. "What *I* feel, too, and I hate that. I've been practicing projecting emotions that aren't my true ones, and she still got down to the core, from what I could tell. Curse her scaly hide!"

Traedis shuddered, wishing she could be a fox for a few hours, but not daring to let go of her control. "Daymet couldn't have been trying to find something, because Aris didn't go anywhere of note. There aren't any runes on any of us. I should ask Master Tagg to check us over for other magic, but I think I or Rose would have sensed anything significant."

Rose sang out a pleased phrase that sounded like tiny bells.

"There," said Traedis. "She's just confirmed that I, at least, wasn't hit with a spell or a curse—I think."

Rose played two notes three times over, a sound that managed to be cheerful and to give the same impression as a nodding head.

"I still want Tagg to look you over," said Vandeyr. "All of us, in fact. I've been doing some study of ciriin, and they have some unique magic." She glared at Rose. "And I'm never going to get used to that blasted thing playing by itself."

"You have a point," Traedis said. "*Sagathas* against watered down dragon magic; I'd be hard pressed to say which would prevail. I'm still of the opinion that Rose is right."

"You can't afford to have an opinion," Vandeyr told her sourly. "You're the king. At least we don't have to deal with Aris anymore. I'd rather play fetch with one of the lightning hounds."

"At least we don't have to give Aris another sheep," Traedis she said, only half-joking. "I don't think the servants would appreciate—"

The realization struck her, and she inhaled sharply at the same time as Vandeyr's own indrawn breath. Vandeyr's head snapped around to face

Traedis.

"The sheep!" they both said, their words overlapping.

The remains of the sheep were in the midden heaped behind the kitchen wall. Though it was unseasonably warm, Traedis and Vandeyr had both changed into worn clothing and boots; the work was likely to be messy and unpleasant, and Traedis was still not sure precisely what they were searching for. Several guards and two pages waited for them in the grassy sward which led to the kitchen gardens.

The midden smelled mostly of rot: the tag ends of fetid vegetables mingled with the stink of viscera and decaying flesh, rinds of fruit and unidentifiable black pulp adding a disgusting pungency to the mixture. Old bones were everywhere, variously festooned with bits of meat and gristle. Flies and gnats swarmed over the whole, a buzzing storm of life gorging itself on death.

Traedis gagged. She quickly moved back and turned her head to catch the wind, which mercifully blew from a fresher corner of the palace. From her pocket, Vandeyr produced a pair of long linen scarves, one of which she handed to Traedis. She wrapped the other around her own nose and mouth, tying it in a decisive knot at the back of her head. Traedis followed suit, glad that her sister had thought to prepare for the ordeal.

Stepping into the soft pile of garbage, Traedis began to search for bones that might viably belong to the sheep Aris had killed. Without knowing exactly what they were searching for, the sheep's remains were their only clue. No expert in identifying bones, Traedis still remembered the size and shape of that sheep as clearly as if it lay spread out before her. She was not sure she would forget the carnage Aris had wrought after years had passed.

"Ugh," Vandeyr murmured, her voice muffled from the cloth across her mouth. "We'd better be right. This is worse than stepping in goatshit."

To answer would entail breathing more deeply than Traedis was already forced to do. She shook her head, denying an answer, and grasped something that appeared to be the shinbone of a deer, hoof still attached by one drooping tendon. She dropped it, reached down, and brushed away two peaches filled with maggots to reveal the partial skeleton of a fish cradling a large wishbone. The ground under her squelched and shifted, almost causing her to lose her balance.

"Got one!" Vandeyr held up a rib plastered with a sickly yellow-green sludge. Tossing it onto the edge of the heap, she bent to continue the search.

The stench was still hard to bear, even with Traedis' nose and mouth covered. She moved closer to Vandeyr; the pieces were likely to be near each other. No one else would disturb the midden in any way besides adding to the pile. Luckily, mutton was seldom served at the palace table, though seasoned lamb was an occasional entree. They would find few bones from any other sheep, and the ones they were looking for were fresh and uncooked.

"I know whose face I'd like to rub in this." Vandeyr retrieved two more ribs and a shinbone. Just as she cocked her arm to throw them after the first, Traedis caught a glimpse of something that flickered on the underside of the shinbone. She made an inarticulate sound and grabbed at Vandeyr's wrist. Vandeyr stopped instantly and lowered it so that Traedis could get a better look at the bone.

Amidst the filth, flashing like a minnow through water, Traedis could see the *quixil* curve of a rune. She immediately snatched the scarf off her face and draped it over Vandeyr's prize. The wash of smell that assailed her left her momentarily sick and dizzy. Holding her breath, she slogged out of the garbage as fast as she could manage, Vandeyr close behind.

Flies followed them, buzzing and biting. Brushing them off was ineffective; Traedis and Vandeyr seemed to have joined the midden as a favorite insect treat. It was hard to ignore them, and even harder to ignore the awful stench which followed them into the soft grass on the garden's edge. Traedis kept her stomach from heaving by concentrating hard on the danger this unknown rune undoubtedly posed.

Two pages, both girls, were equipped with buckets of water, soap, a large tub, and simple but clean clothing, all under a protective tent. But before Traedis or Vandeyr would consent to wash themselves, they summoned Lieutenant Tethyn, who arrived in moments. Vandeyr held out the scarf-draped bone to her second-in-command. "Get something to put this in until we have a chance to examine it."

"Yes, captain." Tethyn sent one of the other guards for a box in which to set the shinbone. Vandeyr let no one else handle it, but laid it carefully inside, touching nothing but the scarf. Only after the lid was in place did Traedis relax and look at the tub. Tethyn stood over the box like a mother bird protecting her nest, awaiting further orders.

"One of the privileges of being Tolin's king is that you get to take the first bath." Vandeyr looked ruefully at her boots. "I'm going to have to throw away these boots. Nothing will ever get them properly clean again, I'm afraid."

Having reached the same conclusion about her own boots, Traedis smiled a lopsided smile, and stripped down to her skin only marginally faster than she climbed into the tub. "I'm going to have to take six baths before I get this smell out of my hair."

"That's what perfume is for," replied Vandeyr, who never wore scented oils or perfumes of any sort. "To make you smell like a rotten flower, instead of rotten food."

Traedis was grateful for her sister's banter; it helped to keep her anxiety from breaking into full-fledged panic. She was not sure what the rune on the bone did, though she would have to find out. That was for later, when privacy could add some measure of safety to its examination.

After a bath and a thorough change of clothing, Traedis took Vandeyr and Ruth into her private quarters for a serious discussion. Vandeyr perched on the edge of an overstuffed chair nibbling on a mixture of dried fruits and nuts which sat on one of the low tables next to her. Traedis wondered how her sister could possibly stand to eat so soon after their search through the midden.

Ruth spoke eagerly. "You found something? What is it?"

Even though she had scoured every trace of filth from her skin and hair, Traedis felt as if she were still wading through garbage: likely the result of Aris' visit to Tolin. "It's a rune on a sheep bone. I'm not sure exactly what it does—I didn't think it safe to examine it without protective spellwork." She closed her eyes briefly, then snapped them open when the rune began to take shape behind her lids. She did not intend to be caught so easily.

Ruth's brow puckered. "What do you think it's for? And what do you intend to do about it?" She hopped up on a chair and crossed her legs at the ankles.

Stopping in mid motion, Vandeyr's hand hovered above the bowl. "Farting Kyaan! I should have strangled Daymet years ago. Aris wasn't here to undermine 'Councilman Atenel.' She was here to assist darling Uncle Cordelayne in planting a rune, and then so thoroughly confusing the matter that we didn't know which direction was up. No wonder Aris didn't have anything to offer. She wasn't here to offer anything at all."

Ruth said, "It seems quite a conclusion to draw from what you've told me."

Vandeyr shook her head, her hand still poised above the bowl. "You don't know how Uncle Cordelayne thinks. Or Daymet, for that matter. How do you slip something into Tolin in secrecy? You bring it in publicly, then pile distracting elements atop it. In other words, we were so focused on what Daymet might be planning, we forgot to think about what Aris was actually doing." Ruth still looked doubtful; Vandeyr finally lowered her hand and scowled. "He taught me, don't forget. Uncle Cordelayne. He's a brilliant strategist, but I learned strategy from him. It's one of his classic patterns."

"But we both thought of the sheep." Having grown up with the mystique of Uncle Cordelayne's brilliance, Traedis found it hard to accept that his plans could be soured by her own less brilliant guesses. "Wouldn't they know we'd figure it out sooner or later?"

Vandeyr gave a short bark of laughter. "My guess is that whatever the rune was supposed to do, it's already done. They know I'm trained in strategy, and you're a sharp thinker, when you bother to think. They didn't need us to ignore it forever, just long enough. The real question is: what does the rune do? And you're the only person in Tolin who can answer that question."

"I'm not sure I can." Traedis shook her head in denial. "I couldn't get a good look at the one which sent Elben mad, even through his memory. I could easily have been caught by it—those glyphs are so amazingly strong.

How do I analyze this and still avoid any negative effects?"

Ruth swung her legs. "Maybe you need to make protection part of your own spellwork. Besides, you know Myssa is a rune. That might help you tailor your magic better."

Traedis ran her fingers across one of Rose's carven flowers. What choice did she really have? Without knowing what the rune was for, she could not dispose of it, leave it to sit in the midden, or even safely bury it. Likely it could work in silence while it performed its function. She could hardly send it to Kenrydh or Emmen; its effect might be specific to Tolin, but it might not be. It was not safe to deposit it in esch lands, for fear that its purpose might be adaptable to King Llyrach's will. Lord Ymre would not take that active a part in mortal affairs. Even sending the bone into the Dragon Mountains had an element of danger; such an action might end up multiplying its effects rather than neutralizing them. It also might annoy any number of powerful creatures.

Traedis heard a faint thread of harp music in her mind, a melody which pushed some of her fear away, leaving room for clearer thought. Heartened, Traedis weighed her other options.

She could not safely use spellwork on the rune inside the City walls. Whatever the rune's intent, it had a deadly potential. The best place to study it was outside the walls, but within her borders.

Slowly, Traedis formulated her intent. "I'll need Tagg and another mage. Ruth, I'm loath to take you; you've endangered yourself enough for my sake."

"But you need my scrying." Ruth shrugged. "It's not the most dangerous thing I've ever done. I'd be glad to help you out."

"No." Traedis held firm. She could still hear Ruth's skull crack against the cobblestones, and was determined not to risk her friend against the authors of those runes. "I'd like to hold you in reserve, in case we learn nothing new." She felt her anxiety calm as she turned over what elements she needed in a chording.

"All right." Ruth nodded. "But if you need me, I'll be here."

"Thank you," said Traedis, warmed to the core.

Vandeyr's shoulders tensed, and her lips tightened. "Where," she asked slowly, "are you planning to wrestle with that cursed rune? The palace is well screened. If we do it here, we might be able to protect most of Tolin if something untoward happens."

Traedis noted in amusement that Vandeyr had included herself in the spellwork, despite her lack of magic. "Not here," she said, jerking her chin at the walls. "Aris left the rune in the palace. That means it's capable of working here. She has to have known it could end up in the midden." She wiped a bead of moisture from her suddenly sweating forehead. "I want to take it into one of the fields outside the walls. Whatever it's for, I refuse to believe it's harmless."

A muscle jumped in Vandeyr's jaw. "I don't want you to be right, but you are. That would probably lessen the danger to the rest of Tolin." She brushed at an imperceptible speck of dust on her sleeve. "One thing I insist on, though; you're going to think your spellwork out from beginning to end, and you're going to have a solid plan in case anything goes wrong. The dragons only know what Uncle Cordelayne means to do. These days I wouldn't put anything past him. And neither should you."

She was certainly right, but Traedis still trusted that Uncle Cordelayne would not cause her permanent harm. Sadness washed through her; he was opposed to them, but she was certain he loved Vandeyr and her. Still, there was no way to reconcile their paths now.

"We'll find out what this rune does. Then we'll go after Myssa," she promised.

She left unspoken the words, "If we can unravel her magic." That would be far more difficult than a single glyph.

Chapter Twenty-Seven
A Touch of Gold

Early in the afternoon, Traedis set out with Vandeyr, carrying the box which held the sheep's bone and its embedded rune. Traedis had brought Tagg and another mage, Gaddiere; Vandeyr had insisted on several guards. They had decided on an empty field some distance from the gates as the safest location. No houses or farms stood nearby, and it sloped up to the forest's edge, which would conceal them from casual discovery.

They rode in silence, their horses' breathing unnaturally loud. Traedis felt her mare dance across the field; she patted the creature's sturdy withers, glad for a little extra warmth from her mount. Beneath them grew brown-edged grass still pale with hoarfrost; the autumn chill's sharp bite augured a cold winter.

The field was cupped by Tolin's dense, broadleaf wood and lush pines, giving way to straggly bushes. Above them, rocky hummocks rose out of the mountain's slope like the shoulders of sunken giants. The track from Tolin wound through the trees in a labyrinthine snarl.

In the center of the field they dismounted, while two of the guards took the horses to tether them at the tree line. Rose banged against Traedis' shoulder as if demanding attention.

Vandeyr had demanded to carry the box that held the sheep bone. "It's my job to protect you," she had said firmly, when Traedis questioned her safety. "Let me at least share some of the risk." It was hard to argue the point, and Traedis conceded the danger to her sister. If this were a lethal trap, Vandeyr would be first to take the blow. Unlikely, however, since Uncle Cordelayne would not risk kin-murder and the wrath of Shorr.

It was a clean, clear day. A cloudless dome of blue shimmered beyond the mountain peak. The grass streaked tendrils over Traedis' boots and the hem of her skirt. A late season moth flapped sleepily from near her feet, fluttered to less disturbed terrain, and settled back into autumn slumber.

Traedis stopped in the center of the field, and gestured to a spot directly in front of her. "Put it here," she told Vandeyr. "I'll open it."

Vandeyr started to speak, then stopped and nodded: a curt nod, but Traedis knew it came from worry rather than anger. Vandeyr set down the box gingerly, as if a small jolt might trigger whatever effect the rune was meant to have. The guards fanned out to encircle Traedis' position in the field. Tagg stepped forward, together with Gaddiere, whose beard was grayer than brown; a deep crease scored his nose. "We're ready," Tagg said, his voice even and calm.

"Protect your king," Vandeyr told them, and took a stand next to Traedis.

The older mage nodded, and the two set their jaws. They would form a dual wall of protections between Traedis and the rune so that Traedis would be able to focus her entire effort on dealing with the potential effects. She could feel the tingle of defensive magic like a mantle shielding her from direct contact with hostile spells. Tagg would defend her first. Gaddiere would serve as a double safeguard; the magic of protection was his specialty. Should any attack penetrate their armor of enchantment, they would suffer its effects before anything reached Traedis.

Taking a deep breath of leaf-mold scented wind, Traedis attached the carrying strap onto Rose, then knelt by the box. She paused before lifting the lid, feeling suddenly wary. But nothing happened as the morning sunlight touched the bone. The rune shone from a surface still containing scraps of flesh and deeply indented tooth marks. Whatever mischief Myssa had instilled was concealed.

"I don't like this," she murmured as she gazed at the rune. The *quixil* was easily visible, winding in and out of the rune like a thread. Overall, this was the most complex rune she had yet seen. Multiple lines balanced against each other so perfectly she could not imagine the mind that had penned it. At the same time, something about it felt unfinished, as if she looked at the clockwork inside a music box. She could not define to herself what she found lacking, but she was certain of its absence. She felt a fizz in her veins: excitement or nerves, she was not sure.

She did not want to immediately tackle the magic itself; that was inviting unreasonable danger. Instead, she would start around its edges and see how that affected its surroundings. She needed to know what it did before she could counteract it effectively.

Nodding at the mages, she signaled her readiness to begin. She picked up Rose and fitted the strap over her back, the harp to her shoulder. Flexing her fingers, she picked out the opening notes of a spell chording.

Rose's tone rang with surprising power, echoing unaccountably in the open air; Traedis' fingers pulsed as they met the vibration of the strings. It seemed her harp was more eager to confront Myssa's malice than was Traedis herself. She spent several moments taming the sound so that it would not overpower her voice, then opened her mouth and added her song to the spell, threading it into the weavework. Then she gathered in the mages' protections and began her exploration of the rune.

Piercing crystalline notes helped her to define the area just outside the rune's influence. Traedis was not sure what sort of trap she was sounding, but it would not be simple. Whether it was set to release its magic at a set time, or to spark at the touch of Traedis' spellwork, it would be imbued with all the care and cunning that Uncle Cordelayne could bring to bear.

The rune remained unchanged, but Traedis knew better than to relax her guard. Carefully, she delineated its boundaries, using a combination of notes that echoed off the actual runework without leaving a magical signature that would provoke Myssa's spell to life. Nothing seemed tied to the glyph as far as Traedis' magic could perceive.

The trap was in the rune, then. Traedis tightened her spell, using a net of quick triads to touch it lightly before the notes slid off and congealed into heavier complementary chords. Harmonics whispered from Rose's strings, the air itself ghosting back the harp's voice. The sound picture began to solidify.

The rune felt like gold. That was the only way Traedis could perceive it: she was not sure why. She snaked in a unifying countermelody which would help her to make sense of the whole, to understand what Myssa had written.

As melodies clung to each other and diverged, it clarified: the word for gold magnified and split into similar meanings, a prism dividing bands of sunlight. Confused, Traedis continued to play, unsure of how to proceed.

Like a flash of fire, the rune grew, resolving from the glass of her chording into something she had never seen but still recognized; the portion of a life rune which carried emotions. Traedis felt the frigid shock of recognition as fear forced shards of ice into her blood.

This was the same piece of rune Aris had offered.

She had been trapped doubly. If she had accepted Aris' offer, the ciriin would have given her this piece of magic. Denying the offer would bring the same outcome.

Even as she realized her danger, the rune seemed to grow yet more, not in volume, but in complexity and power. Like a pen sketching over lines, the bones of the structure filled, adding flesh to its skeleton. For a brief moment, Traedis saw the whole of it in her vision, coiled and detailed and beautiful, more intricate than the finest aelin writing.

The rune clouded as something coalesced into reality. Traedis stepped back several paces, confused and alarmed, her pulse strangling in her throat. Cloudy swirls of skin and hair misted up from the sheep's bone, flashes of gold punctuating them with brilliance in the damp morning light. As Traedis drew breath to sing the cloud away, a woman's form consolidated: Myssa.

Traedis backed up further. Rose held at the ready, she prepared to defend against an assault of unknown nature. Beside her, Vandeyr drew a startled breath.

As before, Myssa wore no clothes, but now she dripped with gold: gold chains, bracelets, anklets, and rings dangled from her. She wore them with pride, as if she were dressed in more artistic finery. She had, Traedis thought, added excessive amounts of vanity to her life rune without adding a firlot of good taste.

The runecaster stared straight at Traedis, her black gaze unwavering. "What," she asked, in a voice as contemptuous as her posture, "do you think you can do with my rune?"

Traedis swallowed hard, but kept her fingers moving on the strings. "I'm trying to determine what it's doing here." Her voice shook as she recalled her last, nightmarish encounter with Myssa.

The runecaster gave a short bark of mirthless laughter. "You want to know what my rune is for? You've been a festering sore on my ass for months now." Her lips stretched into an unpleasant smile. "Here's something I've designed especially for you."

A dagger appeared in Vandeyr's hand. She struck Myssa full in the back. But instead of sticking, the weapon dropped dully to the ground, melting as it fell. Vandeyr gave a grunt of pain, but pulled out two more daggers that met the same fate. She drew her sword. The guards sprinted toward Traedis.

Myssa snickered dismissively and flashed a wink of gold from her smallest finger. Vandeyr's motion slowed almost to a stop, as if she were a snared insect in a spider's web. The veins at her temples bulged, and her muscles strained, but she appeared as trapped as she had been when bricked up inside the wall. Anger dominated Vandeyr's expression as she struggled with Myssa's runework.

Myssa swept her hand in a circle; the guards dropped like sacks of grain on a farmer's wagon. Traedis hoped fervently they were not dead.

She stiffened as Myssa slipped another gold ring to the end of her forefinger and began to sketch in the air between them. The ring left golden lines, which spun like coins as Myssa completed her spell.

Tagg cried out and dropped to the ground. His magic held, though he soon curled up and began to twitch. Traedis let him do his job; if she were not protected, the spell would fall on her and disrupt the chording that was their only hope of surviving. All of Tolin was her charge, not simply those who stood with her. The kingship rode on her shoulders and her heart as a heavy weight.

Myssa smiled even more unpleasantly. "Do you think his heart will stand it?" she asked, almost conversationally, and lifted her forefinger back to the air. The *quixil* curve jumped to life within another glowing rune, quite different from the first.

Heart racing, Traedis searched for an entry point to the life rune; she needed to pry it apart or set it dancing into oblivion. But she could barely understand it; it was too tightly wound, and Traedis had no time to study it and decide on the best approach. Rose's *sagathas* strings might have the power to destroy it, but Traedis did not have the knowledge.

A weak cry sounded from Tagg. "I can't hold the spell, Gaddiere," he said, agony thickening his voice. "Protect the king!"

Gaddiere firmed his mouth and nodded. "I'll take it." He took a deep breath. "Let it go, Tagg."

A guttural sound came from Tagg's throat, and his entire body spasmed. Traedis could feel the spell transfer to the older mage. For a brief moment, there was a hiatus in their protection.

Myssa's rune hit with bone-breaking force, as if she had slammed Traedis into a tree; only the unbreakable connection between Traedis and Rose kept her from dropping the entire chording. She spasmed, realizing that this pain had no variance, unlike Myssa's earlier torture. Then the agony passed, and she heard Gaddiere cry out.

"How many people are going to suffer and die for you, Traedis?" asked Myssa, her tones halfway between anger and satisfaction. She finished the second rune, moved her hand to one side, and started on a third.

Traedis glanced briefly at Gaddiere, then recoiled in horror, almost losing her spellwork. The part of his hair was separating, leaving a thin red line from which blood welled. The split deepened, as if a knife were severing him in two. He gasped, and his magical protection dropped. The mage fell, his head opening like a sliced apple. A line continued to bisect him, splitting him open from peel to core.

Traedis had to keep going. Those here had chosen to give their lives for her and for Tolin. She must accept that sacrifice if she were to defend the innocents in her care. Mist clung to her vision, but she blinked it away, forcing herself to listen to Rose's voice and her own will. There was nothing she could do but continue her efforts to counter Myssa's magic.

The crushing force of the initial pain rune returned. Her fingers splintered, jagged bones severing nerves and tendons. When she looked, they were whole: she forced them to continue their dance upon the strings. A crushing heaviness attacked her windpipe, but she continued to sing. She *would not* give in to the runecaster.

Then Tagg took back the protection, leaving Traedis with ebbing pain and guilty relief. She concentrated on the emotional section of the life rune; Myssa's arrogance and malice might be a weakness Traedis could exploit. She needed to expand and dilute at least part of it in order to fight effectively.

Myssa laughed, finished the third rune, set it spinning, and started on a fourth. The second rune shrank to half its original size. Looking sidelong at Gaddiere's body, Traedis saw that not only had he split completely, but that the process was beginning again, cutting crossways through his waist. Her stomach roiled.

A groan sounded to her left; Tagg was also beginning to split at the top of his head.

"Let the protections go, Tagg!" she called. He could not help her if he died here as Gaddiere had.

If she could not protect her people, Traedis should not be king. Desperately, she called the two things which she knew were greater than Myssa: the Star Cavern, and the strength of her land.

Tolin roused easily, eager to protect its king. Thunder cracked through the air, splitting the sky with lightning so bright that everything in Traedis' vision went briefly white. The storm clouds that had ridden the horizon for days pressed down the mountain, darkening the field as much as its fire had brightened it moments before. Deep in the Star Cavern, Traedis could feel the constellations stir, their elemental power responding to Traedis and to Tolin.

She grasped frantically for any of them, and found the Firebrand. It was the constellation of fire and war, and ruled wildness and power, both of which Traedis needed. Like dry kindling, Tolin's power met the Firebrand's. It ripped through Traedis' *falmyros* and coursed through her spellwork, burned in her veins and her voice and her eyes, causing an explosion of power in her chording. She struggled with the immense energy, to contain and direct what she had summoned. The lightning in the air echoed the Firebrand's luminous strength.

"Very pretty, Traedis!" Myssa laughed at her.

Only then did Traedis realize that her entire body was alive with phantom flames and sparks. She felt like a forge trying to contain a fire meant to melt *sagathas*. Every part of her body prickled and burned as she tried to absorb the power flowing into her from the Firebrand.

On the ground, Tagg slumped, though the separation of his scalp slowed; he must be fighting the rune with every skill he possessed. Traedis swallowed against sickness, and prayed hard for his survival, though fear for the mage was distracting. She must concentrate if she were to have any chance at all.

The pain returned, this time amplified. Traedis would have screamed, dropping her spellwork, but now Tolin was playing her, harping on her bones, singing with her flaming lungs. She knew she could not outlast this assault. She was caught between forces too great to survive. Her own magic seemed to dissolve into the radiance of the constellation's light.

With a supreme effort of will, she turned the power playing her toward a spell of unbinding, feeding it into the chording. For a moment, Myssa's form thinned, and Traedis could see light through her. Even the runecaster's hand slowed, where she drew the fourth golden rune.

Then Myssa was solid again, and as magically impenetrable as before. "You poisonous, weasel faced bitch!" Myssa screamed at her, and continued to draw. "Leave my rune alone!"

Fox-faced bitch, you mean, Traedis thought hysterically. The backs of her eyes exploded with light, flared over her vision, starbursts of brilliance and pain. There was no chill left in her veins; it had burned clean out of her. Her fear was hot, arid tinder that threatened to transform her into a living torch.

Traedis needed a way to see the totality of Myssa's life rune; the moment of clarity before the runecaster had appeared had not been enough for Traedis to unravel the entire glyph. Skilled as she was at seeing the *quixil,* Myssa's physical form obscured too much of the fine detail.

Overwhelmed with fire, she opened fully to the *falmyros,* anchoring herself in Tolin's unyielding stone. It responded with enthusiasm, rushing to fill her with the gods-given right of rulership, expanding her inside, making room for the Firebrand's strength.

Beneath her, a rabbit warren teemed. Pine roots burrowed through the rich earth, warm under many years of dead needles. Stone cracked and fell with the stress of the mountain's angled movement, slow to change, inexorable as Shorr's law. Wind whispered into hollows in the stone, ruffled the wings of butterflies, angled off peaks and gained speed as it flowed downhill. Ants, tiny but unified in their purpose, built structures to house their determination, and warred with each other in a struggle as old as the world. Traedis could no longer see through her own eyes, immersed as she was in Tolin's imminent and urgent presence. She had no body; only Tolin's will and need.

And yet, she saw. Myssa's fourth rune seemed to be taking longer than the other three, but it was still forming with frightening speed. Traedis felt lightheaded; dark specks floated across her vision, followed by trails of colored light. She wanted to stare at the grass, losing herself in every blade, or to touch the gentle wind with her enchanted link to Tolin's heart. As Myssa worked on the rune, it became harder for Traedis to separate which strands of power were her own, and which belonged to Tolin.

The smashing, splintering pain of Myssa's first rune suddenly gave way. Tagg's hoarse voice whispered, "I have it, King Traedis."

With the surcease of agony, Traedis' hold on the Firebrand—or its on her—gave way. Tolin's power swamped her, then ebbed. Without their resistance, the fourth rune spun into her with a crash, silencing her voice.

"Can't find the words, Traedis?" Myssa crowed, her eyes sparkling with malicious glee. "Something happened to your golden voice?"

Traedis tried to squeak, to whimper, to force any sound from her throat. All was fruitless; the only noise she could make was the brush of air sliding in and out of her lungs. She desperately needed her voice, needed the song that would direct the magic of her harp, tying the forces of the *falmyros* and the Star Cavern together.

A single encouraging note rang from Rose's golden strings. Traedis lifted her fingers, determined to fight with everything she could still muster.

She paused.

Her *golden* voice.

Traedis did have a voice. It was Rose.

She had closed off the *falmyros* herself, in her fear of falling into it so far she might never come out. But she had an anchor, and that was also Rose. She could not be separated from her harp, not while its spirit lay in the *sagathas* that also clad her strings and the single hair of Traedis' head.

Her *falmyros*, likewise, could not be separated from her by any spellwork, runecaster or otherwise. It was given by the gods, and only they could withdraw that gift. And the constellations chose for themselves who to aid. The Firebrand had come to her.

She opened herself back up to the *falmyros* and simultaneously to Rose. *Sing for me*, she urged the harp. *Sing my power. Sing my heart.*

The voice that emerged from the harp was startling. It belonged to Traedis, she had no doubt, but she had never heard herself like this, outside her own head. It soared ethereally over the entire field, ringing with a power that Traedis did not know if she truly possessed.

The *falmyros* followed, with laughing waterways and trees adorning themselves for their last gaudy show before winter's slumber. The dreams of children came, full of bright toys and mysterious paths that guided them to tea with luna moths and supper with eagles. Deer delicately picked their way through an autumn abundance they had not seen in years. Traedis had wrought these things, protected the children, brought abundance. The land loved her.

The Firebrand was no gentler than it had been before; it was fierce, made for war, not peace. But the *falmyros* coated Traedis, insulated her from the worst of the burning. Perhaps—perhaps—she could win against this monstrous *rûntazent* after all.

"Oh, Traedis," said Myssa in a fair imitation of Cordelayne's tone. "You don't think that's going to help, do you?" She slid another ring down her fourth finger. This one was a ruddier gold, almost like—

"*Sagathas*." Myssa snickered. "Just a shred, but it serves. You don't think you're the only one to have found a treasure trove, do you?" She sketched the barest tip of a *quixil* tail, and a rune flashed to life. "I have such a surprise for you. Cordelayne has no idea how much he really wants to be rid of you." She flicked it outward.

Traedis was prepared for blatant pain or even death as the rune reached her and winked out of sight like a firefly. A moment later she felt a stirring in the depths of her mind, like the trail of a slug or a leech. She shuddered as a sticky, clammy darkness descended over her thoughts, clouding them with knowledge of her own worthlessness.

How had she thought she could protect Tolin? Uncle Cordelayne had knowledge and skill far beyond what she had ever learned. He had been right; she was unfit to rule. He had plucked her out of Tolin without difficulty. Rose could not protect her; Myssa had almost cracked the harp apart with her runes and her skills. Vandeyr was powerless against magic. Even the gods could not expect Traedis to succeed. Her chest felt heavy and full. She was completely alone, no one to come to her aid or give her support.

The curse she bore was too much. Wingblade had taken her freedom, and with it, her hope. She was not strong enough for the faith her loyal subjects and friends had put into her. It was time to admit defeat.

The dank, slimy sensation crept into her chest, filled her ears. All Traedis could see now was her failures. She shouted at her father, telling him how much she hated him. He had died before she could make that right. But even before that she had been useless, stupid, worthless, obstinate. Mitheira had tried so hard to teach her everything she must know, and Traedis had thrown those gifts away by fleeing Tolin. Master Celdon had been hard, but who would not have been, faced with such an obstreperous student? Maybe she belonged in that closet, among the moth-eaten furs and the darkness. He should never have let her out.

She was a failure as a daughter, a sister, a friend. She could not live up to the least of anyone's expectations. She could not even live up to her own.

Despair was a seeping, sucking morass: thick mud that clogged her heart. Atchûk had died because of Traedis. Vandeyr would also die because Traedis could not protect her. Ruth was next. Tagg might already be dead. Better Traedis should cede her life than make others pay for her vanity and overreaching ambition. The gods had indeed been testing Tolin when they had made her king.

"I won't have to do another thing," Myssa said, her voice sly. "But I'm going to enjoy watching."

Traedis had a knife. It would take little for her to hold it to her own throat, to open up her arteries and pour her blood out as a sacrifice to appease the gods. Uncle Cordelayne could not make a worse ruler than she. Even Daymet would be better.

She choked on despair, swallowed darkness. The future held nothing for her but misery. She would destroy Tolin. Rose was not enough of a reason to go on.

Then, like a star in an endless night, something shone inside her. The memory of rushing wind brushed past her, a cold mountain wind that braced rather than froze. The wildness of the upper air teased out another memory, one that could not be tainted by mortal magic. A woman's form, covering half the sky, the stars within shining eternally. That shape transforming to a wren, gliding into Traedis' mind and body. The touch of Kyaan.

What did it matter if she were nothing more than clay and spirit? Kyaan had regarded her, had found her a worthy vessel, and had left her with traces of wildness that still streamed through her lungs and her spirit.

There was a rune on her. With a jolt, Traedis realized what Myssa had done, and why. And she was not willing to give her enemy that power.

She could still feel the effects of the rune trying to destroy any sense of her own power. But now Traedis again called the *falmyros*, the Firebrand, and the truth of her own heart. Cursed she might be, but she was also blessed. She aimed Rose's magic at the rune that—she suddenly realized— covered half her face. Now she sent it dancing into oblivion.

Lightning blazed from the skies as the union of the Firebrand and Tolin rose to defend her. A The storm from the mountains erupted supernally fast, its thunderclouds promising an autumn storm that would wreak havoc for days. A host of sparks engulfed Traedis in a maelstrom of radiance.

Another rune hovered before her, one she had been too preoccupied to see Myssa draw. It hung long moments outside the shield of sparks. It would not stay there indefinitely; Traedis braced again for death.

Instead, she felt Tolin's love, like supportive hands against her back. It bolstered her spirits, guarding her from the harm Myssa had sent against her. It reminded her she was not alone; others cared for her more than she might believe.

The *falmyros* reclaimed her mind. Traedis sank into the earth and stone of the mountain, where she felt again the protective presence which shielded her from Myssa. She jolted, as if someone had shaken her in a way both kind and firm. Definition returned to the world around her, and she realized that Myssa was nearing the completion of another rune.

There was no time to consider further. She seized a strand of starlight and focused it on Myssa, hoping to bring the other woman's life rune into clarity. With the strength of the *falmyros*, Traedis reached out and concentrated the Firebrand's light to snap it into focus.

She could feel the spell take. Myssa turned translucent, then transparent. Traedis could finally see the life rune which spun around three flat balance points in her chest, almost like a faldren toy. Traedis coaxed it with a spell that encouraged it to remember all the languages and meanings and words that had gone into its creation, to expand into what Lord Ymre had meant it to be. Unbidden, the old song rose to her lips:

Dance and sing! Dance and sing! Gather all into a ring!

She followed the lilting tune, calling the runes to dance, to become more than flat symbols describing flat ideas. True art danced; it flexed; it shaped itself to the moment and to the purpose. Even the *quixil* had a helix hidden within its unbreakable circle. She reached out to gather the runes into her chording.

A piece of the life rune detached.

Myssa made a startled sound, and the rune she was working on dissipated. Tolin's power released its grip on Traedis' attention, and surged into her through newly forged channels, like the Council Spring.

Shifting into a fierce song of unbinding, Traedis used Rose's *sagathas* music to create and dismantle a dancing tune that resonated with Myssa and her rune. More showers of sparks erupted around her. Overhead, lightning lanced through the sky yet again.

"Let go, Traedis!" Myssa screamed, but did not vanish, as Traedis half-expected her to.

Traedis reached out with her magic to seize at least part of Myssa's life rune, so that the runecaster could not leave Tolin without tearing herself apart. Sparks flared as the Firebrand seared the *rûntazent's* magic with a potency Traedis could barely encompass.

Containing the constellation with the last of her strength, Traedis aimed its fiery power directly at the spinning gleam in Myssa's center.

Myssa's rune exploded with a silent shock that toppled everyone in the field. The runecaster splattered into shards of words; pieces of glyph and smatterings of letters flew everywhere. The few bits that might have reached Traedis were deflected by the power of the *falmyros*. Vandeyr lowered her sword, and Tagg gave a faint moan.

Myssa herself was simply gone. Wherever her original body had lain, all Traedis had ever seen of Myssa was a woman long dead.

The field wavered in Traedis' vision, and dizziness darkened her sight. She drew breath to speak, but lost consciousness as the storm broke over

Tolin.

A prickling on her skin roused Traedis from restless dreams. She opened her eyes a bare slit, wondering where she was. Lightning-hued sparks met her vision.

"Ow," she said, and tried to move her hands. They seemed to be weighed down by something soft.

Clarity seeped into her mind. She was in her own bed, under a blanket. She was also exhausted.

Then she remembered Myssa. Forcing her eyelids up, Traedis managed to move her gaze to the ceiling.

"You're awake!" Vandeyr's voice said beside her. Traedis turned toward the sound, struggling against the enveloping blanket. Before her motion was complete, Vandeyr was peeling the blanket off, freeing her hands.

Traedis lifted her head, then dropped it with a thump back to the pillow; her skull hurt, and sparks still skittered before her eyes, obscuring everything around her.

"Don't try to move too fast." Vandeyr's tone was level, but Traedis recognized the sound of strain in its cadence. "You've been asleep for two days. A little more time won't make any difference."

Traedis' throat felt sore. "What happened?" she tried to ask, and raised her head again. This time it only ached.

"Water?" Vandeyr asked. Traedis nodded. Vandeyr disappeared for a moment, then reappeared with a half-full cup, which she held to Traedis' mouth. Traedis swallowed, then jumped as a cloud of sparks shocked them both. Vandeyr uttered a mild curse, but remained steady.

Drawing strength from the water, Traedis raised herself onto her elbows and blinked several times to cleanse sparks from her sight. It did no good; they continued to dance in a firefly pattern that she almost felt she should recognize. As her thoughts cleared, she realized they were no product of her overtaxed mind; they were truly there, and Vandeyr was reacting to them as well.

The silence stretched as Traedis tried to think of anything to ask. She should have dozens of questions, but it was hard to grasp them with her head full of wool and her eyes full of sparks. She struggled into a sitting position, wincing at the jab of fresh pain behind her eyes. Vandeyr reached out a hand to support her.

"All right," Traedis said, as dizziness flooded her vision with even more sparks. She was as exhausted as if she were recovering from a terrible illness. Something nagged at her memory, but she could not piece it together. "I remember what happened—but what happened?"

Vandeyr's mouth twitched, but she kept her expression solemn. "I'm hardly the person to ask about that. I'd suggest you talk to Tagg." She scowled. "Gaddiere's dead. There was nothing we could do—he was in sixteen pieces by the time we got to him." She shrugged, a little too casually. "Myssa's gone, unraveled by your spell. Good riddance to the repulsive tick. And good work, Trae." She opened her mouth, as if to say something else, then closed it again.

A combination of relief and deep sadness and guilt welled up from Traedis' body into her consciousness. She had done her best to ignore what had happened to her protectors, and had apparently succeeded enough to forget about them altogether. Gaddiere should not have died; perhaps Traedis could have borne the pain rune, though it would have damaged her concentration. "How is Tagg?"

Vandeyr frowned in thought. "Alive, healed, but shaken; he knows how near he came to being sliced up like Gaddiere." She pulled her chair to the bedside and cleared her throat. "I've never seen anything like what you did," she said in an uncharacteristically soft voice. "Not only were there sparks everywhere, but lightning lit the whole sky, all the way back to the walls. No one can even touch your harp, it's sparking so much."

Traedis jerked her head around to look for Rose. "Where is she?"

"It's over at the Kyaan church." Vandeyr frowned. "Good thing it doesn't break, because at least three people dropped it, including me." She shook her head in seeming annoyance. "I don't remember the last time I dropped something by accident, but it was simply impossible to carry. The sparks made my fingers spasm open."

Traedis raised her eyebrows, and waited for her sister to continue.

"Master Shorarit ended up floating it to the church, because we weren't going to leave it out in a field. And Elben came from Faldrohaven, picked you up despite getting a bad shock, and carried you home. Seems some fool guard captain went and told him what happened. He's back in Faldrohaven now." Vandeyr's tone turned wry. "Now you're awake, can you do something about those sparks? Tolin seems determined to protect you, but they're getting in the way."

"Oh." Traedis' mind felt thick and slow. "Of course. I think." She concentrated on the land's power, which had been imbued with the Firebrand's fury. A new shower of sparks cascaded to life, brought by Traedis' concentration. Vandeyr let out the tiniest of squeaks.

That would not do. Traedis reached into her *falmyros*, which leaped eagerly under her attention.

Something had changed. The new paths that Traedis had formed during the confrontation with Myssa had altered the expression of the *falmyros*. The autumn storms with their attendant lightning, the Firebrand's strength, and Traedis' need for both protection and fighting power had brought something new into Tolin.

Sparks ran up and down her hands, tingling without pain. Traedis tried shaking them, but they moved with her. She bent her mind to sending them away, to pacifying the land. Slowly, as if reluctant, they faded. Traedis reached out gingerly to touch Vandeyr, and no shock met her questing fingers.

"I'm not sure," she said, "that what I've done will suffice." A prickle behind her eyes suggested she could call up the sparks again at will. But now, she needed to deal with the kingship.

"I'd like to see Tagg." Traedis scraped her hair back from where sweat matted it to her forehead. "And then I'll want a bath."

Traedis sat in the roof garden, looking up at the night sky. Winter was on the horizon; the peaks of the Dragon Mountains were already laden with snow, and Traedis could feel Lord Harfast's approach like the solemn tread of mourners in a funeral procession.

She had too little time. Months were passing, and she had made no progress on bringing Uncle Cordelayne to the thane's justice. She could almost feel the raspy presence of Thane Bi'ia's bone knife, secreted in her office safe. It still hungered for blood, still tugged at the edges of her dreams. Or her nightmares.

Around her, flowers had shrunk into seedheads, marigolds and asters and purple coneflowers. Sharp spikes of withering lupine grew along the short wall that enclosed the garden to the east.

Above her, the constellations wheeled. She could make out the barely visible tail of the Southern Dragon; the Twin Lions stood proudly, prominent in their quarter of the sky. The Firebrand and the Bowl would not rise till much later, but she could see the Great Road, a seam cutting across the heavens. All of it reminded her of the relentless march of time.

Myssa might be gone, but her uncle still had at least two ciriin with him, and Daymet at his side. That was not even taking into account the others who followed him, seeing in him the salvation of the City.

The door that led onto the roof opened with a creak. Vandeyr appeared, followed by Ruth. The two of them took a seat on either side of her. Ruth craned her neck to look upwards toward the stars.

"We'll find him," Vandeyr said softly. "We'll make it right."

Traedis cast her a wan smile before realizing that her sister could not see her in the heavy velvet night. "I know."

Ruth puffed a short, clouded breath of air. "You're not alone, Trae. Whatever happens, you're not alone."

But she was alone; alone to bear the responsibility for saving Tolin. Myssa's runes might have lied, but there was a core of truth to them, like the best lies. The *falmyros* could not be wielded by Lang or Vandeyr or Gavaya. Traedis was the core and the heart. She held the future in her harpstrings, and held off the past with her will. The responsibility weighed almost more heavily now than when she had first learned about the Red Man.

A year and a day.

Inspired by authors such as J.R.R. Tolkien, Lloyd Alexander, and Madeleine L'Engle, Beth determined to become a writer when she was still in grade school. Deciding to focus on her writing, she began to publish fantasy short stories in various magazines and anthologies. *The Herd Lord*, a novella about a war among centaurs, was published in 2011, her first full-length novel *Etched in Fire* was released in 2015, with its sequel *A Gift of Flame* following in 2018, and her short story collection *Seeing Green* came out in 2017. Beth's ideas are sparked by music, artwork, designer coffee, and the question, "What if?" But it is her children who keep her striving for excellence, so that she can make them proud of her.

Goldsong, the first in *The Sagathas Bard* series was released in December 2020. Watch for *Ravensgame,* the third in the series!

Praise for *Goldsong*

"Traedis is a dynamic heroine who will appeal to readers of all backgrounds, and she and other strong female characters have a sincerity and richness of personality that effectively brings them to life on the page."
on the page." – *Kirkus Reviews*

"Goldsong is a beautifully-written fantasy novel, with detailed character development and wonderful worldbuilding and lore. Traedis is a main character everyone can root for."

– Maria Johnson, Author of *The Boy from the Snow*

"*Goldsong* is a book where some of the characters have darker shades to them, where people can be complicated or quite messed up or even evil… but where there is a fundamental goodness, a simplicity and purity that does not equate to one-dimensional or undeveloped characters."

– Raina Nightingale, Author of *Heart of Fire* and *Kindred of the Sea*

https://www.amazon.com/Goldsong-Beth-Hudson-ebook/dp/B08K7X35J3

9 798218 253851